ARIZONA DYING

Days of Lust and Murder

John Woodmount

ARIZONA DYING
Days of Lust and Murder

Table of Contents

Present Day

It's the morning of the Bank Holiday, Monday, 27th August 2018...U-boat has surfaced in the Gulf of Mexico...on board Patrick Dempsey, Wendy Summers, and others. Also present at sea in a belligerent mood is a contingent of the British Navy in a Mexican standoff with the German Navy.

Chapter One

A Taste of Violence

It has been 444 days since the accident on the newly constructed mountain road. A head-on collision caused the tankers to split and spill their loads. Both drivers died, and the tankers careered down the mountainside, finally resting in a densely wooded ravine, totally hidden from the outside world. Their contents continued to ferment in the heat of those long summer days. They remained undiscovered for three days.

On the morning of Monday, 12th June 2017, Bill Cummings, an odd-job driver, stopped to take a leak around midday. He noticed what appeared to be snow on the ravine floor below. As he watched, it spread across the ravine and headed towards the town of Little Tonto, thirty-two miles as the crow flew from where he stood. It flowed through the trees and brushwood and intertwined with the chaparral growing abundantly on the valley floor below. It seemed to Bill an invisible hand was painting the landscape with a broad brush. He observed it had ceased climbing the rock face one hundred feet below him.

A female hitchhiker was the sole witness to spot the tankers colliding and toppling down the mountainside.

Like the useless citizen that she was, she never reported the accident.

First reports of the mysterious landscape around Little Tonto came over on CNN at approx. 18:30 hrs, which was the evening of 12th June. She was the one solitary witness to the beginning of this earth-shattering disaster to befall the continent of North America. Since then, wild birds and animals have fed on the massive heap of waste product spilt across the valley; both loads have melted together in the blistering summer heat.

Time is crucial when a disaster strikes. Armageddon America began at 09:15 on Friday, 9th June 2017, when the tankers went over the edge and down the mountainside.

By 16:00 on the 12th, Bill Cummings had reported the snow to his neighbourhood paper in Little Tonto.

By 18:00, breaking news was coming from CNN. The following day, they interviewed our hitchhiker, who said she thought no more about the accident. However, the stench of interview money brought her to her senses. She was a hooker dropped off by a driver who forgot she was asleep in his rig. She watched him drive away in anger as she delivered a torrent of expletive-laden insults for leaving her stranded. The police arrested her for failing to report a serious accident.

By the 13th, a sizeable white carpet was creeping in the town's direction. It was like a coin dropped in a pool of water, the ripples spreading in an ever-increasing circle. This circle would halt for several hours to regenerate and give itself the strength to carry on. The land was a parched whitish colour the vegetation dead and the water lifeless.

On the evening of 15th June 2017, I found myself gazing upon a landscape from my vantage point on Little Hump Mountain (thirty-two miles from the town of Little Tonto, fifteen miles from the city of Tucson), where nothing seemed alive except for odd-shaped animals. Countless events had altered my life during the past week, but this scene of utter desolation on Thursday evening took the biscuit.

According to CNN, the indigenous mammals and insects had begun to devour one another. Some were mutating into grossly contorted creatures with jet-black bodies and glowing white stripes down their backs. Hunger would force them to charge into each other's territory and tear chunks of flesh from one another's bodies. These animals were not just overgrown; they were vicious and cannibalistic. Their hides were made of bone, and their teeth had the toughness of steel. I thought this was science fiction on Earth. They were attacking outlying homesteads tearing the occupants to pieces and devouring their flesh. They were unable to digest the bone. Local folk had assumed they could incapacitate them with ordinary hunting rifles, but their shots bounced off. The terrified screams of men, women, and children could be heard in Little Tonto. The snow continued to advance in the wake of these beasts, eating the remains of homesteaders who would have been looking forward to the 4th of July Independence Day celebrations.

Innumerable animals had been slaughtered with guns that would have destroyed a tyrannosaurus. The army was in Little Tonto, setting up a defensive perimeter. Anti-tank missiles and attack aircraft were shipped from Davis Monthan Air Force base, and tanks and soldiers from Fort Huachuca. Upward five hundred people were dead.

As night descended, herds of creatures could be seen from my vantage point, their backs glowing white in the dark. Gophers or prairie dogs would howl in agony as they stuck their heads out of burrows into ravenous jaws. I had not seen an animal mutating yet, well, not close-up. CNN was arranging to let the population of Arizona and elsewhere view the horror that lay ahead for anyone foolish enough to get caught by these mutant carnivores.

CNN was preparing to show the world an attack on a herd of eight thousand cattle by a town of mutant prairie dogs, roughly 100,000-200,000 strong. It was going to be a horrorfest. It would show a stampede of enraged cattle bellowing in terror as the ground trembled during a particularly violent thunderstorm. The Earth was completely soaked in blood from these animals as rodents ate them alive.

It was to be networked worldwide with an estimated viewing figure of four billion. CNN was lucky to have two choppers in the air and another three on the scene within twelve minutes of first noticing this unfolding phenomenon. They would have the footage of thousands upon thousands of prairie dogs leaping from their burrows with their bark-like yips. No one else would have this footage of the initial attack on the cattle. The pilots were instructed to fly in close formation and keep competitors out. This event was the big one, and it was theirs; millions would be paid for the best shots. History was now made, and they were living it. The footage was streamed to headquarters in a never-ending run.

Little Tonto's evacuation had been completed hours earlier, and the army had pulled out, leaving tanks and hard-skinned vehicles. Soldiers on the ground would only serve as meals in boots. There was absolutely no point in feeding mutations if it was helping them mutate.

Here I was in the arsehole of nowhere with no food, transport, and worse still, surrounded by hungry carnivorous scavengers. How was I to travel fifteen hundred miles to save my children? Sod the wife; she was an obese lardball and would keep my two kids alive if they could tempt these beasts to eat her. Fifteen hundred miles is a marathon journey, and this snow was travelling at the rate of a mile an hour, or so I guesstimated.

The mutants were a different kettle of fish. They were eating everyone in sight, and whatever was travelling with them was devouring the vegetation. A bizarre occurrence was taking place, and I greatly desired to exit Arizona, if not the country. I learned facts recently that made the urgency of clearing off from here imperative.

What had happened to involve me in such a catastrophe? A fortnight previously, I had been chosen by Bob Fisher, head of transport, to do what he titled bonus runs. My job was to collect tankers from the parent company at Rosemount Heights, Seattle, and deliver them to EARTHCO's depot outside Tucson, Arizona.

Sunday, 4th June 2017.

On this day, it was 10:16 am; I had taken delivery of my usual consignment from the Lonepine Ranch outside Tucson. I presumed it would be residual liquids from the production of youthful cosmetics. These were used to keep extremely wealthy and mature women attractive. I had been allocated a different lorry each month. I was never told why this should be but advised to button my lip and keep my job. Jobs were scarce in these recessionary times. I pushed my lorry hard to keep up with the weekly target to continue earning exceptional wages.

My peaceful world was turned upside down for me on that summer day. The sky was blue, the grass was green, and I had arranged to meet a housewife in the foothills of the Catalina mountains. She had taken a shine to me the previous week. I was to meet her at her grandfather's adobe house, which she informed me was vacant and cosy. I stopped at a restaurant for coffee and a phone call as my mobile had gone walkabout. As I entered, I saw a man with broad shoulders and muscly arms slide a plate of food onto the counter, shouting table seven. He looked rugged and robust, and I put his age around fifty. He reminded me of the Russian actor Oleg Taktarov. Little did I know this was the tastiest truckstop grub in all of Arizona, and it would turn out he was Russian.

One step at a time. 'What happened in the restaurant?' says Dempsey.

I was there to phone Mary, my unfaithful wife, to tell her I would be away all week on double shifts. The company was moving enormous quantities of stock to its new warehouses for security and distribution purposes. The warehouses were built hundreds of feet up the side of a mountain with the odd name of Little Hump. A single-file road had been laid with more twists and turns than a mystery weekend. This road wound around the mountain mile after mile, climbing steeply. The road was reasonably wide and gave much-needed comfort, considering the sheer drop one would view from the safety of their cab. We had to deliver to the vast caverns near the summit. It used to be a silver mine, and James Sturgess (chief of security for EARTHCO) felt it would be an excellent storehouse. No two truckers were to travel in opposite directions simultaneously on the road. Hillbilly Joe never checked in with security but would speed down the mountainside and, lo and behold crashed into Tom Dickens, who was racing up the hill. Greedy bastards did more runs than anybody else. They would be driving for the devil now. The escalators to hell would soon be full of souls delivered 24/7. We were chasing generous bonuses hence the haste to meet our schedules. We could be in deep shtuk if we had an accident on a major highway; spillage they said would cost a fortune to clean up.

Security would send out a patrol to monitor the speed and behaviour of their drivers on the highway. If caught, you would be fired on the spot. The cops seemed to be in the right place to nab a reckless haulier. You would end up in court and lose your licence regardless of the speed you were doing. It was common knowledge amongst the teamsters that specific stretches of the freeway were fatal for the health of ones driving licence. Momentum was built up in the most dangerous places, even if it involved a few hundred yards.

Entering the restaurant, before him stood this sexy little thing in a short black skirt and pert, firm breasts. I recognised her straight away. She was as hot as ever. I stared at her, and she stared at me. I gave her a gaze of pure sexual hunger. The cook decided this lump of a trucker would not enjoy flirting with his wife. Recognition dawned on his face, and with a look of murderous hatred, he decided to belt me one. I never saw it coming; he moved with the speed of a gazelle that was about to have its rump devoured by a hungry lion. My lights went out, and I was securely asleep in Noddyland.

I awoke at 4:07 pm with an almighty headache. I reeked of pig shit from having shared the sleeping quarters of pigs. Doubtless, his relatives were giving me dirty looks. They were eyeing me with *you could-be dinner* thoughts. I dragged myself out and stumbled to my lorry. It was fully hitched and ready to go. I was furious. I wanted revenge.

To make a boring story interesting, I strode across the road to his greasy spoon diner with my baseball bat. I glared through the window and saw him munching on a sausage. I wondered what had happened to mini-skirt, and I rushed through the open door. I swung to whack him with all my might across the head. He grabbed the bat and beat me senseless. He dragged me outside and picked up a whole bucket of food slops as he went. He kicked me in the balls, which brought a roar of intense agony from me, and half the drunks from the adjacent dive bar came out to guffaw and sneer.

'Silly bugger got caught sniffing Wendy's armpits,' they said.

'Should have waited 'til he was in bed or gone to feed his pigs.'

'He regularly pops in for a beer. He could have sneaked over and slipped Wendy a length.' Blah blah blah, they laughed and chuckled.

He dragged me back to his pigsty. Giving me a farewell boot up the arse, he threw his bucket of slops over me, hoping the pigs would finish me off. He even delegated my murder. I hope he chokes on his Buds. I lay there, half-blind from pain, listening to the pigs grunting and snorting. They thought a nice piece of Irish meat would go a treat with their rancid slops. They were nudging my feet while snorting and guzzling their way through their pig swill, occasionally nipping my ankles. They were going to eat me alive. I had to get away from them. I could not move; what could I do? A few rapid prayers passed my lips. A pig bit my ear, and I screamed. Hands were suddenly dragging me from my tormentors, and everything went black. I was back in Noddyland.

I woke up in pitch darkness, confused about where I was. Slowly my brain, or what was left of it, escaped from the fog surrounding it. It went into reverse, rolled backwards, and stopped in a pigsty. Yep, I recall being in a pigsty. I recall the shit kicked out of me. I remember mini-skirt's tight little arse and that cook. Where was he? Was he watching and waiting to give me another good pasting? I swore if he touched me, I would buy a machine gun and turn him into a fishing net. The door swung open with a bang, and two pissheads staggered in, holding cans of Billy Beer and sniggering in the way only pissheads can. To my delight, mini-skirt was with them. She seemed pleased I was alive. She gave me a swig of beer and asked if I was OK.

'Yeah, I'm on top of the world,' I replied, full of sarcasm. 'How do you think I feel?' She looked hurt, and I swiftly apologised.

She said, 'Don't worry. I will come and help you later.'

She went off with the two laughing pissheads. I could hear her in the next room. They were riding her like they would a bronco with raucous yee-hahs. I wondered what kind of sex she had come to enjoy. I imagined her fanny had become a horse's collar, tough as old boots and sufficiently spacious to accommodate my arse.

'Oh, my Wendy, what has become of you...' and I drifted off to sleep.

I awoke with a start. What was nibbling my pecker? The pigs were back; no, they weren't. Instead, it was Wendy, the mini-skirted sex-starved tart. She sucked like an alcoholic with a straw in a beer barrel, drawing in great gulps of air and spitting on the ground. Blimey, she had graduated into a rough blow-jobber.

'I'm in terrible discomfort, Wendy-baby. Can I take a rain check? I'm suffering from retarded ejaculation.'

Best keep her in a cheerful mood until I engineer my escape from this place. I congratulated myself on not visiting here before and decided my guardian angel had been protecting me from these two violent and depraved lovers.

'Wendy, how long have you been here? You never said where you were going when you left town with your parents. Nobody knew, but your family never spoke to anyone. It would have helped if they had studied English.'

'After we moved,' she says, looking at me as if I was something obnoxious, 'I left Mum and Dad to live with my uncle outside Tucson at Cunningham's Creek. And yes, my parents spoke English but not to the bullock-eyed racists where we lived. You know people's attitude towards Iraqis with their snide comments? How did you think they communicated as chemists by sign language? By the way, they work for your company, EARTHCO, keeping old ugly American women attractive for their fat, baldy, ugly men. Is that your rig outside with the EARTHCO logo?'

'Yes, it is,' I reply cautiously.

'My uncle died six months after I lodged with him. To make a long story short, he left me his house. I sold the house and relocated to Fiddlers Elbow. I got a job in a nursery. I met Dimitri, the Russian, and his two boys there. You had the pleasure of meeting him earlier. I heard his wife had gone back to Russia, leaving him with their boys. He had been a cook in the Russian army. He had cooked for Gorbachev. He offered me a job in his restaurant at inflated wages if I would nanny his kids. To be honest, I had a kid of my own, so I rolled them together and made one unhappy extended family. He was an alcoholic. Nonetheless, he cooked the finest of food. The local community and truckers had taken an appreciable liking to his culinary skills.'

'After six months, I learned a great deal about Fiddlers Elbow. Everybody was a pisshead or smackhead, and the women appeared to be in a perpetual stupor. I had decided to get my boy James away from this place, and to do so, I needed money. Dimitri was emotionally good to James and me, and you could say love blossomed. You never inquired about me. If you did, you would have discovered you had a son. You loved me for a week and double-crossed me with Mary, that obnoxious pig. You married her, and in cow fashion, she spawned you two brats.'

'Peter and Susan,' I said, smiling and looking stunned.

'My God, what attracted you to her? She was a weighty girl at sixteen and could have been mistaken for a sumo wrestler at eighteen. Did she rape you, for she didn't half-frighten the boys at the graduation ball? Many left early to avoid running into her and getting their girlfriends knocked out.'

'A slight bit of an exaggeration that I was drunk. I walked Mary home, and we had it off in the bushes, or to be precise, she had me in the bushes. I woke up the following morning and realised I was not in love with this obese honey monster. She and her parents had me up the aisle so fast that I was married, honeymooned, and presented with a bonny boy in less than one year. How I wish I fired blanks. I would have escaped her clutches.

'Things were fine for the first year, and she presented me with a bonny bouncing girl in the second year of our disastrous marriage. That was it; she shut up shop, the excuse being she was ruining her figure, and I was hurting her having sex. What a lame excuse the expansive lump came up with. The dirty dog was a lesbian. She didn't give a damn if I knew, and us less than two years into our sacred marriage. I came home from work one day and caught her in our marriage bed with Anne Butcher, that skinny-arsed, po-faced bitch, and she a married woman. As the years passed, I caught her with no less than six other women, half of them married. She must be one heck of a muff-diver.'

'Mind you. They were a rough lot at Skipton Lakes. You were the prettiest at the high school.'

God works in mysterious ways, and he provided me with the Nolan sisters, who reside on the outskirts of town. They are unhappily married and hungry for extra meat, and I was ready to oblige. The populace was happy, including those cuckolds they married, for not one of those kids was sired by their husbands. I got a job as a haulier and ended up being absent a lot, especially overseas. Mary did not care as long as I lodged plenty of moolah in our account, and I cared even less. Five years back, I became a driver for EARTHCO. Bob Fisher phoned me to say I would be on double shifts this week. I wandered off the beaten track to this godforsaken place to ring my lesbian lump.'

Here I am lying in pig shit, battered and bruised, and my job has gone up shit-creek. I peer around and wonder where the pigs have gone.

'I have to get back on the road and deliver this load. I want to see you again. I want to hear about my boy and you. Why didn't you come to me? I would have helped you. I would have supported you.'

'Listen, dickhead,' she snarled, 'you invited hippo to the prom to spite me for hanging out with Billy Elliot. He was my next-door neighbour; he wished me good luck in my new home. You were a jealous shit, and I'm delighted you ended up with the girl of your dreams.' She cracks me one across the face. 'Take that, you rotten bastard, and let it be a lesson to you not to mess with a young girl's emotions. She told me the following day you had made love, and you promised to marry and love her forever; hah, isn't God good? My marriage is in trouble, and I want you to help me sort it out.'

'Trouble in paradise, eh, but yes, I'll do my best.'

She spun on her heel and said she would be back later.

I squinted at my watch; it was 4:27 pm. I've been in a coma. I've been asleep for a day.

Monday, 5th June.

I'll never deliver on schedule; they'll be searching for me. I'll straighten Cookie's marriage out with a shotgun blast up his arse. I fell asleep and dreamt I was culling pigs. I awoke hours later to hear Dimitri bawling and yelling in his thick Russian accent that he would rip off my *golovas*. My balls and I exist happily together. We hang out together, and we would never want to get separated from one another. What a shagging disaster that would be. I heard Dimitri come to the door and try the handle. I held my breath and waited. Nothing happened. An almighty boom rattled the building to its foundations, yet the door stood firm. Effing and blinding followed, and then silence. Through the silence, I heard a fart, rumbling and drawn out. 'I need a shit,' he mumbled, wandering off.

Moments later, a key unlocked the door, and the lovely Wendy entered in skin-tight jeans and a blouse.

'Let's hurry,' she said, 'he might be back at any moment, and he will murder us. I am not dying for you, you weak, pathetic excuse for a man.'

I hauled myself to the door and limped across the road to my rig. Wendy locked the door and followed me. We made it to the lorry and climbed aboard. I was astounded the truck was untouched. Wendy was pretty, and over the last hours, I learned butter would melt with the speed of a snowball in hell in her mouth.

I wished to entwine myself to her lithe body, tasting and savouring her perfume, sweat, and sexual aroma. She appeared so young for her age. She was in her late forties, yet she could pass for a woman of thirty. I wanted to do so much to her. She was beautiful and promiscuous. I ran my hand through her chestnut brown hair and felt the softness of her skin as she rested her cheek on my hand. Tears came to my eyes as I realised, I had always loved her. I hugged her tightly. I told her I loved her. I understood she would never care for me again, for the past decade's sadness would firmly be planted in her heart and soul.

A double-barrelled shotgun discharged into the storage room door, and in went Dimitri swinging the gun above his head. It was time to exit Fiddlers Elbow. Wendy had left by the passenger door and sprinted across the car park. She made a detour to come up the road to the storage door.

'Dimitri, Dimitri,' she cried. 'Are you hurt, my darling? Oh, my baby, what has he done to you?' Hearing Wendy's voice, he came running out to the middle of the road and stood to stare at her. I deliberated on the idea that he was in love with her as tears rolled down his cheeks.

'Oh Wendy,' he said, 'I imagined you didn't care.'

He held her hand, and slowly they walked to his house. Wendy was a nymphomaniac, but she loved Dimitri and would never leave him. It excited me to know her marriage was in trouble. How could I see her in the future, and would we ever make love? Time was running out for Arizona, with massive destruction lurking in the shadows. Sod the lot of them, and I climbed into my bed in the rig. I'll show that bloody Ruskie who's boss if he turns up. I fell asleep clutching a vicious-looking carving knife.

Tuesday, 6th June.

I was starving. I could have eaten a horse stuffed with chickens. I decided I would continue fasting and complete my delivery. I would tell the company manager that mafia types had tried to hijack my load, but I fought them off. I suffered superficial bruising in the process. I was a company man who would protect their property with my life. Hopefully, it would give me leave to recuperate and extra cash in the wage packet. He might be so overwhelmed he might offer me his wife's enjoyment for the night. Well, he might, you can never tell with yuppies. I could plan how to get Wendy and her tight little ass up the woods, but first, I wanted to see my son. He would be in his thirties, and I assumed he spoke with a Russian accent. I was curious about his stepbrother's names and whether they liked him.

I climbed out of my bed, aching and groaning, and fumbled in my pocket for the keys, which I duly found. The engine fired up with the first attempt, and as I prepared to drive off, I peered across at my prison and down the street at the restaurant. I saw Wendy and Dimitri waving and gesticulating in the most obscene of ways.

I rammed it into gear and gently pulled out onto the highway, and drove for Little Tonto. I would take the left fork on the road and commence my climb up the mountainside. With any luck, by late afternoon, my load would be delivered. I would be booted, suited, and anxious to plot my next move for Wendy.

I slipped on my Ray-Bans and drove south to Little Tonto. My eye caught my name on the envelope on the floor. She had not forgotten me. I sang a few bars of a rebel song I had learned as a child in Ireland. I ruminated on the riches that had burst into my life and if they would turn to shit, as everything else had. I sang out loud, *and side by side, they fought and died in the valley of Knockanure.*

The hours passed, and the ache in my ribs returned with a vengeance. I thought about the housewife I should have met and whether she would agree to another rendezvous.

I checked in at The Sandy Sky Motel in Little Tonto to wash and clean myself. I phoned a doctor, who prodded here and there and casually informed me nothing was broken. I should relax and sleep for the rest of the day. I slept all night, waking up to eat a hearty breakfast accompanied by a frosty beer. I phoned the office and advised them of the situation. James Sturgess, head of security, came online and informed me to wait where I was. He suggested to me not to discuss with anybody what had happened. Had I contacted the cops?

'Best to check in with you first, sir,' I said. I reckon you would rather deal with this situation. I believe you would prefer the cops kept their noses out of our business,' intimating I was part of the management.

'You are an essential team member,' he said. 'Listen to me, Patrick; you will be rewarded for your tenacity and bravery.'

'I need a week's holiday, sir,' I said.

'That, my fine fellow, you shall have and a thousand pollars to help you enrich the time. May I suggest you lock your rig and keep an eye on it? Our man, Winston Dillon, will be with you within the hour. Thank you for your effort. I shall speak to you at headquarters,' and the phone went dead. Things were definitely on the way up. I contemplated my life with my son. Mary would go mental if she knew I had a spare son, she must be kept in the dark. I would not be able to let him meet Susan and Peter. Divorce wasn't an option as I would gain one child and lose two, and perhaps my head with that lunatic family of hers. Never mind, secrets are the best way of keeping things hidden.

Wednesday, 7th June.

My room phone rang, and I got up to answer it. 'Mr Dillon is in the lobby,' a bitchy voice squealed. A key rattled in the lock. I presume it's Dillon and his two henchmen in sharp-cut suits who burst in and pin me to the floor. 'What's your name and occupation?' the fatheaded one yells at me.

I look him in the eye and tell him to go home and bang his mother — a terrible suggestion, as the skinny one kicks me in the balls.

'Don't try to tell Mr Sprangler how to run his sex life,' he screams at me. 'Answer the bloody question.' He takes out a cattle prod and gives me a taste of electricity.

'Thank you for such an excellent contribution, Mr Rugosa,' the Fathead says. 'How do you fancy that, you smart-arsed bollocks?' the Fathead continues.

He kicks me in the bollocks to go with his speech. Crikey, if they keep this up, I'm going to have the biggest goolies in the Americas. I figure the one who keeps staring at me is Winston Dillon, and I pray salvation is at hand.

'Mr Dillon, I'm tremendously pleased to meet you.' I offer him my hand in a gesture of goodwill. 'Patrick Dempsey is my name, and I am a teamster at EARTHCO.'

He gives me a hand-up and says, 'Yes, I believe you. My man will ask you a few questions, reply promptly, and you can be on your way.' He removes an envelope from his left-hand pocket and places it neatly on the left of the table, and from his right-hand pocket, he places a small glass case and leaves that on the right-hand side. I can see a syringe and phial in the case. These people mean business, and more to the point, what have I been hauling all these years? It certainly isn't baked beans by Heinz or any other fart-maker.

'Mr Dillon, you only have to ask,' and I start singing like a canary. 'It happened yesterday as I passed through

Miners Gulch, that abandoned town saddling Silver Springs. I had pulled over for a slash when three men dressed in long dusters and carrying baseball bats came running towards my rig. I zipped up and ran for my truck, only to trip over a gopher hole. They battered my head and body, shouting, give us the keys. 'I will; they are in the cab. Let me get them,' I shouted.

'I'll get them,' says this cock-eyed Cletus Spuckler doppelganger. He climbed into the cab and poked around. As expected, he came up empty-handed because they were in my tunic pocket. He threatens to break my head, I continued.

'You're looking in the wrong place,' I yell at him. 'They are definitely on the floor, for I am positive I left them on the seat.' I climb in beside Cletus. Aaah, they have fallen down here,' and I clamber over him. Taking the keys from my pocket, I dangle them in front of him, and with one powerful kick, I send that cock-eyed-toerag flying out the open door. They were whooping, hollering, and beating my truck up. 'Get in the cab Moses; get the keys,' says an inbred scumbag.

'Too late,' says I, ramming the gear stick and shooting off with three tossers in hot pursuit. I built up speed and sped into Tin Town, where those stinking hippies squat.'

'Why did you not phone this office?' says Dillon.

'I wanted to shower and freshen up; I was a bit shook up from my experience.'

'He thinks he's Elvis Presley going on a date,' says the skinny one. 'Your aftershave smells of lies.'

Dillon tells Skeleton (Alphonse, Rugosa's nickname) to phone Higgins and ask him to take this rig to the warehouse. 'Patrick,' he says, 'take the rest of the week off and take this as a thank you from the firm. Report to me first thing Monday,' and he strolled to the door accompanied by his two goons.

He took a mobile from his pocket. 'Luther, meet me at the Windsor bar in Tucson shopping mall tonight. We have a problem with a driver who has fed me a cock and bull yarn.' He kills the call and gives the phone to the fatheaded one with instructions to destroy it immediately. 'Don't give it to that boy of yours, or I WILL bugger and kill him and you too. Do you understand?'

'I do, boss; it will not happen again.'

'It better not. I don't tolerate liars, and I certainly don't like yes-men ignoring my directives.' He gives Fathead (Helmuth, Sprangler's nickname) a hard slap across the face. 'That should help you remember. Keep an eye on him until you are relieved. I will send another driver in the next hour,' and with relief showing on their faces, they observed their boss drive back to base.

'I hate him,' says Fathead. 'He gives me the willies. Let's get breakfast; I'm famished. You go and order,' he says to the skinny one, 'I need to go and destroy this phone. My little sprog is always mucking in my stuff. Best take no risks; it's my arse on the line as well.' He heads to his car, takes out an engineering hammer, and smashes the phone to smithereens. He returns, and they tuck into an excellent hearty southern breakfast with all the trimmings, and why not?

Having scoffed their big breakfasts with their grits, pancakes, and double helpings of hash browns, both scrutinised me eating my lunch, which consisted of a crisp salad and coffee. My stomach felt knotted. A thumping headache had popped up to let me know I was on shit street. The truck was in pristine condition, yet I had told Dillon those inbreds had knocked lumps out of it. What if these two tossers go to have a look? Would they detect the bodywork was intact and undamaged? Why are they waiting? A terrible thought crossed my mind: what if Dillon had noticed? It would be best to have a word with them. After all, he had abused Fathead with a slap.

'Fancy a few beers, lads? It's going to be a roaster of a day.' I sat down, and they scowled at me as if I was trash. 'Alright, I'll take myself elsewhere.'

Skeleton spoke. 'Certainly, we will have a drink with you; we are all on the same team. Let me get you a cool Bud,' he says, laughing heartily. 'We were obediently doing our job. Dillon might have put us through the meat grinder for being disobedient. He is a hard boss to graft for.'

'Shut up and get the beer?' says Fathead. Skeleton went off, and ten minutes later, he returned with three bottles of Moose Drool.

'Where have you been?' says Fathead.

'I've been to the john. Is that alright with you? Stop bossing me! It was you who got slapped.'

'Got slapped?' says I.

'Yep, Mr Dillon slapped him right across the chops,' says Skeleton. He seemed chuffed with his grassing. I could imagine these two squaring up to each other.

'Why did he wallop you?' I ask, hoping for a reply.

'None of your business,' says Fathead glancing at his watch. 'What do you want?'

'Oh, simply curious if your gob was sore after he slapped you like a little boy.'

'Listen to me, Irishman; you won't be laughing soon; you'll get your comeuppance, piss off.'

'Explain yourself? What's Dillon going to do to me? Help me out, guys. What's going on?' I consider Skeleton is the weakest link, and he would love to see Fathead taken down a peg or two.

At that moment, Higgins entered and made for our table. 'Get me a beer, Sprangler, and be quick!' He turns to me. 'I'm here to collect your rig, hand me the keys and get any belongings you want out. Now!' he yells, and I jump to attention, and off I go. He's built like a shithouse and stinks like one. His arms are rippling muscles, and his chest is muscular. I had no intention of back lipping that mother. Higgins may have instructions to put little old me in traction until Dillon was available to deal with me. I collect nothing and return to discover Fathead and Skeleton sitting at the bar.

Where has Higgins gone? I go to join Laurel and Hardy.

'What's the craic with Higgins?' I ask.

'Open your eyes and look out the window; he's on his way back to base with your rig.' I watched Higgins speeding down the road.

'A Speedy Gonzalez, that bastard,' I said to Skeleton. 'I bet his wife doesn't have time to blink before he's shot his load.' Skeleton is giggling, and Fathead is red-faced and scowling at him. Skeleton snidely remarks, 'Fat men hardly last a minute, often less.'

'Would you enjoy another beer, Helmuth?' says Skeleton, getting up and heading for the bar.

'I intend to murder that starved wanker,' says Fathead. 'That advertisement for famine rations is married to my sister Greta, who is not the sharpest knife in the family drawer. I stifle a laugh pretending to be in agony, and ponder the value those two wankers could have for EARTHCO's security. Sturgess probably employs them to annoy Dillon, or Dillon keeps them as cannon fodder for a rainy day.

'How long have you dogsbodied for Mr Dillon?'

'A while,' says Fathead. 'He promoted us to security when three of his men went to Los Angeles to the Rimini complex.'

'What were your previous occupations?'

'We attended his goldfish lake and groomed his horses.'

I hoped to get information without killing them. I had begun to enjoy listening to their stupidity. 'How long have you been with security?'

'A while,' says Skeleton arriving back with beer bottles,' and believe you, me...' and his mobile rang before he completed his sentence. He fumbled in his pocket and found his phone, only to drop it on the floor.

The phone ceased ringing. Fathead says, ' you clumsy oaf.'

Fathead's mobile rings, and like lightning, he has it to his ear. It is all Mr Dillon, yes Mr Dillon, right Mr Dillon, and he's on his feet, ready to leave the bar. 'Boss wants us pronto. Get your arse in gear, Alphonse Rugosa, and goose-step to our transport. You are nothing but a *flachwichser*, Alphonse, and an Italian *flachwichser* to boot. I bet Italy had a day of mourning when you were born and a day of rejoicing when you sailed off to America with your spaghetti-munching, cocksucking family.' They hurried to the door when suddenly Fathead turned and came up to my nose and said, 'Have you been munching blinis lately, Irish pig? I wish you to rot in hell **untermensch**,' and he strides off after Skeleton.

A sense of foreboding overcomes me, and I'm convinced the banshee will wail for me tonight. The haggard old hag will be letting out a piercing screech so blood-curdling it will shatter glass and my senses. A few prayers pass my lips for the second time. Blinis, blinis are a Russian type of pancake; they must know about Dimitri and Wendy. I resolve to go and see them and find out what may have been said or done. One thing is for sure, you cannot judge a book by its cover.

I've got no transport, so I head to the information desk. 'I need to hire a car, a four-wheel drive, a Rover would do. I would appreciate it a.s.a.p.'

'It's gone three o'clock,' the receptionist says. 'I can get you a car here for the morning.'

'I must have wheels tonight. Can you make it happen?' says I, shoving a hundred pollar bill in her hand. 'For you.' Her eyes opened wide with delight as she grabbed the greenback and was on the phone like greased lightning to Hertz Car Rentals. She fired through the details, asking for my driving licence and credit card, which I swiftly produced.

She hung up and dialled another number and asked for Tony. 'Go to such a place and pick up such a vehicle,' she said. 'Go now, and I will give you fifty pollars,' and she hung up.

'It's in hand,' she said. 'It will be delivered within the hour.'

'Thank you ever so much,' I said. 'Isn't the American pollar wonderful? They can achieve the impossible when they are in a gang. I'll be in my room when he arrives.'

Off I went to pack.

A half-hour later, the phone rang. 'Your vehicle is prepared for collection, sir. Shall I have Tony bring it to the front? There is no waiting, all this terrorism.'

'I'm on my way. I'm ready to go.'

She hung up. Hoping to return this way, I slithered to the information desk like the snake I could be. I was in the presence of a beautiful woman, and I thanked her once more. I asked if we could have dinner. She was in her late twenties and was exceptionally physically attractive.

'Oh yes,' she said. 'I'd love to; please hurry back.'

I noted she wore expensive jewellery and weighed up the odds on her sharing nights with the clientele. Tony came in with the keys. I thanked them while making sure she saw I was admiring her curvaceous bum.

Outside sat a brand-new Range Rover, tank fully laden, and within minutes I was on my way back to Fiddlers Elbow. How did Sturgess get wind of what happened at Fiddlers Elbow? I guess one of their drivers reported my rig. I was three days overdue and off the beaten track. What is Dillon contemplating? Why did he give me a thousand pollars? He must have wondered where I was for three days. I haven't heard the end of this tale by a long chalk. Questions, questions, questions, and not one satisfactory explanation can I come up with. I am in deep shit all the way up to my lugs. I wish I had told the truth. Dillon would have had to suck it up and move on. He could have fired me on the spot or returned me to Dimitri and helped him feed me to the pigs. I cursed myself for being a liar; now, they were convinced I was hiding the truth. Still, you can never tell; Dimitri might knock seven bells out of them.

I made the journey in two hours and nine minutes and screeched to a halt in front of the Russian Bear Restaurant. It was 7:21 pm, and the restaurant was empty save for a cleaner wiping the tables. I fire off a list of questions.

'Where's Wendy and Dimitri?'

'Why's the café shut?'

'What's the problem?'

'Where're the customers?'

'Dimitri is helping the FBI,' says the crone in a manly voice, and Wendy has gone with him.'

Christ knows what part of Russia she's from. However, her English is excellent. 'How long have they been gone?' I ask.

'Two hours. An awfully nice man came to the house with a fat man and said my son would be back tonight after viewing photographs of a man they called Bin Laker. No, that wasn't his name, Bin Lager, Bin Laden, yeah, that was his name. They said he had destroyed expensive New York City buildings without permission, and the Whitehouse was still going crazy. They said Bin Laden was wild and had been living in caves. My son would recognise him; he had shot him up the arse years before in Afghanistan. He would recognise him because Bin had a unique scar on his left cheek you could only describe by looking at it.'

'What colour was the FBI man who did the talking?'

'Black, and a nice man he was. He said I should be proud of my son.'

'And the other one, what was he like?'

'Oh, he had an oversized head, and he kept quiet. He hardly said a word.'

Winston Dillon, I thought, and Helmuth Sprangler, my fatheaded enemy. I cerebrated on what I could do to initiate a search for them. Should I go to the police? I had committed no crime, yet on the other hand, Dillon was not going to jail for kidnapping. He was nasty, and no doubt he enjoyed the high life. He wasn't about to give that up for a pisshead Russian and an Iraqi slapper. Skeleton and Fathead might take the rap after committing suicide from the shame of what they had done. No, the cops would come and investigate and ask a few questions. A few glances here and there and an investigative nod of the head, and that would be the end of the law and poor Wendy Summers.

Was Wendy looking in terror at a syringe and an envelope? There was optimism while Dimitri was alive. Wendy might shag her way out with a grand in her purse. It was three hours since the abduction, and damn little I could do about it. I drove out of town and booked into The Arizona Sunrise Hotel. I sat miserably, contemplating what move I should make next. It better be a good one. On the other hand, they might be cooking me bacon and eggs tomorrow after I'd gone to see if they were back. Dillon would not be foolhardy and inflict injury on them. He would be sympathetic when Dimitri described the tale of the night before. Yeah, I'm worrying about nothing, making a mountain out of a molehill. I better get a restful night's kip, for tomorrow will be a day of happiness or sorrow. I fell asleep and dreamt Winston Dillon and Dimitri Ivanovo were pigs on their way to the slaughterhouse.

Thursday, 8th June.

I gave myself the Treble S treatment. A shit, shave, and shampoo, and I wandered off for breakfast. I felt refreshed; it's surprising what a splendid night's kip will do for the weary noggin. The dining room was packed with guests, and I figured I was being spied on. There was no sign of Skeleton or Fathead.

I judged my best bet was to visit the receptionist at the Sandy Sky Motel and hope to glean information from her. I sat down to have a continental buffet, and having finished, I decided to have a fresh coffee. As usually happened, the sugar had run out. I turned to the chap at the next table and asked if he would mind passing me the sugar sachets. By all means, he said, and as he handed them over, I inquired if he was from England as I detected a hint of an East End accent.

'Yep,' he said with absolute surprise on his face, 'born within striking distance of the Bow Bells,' he stammered.

'Born in the Borough of Stepney close to the Mile End Road, do you know it?'

'No, I can't say I have been there.' Something familiar about his eyes, but nothing came to mind.

'My name is Gordon Thatcher, and this fine lady is my wife, Sheeree; we are on an extended holiday.'

By the gods, she can't be twenty years old. I've never seen such a beautiful head, with its cascading brown hair overflowing her shoulders, like the Puerto Rican actress Lamar Nidal.

'You do have a fascinating face; been sticking it in the wrong place, or are you a bit of a boxer?' Gordon asks. 'Used to be one myself, often woke up with a face like yours; it comes with the territory.'

'How long have you been here?' I enquire.

'Since mid-April, we're on vacation for the summer months. We are staying at the Arizona Sunrise for the next few days while waiting for our friends.' Sheeree is in full vocal, and she tells me they have been to the Grand Canyon, Monument Valley, Tombstone, and many other places.

'I haven't introduced myself, my name is Patrick Dempsey, and I am a teamster for EARTHCO out of Seattle. The other day I lost contact with a dear friend, Wendy Summers, and I intend to meet up with her. We had been at school together. She moved away thirty years ago, and I met her serendipitously at the Russian Bear Restaurant.' I saw a horrible evil look in his eyes, and it was gone. Sheeree frowned at him, puzzled.

'We have been there,' says Gordon. 'Great food and great service must go back.'

'Her husband Dimitri served this up to me for having known her. Reflecting on it, I have no clue as to what yarn she spun him. I would still like to meet her, even if it's only to say goodbye.'

'I don't think Dimitri wants to say goodbye to you,' says Sheeree.

What caused Sheeree to have such an old voice?

'How long have you two been married?'

'Oh, twenty-two years,' he says, smiling at Sheeree.

'No, Gordon, what I meant was, how long have you two been together?'

'It's still twenty-two years, and it's thanks to your company Sheeree looks youthful. I'm afraid my DNA is unsuitable; it rejects all types of renewal hormones, et cetera, et cetera. Sheeree was the perfect patient, according to Professor Haslett of the 60/20 Reborn Medical Centre. It is here in Tucson. It's a specially designed town where everybody works and lives if they wish. It has the prickly name of Cactusville. The reason is that the patients, once or twice a year, depending on their age and physical health, would find their skin becomes prickly. For the following five/eight days, you would suffer bouts of ill temper with powerful impulses to commit murder. By this stage, one should be booked into the clinic and be receiving their treatment to be reborn. Hence the secrecy; otherwise, it would have failed as a business ages ago.'

'Its benefits far outweigh any drawbacks, such as taking a knife to your next-door neighbour's kids because the little scroats run wild in the street. We book into the clinic and spend a week/month in isolation on a drip feed of replenishment liquids and a mud bath. Then out we'd come remodelled as new, with our screws tightened in alphabetical order. You mentioned you drove for EARTHCO. I expect you have delivered tankers of rejuvenating creams and liquids to the clinics.'

'Not as such, we would deliver to a warehouse on the Lonepine Ranch, which is a huge warehouse fifty miles south of Tucson. What happens afterwards? I don't care. I know one thing; we have a different tanker each month. We know this because each one has four letters of the alphabet etched on its underbelly. The last time I checked, my tanker had the initials DEAY. I can't understand the reason for so many tankers. The chances are it is corrosive, making more than a few trips impossible. The tankers have seals, precoded keys and lockout codes on the steering mechanism. These make it impossible to hijack without the driver being present. It's a significant amount of security. We are carrying rejuvenating creams residue or whatever the hell they are. I find a pint of Guinness to be a great rejuvenator, anyhow. Sheeree appears completely bored with this topic of conversation.'

'Just a trifle,' she says. 'Tell us about yourself. You are from the west of Ireland because my first boyfriend was from there. Your accent is Irish.'

'Yes. My parents emigrated to Seattle to join my father's parents. They emigrated in the 1950s. My grandfather is in his eighties, and my mum and dad now manage his haulage business. My grandmother died years ago. I've been here on and off for forty years. I have never lost my accent. In fact, I hone it at Irish festivals. I enjoy participating in the St. Patrick's Day parade here in Tucson. I enjoy the *craic* along the west coast, especially in Vegas. I must admit I find few English festivals considering the size and influence of England.'

'Maybe so,' says Gordon, 'we sure know how to steal another man's country and get the locals to administer it.'

'That's to be sure,' I say.

This jabbering has brought us up to lunchtime. 'I think I'll have a salad and a beer. Would you join me? I ought to go and check if Wendy is back from her ordeal.'

'We'd love to,' says Sheeree. 'Salads will be fine for us too. We need to move on; our friends are arriving mid-evening.' Gordon queried if I would join them for dinner at eight, to which I replied, 'I'd love to.' I had no intention of letting Sheeree slip through my fingers without first trying to get a leg over. Imagine screwing a twenty-year-old pensioner. This woman was beautiful; she wore a high-neck dress that perfectly adorned her body. I was standing in front of her, daydreaming, and she was staring at me in amazement. Thank the lord, Gordon had gone to the toilet. I stood with a boner in front of her.

'What can I say? Old Willie recognises beauty when he sees it.'

'You presume a great deal,' she says.

'I do not, he does, and I will never forgive him. He thought you were his C.O., and he was standing to attention. Perhaps he misheard the order.'

She smiled and accompanied Gordon, who was on his way to the pool restaurant. I joined them. I beckoned a waitress and assumed Sheeree wouldn't say anything to Gordon.

During lunch, he told me they established an enterprise renovating large Victorian houses in the Home Counties. They sold them to wealthy Londoners who appreciated a breath of fresh air and a bit of space from the wife or vice versa. They would take their latest squeeze there for the weekend. It was fashionable in the nineties to have a country house. Wild parties were held at the drop of a hat with coking and smoking, shagging and fagging, and the odd bit of human sacrifice thrown in to please the sexually depraved. The young bucks would head into the towns to collect a motley array of fanny and cock to satisfy the variously sized arseholes that would come from the cities to enjoy our parties. The locals would name these parties Quad Ds because of the drinking, dining, dancing, and dicking. With a cracking flow of alcohol and a vast array of marching powders, they would spend the nights as happy as pigs in shit. Of course, the neighbours were going mental, and who could blame them? Their sons and daughters were getting shagged stupid and wandering home at the crack of dawn, clutching fistfuls of fifty-pound notes and bags of ice to cool their ravished privates.

'Anyhow,' says I, 'did you go partying?'

'Of course,' says Gordon, 'we had invitations, and as they were excellent places to meet new clients, we could not refuse. We were selling dozens of properties monthly. We would not take advantage of our host's generosity.'

'What about you, Sheeree? You must have had men and women knocking on you non-stop.'

'I had my groupies; it was not my scene. Men readily enjoy that type of shenanigans. It is their primal instinct to bang anything that breathes,' and she smiled at Gordon.

'Tell me about Wendy.' I drolled on for another half-hour rabbiting with Dimitri and Wendy about my exploits. Fresh food and soft drinks are ordered, and he says she will make a few calls and see what's afoot. 'It's challenging to hide in America; you are monitored more than any other country, and England takes some beating.'

'You can say that again,' I say, remembering the receptionist at The Sandy Sky Motel. It's 3:56 pm, and I marvelled at how time flies when you're engrossed in conversation. I promise to meet for dinner. I wanted to go and see if Wendy was back. I wish them a pleasant evening with their friends, giving Gordon a firm handshake and a slap on the back. He held my hand firmly, and his eyes glowered with evil intent. The odd thing was his eyes seemed familiar, but nobody came to mind. I whisper to myself, keep a cool head and watch your tongue while you study a potential enemy. I berated myself for having divulged information about Wendy and especially my family. Who are they?

It was time to freshen up the body and make use of the four-by-four. I made it up to Fiddlers Elbow at 5:47 pm.

I reckoned Sheeree was under the clinic's auspices and in the process of having her tea and biscuits, so to speak. Gordon had offered an EARTHCO card at the hotel.

The whole procedure was being charged to the company and onto him. There would be no money trail, which would be very practical for many stars who required help. Mind you, quite a few women of note had been redesigned over the years. I recall a game show host from England with a new face. I recollect a few sensational murders during the last few years. Those wealthy-now-penniless-biddies had been knocking off their relatives to get the necessary bucks for their tea and biscuits. Worldwide psychiatric units were filling. They were blind and crippled, and the blame lay squarely at the door of EARTHCO. It's all falling into place, the raids on the clinics, the failures to discover any incriminating evidence, the countless lawsuits, the questioning by FBI agents of work colleagues, and the general nosiness of state agencies. EARTHCO continued to deceive and function. That would explain the new complex at Little Hump and Dillon getting nasty in a kind sort of way.

I reached the Russian Bear Restaurant to find it empty of patrons. I asked a cop for directions to Dimitri Ivanovo's house. He promptly demanded to know what business I had with Mr Ivanovo.

'If you must nose,' I say, emphasising the must, 'I'm seeking Wendy, the waitress, and a fat Russian cook.'

He replied, 'Hop in. I'll give you a lift. I have a car.' I grumble, and he says, no probs, we'll drop you back.

What can I say: out of the frying pan and into a big roaring fire? As I sat in the car, my arse warmed up, and off he sped like a Scotsman after a ten-pound note. He screeched to a halt in front of a double-fronted mansion.

Dimitri's mother popped her head out the window and pointed at me: 'That is him; that's the *govno;* he came here last night. He tried to steal my son's wife. Take him away.' She sprints to the police car, the wizened crone and gobs in my eye. She strides back to her mansion, still banging on about the Irish, damned old babushka.

A cop darts up and shows her a mugshot of me, and she is going *da da dada* ad infinitum.

'*Spaseebo spaseebo,*' he mummers as he hurries off at double speed to get away from her. He jumps in, and off we go, and when I open my mouth to ask a question, I'm warned to shut up.

'Or what,' and he offers me a can of pop. I put my hand out and get rapped across the knuckles.

'Shut up, will you shut up?'

I close my eyes and dream of Sheeree. They race to South Tucson Police Department, siren blaring. I was informed I was not under arrest but helping with enquiries regarding my movements in the past twenty-four hours. It's 8:07 pm, and I'm hungry. 'I want to phone my hotel, and what about my car?'

'A bit later,' he says, asking me to empty my pockets and hand him everything I could kill myself with. I am escorted to a cell and informed I would be interviewed in the morning, the excuse being the lawyers are busy or out of town. If I required one, they would do their best.

'Don't worry,' I say. 'I'm innocent; you can interview me now. I'm not detained, am I?'

'You are not under arrest dickhead. You were the last person to see Mr Ivanovo alive, and you did attack him last night with a baseball bat.'

'Get me a lawyer, or I'll have your job. Who do you think I am? Who do you think you are, Officer Lopez? You are a knoblicking wetback.'

'I shall report you for racial abuse Paddy, and you'll get five years.' He slams the door shut, shouting murderer at me and a host of other profanities to match the current mood. I'm in deep shit now. I have been swimming in the bloody stuff for the past forty-eight hours. Why didn't I keep driving? I'd never have seen Wendy to remind me of her juicy pussy from long ago. I read the graffiti on the wall about the death row inmates at the Browning unit at Arizona State Prison. I fell asleep and woke up in a cold sweat. I'd dreamt I'd been electrocuted, shot, gassed, and buggered to death. I spent the rest of the night in a semi-conscious state, deliberating if Cagney went yella on his way to the chair or was he doing Pat O'Brien a favour? Either way, I will scream my head off as I walk the green mile.

I awoke, it was daylight, and the door was open.

'Hi, I'm Sergeant Mendoza. Would you be ready for breakfast? Would the full Monty be to your satisfaction, as they say in England? We can deliver it from The Morning Meal restaurant across the road, and it's got a British chef.' This is a momentous change in attitude, but as my father would say, beware of Greeks bearing gifts. I think, what a spiel of codswallop, and I tell him to get my food and a lawyer.

'Oh, don't worry, sir, one is on the way.' He slams the cell door, clarifying who's in charge. What is going on, and how is Officer Lopez? Is he busy filling out racial abuse forms helped by his sergeant with his misspelt

Nordic name? What's his problem, or did last night never happen? An hour passes by, and no sign. Five minutes later, Officer Lopez darkens the doorway carrying my meal. I bet he's gobbed and shat in it and pissed in the coffee for good measure. I don't care, I'm starving, and I'm going to swallow bogeys and all.

'Muchas gracias,' I say.

He smiles and says, 'Enjoy,' and he's gone slamming the cell door violently. Should I tell them the truth? What information do they have about the restaurant fiasco and its aftermath? They nosed around and got witness statements. Lopez may try to make the cap fit; never mind, the cap is ten sizes too small. Winston Dillon would not hesitate to kill Wendy and Dimitri if the cops were on his trail. I figured it was best to keep shtum and see how things panned out.

I ask to shave and shower. Nothing was problematic for those two coppers. I wonder if these detectives will kill me and bury me in the desert as Joe Pesci did in the movie Casino. Detective Sven Gudjohnsen opens the door to tell me my lawyer will be with me at 14:00. He informs me Detective Pedro Lopez will not be pressing charges over the verbal assault he suffered last night, which led to me spending the night at their precinct. If I were to babble on about my rights being refused, I would be charged with assault. I would be detained, and with a bit of 'gilding the lily,' I would find myself doing the Riverdance at Browning. He was sneering at me. I was boiling with rage. I heard him asking if we had an understanding. I couldn't reply; my mouth wouldn't open. It was sealed dry.

At 15:43, my cell door opened, and a Captain introduced me to Sergeant Mendoza, Officer James Capriati, and Detective Sven Gudjohnsen. Detective Pedro Lopez would be present at the interview later.

A right shower of bastards this lot is, I thought to myself.

The captain asked, 'May I walk to the interview room with you? Your lawyer, Delano Hunt, is accompanied by Miss Bernstein from the mayor's office. Political manoeuvres are taking place right at this moment because of you. You can be confident the chairs will be in the same place when this ends. An English hotshot with an American couple has been inquiring about you and your whereabouts. Our reports indicate you were tucked up in bed at the Sandy Sky Motel on Route 51 when Dimitri went walkabout.'

'We will commence the interview with pleasantries, and you will be free to go at the end. Last night's behaviour was not in keeping with the American spirit. You, an immigrant, should have known better, as should Lopez. We will leave as friends. Nevertheless, should you feel that this is not the road you wish to travel...' he suddenly grabbed me by the balls.

'I will pop your nuts into a saucepan of boiling water and serve them to you in a glass of Dublin Guinness.'

He scowled at me with murderous eyes and spoke with a voice as hard as granite. I felt I was in the presence of evil. Here was a man who had frequently killed for his country in close-hand combat or for his own pleasure, whether for drug cartels, sexual gratification, or other death-bringing events. No words came from my mouth;

there was no need for any. The captain knew I would never speak of it as he relaxed his grip on my nuts. Jesus, I'm leaving Arizona for good, and I'll bypass this state in future and its Arizonian psychos.

'By the way, the final word of warning, the FBI may want you for questioning. Refer them to the mayor's office; do not speak of what happened to anyone. We will not lose our pensions and nest eggs we have been harvesting for the last twelve years because of an immigrant farmer. Get in there and do what's right, as this situation is bigger than all of us.' As a final reminder, I got a slap on the back of the head. 'I'm the daddy, and don't you forget it.' We entered the room.

Delano Hunt enquired if I would like to converse with him privately, to which I retorted no.

'Have you had your rights read to you?'

'Yes.'

'Have you been treated with respect and dignity?'

'Yes.'

'Let's get to the interview if that's OK with you, Mr Dempsey?'

'Let's crack on. I am excited at the prospect of getting out of here. Roll out your questions, and I will roll out the answers.'

'My name is Delano Hunt. The lady is Miss Bernstein, whom the mayor has appointed to oversee this interview as Mr Gordon Thatcher and Mr Austin Cahill-Grant have requested. So, Detective Gudjohnsen, as it's your interview, would you read out the charges, if any?'

'None, Mr Hunt, none,' says Gudjohnsen. 'Your client was requested to help us in an interview about his movements, but from inquiries made, he was at the Sandy Sky Motel when the abduction occurred. He is free to go.'

'How are you, Detective Lopez?' I ask. He did not reply. Detective Gudjohnsen ended the interview, wished me well, and left the room with his compadres.

'You are free to go,' says Hunt. He collected his bundle of papers and made a beeline for the door at double-quick time. "Slimcea" followed with her little round arse and cute cleavage, leaving little to the imagination. Delano gave me his card outside the building and informed me Mr Thatcher would be waiting for me for dinner at eight o'clock. He shook hands as did "Slimcea" and wished me a prison-free life.

Delano, following Miss Bernstein, felt her arse as he went. There goes a man who likes his meat close to the bone. I raised my arm, hailed a taxi, and thought, what a pair of snobs; they could do with a resounding shagging.

Chapter Two

Where's Wendy?

Friday, 9th June.

What a birthday surprise, I jumped into a cab and requested the Arizona Sunrise Hotel. I saw Lopez watching me. I reflected on the drama I had caused and wondered what the drama was. Gordon must have some pull to get the mayor to send his secretary. She looked delicate and brittle. You would be frightened to love her roughly in case she snapped in two. I asked to be dropped off a block from the hotel to allow myself time to meditate and see if there was any sign of Dillon. All was quiet as I approached the foyer. There was no sign of Gordon Thatcher and his friends.

It was 5:06 pm, and they were most likely up in their suites, getting dressed for dinner.

My imagination roamed through haute couture and what the lovely Sheeree would wear. Was she due to commence or finish her treatment? I was looking forward to tonight and thanking them for their help. I'd thank Sheeree personally if I ever got the chance and immediately felt guilty for having such thoughts. I promised myself I would not flirt with her. It bothered me that numerous influential people were eager for me to be pliant and obedient. Did I know something? I did not know, and I laughed out loud.

I slid my keycard into the lock and collapsed on the bed. Best get reception to wake me at six sharp in case I oversleep. The receptionist promised a courtesy call, and I lay on the bed and was asleep in seconds. The phone rang. I lifted the receiver.

'What, what do you want, goddamnit, that time already?' and I replaced the handset.

The phone rang again, and I ignored it. I step into the shower after a shave. Feeling a bit refreshed, I realise how hungry I am. With a pair of Gucci leather sneakers, I pop on a pair of Armani jeans and a dress shirt, one of my favourites, but damn, no tie.

Do I need a tie? Those hotshots look as if they are rigidly formal. I'll ask the receptionist.

'Do I need a tie for dinner?'

'Yes, you do, and you can't take it off when you go in, and no shorts. We do not tolerate riff-raff.'

'I haven't got a tie.'

'Well, well, well,' she says, dreadful. 'Do you not have any ties in Ireland? Could you go without dinner?'

She is taking the piss. 'Have you got a tie?' I ask.

'Oh yes, I have a tie; I am wearing it; it's nice. Do you not have a tie?'

'I have a good mind to complain to your boss.'

'He will do you no favour. I sleep with my boss. I will tell him you are trying to bed me. He will chuck you out like you would a mangy flea-bitten dog. Would you like to borrow a tie?'

'Yes, please.'

'I will have one sent to your room, try and stay awake.' I will find itching powder in my bed and snakes in my shoes. The receptionist has it in for me, and I haven't met her yet.

It's 7:44, and there is still no sign of the tie. I phone the receptionist, and she says it's on the way. 'Good God, man, you are impatient; stay calm; it's on its way.' There is a knock, and I receive a box. I give the bellhop five pollars; damn, I could have purchased a tie at the boutique in the foyer. Lord help me; she has sent me up a Bart Simpson tie.

The phone rings. 'Is it to your satisfaction, sir? You sure can answer your phone quickly,' she says. 'By the way, your guests are waiting for you; please get a move on, old chap, as they say in England.' Ah, to hell with it. I slip the tie on and head for the door. I go to the reception desk, and she laughs at me.

'The dining room is to your left, sir; try and avoid getting my tie in your soup. I want it back at the end of the night.'

I laugh and plead for another. She tells me it's the last one available and better than nothing. 'You can take it off when you are inside; that way, it will not dangle in your soup, sir.' She giggles and goes back to her desk. I apologise for being rude and ask for her forgiveness. I enter the dining room and spot Sheeree and their guests at the bar having drinks. I thank Gordon for his kind help. I shake his hand vigorously and give him a slap on the back, all matey and brotherly. I don't care for the man.

I'm convinced he is two-faced. There is something not right about him.

'You are an excellent amigo,' I say. Sheeree is by my side. I lean over, give her a peck on the cheek, and tell her what a delight she is. I congratulate them on being a fascinating couple. She sits and utters not a word while Gordon introduces his associates.

'Patrick, may I introduce Austin and Abilene Cahill-Grant, from Texas and from Nova Scotia, Donald and Margo McCullough. Donald has sawmills up in Canada and supplies lumber to Austin, who prepares it for his chain stores across Texas. We met them on the island of Jamaica; I remember it was while we were climbing Dunn's River Falls. We were staying in Montego Bay. Honesty is the key to a happy relationship. Are you an honest man Patrick in your dealings with the world?' says Gordon.

I note that strange glint in his eyes.

'Yes, I suppose I am. I've never taken a soul from anyone who didn't deserve to lose it.'

Abilene is looking at Bart and telling Margo that Bart is a well-endowed boy, and they are looking at my crotch and tittering. I check the necktie, and Bart has a tremendous tallywhacker in his tiny hand. People have noticed, and I am sure men in white coats will burst through the doors and whisk me off to the lunatic asylum. Donald is telling all and sundry within earshot it is a bet with Mariah, the receptionist.

'Let's order food; it's past eight o'clock,' I say grumpily.

'I fancy a steak,' says Gordon, 'seafood for the girls and extra burgers and steaks for us. OK ladies, what shall you have as extras?'

'Let's see,' said Sheeree. 'Gulf shrimp, Canadian snow crabs, a few pounds of cold-water rock lobster, and a pound of Alaskan crab legs. We will have baked potatoes with butter and sour cream, pilaf rice, green beans with almond spinach and bottles of white wine.'

'We hope to have extra guests tonight at ten,' says Donald, 'Austin's daughter and my two sons, although it depends on their flight schedule. These one-hour strikes screw up the schedules; they should be banned or have a full day's pay docked, not just the one miserly hour.'

'It's the lady's last supper for the next few days,' says Gordon. 'When they return, we will be presented with one reconditioned and two remakes.'

'Where has Donald gone?' I ask Austin. 'I'll go and have a deco in the gents.'

Going into the foyer, I stumble into Donald, engrossed in conversation with Miss Receptionist.

'Your wife is missing you,' I say. 'You'd better get your arse in gear and return to the fold. As for you, Mariah, thanks a bunch.' Her name was embroidered on her blouse.

'You can piss off,' she says. 'I have been annoyed by guests asking what the bet was and by battle-axe wives as well.'

She whispers a few words to Donald that make him blush. I admire her curves and she is good-looking. Arriving back, no one noticed our absence. We sat down to dine. Waiters turn up with additional salvers of piping hot food. When we were served, Rosaline remained to satisfy our every whim. I noted the ladies wore high-neck silk dresses with light suede boots. By the Lord Harry, they were ravenous. Rosaline served them our food, and another round of Guinness was put on the tab. No longer could I wait; the horse needed to be watered, and I went looking for the jacks. From now on, it was going to be a regular occurrence. I met Margo on her way back and I smiled lustfully at her.

I found Margo and myself secreted in an alcove without any concept of how we got there. I was kissing this married woman hungrily and feeling her breasts. They were soft, voluptuous and hot, her nipples hard and erect.

'I want to ride you,' I heard myself whispering while my hands caressed her dress. I waltzed my fingers around her waist and clasped the firm mound of her fanny's bush. She was wearing nothing underneath, top or bottom. She had gone commando. Her body was smooth, warm, and arousing to the touch. She gave off a highly sexually alluring scent. I tasted it on my lips and smelt it on her skin while kissing her. I wanted to strip her naked and plunge my throbbing cock deep inside to the hilt. I desired her to the extent that I would destroy my manhood in a shower of blood and spunk and roll over and die. I swore I would have her by hook or by crook. What if I touched her erogenous zones?

My hand went to unzip her dress.

She pushed me gently and said, 'Later, be patient.' She walked her fingers along my erection, making me spasm, but for the grace of retarded ejaculation, I would have shot my load. She was gone in the blink of an eye, and I needed to visit the jacks. I shook myself to make sure I was awake. As I slowly zipped up, Donald came in and asked if I was well.

'Everything's fine. I couldn't get JT to switch on his hydrant.' As I left the toilet, I remembered Wendy — another fantastic desirable shag. Returning to the fold, I observed the three women were locked in deep private conversation. Gordon was the worst for wear. Austin was knocking back Lone Stars in pint glasses.

'Bloody aeroplane is still in Denver. She won't get here until tomorrow night.'

I put Austin's age below forty-five and Abilene's about forty. When he proclaimed they were both sixty, I couldn't believe my eyes. She is an attractive woman with a sweet voice and cascading blond hair streaked with red. I ask how old his daughter is.

'She's twenty-one, and she has come through a sticky divorce. I warned her it wouldn't work, but she wanted things her way. He was arrogant and abusive in his language. He was a scrounger who needed a kick up the arse. He imagined he had made it when he married my Maryellen. I wasn't going to feed that waste of space and his relatives. I gave her a small allowance while at college and listened to her harping about how hard he was seeking employment. Of course, he wouldn't take a job in my warehouses. Oh no, that unemployed bum wanted to hang out with his spaced-out-pothead chums idling their lives away.

'She dreamt by marrying him, I would change my tune. It made me determined not to give in to her. His ten-watt bulb lit up in his empty head as he slowly understood I wouldn't finance his lifestyle.'

'One day, I had a visit from his father and uncle informing me he would divorce her for one hundred thousand pollars. They never had a thousand pollars between them, never mind one hundred thousand smackeroos, and I laughed. What could I do? I told them to slither off. I considered phoning the sheriff, but the newspapers would have had a field day interviewing those assholes. People gossiped about Maryellen and Alabama. What a name, only a dimwit would christen a cretin, Alabama. His mother's name was Mississippi,' and he falls off his chair, roaring with laughter. I join him in raucous laughter and drain two bottles of Lone Star and three shots of neat Canadian Club. My focus gets screwed up; however, after a while, it settles. We seat ourselves unsteadily. He orders cigars and cheroots for the ladies.

He informs me Mississippi's daughter was christened Missouri. The locals nicknamed her Misswhorey. That sets us off, and we hit the deck, banging on their luxurious wood floor — I suspect it was maple wood. We head off to the jacks before we piss ourselves. I dilly-dally, hoping Margo would pop along. Austin arrived back to check if I was lying in the gutter. When we return, the women wearing Chinese dresses are busy puffing on their cheroots in the style of those old Burmese biddies. A lady whinges about the smoke and smell to the management. Sheeree tells the well-heeled and well-oiled woman to step outside and discuss it in the chill night air.

The lady's husband is scared and drags his argumentative wife away, given that Sheeree's eyes had gone a peculiar colour as had her face. To tell the truth, her eyes were red and her skin yellow. She didn't look too right in the head, and I certainly would not have fancied a quick left hook from her. Gordon takes her by the hand and says goodnight. He has a word with the manager. An EARTHCO card passes between hands and will be redeemed later.

Abilene says, 'She and Margo are booked in for the clinic tomorrow.'

'You should be retiring yourselves,' says Gordon, 'we will seek out our new friend's ex-girlfriend. We will meet for a late breakfast at The Del Toro Café around eleven o'clock and take it from there. I should have the information at ten in the morning. Hopefully, Austin and Donald will be reunited with their children, and so until tomorrow, I bid thee adieu.'

We go to our suites.

Saturday, 10th June.

It was comparable to any other June day: bloody hot. I crawled out of bed with a massive hangover. I dreamt I was swimming through the air, and when tired, I rested on clouds. I heard laughter and swam, searching for the laughing children, yet I could not locate them. I searched all night but to no avail. I could listen to them chattering, yet I could not see them. I felt a considerable unease within myself, and I made a solemn promise no more 'wakey-wakeys.' I phoned reception for a handful of aspirin. I drank gallons of water. The Treble S Treatment is a necessity, and finally, I'm eager for a burst of fresh air. Heading for the foyer, I noticed Mariah was not on shift yet.

Did Donald get his wish? He was in the mood for loving last night. He was romancing Margo, but she kept giving me the eye and telling him to feck off, an expression Gordon said she had picked up watching Father Ted years before. Nobody paid him any heed until, without warning, she swung towards Donald, informing him in a vicious snarl 'to drop dead.' Donald said, 'Sorry, love,' and slinked off. He never came back to the table. Austin said Donald would annoy her, wanting sex when she was not in the mood, but I suspect Donald does it deliberately to get away from her. Abilene said Donald had it off behind her back. She has an eye for butch lesbians, and even though she is a bit of a bi-sexual, she sails firmly on the hetero. I shall ask him later. I bet he did screw Mariah, and I thought of Margo with the hot bod.

Abilene was a delicate little thing. She was blond with a slim, trim figure, and it crossed my mind they had swapped while on holiday. I fancied a threesome. They said they would be under the clinic's care, and we would not see them for a few days. I reckoned I'd phone the wife and have a chat with her. I'd get her out of bed, the sozzled bottle-kisser. Hearing her growl, I changed my mind. I asked in a redneck's voice if Susan and Peter were in.

'You want to speak to Susan and Peter, you do, do you? Let me think, would Peter and Susan be whom you want to speak to?' I heard her pouring herself a drink; she's been on the sauce all night.

'Can I speak to Susan?' I ask.

'You can, talk.'

'Where is she?'

'Who do you want?'

'Susan.'

'I'll get Peter to get her. You want, Susan?'

'Goddamnit, Mary.'

'Don't get fresh with me, you snivelling prick; it's Mrs Dempsey to you pipsqueak. I'll get her; who did you say you are?' I heard glass smashing on the kitchen tiles; she never came back. I rang several times, but the phone remained engaged. I assumed she was asleep. I remembered they would be at school teaching.

I reached the Del Toro Cafe at the appointed hour, but no one had arrived.

'I'll have the full English with coffee; please ensure the orange juice is freshly squeezed. I'm waiting for my friends; can you serve my meal in half an hour but keep the coffee flowing?'

I felt a tap on my shoulder as I sipped my second coffee.

'*Bon Jour*, Mr Dempsey.' Who did I see, Gordon and Austin dressed as Sherlock Holmes and Dr Watson?

'We wish to render our services and instigate proceedings into the curious disappearance of Wendy Ivanova and her husband-lover. We are the Baker Street Irregulars, and without further ado, let us partake of our meal and set off and search for Madame Wendy.'

They sat and ordered full English with extra toast and marmalade.

'Where is Donald?' I ask.

'Damned if we know. Margo said he had the hump last night and told her he would be in room 448 if she needed sex; otherwise, leave him alone. Margo went to the clinic with Sheeree and Abilene, and they won't be back until Thursday, the 15th of June. Sheeree will be back late Tuesday. Donald can be a real bastard and tight as a duck's arse, as well as being a terrific buddy. It's his Scottish ancestry. He polishes off a whole haggis on Burns Night. He eats it while listening to the Scots Dragoon Guards blasting away on bagpipes. Every New Year's Eve, he stands outside his house singing Auld Lang Syne at the top of his voice, and he's tone-deaf. We spent a New Year with him, although Margo is a different kettle of fish. She sings like a linnet and bakes scrumptious cakes. She has two fantastic sons. Richard is a cop in LA, and William is a biology doctor to do with diseases in Atlanta, Georgia.'

'So, where do we start?' I ask.

'We start,' says Gordon, 'with you telling us what happened to you from when you went to the Russian Bear to when you met Sheeree and me the day before yesterday.'

I launched into my story for a second time, interrupted by the arrival of breakfast, and continued until the story and plates were finished.

'I gotta tell you, Patrick,' says Austin, 'and I have excellent contacts; there is not a whisper in any police department in Arizona relating to Dimitri and Wendy. It's as if they vanished into thin air. When the third recession came in 2014, the world economy was weak from the 2007-2011 recession. There is no need for me to spell out to you the economics, but a multitude of well-to-do individuals went bankrupt. Gold and precious metals were the commodities of the day. The union of the pound and the American dollar in a new currency created the pollar. The law throughout the world had stiffened. In fact, it had a raging hard-on in Britain and America, and if you didn't abide strictly by the rules, you would get shafted.'

'These EARTHCO clinics are being pressurised to cough up their secrets. It's just a matter of time before the international community forces the US to mount raids on them. We had to secure a special haven for our wives to continue treatment if things go sour and Homeland Security shuts EARTHCO. You, Patrick, can help us acclimatise to our new bolthole when the time comes.'

'We have clubbed together and bought an island off the west coast of Clare. We want you to go there with Wendy when we find her. We have paid the islanders to leave; nonetheless, they are kicking in their heels. They are extremely agreeable to taking our euros but reluctant to move to the mainland. They will be shifted one way or the other. We would like you to speak and encourage them to speed up their exit. We understand you are the man who can help us achieve success. Are you up for the mission, for you will be away for a week or so? Those villagers have been paid for their properties. I want them to get out. They have been messing us around for the past six months. Those people on the island of Stonnage are MIRA supporters. The island of Stonnage belongs to me, and I want it. I will murder those cabbage-headed fishermen if they don't leave.'

He is furious and yelling. The waiter returns and tells him in a firm and threatening voice to shut up or get out. Gordon ignores him.

'That will lead to the MIRA sticking their oar in. I will slaughter those MIRA thugs. I have an army,' yells Gordon, rage building up in his neck veins. He was damn near apoplectic.

'I thought you were helping me track down Wendy,' says I. 'I now learn you want me to go to Ireland and evict a grumble of fishermen because you are frightened of the MIRA and you with an army, Mon Commandant. Are visions of Bob Hoskins riding in the back of a cab with a youthful James Bond making your balls shrink? It could be a "Long Good Friday" for me if they sniff me nosing into the MIRA business. I will go and find her myself, thanks for nothing; you are a money-grabbing shit,' and I leave.

'Damn you, Gordon Thatcher, if that is your name.' I suspect our paths have crossed militarily in the past.

I ask myself what gave that bastard the notion I would mediate for him with the MIRA (Munster Irish Republican Army). What does he know about me, and more to the point, what should I know about him and can't relive? Something to ponder. A few enquiries I shall make when I get his mugshot. It dawns on me Thatcher may have had plastic surgery. Why wouldn't he? They are all plastic and Botox.

The waiter stands with his sleeves rolled up, ready for a fight.

'Kick the shite out of that afterbirth,' I tell him slipping him a twenty-pollar bill. I go to the cashier and pay for my food, having grasped that Gordon is a proper vicious killer and Austin, who didn't say much, is as bad. I've wasted a bloody glorious morning.

It's lunchtime, and I head back to the hotel. From the corner of my eye, I spot Skeleton parked on the other side of the road, and without doing a quick reconnoitre, I race across and grab him by the shirt. It's then I twig; it's not him. I opened my mouth to apologise, grunting; I thought it was an old enemy. The stranger jumps out and punches me square on the jaw.

I run away. I don't want the cops turning up, especially Lopez. I take a detour and enter the hotel through a side entrance. I grab a refreshing beer at the bar and pick up the complimentary paper. Skeleton must have a doppelganger or a twin and a vicious twin to boot. I rub my injured jaw. Across the Arizona Daily Star's front page is a picture of three women and a man strutting down some steps smiling happily with a banner headline 'Senate Committee to Investigate EARTHCO's client's deaths.'

That explains the need for the island. Why would they purchase that windswept, rocky island? There is no counting on people's tastes.

I order a coffee and start to read, the cold beer wholly forgotten. It's about EARTHCO's Arizonan clinics and how a dozen former patients have been charged with murder in the last year. They name four people, three women and a man, known as the Four Corners, the principal stockholders and the CEOs of EARTHCO. I read the names Helga Von Feldt, Benedikta Walbeck, Bridgette Poindexter and Henry Preston. I've never heard of them. Why would I? They have been summoned to appear before a grand jury to counter accusations regarding their clinical practices. It says there are umpteen cases of homicide worldwide, principally in Europe. At present, they are interested in the deaths of American citizens, including one Congressman's wife. It goes on to give details of the deceased women, wealthy bankrupts. Many are insane and have been incarcerated for murder. A handful has been jailed for extortion and kidnapping, husbands murdered for insurance monies, etc. The paper asks why no men are charged with murder, and it says the meetings will take place in late July, the exact date to be published.

It mentions the FBI has been conducting investigations without any conclusive proof of wrongdoing by any staff member. It cites James Sturgess, Head of Security for EARTHCO, saying; he has never been aware of any member of the company having committed any crime. The murderous attacks have nothing to do with EARTHCO but with these poor wretches' mental states. They have multitudes of satisfied customers who are blissfully content to return to the clinics for Botox treatments and rejuvenating spas.

Fantasising about Sheeree and her gorgeous head, I thought Botox my arse. What about Margo and her hot body? No way, there is a lot more to this than meets the eye.

Nobody followed me back in, not Gordon nor Austin. Sod them; I'll have lunch and head back up to the Russian Bear and take things from scratch. I decided to check out and stay wherever I dropped anchor this night. I head to the dining room for lunch. This Tucson air doesn't half give you an appetite. Whom do I spot when I go in but Donald and Mariah, busy tucking into their brunchy-lunchy?

'Well, well, well, look what the rabbit dragged in,' says Donald holding Mariah by the hand. 'What do you want? Have you come to insult her, you ruffian, you vagabond? How dare you, and she so lovely? I have a good mind to challenge you to a duel. However, I am aware of who you are. I'll overlook it this time, mind you, this time only, *capish?*'

'Oh, you speak the Italiano, Canadian of Scottish descent. Let me tell you, husband of Margo, singer of Auld Lang Syne, I have just terminated a meeting with your chums, and you would never guess what they want me to do.'

'Oh yes, we do!' pipes up Mariah. 'They want you to go to Ireland and kill those greedy pigs that won't vacate their pigsties.'

'Is there anyone in Tucson that has not been informed I am supposed to commit murder? Last week, I was a lorry driver with a fat wife and two grown-up gimme-gimmies. I've been rebranded and repackaged, and I'm averse to being sent out to murder and maim. What gives you the impression I'm a murderer, particularly of my own people? Furthermore, what information do you have to know who I am?'

'Hold on a moment,' says Donald. 'Mariah and I have been in love for the past year. I met her when Margo first came to the clinic. I was sitting at the bar feeling miserable and lonely. Mariah asked if she could join me for a drink while waiting for a taxi to take her home. We had clocked one another at reception, and I admired her.'

'Yeah, I can see why,' I say. 'Was it love at first sight?'

'Hilarious,' says Mariah, 'we love one another, and we hope to be together one day.'

'You'd better keep an eye on Margo when she's short of her medicine, I tell Donald, she might get the urge to redesign Mariah's gorgeous face.'

'Mariah is on duty in a moment; she is on the two 'til ten shift. Let's grab a bite out of town?'

'Fair deuce,' says I, 'but I am searching for Wendy.' They hug and kiss as if they were emigrating to different ends of the earth. We take the 4x4 and drive up to the Russian Bear, but it's still shut. We stroll to the Dancing Queen saloon at the *plaza mayor* in Fiddlers Elbow and have lunch and a quiet drink. We haven't spoken, and I sense something is playing on Donald's mind. It's best to leave it and decide to chit-chat, and perchance he will open up a bit later.

'You are in love with Mariah? She is gorgeous; you are fortunate to have met her,' I smile at him.

'Why don't you can it, your bollocks? You would be inside her knickers in the blink of an eyelid. I saw how Margo was giving you the eye last night, and if I had been in love with her, I would have broken your head on the spot. You are welcome to her. She will eat you for starters. She is that type of woman; she will suck you in and blow you out as spunk bubbles. You can have her with my blessing. It's Mariah I want, and you can help me keep her; how I do not know. Listen, nobody is what they appear to be, including you. I don't hate Margo; I want her to be safe.'

'The way things are with EARTHCO, they may find themselves before a grand jury. The treatment centres could be shuttered and locked. Then what, how will they cope without their treatments? They will metamorphose into psychopathic old hags frothing and raving at the mouth. They will end up in lunatic asylums, blind and crippled and left to wallow in their piss and shit. Humanity is lacking in today's society, and that is an understatement. I don't want misery for Margo or Abilene, she is delicate, and as for Sheeree, she is sex on legs. I loved and admired these women when they were normal, caring and pretty. Age was not a factor, as I had known them when they were young. They were still desirable in my eyes when they were older, yet they worried about a wrinkle or a bit of cellulite. I saw beauty, and so did Austin. I don't know what that Cockney saw. I hate his brutality. Sheeree kept harping on about her friends and the benefits of being an adolescent, but youth cannot last forever. There is always ageing that gets in the way.'

'When I was a boy,' I say, getting a word in sideways, 'we used to learn mythology at school. One of the stories we were taught was *Tir Na Nog*, translated into English as 'Land of Youth.' Nobody ever grew old, hungry or sad. Sickness or death didn't exist; it was a place of youth and beauty. Valhalla or Elysium would be the equivalents.

Oisin (o-sheen) travelled with Niamh (neev) on a magic horse that galloped over water. This fairy island lay off the west coast of Ireland. With a six-thousand-year history, the county of Clare would be the obvious place for it to be. Though enjoying the pleasures of eternal youth, Oisin missed his homeland and wished to return. Niamh lent him the magic horse but warned him never to touch the soil of Ireland. Arriving back, everyone he had known had been dead for three centuries, and depressing loneliness swept over him. His horse bolted at the sight of wolves, and he fell from the saddle and immediately aged to the tune of three hundred years. Gasping with his dying breath, 'This cannot be, for I have been absent for less than a year. His whole life passed him by in a fleeting glimpse, yet he would have spent his life in slow motion if he had stayed. Perhaps he would have suffered insufferable misery. Perhaps he would have enjoyed exuberant happiness, but his destiny would have been of his own making.'

The girls were now dependent upon the whim of destiny, and their future lay on what might be their *Tir Na Nog*.

'A nice yarn,' says Donald, 'nevertheless, if we don't get control of that island, we cannot protect our wives from the ravages of age. There are famous film and TV stars living under assumed names. Quite a few went to their own funerals. What a brouhaha would ensure if these old farts booked in at emergency wards looking for help.

'I'm Elizabeth Taylor; make me youthful.'

'Go and sit. Wait your turn.'

'Do you know who I am?'

'No, I don't. You do look ancient enough to be suffering from dementia.'

Elizabeth fires off a mouthful of obscenities as she rips his windpipe out with her claw-like hands. 'I bet that was a surprise, you cocksucking turd,' as she kicks a nurse in her pussy-shop. 'Get me a doctor,' she screams, tearing her hair out in clumps. 'I'm decomposing as I wait,' she spits teeth out all over the place. Finally, she stutters incoherently and slumps to the floor, pissing and shitting, and faints into a coma.

'I don't want Margo to go through that in public. If she is to die, I want to help her pass away peacefully in her sleep with me holding her hand. She is the mother of my boys and has earned the right to my love and affection when she needs it. I am hoping Margo is in love with you and it's not a passing fad. I tell you this because I have no option. I know you can keep your mouth shut and would prefer to die rather than divulge confidence. You have morals and standards, and if you do not wish to cooperate, you will not do so.'

'You imagine you know me. Where would you have gotten this information? My family are immigrants, and we are close-knit and do not talk freely about our lives, past or present. I do not wish to speak one more word relating to my family. Is that clear?'

'Crystal!' he says.

'The day is gone. It's six o'clock; tell me the facts or clear off. I might grow old listening to you prattling on. Do you know where Dimitri is, Dillon, Wendy, or anyone who can help me? Put your thinking cap on and get the drinks in. I'm phoning my wife, and when I get back, and you are still here, I will know you will tell me interesting information.'

I head to the mobile phone shop and purchase a phone. I can't be arsed looking in the Range Rover for mine; it's invariably hiding where it shouldn't be. I punch in the numbers and hope the fat cow is awake and sober.

How come other men have sweet wives even if they are sluts, yet I'm stuck with a fat-arsed lesbian? I'm divorcing that bitch if she gives me lip. I don't give a curse about the gimmies; they will get used to it. Toughen them up for the misery that lies ahead when they get married.

'Hello, who's that?'

'It's me, Patrick.'

'Where have you been? You should have been home yesterday. Have you left your loving family? Why didn't you phone earlier? We miss you terribly. We cried most of the night. We dreamt you were injured or kidnapped.' I asked if she had checked with the police.

'No, of course not. We knew you'd be OK. Your paycheck is not in my account; explain yourself. Have you got another woman? We need nourishment; your kids need clothes. Where's the money? It should be in my account.'

'When did you last check?' I ask.

'A few minutes ago, I sent one of the kids.'

'That clarifies why you're sober, Mary; no spare cash, no sour mash.'

'Don't you insinuate I'm an alcoholic; you are a disgrace leaving your doting family hungry and thirsty. What kind of man are you?'

'I've had a bellyful of your miserable gab; I'm divorcing you, suck on that while you're waiting for your Bourbon. I don't know why the money's not in the bank; Sturgess, head of security, has probably blocked it. He is a right scumbag at the moment. I'll ring you back when I check out what's what. Meanwhile, get the groceries on tick. I'll phone Patel and square it with him. I've saved his bacon in the past.'

'How are Peter and Susan?'

'Oh, they are starving, thank you for asking. Would you hang up now and get us our pollars? Be a doting husband, and don't forget we love you dearly and don't forget the money.' She was gone, no doubt, directly to Mr Patel for a bottle of Bourbon. Won't she be in for an eye-opener, the fat lesbian alcoholic? The cow still thinks we have kids, and them banging thirty. They should have coinage. What do they do with their wages? I get Patel's number from enquiries and tell him to give her food but no alcohol.

'She'll not tolerate that,' he says. 'I don't usually give credit.' I've had my fill of crap today. I warn Patel, I'll shop him and his brown-arsed family for buying stolen merchandise from junkies if he doesn't do as he is told. While waiting for her to show, he should reminisce about the junkie who was going to stab him when he was trying to rip the crackhead off.

'Oh, you are right, Mr Dempsey. You are an outstanding customer. I will give her food and no alcohol.'

He hung up. She will get her Bourbon when she grabs him by the balls.

I go to the toilets and relieve myself in case Donald is waiting to punch me in the kidneys. There is nothing comparable to a punch in the waterbags to teach you pain and how to piss blood. He is still sitting at the table and has the beers and whiskey chasers. He tells me they have no knowledge of where they are. They are either dead and buried in the desert or on Little Hump Mountain. That is a death sentence. No way Winston Dillon will set them free without dropping himself in the shit. It hits me like a sledgehammer, and I collapse in my chair, gulp a beer and whiskey chaser, and order more alcohol.

'Will you help me find them, and I promise to run off with Margo? Wendy is in love with Dimitri, and Margo will be an excellent catch if she ends up like Sheeree, and as for Mary, my wife, she is a lesbian. Yeah, things will be fine. You can have your Mariah, and we will have another round to seal the deal.' Another round is tabbed. Who's trying to get who drunk tonight? Time will tell.

'Right,' says I, 'we wish to root out two people, Alphonse Rugosa and Helmuth Sprangler. They will know where she is, and I need to speak to Rachel Bernstein. I require their addresses so we can pay them a visit. Will you help?'

'Of course,' says Donald, excited to have Mariah's fabulous arse to himself, morning, noon and night. I bet he is sitting nursing a hard-on.

'Can I borrow your phone?' he says.

He dials a number and asks for Richard McCullough. 'He's off duty,' dialling another number. He speaks to Richard and gives him the lowdown on the information he requires. 'It's urgent, and yes, we would like it at nine o'clock in the morning, and yes, it's urgent. I'll explain tomorrow. Give Linda my love, bye!' He puts the phone in his pocket.

'I shall hang on to this; better buy yourself another, as it's going under the hammer when I'm done.'

Oh my, oh my, they do enjoy smashing phones down here with hammers. There's nothing to do before the morning. We book in for the night at the Dancing Queen saloon. We eat and sleep and dream of pretty women.

I hear laughter in my dreams. A voice is chanting my name, and I wake with a start.

Chapter Three

Rachel's Screwed

Sunday, 11th of June.

I am optimistic I will find Wendy today, so no more time-wasting. I'm booted and suited and dining at 8:06 when Donald comes in and orders a meal for himself.

'I've had a pleasant stroll, and I've got a clear head on my shoulders,' I tell Donald.

'I rang Gordon,' he says, 'and we chatted. Your name came up. He wasn't cock-a-hoop with your attitude, but he would still like us to be amicable. He is pulling out all the stops to find Wendy. He hopes you will still go to Ireland when you understand what is on offer. If you want to meet up tonight, he will discuss "options and payments" and for you not to worry about the conversation yesterday. What must be done will be done, with or without you on board. That is not to say you and I cannot continue your mission.'

'Be honest, Patrick, would any of us choose to live on a rock in the cold Atlantic? What a dump it must be. No offence Irishman, but would you not prefer to party in the Maldives or the Caribbean? Now that would be spectacular: sunshine, cocktails and dark-skinned money-suckers. Gordon informed me that the island is essential to EARTHCO. It is not the island they want but what it contains. I don't know what that is yet. EARTHCO obviously does.'

'We should take a run-up to the Russian Bear Restaurant and have a chat with the clientele at Dimitri's watering hole, see if anything is blowing in the wind,' I say.

'I shall be an FBI agent,' he says, showing me his credentials. 'I got them off Richard for my birthday. I like to play pranks on new friends.'

'Special agent in charge, nice rank, looks the real McCoy to me. Can you get me one?'

'Sure, sure, I'll have a word with him.'

Who is this guy? He is either a lawman or an outlaw man; I best watch my step either way. I don't want to tread on his toes and wonder if he is carrying. As if reading my mind, he removes his jacket and says, 'No gun, just a badge. I'm not taking my role-play seriously.' We laugh to ease any tension. I have another coffee after fetching the Sunday paper, which weighs a ton. I ditch the supplements, and I'm left with a few pages.

Yesterday's EARTHCO news item is followed by a threat of legal action against the newspaper and a complete rebuttal of their facts. The editorial implies they have two first-hand accounts from clients detailing the medicaments they received for their forty million pollars. They would further tell how it would cost tens of millions per annum or per quarter for top-up youth-enhancing baths. EARTHCO states their treatments are expensive and tailored for the rich and super-rich. Their clientele is informed in the first instance it is a rolling cost, and their clients lodge vast sums for future expenditure. It is deposited in their banking system and earns a discount for the account holder based on time and amount.

This information has been in the public domain for years, EARTHCO states, and much more besides. Donald says he knows all about it. 'It's a true account of the plight of two women who cannot afford the aftercare. Their last hope of receiving help is by suing the clinics on the grounds their health would be irrevocably damaged if treatment were not offered on a free basis, even if it meant the taxpayer footing the bill. They don't stand a snowball's chance in hell,' he says. 'If you can't afford follow-up treatment, whether it be a facelift, boobs, or any enhancing surgery, tough luck, your future is not the clinic's responsibility. They had been forewarned and refused to accept no for an answer. It's the last chance saloon before they end up pissing and shitting themselves. They should have been content with the body they were born with and spent their time honing a pleasant personality.'

After packing our bits and pieces in the Range Rover, we head up to the Russian Bear, and it's closed. Not a helpful sign. We cross the road to the tobacconists and ask why it's shut. It's a Korean shop, and he no-knowee — Bloody immigrants. On their way to church, we collar a group of Baptists who tell us to trust in the Lord, for he will lead us upon a righteous path leading to God and salvation. Fornication and drunkenness are the twin evils that beset gluttonous heathens they preach, looking me in the eye. I tell them to masturbate under my breath. Donald thanks them for their advice.

It's too early to bother with the saloon, and we drive to the babushka's house, and she is outside picking weeds from her driveway.

'Let me handle this,' says Donald. 'Be polite, stay in the car, and wait until I give you the nod.'

'Mrs Ivanova, I'm Donald McCullough from the FBI, and I am here with Mr Dempsey to locate your son.' He waves to me to join him, and as soon as she eyeballs me, she's yelling, 'I'm a govno and the son of a thousand whores.' I give her a murderous stare. She gives me the evil eye, and I keep my distance in case she spits at me. Jesus, Mary and Joseph, and the rest of his family, her mother must have terrified the SS units if she is anything to go by. I wonder what happened to her husband, who probably committed suicide or enlisted in the foreign legion.

Donald asks if she has a suggestion as to where Dimitri might be. Has she heard from him? Has she met Dillon, the Black man?

'Da, da,' she says, gesticulating down the street. 'He is staying at the Dancing Queen Saloon; he is visiting me later. He will gift me real Russian white birch vodka and beluga caviar; he says we will have a party.'

'What have the police done?' Donald asks.

'They ask if my son wants to steal a lorry. I say no, they say OK, and they leave. They have not been back; they don't like Russians, the cocksucking hillbillies.' She tells us to leave, and off we go. I should have stayed in the car and avoided this wizened bitch; what was Donald up to? What possessed me to get out of the car?

There is nothing beneficial to be learnt here except Dillon is in the hotel. Maybe he has been watching me, maybe Gordon is watching me, perhaps I should be watching me. I recalled the letter on the truck's floor; it was the one thing I'd picked up. I'd forgotten it in the excitement of the previous few days. It would be in my work jeans.

Donald's phone, or should I say my phone, rings. It's Richard. I hope he has positive news. 'He is flying from Los Angeles to Tucson, and we will meet him at the airport tomorrow night.' He hangs up. I take the phone.

'What do we do today?' I ask.

Donald reminds me of Rachel Bernstein and Laurel and Hardy.

'Surely, they must be within striking distance. We should go to the mayor's office and see if we can spot Rachel,'

I mutter. 'We might catch her going out for lunch.'

'Damn fine thinking,' says Donald, and off we go arriving at 11:55 am. 'We'll give it ten minutes and see if she comes out,' he says. 'You, Patrick, keep an eye on the carpool, and I'll eyeball the offices.'

A bit later, Donald returns, puffing and panting.

'She's at the sandwich bar on her own. But, goddamnit, I'm not fit. Patrick, go and talk to her, and I'll join you in a few minutes. I've just glimpsed Freddie Smith, and he needs to be reminded to settle his account with Austin. Austin has not paid me yet but keep it under your hat. I have no idea why I tell you this stuff; probably a lack of confidantes.'

Reaching the sandwich bar, I see she is far from being a happy bunny.

She leaves the bar and walks across the road, almost getting run over but for my quick reflexes. I pull her back to the kerb. She has been crying, for her eyes are red.

She bursts into tears, and a woman called me a nasty bastard; if my husband were here, he would give you a thrashing. Rachel says, 'Sorry, sorry,' and hurries to the car park. She fumbles, loses, finds and uses her key fob. She jumps in and thumps the steering wheel with her hands. She would do no damage if she pounded non-stop for a hundred years. Her little hands are delicate, and I try to dissuade her gently. I ask her to slide into the passenger seat to mitigate any chance of a rapid take-off by her. Wrapping herself and her car around a concrete bollard is one thing. To twist me around one is a definite no-no.

She opens her legs and lifts one into the passenger well. She lifts the other one unnecessarily high, flashing her frilly knickers and tanned thighs. She is delicate and angelic, with small, firm breasts extremely pleasing to the eye. A bulge develops in my trousers. I reflected on Delano Hunt feeling her arse, and I thought, there goes a man who eats his meat off the bone, and I am a man who would feed his bone off her meat. I can be a gentleman and would not take advantage of a damsel in distress. Or would I? I ask what is wrong, and she tells me Delano Hunt put her in the pudding club and won't marry or cohabit with her. His career is important, and she must have his baby. He will kill her and her family because he has connections to evil men through his employment.

'He boasted he has seven other children with girls. One girl, he had her murdered, and if I don't toe the line, he will kill me too. He said he would never speak to me again, but he will keep an eye on me. I don't want to have his baby. I want to have a husband and then have babies. He tricked me into getting pregnant by switching my pills. I can't tell Mum and Dad; they would be horrified and disown me. They love having an upstanding daughter in the Jewish community. I want to have an abortion. I'm frightened of what Delano will do. He doesn't like you, nor does Mr Thatcher or Mr Cahill-Grant; they are business associates.'

'What about Donald McCullough?'

'Never heard of McCullough,' she says. 'I've heard them say not to tell Donald. It's easy to remember his name, Donald Duck.' I laugh with her. She is the kind of girl middle-aged men would love forever and never look at another woman. I feel sorry for her, and I vow secretly to end her misery and Mr Hunt if he should encourage it.

'I will make your miseries fade like the morning dew,' I whisper. 'The first thing we will do is get you an abortion, and definitely not here in Tucson. Have it in Europe; you do have savings, I take it?'

'Oh yes, my great granny died and left me millions. I was two, but I wanted a career. Mum and Dad don't ask. My great-granddad was a gangster in the twenties; he fraternised with Charlie Luciano and Al Capone.'

'Tell the mayor you must go to Israel on family business, and you will be absent for a week. When do you want to have the abortion?'

'During the next four weeks?'

'That gives us a wide window of opportunity. I wouldn't guess you are pregnant; you're slim.'

'I know,' she says, patting her tiny navel, 'but it will show soon. Delano is a complete bastard. What are you going to do about him? He can get nasty.'

'Before you go to Europe, Delano will tell you it is OK. I, too, can get nasty.'

She looks at me dubiously with a glimmer of hope and says, 'I hope so, Mr Dempsey.'

'What about a proper lunch?' I ask. 'I'm sure the mayor's office can wait?'

She tells me the mayor wanted her to sleep with him because Delano had said so. 'I asked Delano today in the mayor's office, and he said I should if I wished to keep my job,' Rachel continued, 'Delano flicked up my skirt, flashing my thighs and panties, and they laughed. He denied sleeping with me and threatened to wallop me if I ever spoke of it.'

'Final warning,' he said. I left the room crying and went to lunch.

My blood was boiling, and I swore I'd rip his head off his shoulders.

The contorted look of rage on my face reassured and frightened her at the same time. Instead, she brightened up no end. Rachel said she would love lunch but out of town as she didn't want to run into Delano.

'Of course,' says I.

'What brings you to this neck of the woods,' she asks, and I tell her I was searching for an old schoolmate.

'Let's find your mate,' and she holds me by the hand. I offer a silent petition not to let me fall in love with such a sweet girl. Worse still, she is pregnant with Delano's kid. I could drown Delano and the little brat if she chose to keep it. Two pieces of scum removed from the planet must be worth ten brownie points.

Donald is eating a sandwich and appears overly excited. I imagined he would be spitting nails considering he had been waiting half an hour. He was impatient to tell me Margo had spoken to him, and she was feeling like a teenager. I said I was delighted, but what about Mariah?

'I love Mariah,' he says. 'I want Margo to be attractive for you. I want her to sweep you off your feet.'

I remembered my promise and consoled myself with the fact that Margo gave me a wicked hard-on. God knows what she will provide me with when she returns, a dose of the clap if they have been test-riding her in the clinic. I bring Donald up to speed and he says, 'Away you go, don't forget tonight, the airport at six o'clock. I'll inform Gordon and Austin we are meeting my son. Ask Rachel to meet us close to four o'clock at the hotel, and we can go to the airport together. Having a legal eagle perched on our shoulders will do no harm. I'm off to pamper Mariah.'

I advise Rachel to take her car across town to another car park, and I will follow her to ensure she is not pursued. She parks up, and we leave in the Range Rover. We return and see nothing out of the ordinary. To my dismay, there is no sign of Delano. She takes the car and parks it on a side street at a cinema on Drexel Road. That should be easy for her to pinpoint without dickhead seeing it. She's relaxed with our plan, and we go for lunch at the Cine Complex.

'I need help,' I tell her. 'Anything you can find out about what happened the other day when I got arrested.'

'I remember it well,' she says. 'You were fitted up. Gordon Thatcher wants you to go to Ireland for reasons unknown to me. Mayor Brady has a wife who needs, never mind wants, cosmetic upholstery, so to speak. He can't afford it. He wants to get her and her sister into Cactusville. I suspect they have been keeping it in the family for years, given that both sisters have boys, and they both have elephantine ears and crooked smiles. Bridgette Poindexter and Henry Preston can't stand him. They will not allow those two hags into the Reborn Clinic without full payment. Sour grapes buried in an old blood feud going back to the civil war in Ireland.'

'Any hint what about, what would that period have to do with the mayor?' I reckon he's got Irish in him with the name Brady.

'I never asked, and I was never told,' she says. 'Brady has done Thatcher a favour, for they were sending you to the Browning unit to roast your bacon. Cahill and Thatcher made him an offer he could not refuse. Thatcher was eager no harm should befall you. The mayor wanted you executed; eccentric, very eccentric. They would lend him the twenty million pollars he demanded to make up the fifty million. He gave his ranch as collateral, and the advance would be repaid five years to the day interest-free. The total cost should have been eighty million, but he got a mouth-watering discount. Brady has a lot of power with the police, and he could make life tough for EARTHCO, but they might have him whacked. Of course, he might have secret files and films hidden. Best let the pollar do the talking. Money is another word for diplomacy. I've heard Brady talking to Delano and Detective Gudjohnsen. Remember him, Patrick?'

'How could I forget.'

'With twenty million pollars on the table, the deal was done; the women would have their treatments. Brady was sore having to part with millions of pollars, but what price for two juicy pussies so white and tight? He was now deeply buried in EARTHCO's pocket. He had to look on the bright side and hope they would not scarper; it wouldn't be the first time it had happened to him. His first wife left after hearing about his antics out on the highway. He swore twenty million times it would not happen again. If they had any notion of doing a runner, he would have them incinerated at EARTHCO. He had an international tracker planted in their pelvic bones as an insurance policy.'

'He would often take a spin along Highway 51 with his right-hand man, Lieutenant Harry Parker, and see what pussy they could nick for a misdemeanour. The hitchhikers would oblige without getting too het up; it was transient sex, a knob in the gob and glug a glug. It would be finished quickly, and you would be on your way with forty or fifty pollars if she gave good head. If not, she would spend the night in the cells with a one hundred pollar fine. A hot meal and a shower would often swing it, especially if the boyfriend had a bit of pot and attitude. Harry liked a bit of arse, as did Gudjohnsen, and the gift of a bag of fine weed would encourage our 21st century wanderers to choose the proper route.'

'Sex was like an Amtrak ticket; it would get you onto trains for free and get you to safe destinations. After listening to their sob stories, Brady had tickets issued to minors to get them back to their parents. He never took advantage. He checked they were clean, well-nourished, and untroubled on their homeward journey, knowing a daddy or uncle would be nursing sore bollocks on their arrival. Mayor Brady was harvesting fanny for his future. I know he dined with nice women and may have slept with them. He had a large array of cards on his birthdays, signed with love. He loved to show the younger officers his harem.'

'I have been droning on,' says Rachel, 'and we haven't yet ordered. Let's do so right now.' The waitress is beside us, and I apologise for the delay. Rachel vocalises her amazement with the story. 'My-o-my, what an exciting man our mayor is. He could do much for my family.'

'Yes, I'm sure he would. Can we order now?' I ask.

'Yes, what would you like?'

Rachel says, 'I would like a small Topopo and a pot of coffee.'

'I'll have a shrimp Caesar salad,' I say.

She takes her mobile out and switches it on — the phone blips.

'It's Delano,' she whispers with fear in her voice. From experience, it's best to catch the bull by the horns — tell him she is registering for an abortion at this moment. She practically has a heart attack at the thought of saying such a sentence. I take the phone from her and walk outside to the car park. I hang up and ring back before he can redial.

He answers, 'Where the...' I interrupt in a firm, threatening voice, 'I will murder you, you toe-rag,' and hang up. I see her peering out of the window in terror, and I give her a broad smile. He phones back, and I put him on speakerphone.

'Who are you?' he bellows. 'Where is Rachel? Blah - blah –blah, I'll kill you,' I hang up. Delano phones back, and I hang up. I phone back and tell him I will pay him a visit, and Concannon and Jessop will not help him. 'You have chosen to knock up the wrong girl. We will meet.' I switch it off. I re-enter the restaurant. Our food is on the way, and Rachel is about to give birth to kittens.

'It's all in hand; he will toe the line. It has become necessary to help him adjust his outlook on life a wee bit.'

'Will it be OK?' she whispers. Then, putting her hand on mine, she whispers, 'Will you help me?'

'Of course, don't worry, I'm the boss, not him.'

She perks up and eats her little meal. I place her phone on the table, and she quickly hides it in her bag.

'If he doesn't toe the line, I will put the fear of God in him to such an extent he will be crapping himself for a week. We must get to the hotel,' and off we go. 'We must exchange mobile numbers with our new buddies. No one can contact anybody. Let us exchange our numbers first. Damn, my phone is at the hotel.'

I buy two, one for Rachel and one for myself. I pop into the next phone shop, buy two sim cards and tell her we'll sort them out later.

I have no time to wash or shave, as I recall Donald's advice to have a full tank as we may have a long journey tonight. I gas up and head for the airport arriving at 05:58 pm. We stroll to the concourse hand in hand and see Mariah and Donald talking to Richard. He is reasonably tall at six feet, powerfully built, with a healthy brown complexion. I wonder if Richard eats haggis or wears a kilt. I wonder what he knows and what we are doing here.

I'm starving, and Rachel looks delicious. I want to explore her from head to toe. We join Donald, and he introduces us to Richard. I shake hands and ask if I can see his badge. He's surprised at the request and produces his Los Angeles Police badge. I memorise the number and ask if it's real. He seems puzzled, and I tell him it's vital I find my friend Wendy who is frightfully dear to me but not in a sexual way, in a sisterly way. I'm fully alert that Rachel is standing beside me with her hand brushing mine. I mentioned to Richard that she is a colleague and a lawyer who helped me. I draw her close and give her a gentle squeeze. She smiles, and I clasp her hand, feeling a sense of security running through her body. She is relaxed, for she feels safe in our assemblage. I ask if anybody is hungry, and the answer is yes.

Donald tells us we are booked at the Country Inn on South Tucson Boulevard for the night.

'Let's get going.' I retake Rachel's hand and head out towards the taxi rank.

'No need,' shouts Donald, 'the hotel has sent a limo.'

Richard and his dad get in, followed by the lovely, proportioned Mariah. You would eat a yard of her shit to have a feel of her arse.

My staring hasn't passed unnoticed. Rachel makes clear her disapproval by flashing her thighs as she tumbles in. Donald receives a dirty scowl while Richard tries to appear absent-minded. I get the message. We arrive shortly before 7:00 and agree to meet at 8:45 for dinner. We book a table and put in our orders.

'Yes, sir, you will be served at 8:45.'

Donald has booked separate rooms for us. He could have been a bosom buddy and booked a double and forgot about Margo for one night. We retire to freshen up and bang on 8:30; we are polished and head downstairs. I should have purchased better clothes at the boutique in the foyer. Rachel had bought an outfit for herself.

Down the winding stairs ambles Mariah and Rachel, chaste and demure in appearance. I wanted to make love to both women. I'd never been privy to a duo so much in love as Donald and Mariah. The twenty years + age gap never existed except in the minds of jealous people. His gaze never left her, for he never gave Rachel a second look. Instead, he gazed in awe at Mariah in a short miniskirt of powder blue and cream trim that swirled around her tanned thighs as she did her catwalk into the bar. Rachel, in a white and pink trim mini, followed suit. They were wearing five-inch heels, which gave the impression they were barefoot. Low-cut elegant blouses allowed their flowing locks to nestle on their shoulders.

I felt proud to escort Rachel to dinner, knowing many a man would be divorcing his wife if there was the slightest chance they could meet such an angel. I felt Donald sizing me up. I must make him aware Margo was the one for me. Everything was guesswork with those types when they were in love. He might have her knocked off. I still preferred to be with Margo. She would be approaching my age and adolescence. Rachel was too delicate. This can't be happening to me, all these cute women.

Rachel's tugging my arm. 'Are you daydreaming, Patrick?'

I laugh because it is real. I am in the company of women I am frightened to love, and Richard says, 'Are you coming in, or have you lost your appetite?'

'No, no, I'm on the way,' I say. 'I can't believe how beautiful your mother is.'

He frowns at his dad, who shrugs his shoulders. I shake my head in disbelief at what I am saying. My brain is muddled.

Where is Rachel? My brain asks. I inform it that she has gone ahead with Mariah to soak up the admiring glances and estimate the number of cocks their fannies could enjoy tonight. She must have calculated a lot from the smirk on Mariah's face. I wonder what she's thinking. Can you send up Sylvester Stallone (Paradise Alley) with that block of ice for the morning? Thank you. We have dinner with a little chat, and afterwards, Richard and I retire to the lounge for drinks. What's happened to Wendy, the love of my life?

'Where's Gordon and Austin? Shouldn't they be here, and what is the tank of gas for?' I ask. 'Change of plan due to a lack of clarity regarding Dimitri and Wendy. Don't worry; we have it in hand. Explain later. What I am about to tell you is confidential, and if anybody does not want to be a party to murder, leave now,' says Richard.

Rachel is startled, as is Mariah. 'I don't want to murder anybody; I should leave. I'm a lawyer; I will be disbarred and sent to jail. Why did you take me to meet these people, Patrick? I trusted you with my life.' She begins to cry.

'We are not going to kill anybody,' Richard says. 'They might try to kill us. We would have to defend ourselves. We may have to kill, and courts might consider it murder. If you don't kill on your own property, you could be on the way to Old Sparky. I'm saying they are being held prisoner by nasty, powerful people, and the police can't be bothered to help. We don't know where they are. There are countless ways to end up murdered, which could be accidental,' says Donald.

'I don't intend to kill anyone,' I say. It's Richard's way of grabbing attention.

'Let Mariah take you to your room and tidy your makeup, return, and have a drink.'

I get up and walk Rachel to the foyer.

'Have you said anything to Mariah?'

'No, nothing about our friendship.'

'Don't let on to Mariah. I like you, you gorgeous little creature. Say you are helping me search for Wendy. Tell her what happened the night I was arrested and nothing about Delano and the baby. Let her think you are still with him and looking forward to getting married. I will explain tomorrow,' and she gives me a confused look. Mariah caught up to us after saying a snoggingly goodbye to Donald. They head for the lift.

'How trustworthy are those two?' asks Richard. 'Would you bet your life on them to keep their mouths shut?'

'She will say nothing,' I mutter.

'I agree,' says Donald. 'You were abrupt with your language bringing murder to the table.'

'What about you, Patrick? Feel inclined to wipe out a dozen civilians? Have you got murder in your blood?'

'If you continue to speak like that to me, I will introduce you and your son to drip feeds, do you understand? Don't play me for a loser, or I will walk. So far, I've been enticed to commit murder by your friends, and now he's talking murder. What is the matter with you people?'

'Have you got information for me or not? If so, spit it out, and let's see if it can stand. I don't want Rachel involved in any shenanigans, and if I were you, Donald, I'd keep Mariah out of it even if she knows what's going on. If any heavy stuff happens, I don't want the girls getting splashed with it. Best to have a true accomplish on the outside, a person you can trust.'

'Well said,' said Richard, and he shook my hand. 'You are dead right, but I wished to witness everyone's reaction.'

'Indubitably appropriate,' I say, 'you can be a special agent in charge, Donald.'

I noticed Richard reacted to the special agent. These two are something else, and I'm not lowering my guard with either of them for one second. I'll screw his bird because she has a classy chassis. I'm fed up with this rigmarole. Got to make her feel she must let me ride her, as it will strengthen her love for Donald. It must be kept secret so her love and my friendship with her lover remain strong. Hopefully, she will find it therapeutic and, like Oliver Twist, ask for more. I'll sweet-talk her into bed. Letting such a body slip through my fingers would be a crying shame.

'EARTHCO's head office is in Beverley Hills, and the receptionist is my friend,' says Richard. 'I requested a list of clinics for the Tucson area, which she said she would gladly supply. I asked her to find out where our three musketeers were bivouacked.'

'You mean Dillon and his sidekicks?' I ask.

'Yeah, that's who I asked her to check for, and Dimitri and Wendy Ivanova.'

'Don't let up now when the story is getting exciting; what did she give you besides a shag?' I ask.

'It's not that kind of a relationship. Are you fit, Paddy? I should give you a manly workout, preferably with a size twelve boot up your arse.'

'I'll bury my boot up your arse. I will have a brown ankle when I pull it out,' I snarl.

'Stop it!' shouts Donald as people give a sly glance to see who's yelling.

Finally, a security guard turns up. 'Sorry, sorry, family problem, we will be off. My son hates me, thank you, goodnight,' and we sign the bill. 'I don't want to hear another word,' Donald whispers. 'They are listening to us; let's talk about the weather,' and we head off.

'Where are the girls?' I ask. 'I'll phone Mariah's room.' No reply: I try Rachel's, no response. A waiter from the restaurant informs us they are in the Oliver Reed bar. We spot them bold as brass talking and laughing ten to the dozen to two attractive men. The green-eyed monster is up in me and rearing to attack. They are drinking. Mariah spots us, comes, and queries why we took so long to find them.

'You could have come back to the restaurant,' I grumble. 'I suppose it was out of your way by twenty feet.' I feel uneasy, and Mr Watchit, my warning man, is on high alert. This is a setup. Rachel would never throw herself at another man. Donald is ensuring I am available for his wife once she's out of the clinic. Why he should assume I want his wife above anyone else's is a mystery, but I will play his game. Nevertheless, she is a fantastically alluring woman.

'Rachel has been upset today, and you should not encourage her to double-cross her boyfriend,' I say.

'I'm doing nothing of the kind,' says Mariah. 'She wanted to let you discuss your business with Don and Richard. She would have had the waiter find you. Let her enjoy herself, and if she wants to sleep with one or both, let her. What does it have to do with you?'

'I want her to do a job for me. I'm tired of these antics. I want to trace my friend Wendy.'

'Do you love Wendy, Patrick?' she asks in a soft coaxing voice.

'I did once, but not anymore. I care for Wendy's safety, and she is the mo . . . most annoying person.' The game could have been up if I had continued talking; he might have had Wendy bumped off. He must never be aware that Wendy is the mother of my boy. Donald possibly saw me molest Margo, or she told him. He is cocksure of his position.

'We have business to discuss, so away with you to your lovers,' I say. 'Donald won't mind, have both in case one is not up to the job?' Donald doesn't seem distressed. Are they trying to take advantage of Rachel? Mariah leaves smiling and laughing and joins Rachel and the two men.

'Right, Richard, let's be having it; cut the bullshit. What you got?' I nod at Donald to get the drinks in.

'My friend ferreted out three clinics in the Tucson area,' Richard produces a sheet of paper and gives it to me. 'You have the addresses of three men (Winston Dillon, Helmuth Sprangler, and Alphonse Rugosa) who are employed as security for EARTHCO. There is a fourth name, Luther White; he is Winston Dillon's chief assassin. I've checked him on our files, and he's suspected of several murders in Tucson in the past twelve months. They were in Fiddlers Elbow with Mrs Ivanova last night and had a party, according to the cops. The old lady died this evening following a heart attack. Dillon and his two goons left at noon. There was no sign of Luther White; it's been written up as a cardiac failure. Her son can't be located. The Russian Embassy has been informed.'

'Now for the bit you want to hear. Dimitri, unconscious, arrived at the Rosy Cheeks clinic on Apache

Drive yesterday with Wendy in an ambulance. She was to be transferred to Little Hump Clinic. How do I know?'

'Patient notes and files go on the mainframe, which my friend has clearance for, and she tapped Wendy's name in, and up she popped. What a stroke of luck! According to Wendy's notes, he informed the doctor they had been kidnapped and taken to a warehouse known as the Lonepine Ranch. I googled that, and it's leased to EARTHCO. Dillon kept accusing him of being a hijacker and responsible for losing another lorry that should have been delivered to the Lonepine Ranch. Dimitri said Dillon knew he was a Russian army officer and hijacker for the Russian mafia. This time he hijacked the wrong truck.'

'They gave him a shot of heroin, but not only is he a pisshead, but he's a smackhead to boot. He played their game which got them nowhere. They threatened Wendy with rape. He wouldn't tell them nought, so Dillon brought back two of his goons to shoot her full of heroin. That sent her into respiratory arrest. They said Dimitri went mental and killed both men instantaneously. Dillon went for his gun but was knocked out by an enormous fist pile driving into his head. He is in a coma. According to the notes, Dimitri revived her with great medical skill; he left the building and approached a parked ambulance. The ambulance driver said he would take them to a clinic for further assistance. Dimitri cottoned on to Dillon, intending to interrogate them violently but not kill them. He wasn't amused but stayed tight-lipped.'

'Wendy's breathing became difficult, so he asked the driver to take her to the nearest surgery, which turned out to be EARTHCO's. They treated and stabilised her and advised him she should stay overnight for observation. He said they assumed she was an EARTHCO patient. The driver had phoned Sturgess, who sent a helicopter and whisked Dimitri away. It was then Dimitri wised up to his second mistake. Though he is old, I must tell you that he has the strength of several men combined. He nurtures a brute force within him and is an ex-member of Spetsnaz. He kills with his hands. If he gets a grip on you, he will rip your head off or give you a high-pitched voice.'

'The helicopter crashed outside of Little Tonto, and when the police arrived, there was no sign of Dimitri or the pilot. Three security guards were found lying out in the scrub. Wendy Ivanova is recuperating in the Rosy Cheeks Clinic and should be released within forty-eight hours. The FBI has shown an interest in her to the extent they have placed two guards outside her door. EARTHCO has placed two more. She is going nowhere without being spotted.'

'Mighty fine sleuthing Richard, let me get you a drink. You do drink, don't you?'

'Oh yes, I'll have whatever you're having.'

'I'm on the Guinness.'

'That will do nicely.'

'Let's get the women back if they haven't been knocked up,' I say.

'Don't let Dad hear you bad mouth Mariah for he's madly in love with her.'

'I heard what you said,' says Donald as he returned from a piss. 'I'll get the drinks.'

'If you are going to screw Rachel, don't let Dad know.'

A lady appears with waist-length blonde hair and a short skirt, legs up to her ass, lovely tits, and heavy sophisticated makeup. I wouldn't half fancy screwing her myself. She is pretty, yet she fires my curiosity. I've seen her type elsewhere, but where? She's about thirty. He introduces her as Apsara. She cheek kisses Donald, who has shown up with his precious Mariah and Rachel, accompanied by two gigolos. What is she up to bringing those-pussy-fillers along?

Mariah introduces her brothers, Peter and Jack. A sense of relief flows through my heart, loins, and brain. We are heading to a country & western bar, Rednecks. Taxis arrive, and off we go. Rachel and Apsara travel with Richard and me in one taxi while the rest bugger off in another.

'Where are you from, Apsara?' I ask. I already figured out the answer and what she is.

'She is a Thai ladyboy,' Richard says. I turn to Apsara and tell her she is fascinating, and if you don't want him, I'm your man. I've been to Thailand.'

'Don't take the piss,' says Richard. 'I love Apsara.'

'Fine by me,' I say with a grin, and Rachel is laughing and whispering to Apsara. She is jovial, for she's free from her tormentor and safe. We arrive and pay the entrance fee. The music is foot-tapping, and we order bees and berries and monkeyshine.

'I want to make love to you all night,' I finally say it. She doesn't seem overly surprised and says, 'Yes, I'd love to.'

She squeezes my hand. Donald doesn't care; he has Mariah in deep conversation. Apsara is engrossed in a perverted sex scene Richard is detailing to her. We order burritos and tacos and replenish our monkeyshine. I want to dance, and Rachel is happy to oblige. I embrace and kiss her full on the mouth, feeling the warmth of her breath and the wetness of her lips. I have a wicked hard-on. I manoeuvre it upward and push my mushroom against her flimsy dress. She moans; she's wet, and I say I want to slurp from her furry cup. She takes my hand, places it on her breast, and tells me I can do what I wish. I take my hand away, and we dance to, 'Please don't stop loving me' sung by Dolly Parton. Having enjoyed our dance immensely, we take our seats at the table. Donald gives me a funny look.

'Fancy a slash, Donald?' says I. I get up to go to the toilet.

'Don't mind if I do,' and we leave and take a detour outside, and I ask if he has a problem and, if so, spit it out.

'I intend to make love to that delicate girl tonight, and Margo's not here. Unless you want Mariah or Apsara to suck my cock would you kindly feck off and enjoy yourself? I don't half-fancy sticking one up, Mariah; she has an excellently proportioned body. When Margo becomes available, I will be up her quicker than a squirrel up a nut tree, OK? I will have your Margo ravished at least half a dozen times before we hit the bedroom.'

'Stick with Rachel, thank you,' and he scuttled off for a piss, fearful I might make a play for Mariah. I don't know why he should be scared, but then again, people are frightened of competition.

We ate our burritos and drank copious amounts of beer. We agreed we should retire to our beds, preferably with one another. Two hillbillies had been giving Apsara pervy come-ons, and when we went outside to hail a taxi or two, we knew a problem was looming. They made a beeline for Apsara and grabbed her by the leg, which caused her to trip. I attacked both leaving them in a bloody mess within seconds. We hurried to the taxi rank and reached the Country Inn fifteen minutes later. Nothing is mentioned concerning the violent act that has just taken place.

'Thanks for a lovely night,' I say.

Rachel and I head for the lift. We enter her room. Sexual hunger is upon us, and we kiss passionately. She wraps her leg around my thigh. I slide my hand up to her stocking top and round her bottom, floating her lower body into mine. She wriggles free while undoing her blouse and falls backwards onto the bed. She lies with her legs slightly apart, revealing pink lacy knickers complimenting her tanned skin. She leans forward, gripping her toes, and rocks to and fro, flashing her tits, and finally sits up facing me with a "do you fancy what you see" smirk on her face. I make a grunting noise to let her know she has awakened my animal urges. I remove my shirt as she allows her blouse to droop over her shoulders, her breasts in full view. I lean across and kiss her lips, which causes her to collapse on the bed with her arms outstretched. She rolls onto her belly, giggling, legs splayed. I stand naked with a raging hard-on. Sliding a finger into her fanny, I gently tug her panties off and compliment myself on my good luck. She rolls onto her back.

A small bush of hair and pear-shaped titties greet my hungry eyes. I caress those nipples with my fingertips and gently suck. She spreads her thighs, and slowly I lower myself, letting my cock brush her pubic hairs. She moans in satisfaction as I continue to lick and suck. My mouth slides to her navel and onto her outer lips, teasing them open with my tongue. I encourage her to move her body in rhythm as my tongue probes ever deeper within, all the while licking and sucking her juices as I nibble her clit. She rhythmically moves to the music in my mouth.

Having satisfied the hard-on in my tongue, I rise, hinting I want to penetrate her. She slides a hand and guides my cock. I slip my knob inside, causing her to gasp. The hotness of her fanny and the beating of my heart tell me I am in a heaven-hole. She is tight and moist as her pussy gobbles up my manhood; he is straining at his foreskin, trying to break free. I gaze upon her face, sweet and delicate, as are her legs. She wraps both around my waist. I slide my hand under her bottom and push deeper inside. I ride her with deliberate deep, penetrating strokes.

She is fascinating, hot, and erotically virginal. I'm pumping, "in and out, in and out," as an old-fashioned engine piston should do. She is keening a continuous wail. Let's see what kind of wailing she does when I ram him into fifth gear and go to Mach 1. *Aaaah*, this is the life as I stifle a laugh and smother her with kisses. I kiss her lips. And she lifts her head to help. Her mouth is like a bird begging for food, opening and closing, and pouting for kisses. I lock my arms in a press-up position and gaze upon her as she spreads her stockinged thighs high and wide. Her hand is on her clit, helping it to ignite. We are primed to explode; I find it hard not to ejaculate, but I keep control. I slide my hand back down, gently letting her pussy juice moisten my fingers. I push a finger deep into her arsehole; she moans with pleasure. She is a woman in love; her body is shivering with excitement. She is going to orgasm, as am I. She wants to control me, and she rolls me over as she rides my cock. There is passion in her eyes. She has found what she seeks; she has found domination. I'm squeezing her nipples hard; pain and pleasure scythe through her body. Our tongues are fighting one another. I'm parting the cheeks of her bottom wide; she is in the throes of orgasm. She shouts out my name.

'Take me, Patrick; I am yours.'

I am in seventh heaven. I ride her with strength and passion, and she cries out as she ascends to a higher plain. We have reached the house of orgasm; la petite mort's upon her. We are in a union: our souls, hearts, and minds are as one. We have become one; we have completed a sexual experience we may never be capable of recreating to such a degree again. We descend into a state of paralysis and exhaustion. How long have we been at it? Fifteen minutes, half an hour, an hour, two hours, who knows who cares as we cuddle and hug one another tightly and drift off to sleep.

Chapter Four

Murder by Accident

Monday, 12th June.

We woke together bright and early. We kissed, showered, and said very little.

'I loved last night. You are a married man, and therefore it must come to a grinding halt. I will carry our experience unto death or until dementia takes me.'

'I never hid my wedding ring from you.'

'I saw it yesterday. I was happy to love you as you did me. I want my own husband, not someone else's.'

'Will you still help me with Delano?' Rachel asks.

'Don't worry; I'll fix him properly. Have I got a surprise for that shite. He won't be so eager to knock up girls in the future. Let's have brunch for breakfast and figure out what the rest are up to later. I wonder how our resident ladyboy is. What's his name?'

'Apsara,' says Rachel. 'Do you want to love him with me?' she asks mischievously. She slips into jeans, a T-shirt, and sandals. Her nipples are protruding.

'OMG,' she says, 'but what can I do?' Off we go. It's 06:12. We are the early birds. We tuck into waffles, muffins, bagels, and coffee and await the pleasure of our hosts, who are still in bed.

'What time does lunkhead-boy get to the office?'

'8:30 on the dot.'

'It's 07:14. Let's have another coffee and pop over to Delano's house. Do you know where he lives, or was it a desk job?' She blushes, and I'm ashamed of myself; I do love-lust her. She is so sexually appealing.

'No, he invited me to his home; I know his address.'

'Let's pay him a visit,' I say. We drink our coffees, and Rachel starts to fret.

'You must make yourself strong,' I say. 'Invoke your ancestors to give you strength and courage. Being Jewish, they must have had buckets of it throughout the centuries. Call on your great-grandfather to give you his gangster grit. I implore my ancestors to fill me with courage in times of peril, for they faced famine, war, pestilence, and death. We were as downtrodden as the Israelites, habitually getting set upon yet standing up for freedom and our right to live as free men and women. Mustn't forget the women, a powerful lot they are. So best foot forward and let us destroy your tormentor by hook or by crook. We must take him by surprise, or he could shoot us entering his house. Then say it was self-defence, and Lopez would have a field day with me. The consequences are too ghastly to contemplate, but the show must go on.'

We parked at some distance from his house and walked up the opposite side of the avenue. As we crossed the road, his front door opened, and a Rachel doppelganger stepped out and flounced along the footpath. I pursued her, beckoning Rachel to follow. We reached her car and closed in on her.

I said, 'Excuse me, have you just left Mr Delano's house.'

She seemed rattled. Rachel shoved her credentials up this lady's nose and said, 'We are investigating sexual harassment of women by Delano Hunt. He enjoys creating a pregnancy and bullying them into keeping the baby with threats of violence.' Bingo! We hit the nail on the head. She said, 'Get in,' and she drove half a mile to a coffee house. She ordered a coffee, demanded Rachel's I.D., scrutinised it, and said to me, 'Who are you?'

'Patrick Dempsey, private investigator.' I reached into my pocket and produced a driving licence. 'Where's my I.D.?' Rachel stared at me sternly. Then, with dictatorial authority in her voice, she cautioned me that the Senator would not be pleased to complete my assignment in a slipshod manner.

'You know this investigation is secretive due to Hunt's contacts within the mayor's office. Let it not happen again.'

'Please accept my apologies, Miss . . . Goldman, Elisabeth Goldman.'

'Miss Goldman, may I ask what you were doing in his house? Are you his girl or just a friend?' I ask.

Elisabeth spills out a detailed account of her employment as a legal secretary at Concannon and Jessop. How he coaxed her from her fiancé with tales of his love for her and how they would live happily ever after in a land of milk and honey. She lapped up the usual half-baked reasons men and women offer one another to get their way. 'I got pregnant, and I had his baby, a boy. He visits him now and then. He never gives me any financial support. I lost my job, for he insisted I accept welfare and stay home. I am frightened because my brother was assaulted when he complained about how he treated me. My parents live in Israel and know nothing of this. My boy is four months old, and I plan to have him adopted to escape his clutches. I stayed with him last night, hoping he would agree to let the adoption go ahead. Otherwise, I will have Delano bumped off. My family in Israel is in the military and would present themselves in a jiffy to avenge my honour. It would lead to problematic questions I could do without answering.'

'Your traumatic lifestyle does not perturb you,' I say. 'You would have Delano murdered if you could make it happen, as long as there was no fuss?' I mutter.

'Too right, and you can tell that to the mayor who tried to get me to have sex with him. Hunt was culpable for that as well. I met two other girls in this position. He chooses us carefully; he doesn't mess with the Mexicans or locals. We girls are legal interns, and I worked under him as he was a senior attorney.'

'Enough said!' says Rachel. 'We will put an end to his shenanigans once and for all. 'Are you with us?'

Elisabeth says 'Yes,' and drives back towards his house. She pulls from the glove compartment a cannon of a handgun.

'Where the heck did you get that?' I yelp, astonished. 'I haven't seen one of those since Cody Jarrett was waving his .45 on top of the gas storage tanks and yelling, top of the world ma. Let me guess; a dear ancient great-granddaddy owned it during prohibition. I seem to have caught myself up in the Kosher Nostra great-grandchild reunion. What were you going to do with it?'

'I planned to shoot him, but I forgot to load it.'

'You will end up rotting in jail if you blow him away, as you put it. I will teach him the error of his ways and pay restitution to those he has wronged. You can bust a cap in his ass if that doesn't wash. The plan is straightforward: we will kidnap him at his house and make him pay. End of story.'

I give Elisabeth a phone. 'Phone Delano and tell him you have found a briefcase full of government papers and you are at his house. Ask him what you should do. Tell him they are contracts for law firms, and you expect payment. Ask if you should go to his office and give them to the mayor. That will make the prick come running.'

She dials the number as cool as a cucumber, and he is on his way. Rachel becomes excited. I take the phone from Elisabeth for a future hammering.

'Tell him you will leave the papers with him and leave. We will enter when you do, and I will help him readjust his mindset. Elisabeth, go to his door and wait.'

She's off clutching her briefcase. We watch her walking up and down the steps, and Delano is suddenly there. She is outside his door. He rushes to greet her and tries to take the briefcase. She refuses and says, 'No, I need the toilet.'

Nothing is said as he opens the door, and they enter. He shuts the door behind her with an aggressive bang. We head for the steps, and Rachel knocks. She has a laughing smile; I don't think this was in the script. Delano opens the door. There is no sign of Elisabeth; she must be in the toilet. His face drops, and he's alarmed as I push past, followed by Rachel.

Elisabeth comes out brandishing the gun and laughing. She will shoot him if she doesn't take control of her nerves. There is madness in her eyes. I ask her to give me the gun, but she points it at my head. I wonder if she has any bullets in the bloody thing. She takes two or three steps forward and is eyeball-to-eyeball with Hunt, yelling at him to kneel, which he does in a split second. Blood spurts from his mouth as she rams the gun barrel down his throat.

'Huh,' she says, 'you owe me this house.'

She cracks him across the face with the gun butt, 'And for my new friend Rachel, all the cash you have and can borrow. Let's view your bank accounts. I'm going to kill you,' and she cocks the gun. A foul stink permeates the air.

Delano has shit himself and begins to weep. 'I'm sorry,' he laments.

'Yeah, distressed you are in this position,' I shout at him. 'What we should do Rachel, is cripple him. Shoot him up the arse and cut his bollocks off.'

He begs me with pleading eyes, and I can sense he is remorseful for his actions. He would do anything to make things right. They can see this as well.

'I understand you have learned your lesson, and you are deeply remorseful, and you will repent and be a virtuous Christian,' I say.

'I will, I will,' he cries, whimpering childishly. I have met this kind of bastard before, two-faced and willing to renege on any deal at the drop of a hat.

'I'm glad you've grasped your lesson.' He shows relief as I offer him my hand to get up. As he takes it, I knee him in the mouth. Then, enraged at the pain I inflict on myself, I land a flurry of kicks to his sexual anatomy. Finally, I give him a kick that would kill most men –unfortunately, it kills him.

'You have murdered him,' cries Rachel feeling for a pulse.

'Ah, to hell with him,' says Elisabeth, 'he would have made my life miserable.'

'True,' says Rachel, 'but...'

'I suggest you register your baby as his Elisabeth, after he's discovered. If you are not up to it, keep your mouth shut. If the coppers arrest you, stick to the truth, you phoned him to tell him you found legal papers. You are intelligent and dangerous; fill in the blanks and leave us out. 'Tell the coppers you left a bit later. What about CCTV?'

'No, nobody has security cameras in the block. They don't advertise their dirty washing on television. We will firebomb the joint later.'

'Elisabeth, go on your way and remember we never met you. I don't know why I killed him. Something came over me; a red mist descended; it created a mess. You leave now and goodbye. Get rid of the gun, and we may meet again.'

We hug and leave the building. What a woman Elisabeth is. I hope I never see her again. Rachel's phone is blipping.

It's the mayor's office. 'Have you seen Delano?'

'No, why?'

'He has not turned up at work. Have you phoned him?' the mayor asks.

'No, maybe he is riding a pretty gullible intern.'

'Don't be impertinent; don't speak like that to me. Where are you? Go and check what his problem is and get your arse back to the office. It's not the end of the world getting pregnant. I could be loving to you, Rachel.'

'OK, boss, I am your obedient servant; I'm on the way.'

'You best go and knock on his door,' says I, 'but first, get your car and park in front of his house. I will wait in mine. See if he opens the door,' I said, laughing aloud.

'You are a dangerous and violent man,' she says. 'I like it.'

We walk to the cars, and a little later, she returns and says a zombie opened the door.

'Was it Delano,' I ask as I try to bite her on the neck. I ask her to go and buy sweatshirts, jogging bottoms, trainers, and size twelve for me. Book a hotel and phone me. Ring Brady and tell him there is no response, and you are off to Europe for an abortion. He is not to mention Hunt your destination. Keep dialling Hunt's phone to keep the pretence going. Christ only knows how this tale of murder will end.'

We meet at a motel and have another brunch. I whisk Rachel off to our suite, and we shower. I tell her I want to bugger her.

'I feel so horny, Rachel; nothing like a bit of violence to give me a sadistic sexual hunger.'

'No, you can't, not here. I have not done it previously, not entirely anyhow.'

She slipped down to my throbbing hard-on and began to suck, twist, and bite, and I was in agony and ecstasy.

I shot a bowlful of hot jiz into her red-lipped mouth without effort. I clamped her head tight between my hands and buried my cockhead deep in her throat. She sunk her nails into my arse cheeks, adding pain to my pleasure. She ended up sprawled on the shower floor, half-drowned and half-choked. She called me a bastard and informed me she had an intense rape orgasm.

'Bugger me,' she yells as she clambers up the shower wall and grabs the handrail with both hands. She stuck out her arse and splayed her legs, and it was an inspiring sight. 'Can't do it,' says she, 'can you shoot your big steaming load?'

Slipping my hand around her belly, I press her close and let her feel my hard knob on her ring.

'Oh my god,' she yells, 'you can. Will you let me get the...'

A few hours later, we woke. It is 1:01 in the morning. We go at it hammer and tongs, pure raw sex, so exhilarating; shower and dress, and we grab a taxi and head for her car at the cine complex. We have a meal and a few drinks and watch a late-night movie and fall asleep. The usher wakes us, and we leave. We take a walk to her car.

'If I turn up tonight, all is well; if not, stay shtum,' I whisper in her ear.

Tuesday, 13th June.

I chuck the clothes and phone in a dumpster as tourists use these. I grab a taxi and ask to be dropped off a couple of blocks from my car. I take a leisurely stroll; his house is ablaze. Fire engines are arriving, and I spot a single police car. He has not been missed; otherwise, the area would be swarming with coppers. It's 06:11 in the morning, and I head for my car, fearful of running into Lopez. I return to the Arizona Sunrise. DNA is a significant problem. No one has my DNA. They will know I am Irish if they discover DNA. It should reduce the odds to forty million or so. I feel Elisabeth has had a hand in tonight's bonfire. These two Jewish lasses are the spawn of gangsters.

I return to the Sunrise and spot Donald and Mariah having coffee. I ignore them. I sleep for a few hours and have dinner. I drove to the clinic to see Wendy; I couldn't believe what I saw. SWAT teams and FBI agents are swarming over the place. Helicopters were landing and taking off with, I presume, casualties.

'What's going on?' I ask a copper.

Bugger me blind with two stiff cocks. It was Detective Sven Gudjohnsen, the psychotic bastard. He was overjoyed to greet me as he grabbed me by the shoulder. His grip was steely. I forewarned myself if I ever shot this maniac, he would get the entire magazine.

'I'll tell you what's going on,' he says, 'your girlfriend, yeah, that tart Wendy Summers and her 7/11 fanny has been kidnapped or eaten. Definitely not eaten; otherwise, we would have found her fanny. Either way, she is not here. I have fifteen officers, approximately thirty nurses, doctors, and orderlies, and countless patients and visitors dead and dying. They have doubled in weight from the amount of lead pumped into them. It's a complete massacre. What do you have to say? You are a vicious criminal. Have you been here today? We are going through the CCTV scanning for your mug as we speak. When was the last time you saw Wendy Summers?'

'The last time I saw her was when she sat in the cab of my rig. Cross my legs and hope to die; that is the truth.'

'Somebody wanted her really bad smarty pants,' and he increases the pressure on my shoulder.

'This has to do with EARTHCO. She knows a secret that has not yet been made public. She told everybody Winston Dillon and Luther White had kidnapped them. They were accused of hijacking two trucks on the 9th of June, and another attempted hijacking on the 4th or 5th of June. Once again, you are in the picture; it was your lorry. Summers had associated with EARTHCO management in the past, that one is a dark horse. We need to question you in-depth, seeing as this situation is dire. Dimitri Ivanovo is missing, presumed alive, and Winston Dillon is in a coma, compliments of Dimitri. Their copter lies miles outside Tonto, with security guards and a missing Russian pilot.'

'SWAT is mounting an operation into EARTHCO's complex at Little Hump, and you are accompanying us. You will recognise Luther White, James Sturgess, and Wendy at first glance. Those two dickheads Rugosa and Sprangler, you may spot them. Chop-chop, into the wagon with you, be an obliging laddie.'

'I need to go to my hotel to spend time with my mates, you blubber-chewing Eskimo. I will return in one hour.'

'I don't think I made myself clear. I have dead people all over the place, upwards of forty climbing towards fifty, a complete ward wiped out, including reception. This was a deliberate attempt to silence any witnesses to this murderous mayhem that had taken place. It has to do with those trucks, and we will unearth what is going on. EARTHCO has gone beyond the pale and will suffer the consequences. Here, wear this.'

He tosses me a bulletproof jacket and a phone.

'We will listen as you dial your numbers.'

I phoned Rachel and told her what's happened. She tells me Gordon and Austin are looking forward to seeing me. Donald and Mariah have gone to Las Vegas with Richard and Apsara for a short break. She asks if she can accompany me, and I say, 'No, it could be hazardous.'

Immediately Gudjohnsen is on the line telling her she is welcome. Now he will make me play ball and be a good boy, but he has taken me offline. She is on her way with her cute little butt. I hope she doesn't get it shot off.

'Your girlfriend will be keeping an eye on you.'

Two choppers land a half-mile distant.

'Get in the jeep; let's go,' he snarls. If this blows up into a gun battle, I intend to kill Gudjohnsen. When we get to the helipad, two dozen SWAT members are milling about while checking their equipment. There is a display of weaponry that wouldn't go astray in Afghanistan. They have Remington 48s and M16s if you fancy doing a spray job like was done at the clinic. Mp5 is essential for the man with a trench coat and Glock '40s. Wow, they have been so updated. I love European weaponry.

'Are the guns dangerous, iceberg head?' I ask Gudjohnsen.

'Not as dangerous as you.'

The SWAT has broken up into four teams, Alpha, Beta, Gamma, and Delta; very Greeky tonight. We are with Delta, one of the SWAT members. He is the quartermaster, and there are weapons aplenty. I must get my hands on a firearm. Rachel has arrived to join me. I feel uneasy, and I plead with her to leave. Gudjohnsen butts in and tells me she is coming, so accept it. I embrace her and implore her to leave, but it's too late. We are boarded and soon airborne, and we circle the field, as do the other choppers. We are being held back as the other helicopters head out into the desert en route to Little Tonto. It's 06:04 pm, and I will be late for dinner. Let's see Gordon get me out of this one.

The pilot says, 'We've got the green light,' and off we go in the direction of Little Tonto with the sun shining through a cloudless sky. I hold Rachel's hand, for she thinks it's a magnificent adventure. Gudjohnsen is an evil bastard; he is capable of anything. He might be mulling over killing us, thinking Wendy has told me something. I am going to kill him. I am going to murder him in cold blood. We are sweeping in from the West; the sun is shining on a plateau further up the mountainside. I sight a vast aircraft hangar cut into the mountain where the others have landed. As an explosion rocks the helicopter, we swoop and touch down on the plateau.

'Apologies, Mr Dempsey!'

'What are you on about Gudjohnsen?'

'Oh, we are a few seconds early,' says Sven, 'come on, on your feet, quick march. Tell us what you know, or petite Miss Sexy will get a taste of black banana.'

Pistol shots follow a burst of automatic gunfire in rapid succession. Gudjohnsen looks startled. The pilot and the SWAT man are in deep conversation. Rachel is terrified and sobbing hysterically. This is not how she envisaged spending the evening. Three SWAT men come running out of the hangar as the pilot jumps from the chopper, followed by Sven. Sven's pilot shoots two with semi-automatics and the other scampers like the clappers back into the hanger. Sven shoots the one in the chopper. I grab Rachel and run inside. I am searching for ammo, and I grab a rocket launcher as the pilot tries to shoot Rachel and me. His gun is empty or jammed. I grip his throat and strangle the life out of him, crushing his windpipe. We race further inside the hanger.

Sven shows up bawling and yelling, probably shouting, I'm a murderer. I swing the rocket launcher and hit him on the shoulder, and he crumbles to the ground. I grab him by the windpipe and start strangling the life out of him. Surprise is on his face. He needs murdering, and I'm the man for the job.

'That should have done him in,' I yell, kicking his lifeless-looking body in the bollocks. She is terrified beyond belief. I carry her out to the chopper and strap her in. I'm seated, but I can't fly the machine. I can't get the controls to move. What's wrong with the controls?

'Are you a pilot, Rachel?' She sits like a statue, petrified, unable to speak.

I best get tanked up with firesticks. Whoever exits from that hole in the mountain will kill us. I need a pilot, and we can go for dinner with Gordon. He's a right vicious bollock, but he is a necessary evil in my life right now. We jump from the chopper and through the entrance of the hangar. I see no one alive in there; Sven has risen from the dead. We move further into the battlefield. The choppers are burned out, and all about lie the bodies of SWAT members. The place is awash with blood and water. The sprinkler system is still dripping; they had waited until they were in and hit them with grenades when they were getting off. I bet they didn't expect that.

EARTHCO has definitely gone beyond the pale; they will be shown no mercy. The Air Force is going to reduce this place into road chippings. I wonder if they already know. I need to move fast, and I've strangled the pilot. Talk about throwing the baby out with the bathwater.

Sven Gudjohnsen is nowhere to be seen as I step over bodies in civilian clothes, possibly security for EARTHCO. We move further in, and I collect magazines for my Glock and a couple of Mp5s. I give Rachel a Glock, show her how to use it, and tell her not to point it at me. I wish Elisabeth were at my side, for she would shoot the bloody lot. We continue up the stairs and stumble over bodies; it must be Sven and that SWAT guy moving up to the central building. Where is he going? He must know otherwise. He would not be here. He is meeting Winston Dillon, huh? I'll give him a black banana. I feel frightened for her; she is such an innocent girl, so immature and delicate. Gudjohnsen wants to abuse her. I am worried for her. I will kill her before they can hurt her; they want to shame me by violently molesting her.

'You gotta kill yourself,' I tell her, shoving the Glock against her temple.

'They intend to hurt you, rape you, torture you to get at me. They hate me; please tell me you will do it. How can I protect you?'

I am falling, and darkness surrounds me. I wake up hanging upside down from a meat hook in an empty room — hooks and chains in abundance hand from the walls. Nothing I can see would burn; it's a torture chamber. My wrists and legs are bound with a thin nylon rope. A set of fire hydrants stand like sentries on each side of the door. Where is Rachel? She is on the floor beside me, conscious.

'What happened?' I ask.

'They shot you with a stun gun, removed my weapons, dragged us to a jeep, and drove onto a lift. I think we are on the mountain. Detective Gudjohnsen was talking and laughing with a Black man. It was Dillon, Winston Dillon.'

'I heard them say the whole place is going to the dogs, and it doesn't matter what happens now. Winston said there was no way to stop it, and they will be evacuated with the rest of the chemists. He said the Four Corners fled to Tahiti. Winston kept back a shipment of British sovereigns and South African Krugerrands; he said it would help them rectify their unexpected unemployment situation.'

'Have they touched you? Did they say what they want?'

She shakes her head. 'I am frightened. I'm regretting I came,' she whispers.

'It's too late,' I say. 'Can you undo me? See if you can untie the rope.' I pass out.

I awake, and I am in the same room alone. Rachel is in the adjacent room, and she is screaming. Sven Gudjohnsen and Winston Dillon are with her. Both men are naked. She stumbles to the far side of the room, and Winston gives chase dragging her back by the hair. He lifts her up in his arms. He throws her onto a table, and Sven grips her by the throat. Winston undoes her jeans and removes them. Her legs are flailing in the air as he yanks off her T-shirt. Sven cuts the shoulder straps on her bra and rips it off, almost pulling her off the table. Winston cuts and waves her knickers in the air. She is shouting out to me. She can see me, and the men are fully aroused. Winston has her pinned to the table by the shoulders, his outsize hands clamped upon her breasts, his elbows locking her head in position. Her arms are flailing in the air as Sven grips her ankles, forcing open her legs. He raises them high and spreads them wide. Winston leans over and opens her pussy lips for Sven. Sven penetrates her, and she lets out an agonised scream. She gasps in shock as she is dry and frightened.

He slurps from a whiskey bottle and pours the rest over her. She screams as the raw whiskey mixes with her bloodied privates. He rides her with a viciousness that lays him out as a sexual deviant of the worst kind. He twists her nipples and raps her across the shoulder blade with the bottle. She screams louder, and I yell at them to stop. He pulls out, and they flip her over like a side of beef. Winston moves behind and slams her face into the tabletop. His left-hand grips the nape of her neck, and his right hand her fanny. She rises, and Winston enters her butt. She screams in pain and horror.

Sven makes obscene gestures to me. Winston lifts her head so I can see her eyes bulging from their sockets. Blood is pouring from her mouth and nose. He is howling like a wolf, and blood shows as Sven takes his turn and drags her to the floor, and rapes her broken body. He has a grip on her windpipe, and she is suffocating. I'm crying with frustration and beseeching God for a speedy end to her agony.

She knows they are going to murder her; death is staring her in the face; she will die. She is pleading for her life and her unborn baby. She will do anything.

Sven drags her to the table and throws her on it once more. Her head hangs low as Winston rams his cock down her throat. She is choking. Rachel pleads with her eyes to Sven as he brutally rides her. He is shagging the life out of her as she slowly suffocates from Winston. She cannot remove his hand from her nose and stares at me in desperation. I'm praying for her. I say Kaddish, which I have watched in films using the Lord's Prayer. In my mind, I can hear the Hava Nagila from afar as she laughs and dances at her wedding. She no longer shows any signs of life, for she is dead. They killed my angel.

They drag her by the hair into my room and throw her against the wall. She's slumped in the corner, her lifeless eyes accusing me, terror etched into her face. I stare at her broken body lying in a pool of piss, shit, and blood.

I should never have allowed myself to be forced aboard that helicopter. I should have slapped her hard and sent her home. I might have saved her life.

'We will give you the works later, you old murderer. Something interesting on CNN news that is weird but expected.'

Sven kicks me in the face, and I pass out.

Chapter Five

Fathead and Skeleton

Wednesday, 14th June.

I recover consciousness; my heart is grief-stricken, my soul devoid of mercy, and my head hurts. I tried to open my eyes; I recognised a voice in the distance. I could glimpse a chink of light as I lay on the floor, and I sensed movement. The taste of orange juice was in my mouth. I tried to drink and began to cough and splutter. The horror of what I witnessed came flooding back, and I cried out in anguish. I cursed God for letting evil loose upon the innocent. I cursed her tormentors and swore I would chase them to the ends of the earth. I would revenge her murder with all the hatred and malice I could muster. I would show them evil on a scale they never dreamed of.

I heard footsteps. I tried with success to open my eyes, and the voice and face became visible to me: it was Alphonse the Skeleton. I was confused. Skeleton held my hand, and I tried to withdraw it. I cried and lamented. The wretchedness of my loss overwhelmed me. I cried and lashed out with my arms and legs. I was being punished for my past sins. I could no longer bear the physical and mental anguish and fainted. The horror was embedded in my mind when I regained consciousness.

I opened my eyes and saw I had not been having a nightmare.

I could make out Skeleton and Fathead staring at me.

On the table, the table that witnessed such horror lay the body of Rachel hidden beneath a blanket-type shroud. I tried to sit up but could not. My hands and legs were bound. I had dreamt I had lashed out with my arms and legs, but my hands were tied. Was I still dreaming? I bit my lip and waited for the blood to drip onto the cold concrete floor. I was trapped in a world of suffering and misery.

'I am going to cut your bonds and release you,' says Skeleton. 'I am not your enemy, and neither is Helmuth. Winston Dillon sent us to kill you. Something is amiss with the ground outside; outlandish creatures are roaming the countryside. Come and watch the news. Dillon, Sturgess, and the cops left hurriedly yesterday and took a lot of equipment. Dillon said they had ridden your girlfriend to death and would send you to hell.'

'We never killed anyone, and we would never hit a woman. You do believe us, don't you? They did terrible things to her, and we are sorry for your troubles. We are alone; we must escape this place.

They were unarmed, and I wondered how they would shoot me.

'Where are your guns?' I ask.

'Why,' says Skeleton, 'are you going to murder us? We mean you no harm. We have guns, and you're not getting one, so let's go and watch the news.'

'No funny tricks,' says Fatman. 'I will break your neck. Don't get confused and think a bit of kindness is a spot of weakness. No man should have to suffer what you saw, and if you heard what they said about Wendy Summers and what they intend to do to her, you would be in a killing mood.'

'We need to go elsewhere,' says Skeleton, 'definitely out of Arizona. A chemist mentioned they had been trying to hit on a way of destroying growth hormones. They kept mutating if they were not in a human receptacle. There was no way to stop them, but I didn't know what they meant. Thousands of tankers are hidden in out-of-the-way places. It was inevitably a gamble if these growth hormones would leak into the environment. Their annual profits were enormous, billions of pollars rolled in. Each client would pay ten/to fifty million for follow-up treatments, which involved a bath and injections. We would never have laboured for such a terrible firm if we knew what they did.

There is a shedload of barrels below us. 'The mineshaft is full of leaking containers. The roof has collapsed and busted the tanker's linings. It's been leaking through the mountain for weeks, months, and years. I don't think anyone suspected what was happening.'

'It's all over the news, and thousands are dead. The President was in Arizona yesterday to see for herself. The President of Mexico and the Prime Minister of Canada came and had a gawp. The borders are shut and lined with troops and heavy weaponry; they kill everything that moves, including the flies. Arizona is a no-fly zone, no pun intended. Arizona and the surrounding states have been sprayed with pesticides, insecticides, and all kinds of...cides. The air stinks of death. Come and see for yourself; we must stick together.'

'Yeah,' says Fathead. 'We must stick together, be the best of chums. I don't trust you; you have the demeanour of a killer. I may not be the brightest spark, but I know how to spot a killer.'

'Let's see this television of yours and what you're babbling on about.'

We enter a lounge with sofas and a large-screen TV. News reporter Eve Hannigan updated the recent casualty figures and the latest advance of the snow. She showed footage of beasts with huge mouths full of fangs, for want of a better word. They were tearing buffaloes apart at the Montana Ranch, a favourite place for newlyweds from Tucson and Phoenix to spend weekends learning to ride and be cowhands.

I asked Skeleton what was happening, and he said the country was going to the dogs.

'What is that supposed to mean, Alphonse? Is the country going to the dogs? What is that snow, and where do they get those funny-shaped hippos? Why are people dying?'

He told me about the evacuations taking place. The ground is dead. I would die if I touched the snow, specifically when it moved. No explanation was required for the animals; they were mutants, and if I wanted first-hand information, I would have to watch the news.

'Yeah, watch the news,' says Fathead. 'Yeah, what do you think we are, talking newspapers?'

'Sorry Helmuth, I thought your big square head was a television, terribly sorry overfed fat chap.'

'I'll fix you, Paddy, me boy, just wait. I know you and what you are, and I have met your type before.'

'Yeah, all right, fatty.'

For the next few hours, I saw all kinds of horror. I woke, slept, and cried. My blood boiled, and murder was on my mind. Hate is an invigorating weapon; it gives you the strength to live. No rabid animal would keep me from slaughtering a pair of mad savages. I intended to catch up with them. I would make their last forty-eight hours on this planet the most miserable and painful that any human being had ever suffered. I would treat them to the bloodiest tortures devised by man. I would invent a few of my own. I might keep them in a soundproof basement and torture them for years on end while keeping them one step from death. I would get Gudjohnsen to bugger the arse off Winston. See how he relishes a bit of cock up his arse. I would warn that Viking Eskimo to bugger him with maximum brutality. I'd whip his white arse if he didn't do it right. I would insist that they wore protection coated with sharp sand to increase their inner mutilation and so increase their wolf howls that they inflicted on my Rachel during her murder.

Unlike Pulp Fiction, I'd strap a jumbo vibrating dildo in his mouth and see how he would savour that. I'd persuade Sven to brutalise him. I would encourage them to swap places, knowing Winston would need no encouragement. I'll watch you on CCTV, I'd tell him, make sure I don't have to come back. I'll say bye 'n bye, for now, bumboys. Remember, a sore arse is a satisfied arse.

Winston appreciates a manly buggering, so squeeze his balls hard. I'll watch and help him wank when he gets a stiffie. I would have to find a way to stop them from mentally giving up on life. I would keep them suffering on a grand scale. Yes, that is what I shall do. I felt satisfied.

'When are we off from this godforsaken dump?' I enquire from Fathead.

'I will let you know when I have to let you know, OK.'

'I want to leave.'

I'd love to kill him. He is a robustly built mother, and he might put me in a coma, which reminds me, where's Wendy, and more to the point, what's happened to Dimitri. I wonder if Mary got her Bourbon. I'll give her a buzz later.

Skeleton says he heard Dimitri forced a helicopter to crash. It was taking him to where Wendy would be nursed back to health after her drug overdose.

'You know that was not the idea,' I say. 'They want to rape and kill her as they did to Rachel. They would get a buzz out of doing it in front of me. Has anyone got a clue why they hate me? I never clapped eyes on those two bastards before this week.'

I shake Alphonse's hand in friendship as I snort at Helmut. 'I expect you are descended from the spawn of a goose-stepping SS soldier.'

'You are a murderer, Dempsey, and you allow your women to be murdered.'

I ignore his provocation. 'We ought to leave, and I need to find Wendy. Any clues where she is?'

'We could check the wards,' says Skeleton. 'There might be medical notes. It might be worth a deco. She could have been here.'

'What transport is available?' I ask.

'Absolutely nothing,' says Fathead. 'Not even a bicycle; The bastards have taken every bit of transport. It was absolute chaos here yesterday.'

'Hang on, what day is it?'

Thursday, 15th June.

'What time is it?'

'It's three o'clock.'

'I have been unconscious for two days. When did you discover Rachel?'

'Tuesday afternoon,' says Fathead. 'We were sent to get a shot of you...'

'Why didn't you call the cops?'

'It was impossible; the army was in Little Tonto. The snow was everywhere, it didn't get up the mountain for some reason, and the place was full of mad dogs and rodents attacking and eating one another. The news showed a re-run of a prairie dog attack on a herd of cows. What could we do?' I need to find Wendy's son, our son. I wonder where he is. I'm leaving this godforsaken place asap.

'Tell me, Alphonse, what's Tucson like?'

'It's been semi-evacuated; the countryside is infested with mutating beasts. They are easy to spot at night-time with their backbone showing a bright white stripe.'

'So, how do we get out of here?' I ask. 'What about the army?'

'Och, no way,' yelps Skeleton. 'The agencies, including the police, have authorisation to kill. Don't forget the SWAT teams; they lie outside, dead and rotting. They wouldn't take them in case they were contaminated. They suspect we are terrorists. They will tie us to crosses welded to the outside of jeeps, so we don't pollute anything. Dillon told us what was going on. We are to blame for this plague sweeping Arizona, and there is worse to follow. We will be executed for mass murder for keeping it quiet. They will torture us to make us grass up the Four Corners.

'I don't know where they are,' wails Fathead. 'I don't want to be castrated for those horrid bitches.'

'What do we do?' I ask.

'I have a suggestion,' he says. 'We could stay put. There's plenty of food and drink.'

'That's fine, but what happens if the snow spreads in an ever-increasing circle? It's outside Tucson; what if it doesn't stop? We will starve. We will have to eat you, Sprangler,' I say, laughing with Alphonse.

'What did you say?' bawls Fathead.

'Shuffle off Helmuth and find our transport, or we will feed you to the hippos.'

He leaves, grumbling. Alphonse and I head for the wards. He is nervous, and when I ask why, he says he is frightened of the women as they're frothing from the mouth with protruding red eyes. He was happier when he was pond-keeping.

We enter the ward, and I spot Margo McCullough's name as we pass the empty beds. I had plain forgotten the sexy Margo. Was Donald at this moment waiting for me to take Margo off his hands? Would I ever see them again?

In the next bed lay Abilene Cahill-Grant. Her features were frightful, with monstrous red eyes staring into space and her lips curled back, showing white teeth in a death grimace. She was horrendous.

Next to her was Sheeree Gordon's file, and in the next bed was the cause of my anguish, but not in body form; PATIENT 21, Wendy Ivanova, a drug addict. None of their files showed they had been discharged except Sheeree. She had been released on Tuesday and was picked up by her husband, Gordon, in a helicopter.

'So, where's Margo and Wendy?' The lights went out in my head.

I woke with a headache and realised I had been knocked out again. This was becoming a menacing inconvenience. I staggered to my feet and see-sawed out of the ward, following the signs to the helipad. I staggered out and sucked in enormous gulps of air, foul air. I staggered over to where the air was fresher. What if it was contaminated? I moved out of the cavern with its burned aircraft and mangled bodies. I collected an assortment of weapons, but nothing with sufficient firepower to destroy one of those hippos. The sun would be setting soon. In the distance, I could glimpse Laurel and Hardy trudging down the mountainside. They must be on a suicide mission. I bet Alphonse is hoping Helmuth gets eaten so that he can run back up the hill. As far as the eye could see was a barren waste, and among this desolation, I saw animals roaming the countryside. They said the snow had stopped climbing the mountain.

I need a computer to go online. I felt hungry and went to see what I could obtain from the kitchen. The cupboards are bare. What was Fathead on about? There is plenty of food, he said, but the cabinets are empty, as are the fridges. The freezers are full of defrosted food. Fathead discovered the same menu and concluded it was best to leg it down the mountain. It's a bit risky in the dark; on the other hand, you could catch sight of those hungry hippos and take evasive action. I search high and low, and not a morsel can I detect; the bins are empty.

I settle in front of the computer and learn about the destruction of Arizona.

In a nutshell, Bill Cummings spotted the snow and notified his paper which sold the scoop to CNN and NBC, and the rest of the alphabet. The networks sent out choppers, and they landed in the snow. The crews had been poking in the snow, which turned out to be a misty white smoke. The plants, trees, mammals, and grass had degraded to dust; nothing was alive. They collected specimens and dug deeper into the ground. It appeared normal, with streaks of white here and there. Reports and footage were sent back.

A white foggy mist materialised a few inches above the ground. It was finally established that it would range between one and six inches. It gave off a sweet smell like almonds. The aircrews jumped back in their choppers and took off, swirling the mist like a Dervish. Another crew ran from the fog onto the high ground. Bill and Tina Wimpey stayed, knelt, and touched the mist with their hands. They said it felt cold, and they went off the air. A camera crew caught their last moments. It took ten minutes from contact with the mist to when they dropped dead. They melted before the camera crew's eyes. Later another chopper landed to check out Bill and Tina; barebones and clothing greeted them.

From then on, the camera crews named it the Death Snow, and the name stuck. Whatever it was had devoured their bodies. No one made a sound out of the ordinary as they died. They would do what they were doing and drop dead. You could remain unharmed in the mist if it didn't touch your skin. Nothing was known about it except it proceeded at varying speeds. Periodically it travelled a few hundred yards an hour; other times, it would go a mile an hour.

I saw herds of beasts, contorted and rabid, roaming through Little Tonto. North, South, East and West, the Death Snow travelled outwards in an ever-increasing circle. Nothing could stop it. Test trenches had been dug as an experiment, eight to ten-foot-deep. Success was one hundred per cent. No animal crossed from one side to the other. They could be shot, but this was abandoned as they fell into the trenches and decomposed in the sunshine. It was best to let them stand there bawling. The Death Snow tumbled to the bottom of the trenches and slowly solidified.

It was less than seventy-two hours since the crisis broke upon the greatest nation on earth, with its population at a massive 350 million in 2015. Arizona had a population bordering on seven million; half a million people in Tucson would be on the move. This didn't include the towns within the quarantine area. A map showed the state of Arizona.

The obligatory end of the world is nigh wankers, and Jesus freaks are out waving their placards. They had waited since 9/11 to get back on the streets. No doubt, hordes of freaks were waking up, hoping the end of days had arrived. I could imagine them waving goodbye to their wives as they ate their meals of dry bread and water. They would grab their bibles and placards and head for a busy intersection. They would spend the day quoting fire and brimstone to the travelling masses, and in thanks, they would be gobbed on for their troubles.

Prisoners were being shipped from all states to build a dry canal across Arizona and try to stop this Death Snow from spreading further North. It would descend to the bottom of the trenches and hover six inches high, solidifying. Hordes of volunteers were on the move from every state armed with a pickaxe and shovel, heading for the railheads to join the military trains to take them to this new frontier. Amnesty and citizenship would be granted to illegals who presented themselves to the authorities in the next forty-eight hours. The cost of this priceless reward would be unlimited free labour while the crisis lasted.

It was like the movie, Once Upon a Time in the West, with endless lines of labourers stretching to the horizon, labouring and building this dry canal. These 21st-century navvies would hope a Claudia Cardinale doppelganger would fetch a pitcher of water to quench their thirst. Firearms were issued to the most competent after a one-hour drill. The cities of Tucson and Tombstone would end up with gunfights and drunken brawls like a century before. Undoubtedly, a couple of Henry Fondas and Jason Robards would pop up in this 21st-century epic.

The five states (New Mexico, Colorado, Utah, Nevada, and California) with a state line with Arizona watched apprehensively. Should that fail, they and the US would be doomed. The Death Snow would spread throughout the country with no obvious way of stopping it. It was assumed it would kill the rivers and ride the current to the opposite bank. The endless broadcasts warned the population not to venture from their home state. Members of the public had to carry their driving licence or picture ID. If caught outside state lines, your car would be confiscated, and you would be introduced to blood, sweat, tears, and toil.

Homeland Security had grounded domestic flights. Tourists were shipped out by boat and plane. Overseas Americans were ordered to return; otherwise, their entry would be restricted after the seventy-two-hour deadline. The government was panicked by the virus, which was travelling through Arizona. Could this blasted virus be controlled and quarantined? Nothing comparable has ever happened before, and the big question was, could it be halted? Tens of thousands of Arizonans went on an extended holiday.

Along the border for hundreds of miles, detonations could be heard. Both armies blew up the ground to destroy people or drug smuggling tunnels. The Mexicans were taking no risks. A new fence was put up after a ten-foot-deep concrete wall was sunk. Further in, an army of people laboured night and day to build a trench twelve-foot-wide and twenty to thirty feet deep. Everything was utilised; it was a massive earthwork. Southerners remarked that the South would never have fallen if General Lee had such a barrier. The Mexicans believed the same.

Thousands of soldiers skilled in horsemanship now rode the range killing animals, large and small. Armies of sharpshooters shot the skies clear of birds. They kept an eye on the cavalry horses, as did the soldiers, but none showed any sign of mutating. The scorched earth policy circling Little Tonto had slowed the Death Snow to a complete stop, and practically all the animals and mutants had been killed and collected.

From the South, crackpots with assorted weapons were pouring into the state, the difference being that this lot was hunting the mutations. This was the great chase, the opportunity to pursue aliens without Sigourney Weaver getting in your way. The stink of burning flesh added to the stench of undiscovered rotten meat that filled the air. An army of pick-ups scoured the land, accompanied by tens of thousands on foot, moving like a human wave, driving everything in front of them. Death awaited these animals, big and small, from flamethrowers and grenades. Helicopters swooped with sharpshooters at the ready.

Two massive columns of human beings converged on one another, and caught between would be millions of animals, and waiting for them would be the specialist extermination squads. Nothing like this had ever been attempted — the mass extermination of native wildlife by an army of forced volunteers. It was common gossip that anyone refusing to volunteer would not receive any help financially or otherwise in the future.

Homeland Security had ordered the networks to continue showing the attacks on the Montana ranch. They showed assaults on homestead families by household pets. It was gruesome viewing: a plump furry cat jumped on a housewife walking home from the store and ripped her face right off. In another incident, a dog chewed a baby in its pram. Horror was piled on terror; the intention of showing such terrible brutality by rabid animals was to instil fear in the population. What would be howling along the road would be packs of wild animals followed by an earth-destroying mist, including a massive amount of bloodletting if one wanted to continue living.

The Whitehouse could do little as regards the feral animals. There was a lot they could do to curtail domestic animals. No pet was to cross the border, pets were to be euthanised, and any freed would result in a ten thousand pollar fine. People were being sucked financially dry. Arizona stank of death; gunfire could be heard 24/7. Viking-style pyres burned day and night. Flatbeds roamed the countryside, collecting carcases of animals, and all the while, the state was emptying people.

What was causing it remained a mystery? The Centre for disease control in Atlanta was investigating various avenues. Europe and the rest of the world refused to allow the carcases into their respective laboratories.

The United States of America had recognised the danger to their commonwealth. This plague could devastate America. With upwards of four hundred million people, including the illegals running amok in the black economy, and the Americans who would be sent back in due course, the situation could become apocalyptic. How could you feed the population with America's breadbasket empty? Committees were being set in motion to study specific aspects of the crisis.

Army units were deployed to American dependencies, while massive quantities of military hardware were shipped back from Iraq and Afghanistan. A dozen aircraft carriers, four hundred battleships of various tonnage, and four thousand aircraft were either on or getting authorised to put out on the high seas. Multiple shipping was lying off the coast of California and New York. Hawaii was quarantined, non-residents evacuated, and tourists shipped to their respective countries. Cuba and the Bahamas were invaded and annexed on the third day. At the age of ninety, Fidel Castro offered the first American soldier to meet him a cigar. They sat on his bed and smoked while drinking Bourbon, compliments of warmongering Hillary. 'Well,' says Fidel to the American, 'John and I were great pals. I bet you didn't know that young Kennedy.'

'I bet I did,' said Patrick.

America would not get caught napping; they had put their well-oiled contingency plans into operation with no quarter given to troublemakers and dissenters. 9/11 had been a baptism of fire, so being prepared to kick butt was the motto after that. Over the past hundred years, America had saved militarily weak countries' independence, and payback was due. The time was now, and payback would be expected without any whining. No threats were made, but the language was of the bullyboy. America was facing a crisis of epic proportions. The Americans would show the world it had the balls to fight this horror as it had done at Pearl Harbour, the Cuban missile crisis, the Iranian hostage, and, of course, 9/11.

They had survived economic upheavals from the 1929 crash to the 2014 mega-crash. They moved on carrying the banner of freedom first waved by George Washington. The President, Hillary Clinton, made a speech to her people and encouraged them to show their ancestors' mettle and show the world the American dream. The desire was to show courage and to have the faith to stand for freedom. To obliterate the menace heading down the mountainside, destroying their way of life. This alien monster was killing, yes, poisoning the land of the free and the brave and forcing its people to flee for their lives.

The Americans would stand and fight these ferocious animals as their ancestors had done on this continent's plains and mountains. They had not run back to where they had come from. Those immigrants stood their ground and carved out a life for themselves and their children's children. The poor and huddled masses migrated from all corners of the globe to give their blood, sweat, and tears to the melting pot that would become America's commonwealth. Fifty states were united to provide the nation with a unity of one people that was envied across the world for generations past and present. Here we stand, four hundred million strong, grown from a few pioneers who arrived on ships from

Spain. Those descendants now invite the international community to lend a hand in our hour of crisis.

I fell asleep and dreamed of sitting on a cloud playing hide and seek with my schoolmates. I counted to nineteen and searched for them. I could not find them. I heard laughing, and they hollered, 'Here we are, here we are.' I could not locate them. I swam from cloud to cloud. I flew across the sky. I dived, yet they remained elusive.

I woke up crying.

I was starving. The television was on. It was daylight. The newsreader was saying Alaska had been quarantined. The Canadians were refusing entry to the land route via the Alaskan Highway. America made it clear that they would have stored their treasures beneath Alaska's ice if they kept the roads open for a week. They would compensate Canada with considerable gold and platinum once an infantry had been completed.

Canada calculated that old guff was codswallop. Why could they not airfreight their junk there? Nevertheless, America had its back against a wall, and one had to handle such a beast carefully. It could invade the country in a fit of pique, and what would King Charlie of England do? They would play the game and see how events panned out and put feelers out to England, Russia, and other allies and speculate on what help they could offer.

Their armaments factories would manufacture the components to make a few atom bombs.

If they want to mess with the Maple Leaf, they will find a maple tree up their arse in the guise of a one-hundred-megaton bomb. Let's see if that knocks the crap out of them. Meanwhile, the politicians could politick and spend their nights in luxury suites with Juicy Lucy's slobbering over their wizened old cocks, trying to blow some life into them.

The Russians should have kept Alaska instead of selling it for a few cents an acre. The French should never have traded Louisiana and the Great Plains to the Yanks. Spain and Mexico also grabbed the Yankee dollar. They aren't going to buy Canada. No siree, and they will keep their plague on their side of the border. The Canadian prime minister ordered Canada's combined forces to go on high alert and be prepared to repel an invasion by US forces.

I switch it off. I need to plan to pick up my family and migrate across Canada's border and to Ireland. I'm sick of the mayhem. If I don't come up with new information on my way home, then sod the lot of them. I need to find food; otherwise, I will turn cannibalistic and end up defrosting Rachel and eating chunks of her. I cried and wept as I emptied a kitchen freezer of rotten food. I carried my angel's rigid body and placed it lovingly inside. I swear I will hunt those two rapists for eternity and kill them. I remind myself for the thousandth time.

I search the wards and root out fruit and biscuits in the patients' lockers. I find booze, sweets, and fags. I haven't smoked in years and now marks an excellent excuse to restart. I gather up my food and head back to the kitchen. I eat a hearty kiddie meal and sit and cough as I get used to Camel cigarettes. I sleep for hours and wake up late in the night. I must be tired, the stress, I suppose.

I head out to the plateau and collect a selection of weapons. I find what I am searching for, anti-tank missiles. I plan to leave at the first light and head for Little Tonto. Hopefully, the army will be entrenched in strength, and I can cadge a lift back to their base. I intend to tell the truth regarding this wretched mess right from the moment I set foot in the Russian Bear Restaurant. Let the cops investigate for me, and I will roast them on a spit. I test the weapons and make an incredible din when I fire off an anti-tank missile. I fire it far out on the plain, hoping to hit Laurel and Hardy. Signs of life are absent.

I need a pair of binoculars to study the wildlife roaming the countryside. I bugger off to find a pair, and ten minutes later, I'm back. I am focusing the sights when I hear a shot. I fire off half a dozen, but no reply comes back.

I sit and watch the telly for a couple of hours, but it's primarily repeating, and I retire to bed. I sleep the rest of the night and wake refreshed. My mind is at peace, and my objectives are clear. I am steeled and armed for my mission; to reach civilisation is my No. 1 objective.

Chapter Six

The Dawn of EARTHCO

Friday, 16th June.

Four days since the news broke, it's best not to phone Mary: she could set me back years mentally with her alcoholic ranting. I throw heavy weapons over the plateau and watch them bounce down the mountainside. I scan as far as the eye can see with the binoculars, but nothing stirs; all's quiet on the Western front — time to march. I wonder how Skeleton is holding up or if they have been eaten.

I chuck the anti-tank missiles over the side in their steel boxes and watch them come to rest in the middle of the road. Pity I can't climb down. I set off feeling I was marching into a wilderness. I had known the unknown before as we trained in the mountains of Wicklow, and I felt the urge to sing for my dead comrades, songs we had sung together. I hummed Old Skibbereen, a cover version sung by a Croatian band. I liked the song's tempo and sang it loud and clear. Who would hear me croaking? The words came back to me. I finished my sing-song when I spotted my missile box on the road. That was the end of my reminiscing about Yugoslavia during its wars of independence.

The box was sideways to the run of the road. I was sure it lay parallel and centre; someone was watching me. Was I going to get an anti-tank in the bollocks at any moment? I drew my Glock, checked the magazine, and continued towards the box. There was no point getting cold feet now; if I was being watched, they were in no hurry to kill me.

I could hear laughter and my name being chanted melodiously. It was Skeleton and Fathead. What a disappointment. They were waving to me and shouting what I couldn't make out. As I got closer, I heard the word Dimitri, and I screamed, 'Where is he? I want to kill him.'

'You don't want to do that tovarishch. I have come to help you search for my Wendy; they have related the torment you have suffered witnessing your Rachel being murdered. I know Wendy loves me and you her, but she will not come to you, and you are happy for her to be with me. We will be best friends, and we will find her and keep her safe; we will go and kill your enemies. Helmuth and Alphonse will lend us their skills. I have my pilot friend from the Russian Air Force and Aeroflot.'

'Please call me Yanni,' the pilot says. 'I have copter one mile from here. We will leave this place and not come back.' Imagine my shock when I saw Dimitri.

'The guards,' says Yanni, 'were going to throw him out over the desert. We drank much vodka together when we were in Russian army in Afghanistan. I said there was a fault with copter, and I pretended to crash-land. I shot three guards. We did not want to get chopper back in air, so we agreed to walk here and help Wendy escape. When Alphonse told Dimitri you were here, he wanted to kill you. He recounted a story, a sad story, and now we are allies. Now we go back to the chopper and make it fly. Did you know I was a pilot for Spetsnaz?'

We rambled down the mountainside and continued into the desert where the chopper was sitting.

'Why haven't SWAT collected it?' I ask.

'Oh, they tried,' says Dimitri, 'they could not make it fly. I make sure it could not fly but fly it will.'

We climb aboard, sweating from the heat, tongues parched from the dust. Dimitri removes a switch from the dashboard, throws it out, and puts another from his pocket.

'Old trick,' he says, 'someone always attempting to steal chopper in Afghanistan and Russia. Maybe we will get buzzed as we fly past Little Tonto.'

The town is empty of people, so he flies on to Tucson; gangs of men are toiling in trenches. It will not be successful, it's too late, and the army knows that. We landed outside Tucson and commandeered an army jeep which took us inside the town where the SWAT teams were. They leave us unguarded; they assume we are SWAT because of the helicopter.

'What do we do now?' says Yanni.

'I want proper food; I'm sick of biscuits,' I say. 'I want to go to the Arizona Sunrise Hotel, where Gordon and his associates are. I don't like them; they are treacherous, but they may help us locate Wendy. I might have one or two friends among them, possibly a man named Donald and a woman.'

'What is her name?' says Fathead.

'I don't know her name yet,' I lie to him. I know he is an evil bastard. 'Austin's wife is dead; she was in the hospital. No one should give him the shocking news, is that understood? These people are murderers and would kill you without a second thought. They may have left. Donald and his son were going to Phoenix for a few days, but they should be back by now.'

We are grilled by a SWAT captain for who we are. Dimitri tells him we are specials from Spetsnaz, retired naturally, and here to watch and learn. He tells him we have come from the airport, and they walk together. Dimitri beckons us to follow him, and we march like soldiers. Dimitri marches to a vehicle with Yanni and speaks to the driver. The captain gives him a nod. We go to the Arizona Sunrise, where he drops us off.

The driver asks, 'What's an Irishman doing with a group of Spetsnaz?'

I tell him I am an army ranger instructor seconded to study and evaluate.

'We must be prepared and qualified to help America if requested.'

That was satisfactory for an answer. We headed for the hotel, which was functioning as a military base.

Who was standing at reception with her sister but the lovely-arsed Mariah in military uniform.

'My God,' I said, 'how I love a girl in uniform.'

'Where're your uniforms, old-timers?' she asks, grimacing at this dirty motley crew of fifty-somethings.

'We need to freshen up, and then we will whisk you off for dinner,' I say.

A three-star general arrived, and Mariah left to see what she could do for him with a pleasant smile. A soldier asks where our rooms are, to which we shrug our shoulders.

'You must show authority,' he says, 'this is not your home defence force.'

He marches up to Mariah and stands beside the general, waiting for Mariah to finish. The general frowns and asks his name.

'Murphy, sir, Major James Anthony Murphy, call me JAM for short, sir. I am the President of Ireland's grandson, sir, sent by my father to receive a first-class military education. I regret to intrude upon your space, sir. We have Major Dowling of the Irish Army Rangers trained at the US Army Ranger School at Fort Benning. We have yet to be allocated rooms. SWAT Commander Dickinson will visit us late afternoon with an executive order; until then, hush-hush is the words.'

'Yes, sir, I have been sworn to secrecy too,' says Mariah adding her spoonful to the deception.

'Would the general like to authorise the accommodation for our guests?'

'It's most unusual,' says the general. Mariah shoves a paper and a pen in his hand, which he duly signs, and buggers off on the double in case he is enticed to sign anything else. He shakes his head as he goes.

'They are all the same,' she says, 'wanting everything for nothing. The horny general was hoping I was free later. I would charge him plenty, only joking; only joking.'

Jeez, she has the gift of the gab, but what a mouth.

Donald can't be far; he would never leave his precious one alone in case other dogs came sniffing. I bet he's here. JAM is giving her the eye. He would be attractive competition among his age group, never mind the granddad brigade. It's granddaddy-cock that is brushing her fanny hairs at night and not Murphy-the-stud. He is as American as I am Irish. Maybe his Irish connection is back in the distant past. Presumably, during the famine period, considering there were oceans of food in the country, it was shipped out to feed fat Anglo-Saxon lords and their families.

'So, what's your name? I can't read your nameplate.' I say.

'Do you not believe it's Murphy?'

'No, I don't; what is it? Come on, spit it out; what is it?'

'If you really want to know, it's Dempsey. 'James Anthony Dempsey Ivanovo and I'm from Fiddlers Elbow right here in Tucson, which is in Arizona, in case you don't know, army ranger man.'

I had countless bombshells in my life, many in Croatia and Ireland, but knock me unconscious with a feather duster; what a shock to the nervous system. He stood six-foot-tall with the features of a Celtic warrior and I, his father. Surely there couldn't be two Dempseys in Fiddlers Elbow with connections to Ivanovo, or could there be? I doubted my own eyes; he has my family's eyes and Dempsey's rugged looks.

The others have left in the lift, and we are alone; maybe he engineered it this way; of course, he did.

Dimitri was here, and they saw one another. But, on the other hand, I don't recall Dimitri and Yanni being at the desk. Yet, he was tipped off about my movements.

'How is your mother?'

'She is at home in the Fiddle.'

'Is she? When did you last speak to her?'

'Not so long ago. What's your problem, absent father of thirty years? Why do you care you're a useless lump of rubbish? I will be speaking to you with my fists a bit later. I am a soldier, and I must serve my country first.'

'Now, son, don't jump to conclusions; there is a logical explanation for what has happened throughout the years.'

'Oh Papa, tell me later when I have recovered from the shock that I am related to a turd. Oh, pappy, will you not give your son a hug? I have waited half my life for one.'

'Of course,' I whimper, tears welling in my eyes.

'Daddy, is there a tear in your eye? Let me help you get it out.'

He cracks me one with both fists in both eyes. I will have a pair of shiners tomorrow as I laugh to myself. He has gone up in the lift, got some of it out of his system, and maybe he will feel better in the morning. Christ alone knows what Wendy has told him about me as I head up in the adjacent lift. I am on the top floor. There are lots of suites; better get knocking. I knock on a door which is opened by Dimitri and James, two daddies and one son, grand. What now?

'Dimitri,' I say, 'we ought to have a drink.'

'Too bloody right,' and he slams the door in my face after inviting me in.

Damned rude, slamming the door in my face, and I rub my nose. I go and knock on the next suite, and Alphonse answers. He is happy to see me, and in I go like a bolt of lightning. This is turning out to be a real eye-opener of a day. I think, can my heart take all this excitement and violence as I admire my slightly swollen eyes? Not once but twice, this has happened; father and son have blacked my peepers.

Will it be Wendy next? I seriously consider doing a runner to preserve my eyesight as I skulk off into my room. They tell me they are set for dinner. I haven't washed or shaved, and I come out to tell them. Dimitri and Yanni wear Spetsnaz uniforms, while Skeleton and Fathead wear the Army National Guard dress.

'If I'd known it was a fancy-dress party, I would have brought my battle kit,' I say.

They sneer and laugh at me and say, 'See you later,' and they are gone to stuff their faces. I lay on my bed and daydreamed about Margo the other night and how sexy I felt with her. I wanted her more than ever, the hurt of Rachel's loss was still with me, and it had not diminished one iota. I felt lonely and cried over the loss of Rachel and Wendy. A surge of hate passed through me, and I felt strong and virile.

I phoned Mariah and informed her of my predicament.

'What, now you have no clothes?' she stated. 'I hope you have got my tie. You are a fool, repeatedly losing your rags. You know what they say in Arizona, a fool and his clothes are easily parted. Are you a fool or a part fool? Have you still got your money?'

I can't take this drivel; the day has been full of revelations.

'Mariah, I want to make love to you.'

'Why?' she says, roaring with laughter.

'You ask me why, because you have a body I want to hold, kiss, feel, stroke, and make love to. My heart is broken, my soul is empty, my mind is numb, my body is racked with pain, my blood runs cold. Please help me.'

She hangs up on me. I need to eat, and for that, I need to wash. I use complimentary items, shave, shower, and ponder what I will wear. With a knock on the door, I am presented with an airman's battle dress uniform, which fits me.

The phone rings, it's Mariah.

'Meet me in the foyer in fifteen minutes exactly.'

I've pulled Mariah. I can't believe it; this woman has a body to die for. My heart is racing. Does Donald know? She was in love with him the other night. What happened? Is it a trick? This woman is incredibly sexy; her tits alone could drive a man insane fantasising about them. I mused about what she would wear; apparently, we were not dining with the other military personnel. I feel apprehensive. I recall Donald and his nasty attitude. Mariah was a party to the stuff they wanted me to do in Ireland. There's Austin and Abilene. Is he aware Abilene is dead? What about Richard and the ladyboy? Was that his name? I can't remember. He must have screwed her/him. Aah, Apsara, that was her name; I fancied her myself; what radiant hair and stunning legs, I felt horny.

I wanted Mariah, and I daydream she's dressed sexy. I love hot women.

I take myself to the toilet and have a wank fantasising over the beautiful Mariah lashed to the four-poster bed waiting for me to ravish her. Never in her future lovemaking would she mentally enjoy making love with Donald. That would be my punishment to him. But, if all goes well tonight, Mariah will get the loving of her life.

As the seconds pass, I chew over where that poisonous serpent Gordon is lurking with his horny tart. You can, without fail, get your own back on men by riding their women. It guts them to know you screwed their bitch. They want to kill you, but many things stop them, the most apparent being she was a tart and they should get rid of her. I suppose women do the same thing.

'Your transport is here,' a bellhop informs me as he leads me to the side exit. 'Have a pleasant evening, major,' and he salutes me.

I'm a major in the American Air Force. I salute back, and in I jump to this luxurious staff car to be surrounded by a cloud of perfume. The fragrance was a Jo Malone because of its fruity, flowery, woody scents.

She was with her sister, who greeted me with a huge smile and a pleasant, 'Hi, I'm not a Becky; call me Rebecca. Nice to make your acquaintance again.'

I recognise her as the receptionist from the Sandy Sky Motel. By heck, these women are very edible. I plonk myself between them. The girls are wearing Air Force uniforms with full makeup and crossed legs.

Aaahh, this is the life as the car speeds North onto Highway 1-10.

'Where are we going?' I ask.

'To Phoenix,' says Mariah, 'to meet Donald and his boys.'

'Is Apsara with them?'

'Yes, duckie, he is with them, and so is Richard.'

'I was only asking.' I lean close to her and whisper, 'I meant what I said.'

She laughs and whispers to Rebecca, 'He meant what he said,' and they put their fingertips to their mouths Japanese-style and titter. That Kill Bill movie has a lot to answer. I imagine these two impeccably dressed in school uniforms as Gogo Yubari's. Could they be as mentally deranged as Gogo? If she asks me if I want to screw, I'm going to keep an eye on her hand when I say yes.

'Why are we going to Phoenix?' I ask. 'I've just met my son, which has become the briefest reunion in history. Come on, girls, daddy wants his little boy.'

'Patrick, we are going to Phoenix to carry out a vital mission,' says Mariah. 'EARTHCO is suffering a calamity because the FBI has become an existential threat to them and us. With other people, I have to acquire material that is of the utmost importance for their future.'

'You drive a truck for wages; you can name your price for this mission. Don't ask for tens of thousands of pollars; try hundreds of thousands. EARTHCO is blamed entirely for disposing of liquids that should be stored under licence in secure depots. However, for privacy reasons more than financial, they felt it would be better to hide it inside a mountain and keep their fingers crossed. The chickens have come home to roost with a vengeance.'

'For the past few years,' she says, 'rumours among the clinic's clientele had spoken of mysterious deaths of their loved ones, but next of kin had received compensation for signing a confidentiality clause. No one ever spoke out publicly; if they did, the clinics dismissed their talk as spiteful and vindictive. They would publicly apologise after being threatened with prosecution and say losing their loved one was a terrible cross to carry. They blamed the clinic, just like upset people would blame a hospital, but it was the luck of the draw.'

'Most serious was a statement made to an FBI field officer who happened to be staying in Tucson on holiday with his wife and sister. While dining at a restaurant with his wife and sister Mathilda, Mathilda conversed with a Humphrey Cagney, a teamster for EARTHCO. They enjoyed one another's companionship throughout the week. Before Mathilda went home with her brother, she enquired if Humphrey would like to visit her in Chicago.'

'He said he would, and if it were OK by her, he would want to relocate to her vicinity if she so wished, blah-blah-blah.'

'And so, it happened. He turned up on their doorstep one night, frightened out of his wits, blabbering the company was trying to murder him. Mathilda's brother Jack, who happened to be visiting, invited him in and gave him a stiff drink which he drained in one shot and held his glass out for a refill. His glass replenished, he began to tell a tale of how EARTHCO had invented a concoction of herbs, special water, and body liquids.'

'He had elected to leave his employment and move to Chicago to be with Mathilda. He wanted to retire immediately but with severance pay. Daydreaming, he wandered into the offices of Benedikta Walbeck, the CEO. He didn't know how he ended up there. The CEO's offices were on their own floor with their private lift. He was absent-minded, probably mentally masturbating over Mathilda. He popped his head around the door to see the office was unoccupied. He knew he should not be there. Being a bit of a kleptomaniac, he lifted a DVD off the desk and hurried out. He went to Bob Fisher's office and said he wished to leave as he had fallen in love with a beautiful woman and was off to share his life with her.'

'But Bob refused to clear his severance pay and made him stay for the next week with wages and a bonus. He was satisfied with that offer. Bob Fisher treated his teamsters with courtesy and respect. Humphrey pleaded for an early run, and Bob said to be on-site at seven, and there would be a return run waiting. The following Thursday, Humphrey hitched up and delivered his consignment Friday afternoon. He was back from Seattle on Monday morning, having spent Saturday night and Sunday with Mathilda, who had flown to be with him. On the way back, the rig broke, and Sturgess, head of security, sent a mechanic from a garage to check it out. They took the truck, and he booked into a hotel for the night. He remembered the DVD and retrieved it from his jacket pocket. He wished he had never seen it.'

'I want you, Patrick, to listen to the account Benedikta narrates on this DVD. We are leaving Arizona for the West Coast of Ireland,' says Mariah. 'We have a mission to acquire this island called Stonnage, and in the process, you can name your price in payment.'

'I can't bloody well go to Ireland at the drop of a hat, for Christ's sake; what about my wife and employment? Dimitri will surmise I have done a runner.' She puts her hand up to silence me, 'Listen to the DVD, and I will describe the mission later and what is required of you. Think megabucks.'

'It's a copy of the DVD Humphrey Cagney gave to Mathilda. She gave it to her brother, Jack, the FBI agent. A copy was sent to relevant agencies and the Disease Control Centre in Atlanta. I assume William, Donald's son, got his hands on a copy. Patrick, it does not make pleasant listening. Mathilda's husband, brother Jack and boyfriend Humphrey have all disappeared, as have several sets of neighbours. It is assumed that they have come to harm.'

'It is a confession by Benedikta Walbeck implicating EARTHCO and its age-defying products in mass murder.'

Her statement began with her grandmother Angela, a German schoolteacher. She was sheltering in a Berlin bunker at the beginning of January 1945 when an Allied plane dropped bombs on the building. One exploded, blowing in the wall of the shelter. A steel table was turned on its side as Angela and some neighbourhood children played a blindfolded hide 'n seek game. It was the children's turn to find Frau Angela; she hid beside the table.

The bomb exploded, knocking her unconscious. She awoke feeling rather strange and forlorn. She was out on the street with children lying on top and at her side.

Blood and skin, brains and flesh, were stuck to her hair and skin; she was ragged, as were the children, the blast having shredded their clothes. She did not recognise any of the children, but one or two looked familiar in an infant way. She tried to cry out, but it was impossible. She was frozen with fear. How could these boys and girls be lying here blown to bits when they were laughing and playing a moment ago?

Time stood still as she gazed at the horror that surrounded her. Darkness came, and with it, the screeches of bombs exploding around the city. The inferno raged. It was Dante's Inferno; it was hell on earth, the sky burned red, the wind howled through the street, and the ground shook and moaned as Berlin was bombed into submission.

She passed out whilst calling on the almighty to help her in her hour of imminent peril. She knew God had forsaken the German people because of their leaders' sins, having forced them to partake. This was a taste of the afterlife. Never no more would the laughter of youngsters at play be heard in the great cities of Germany.

The punishment was coming from the East and West; it was coming from the North and South. It was raining from the skies, exploding from the earth, closing in from all sides; there was nowhere left to run and hide; the German race was meeting its nemesis.

Angela was eighty-two years old, and she remembered the celebrations as a child when Germany had risen to be a world power in 1870. She recalled the defeat of the German army in 1918, but its cities lay untouched. From the ashes and burnt earth of the Western Front arrived a demon dressed as a German who promised a one-thousand-year Reich. This Fuhrer brought death and destruction to his Aryan people on a scale never witnessed by man or beast. Germany was in its death throes while its Fuhrer, Adolph Hitler, ranted about future victories.

She felt the thud of bodies being thrown on what became a funeral pyre and copious amounts of liquid poured upon them. It trickled down her face and body, seeping into her mouth, nose, ears, and eyes. It trickled into her belly button, her fanny, her arse; it stung. It was whiskey. Angela had a glass at night with her husband, Walter. It helped to keep the cold frosty winter air at bay. They must be short of oil to be using whiskey. Where was Walter?

She began to cry; she was no longer frozen with fear, for her love for Walter awoke her from her personal hell on earth. The sirens were sounding as a German soldier — she could see he was a corporal with one arm and a large bandage around his head — emptied and threw the containers onto the pile of corpses and ran for shelter. She heard the German civilians cursing and crying while the bombs rained on the houses. They condemned the night terror fighters and the murder they brought to Berlin. She drank the whiskey as it trickled between the corpses mixed with blood and lay in a stupor.

She glimpsed two paedophiles dragging bodies out of the heap of tangled remains and forcing themselves upon them. It was sick. She heard them puffing and panting, but she could not cry out even when a necrophiliac dragged her out and fondled her. She stared blankly as a soldier put a gun to his head and shot him. The bodies were cold and stiff the following day when she awoke. Rigor mortis had set in.

Smoke hung heavy across the sky, and she was smothered in soot and ashes, blood and brains. She opened her mouth and let out a piercing scream — one after the other; the cries reverberated through the shattered buildings. Finally, a child emerged from the shadows, ran away, and returned with a woman. She was still screaming as they dragged her from the pile of corpses. They shoved a cloth with a ball in her mouth, it tasted of blood, stinking blood, and she fainted. She woke up in a lunatic asylum.

The Russian troops advanced on Berlin in April, and the city surrendered on the 2nd of May 1945. Angela would be one of at least one hundred thousand women in Berlin raped by the Russians. She kept and named her daughter Anastasia to remind her of the soldier who raped her. As the years passed, her daughter became a charming beauty as in the fairy tales. Anastasia aged rapidly when she was thirty.

She knew of her mother's suffering in the war's final days and how she had died in the asylum a year after giving birth to her. Her aunt Agnetha Poindexter mothered her with her own raped baby, Sylvana. The girls were the same age, and on their eighteenth birthday, Agnetha announced they were not blood sisters but had been the result of the war.

A year later, in 1964, they fell out when a British soldier, English to be precise, relocated to the town with

Anna, his German-born wife. His name was Albert Preston. They had a son, William, aged eighteen, and both girls fell in love with him. He married a girl from Heidelberg, Elisabeth Von Feldt, who was born in 1946. No record of her parents exists.

One may ask the point of this history.

These four people were the parents of the present Four Corners or the four Chief Executive Officers of EARTHCO. Circumstances were taking place to unite these four names in a city in Germany. That city was Berlin.

'Come put a dram in the glass,' says Humphrey. 'Storytelling is thirsty work, and I know I am a dead man walking. Don't be sparing with the whiskey, as this is a horror story on a par with Oscar Wilde's Dorian Gray.'

Anyhow the family tree of the four CEOs since the war is.

William Preston, born 1946, son of Albert/Anna Preston.

Elisabeth Von Feldt, born 1946, daughter of unknown parents.

William Preston married Elisabeth von Feldt in 1965, separated the same year, divorced in 1968, and had no known children.

Erica von Feldt, born 1987, CEO daughter of Elisabeth von Feldt.

Henry Preston, born 1980, CEO son of William Preston.

Anastasia Walbeck, born 1945, daughter of Angela Walbeck/ Rape.

Benedikta Walbeck, born 1978, CEO daughter of Anastasia Walbeck-Poindexter. Anastasia chose her mother's name Walbeck shortly after her eighteenth birthday.

Sylvana Poindexter, born 1945, daughter of Agnetha Poindexter/Rape.

Bridgette Poindexter, born 1978, CEO daughter of Sylvana Poindexter.

Not one CEO was born into a marriage. All were illegitimate.

Anastasia and Sylvana never married. At the age of thirty (1976), Anastasia began to age. Agnetha was in her sixties, but she was as sharp as a razor. It did not go amiss on her what was happening to her niece. Anastasia needed to tell her aunt about her mother, Angela. She had anticipated that would not be the case, but the ageing was the opposite of what happened to Angela. Anastasia was suffering senility before her eyes.

Angela was never allowed out of the asylum. People assumed she was Angela Walbeck, looking forty going on eighty. They could not release her since her violent mood swings had killed four inmates and one doctor who had tried to get fresh with her. She was certified as insane and would be executed as soon as she was fit for trial, and the baby had been born.

Her neighbours thought she was possessed, and that was what made her youthful. Because of the disease, sickness, and death surrounding Germany, some people believed she was Lilith (The first wife of Adam and a demon to boot). Her age was estimated to be forty/fifty years old. Yet, she had given birth to a healthy baby girl,

Anastasia, at eighty-three. The authorities said she appeared fifty or so when admitted one miserable January night in 1945. She was not who she said she was. She was traumatised by rape and abuse. She would become healthy in time.

After being admitted, she became calm and morose but was raped by a Russian soldier weeks later. The asylum staff detained him, and his commanding officer had the private executed with a few ethnics to appease the Western powers, or so Agnetha said. Those rapists should have been hung out of hand; they were no better than the savages they had defeated. She had her baby, and within weeks, she aged sixty with mental health issues. The country had severe emotional and physical problems, and one more woman would not be noticed or cared about. Something wasn't right about this woman, with her age bouncing from eighty to fifty to forty to sixty.

The most important thing she mentioned to Anastasia was the blood, brains, and whiskey that had poured down on her. It must have caused a reaction to her bodily functions. Otherwise, she had regressed to her younger years. How lucky she was not to be cremated in the funeral pyre. She said she had woken several nights in the heap of bodies petrified. She said the bodies were decomposing. She said she saw angels, demons, and gardens of love and hate. She said many things, who knows what she saw or imagined.

She had written files of her rantings in a locker by her bed.

Agnetha said it was the only time Angela was happy to hear an air raid siren. She had lain in that mess of human flesh and alcohol for days. Sylvana, assumed her mother, Agnetha was a devil woman left behind in the wake of Dante's Inferno when it returned to its subterranean home.

Agnetha had sworn never to divulge the truth to Anastasia about her mother. Something akin to what happened to her mother was happening to Anastasia but in reverse order. It had to be stopped, or she would find herself in an early grave. Agnetha recounted in detail what happened to her mother, Angela, and Anastasia, frightened, threw herself into relationships. She was overcome with the desire to procreate. She gave birth to a girl named Benedikta Walbeck under her family name. She was born in 1978. Not to be outdone, Sylvana had a baby girl called Bridgette Poindexter, using her maiden name, a few weeks later. History was repeating itself for Sylvana. She was expected to be a mother to Bridgette and Benedikta like her mother had been.

They had qualified as cosmetic chemists circa 1970 and were employed at Rebus Pharmaceuticals in Berlin. in '71 or '72. There they met Elisabeth Von Feldt. She was head of department ABC, a beauty treatment research laboratory. They tested mascaras, lipsticks, skincare creams, etc., for department stores in Western Europe.

It gave the customer confidence to buy the products knowing they had been tested independently. The massive conglomerates could not be trusted; they are not believable today. Take the food industry. Take tourists, for instance, mainly the British; you would think they were fed Soylent Green the way they go on about foreign food. They are ecstatic when munching on a bumper bag of soggy chips with something resembling fish with sufficient cholesterol to drive their doctor berserk.

The world had moved on from the days of post-war austerity. People wanted cosmetics they could trust. Animal lovers wanted cosmetics not tested on animals, hence the popularity of Rebus. It was a household name for independence. They wanted to be rid of wrinkles, and they would pay. The testing on animals and humans continued, and everybody pretended all was well if beauty could be bought.

The hypocrisy of humans equals no bounds. Money was available to the masses for the first time in history. Credit cards were easy currency, and the 1980s were approaching, and with it, the age of greed. Chain stores were built. Entrepreneurs of one type or another were waking up to the fact that a stash of cash could be made to satisfy the masses' greed. America was the place to be, the greed was pouring down the streets of Wall Street, and Michael Douglas was echoing what was said by the entrepreneurs: Greed is good, as in his 1987 film, *Wall Street*.

Benedikta and Bridgette were roughly ten, and this Russian-dominated part of Berlin was going nowhere fast. Sylvana agreed with Elisabeth they would die poor if they stayed in East Berlin. Plans were hatched to skip to West Berlin and on to America. They were skilled chemists and close to discovering Angela's secret. They had little money, and that would be a significant hindrance to escaping the Stasi. Sugar daddies from the

West were sought after. Where would you unearth one of those? These women had secrets, and they were now cleaning the kitchen, so to speak. Nothing would be left in their wake to incriminate them.

The elixir of life was within their grasp: they felt it, smelt it, tasted it, but they were still as far out as the lighthouse. They had tested a million formulae with whiskey and blood, brains, hair, skin, bone, adults, children, teens, infants, virgins, non-virgins, males, females, animals, lunatics, dead, and dying. Perhaps it wasn't whiskey. They had tried every conceivable concoction, and nothing had shown results. They had experimented with spa and mineral waters, including spring waters from Germany, specifically the water used by German distillers. There was a strong probability it was the water, but what kind? Perhaps it was the wheat, rye, and barley used to produce the whiskey. Maybe it was a concoction of herbs added to the whiskey.

They achieved a few positive results from batches of spring water obtained near the Baltic coast. It had regenerated the genes in a handful of patients for several weeks. The patients attacked one another, inflicting minor injuries. It had a detrimental effect on animals, making them aggressive and showing signs of mutating. The water source was lost when unexploded ordinance was detonated on the coastline.

Anastasia had been confident her mother, Angela, had regressed to her youth and that she was her mother's daughter. Her blood group was the same, and with the advent of DNA, she had obtained conclusive proof Angela was her mother. Her mother had given birth at the age of eighty-two. Angela had no other family of her own. What had made her youthful? Surely it could not be the sound of war, nor could she have been Lilith?

No, not likely. Angela said it was not the alcohol but the water, yet whiskey was almost water. They had purchased whiskey from distillers worldwide that had been producing pre-1945. No positive results had been achieved. The solution was out there. They may source it in America. They had advanced labs.

DNA was on the scene. No longer guess the daddy?

1989 was the year that changed the face of Europe, the Berlin Wall was demolished, and by 1990, Germany was unified.

'That's it,' says Elisabeth, 'I'm going to America. Anybody coming?'

Plans were finalised. Their properties were sold. With their children, Bridgette and Benedikta, Anastasia and Sylvana emigrated to Phoenix, Arizona. They bonded with the large German community. Property was rented from a German landlord.

Elisabeth and her two-year-old daughter Erica were next to follow.

Anastasia was not in prime health, and at forty-four, she looked seventy-four. She was overly aggressive in her verbal outbursts; soon, violence would take control entirely. She was going the way of her mother, Angela, albeit ten years later.

Anastasia had been incarcerated in a lunatic asylum for a couple of years as a teenager. She had recuperated sufficiently to be released. She continued to have violent outbursts, which led to murder on occasion. She was prepared to kill and main, which helped when they had to conduct their experiments. She never showed remorse for any hostile act she committed against an adult or a child.

Establish the water source, and you will find the cause of your grandmother's youth,' she would tell Benedikta. This made no sense to the child, but it did to Elisabeth. So, it had to be of this earth unless divine intervention interceded that holocaustic night in Berlin. Angela had said she drank a copious amount of whiskey, seeping from a jerry can and whatever else had drained through the corpses. She had felt intoxicated, youthful, energetic, and passed out. Benedikta's mother, Anastasia, died in the early nineties. Her personal belongings were given to her daughter, and Bendikta kept them in a box at the foot of her robe.

She also possessed her grandmother Angela's trunk.

Elisabeth's flight was diverted to Shannon Airport, Ireland. They had to stay overnight while the plane was searched for bombs. Terrorist scares were daily occurrences. A fault was found in the plane's engine, which cancelled the flight for another twelve hours. Sightseeing came to mind, and as it was late summer, why not get out and take in the countryside with its lakes and mountain scenery? As happens in a tourist area, a guide is available and willing to show you the sights for miles in all directions, and this place was no exception.

Elisabeth, Erica, and another couple agreed to share the taxi's cost and visit the Western coastline. Tony, the cabbie, said he would be a few minutes as he wished to have a word with his mum, who lived on a farm with her husband and two teenage sons. Would they like a cup of tea while he chatted? Of course, and in they went. He often did this. One wall was decked with photos of himself with women while his mum posed with handsome men. They were delighted with little Erica; she was such a bonny baby.

The door opened, and a youngster staggered in and said in a slurred voice, 'God bless all here' and fell on the floor, fast asleep. All hell broke loose, was he dead, or was he shot? To his mother's surprise, Tony got up from where he had been kneeling beside him and gave him a kick in the arse.

'The wee shite is drunk.'

'I'll be damned,' she snarled, 'that's twice this year, no more whiskey in the house. Get rid of Uncle Albert's bottles; he has been drinking that poteen his whole life. Before the war, he began drinking that concoction; my mother said so.'

'What war?' says Elisabeth.

'World War Two, Albert's father got them off a poteen-maker up in the hills. The poteen-maker said the village was full of tight-fisted fecks, and he was off to New York to ply his trade. No one heard from him anymore — good riddance to bad rubbish. He practically single-handily turned the village into an alcoholics' paradise.'

'You're from Germany, aren't you? I recall he had a brother working there during the war and probably had a job as Hitler's whiskey taster. I know they sold their whiskey to the Germans, lots of cases. There was another Irishman by the name of William Joyce, yeah, Lord Haw-

Haw they christened him, used to come on the radio and spin you a yarn praising the Reich and its victories.'

'What's poteen?' says Elisabeth.

'My innocent child, where have you been?' says Tony, 'have you never heard of moonshine?'

'Yes,' she said. 'We would call it poncheen.'

'I will explain poteen to you over a drink later.'

'No, you won't, you amorous article. She knows what it is,' says his mother.

The others are chomping at the bit to get on with the sightseeing, and his mother tells him to go with his tourists. They are in the taxi waiting. She whispers to Tony to try and put a smile on that poor woman's face and nothing else. The husband is a miserable sod. He's probably an accountant. As for us, I'm taking you two on a tour of historical sites, you'll like that little lady,' as she gives her a motherly smile, and Erica laughs back.

'It's most kind of you,' introducing herself and Erica. 'What about the boy on the floor?'

'Oh him,' she laughs, 'generations of Clancy's have lain in drunken stupors. He is keeping up the tradition. By the way, my name is Mary.'

Mary says he will grow out of it right now, shaking him like a rag doll. He opens his eyes and sits up.

'I'm sorry, ma,' and he scrambles onto a chair.

'Stay there and don't move. I'm going out for a while. Tell your father I've left him.'

'Ma, I can change,' and he falls asleep.

'He'll be OK,' Mary says, grabbing her keys. We head out to a Range Rover.

'Best take this in case we go up the mountain.' She straps Erica into a car seat.

'Do you do this often?' asks Elisabeth.

'Of course, it gets me out of the house.'

She meanders through country lanes heading towards a town known as Kilrush. A traditional music festival was in full swing. Mary and I became best friends there, and she treated us to lunch. We met a pal of Mary's named Ray, who took an instant shine to Elisabeth. Erica had a bottle of warm milk and promptly fell asleep like Mary's son. They both had drunk too much.

I listened to her yarn, word for word, as Benedikta Walbeck had dictated it. Who to, why, where, and when, God only knows.

I am absolutely intrigued by this tale of longevity as I now know that EARTHCO has been prolonging the life expectancy of the rich and famous. They had discovered the formulae and manufactured them in vast quantities.

Thanks to their greed, America was in the grip of an unknown catastrophe. Aah, well, that is a profitable business. I want some of what they have been having. She must have correlated the information from the Four Corners. I wonder why.

I did not know that Benedikta had her mother's and grandmother's possessions, including her written files.

Elisabeth said as she stood in that village with Mary, she felt she was close to the source of Angela's youth. It was here in Ireland, of all places, right here in this remote backwater. Some people have a nose for sniffing out things; a part of the jigsaw was here and the ingredients. A link between this community and Berlin in the

1930/'40s would be the final piece of a puzzle that took form hours previously.

She was an evil mother, and she wondered, passing a Catholic Church, if God would forgive her. Probably not; her crimes were so heinous she would suffer here on earth and in hell. She swore no more evil would be let loose before this elusive ingredient could be identified. Elisabeth's mind told her it was here; she guessed it was here, she suspected what it was, and she would sip it tonight. She did not want to believe the notion establishing itself in her mind; it was too simple.

The search would be at an end, and the horrors of Elisabeth's nightmares and Sylvana's would subside for a fraction of one minute. This would be heaven on earth to be free from the terrors visited upon her in her sleep, yet the search must continue. She would never stop; this was the most potent drug she had ever dreamed of.

That is what she hoped for, and obviously, some way of controlling the side effects. There is a cure for all ailments; you just have to invent one. What else could you seek? To develop this was to create immortality. How much would one pay? They had spoken about it, millions of American dollars, millions of Deutschmarks, millions in gold and land. Billions would be an appropriate word. They would be wealthier than Medusa. In their eyes, he would be a pauper, as they could have bought his stash with petty cash.

A terrorist bomb threat and a broken engine had combined to change men's and women's caducity for the future.

'We should be making tracks back to my house,' says Mary.

'Is your flight early?' asks Ray. 'You can stay here tonight, and I will run you to the airport in the morning.'

Mary sat at the rear with the baby firmly strapped in. Elisabeth sat with Ray, and he spoke of Berlin, as his family had worked there in the 1960s and '70s. Ray had qualified as a chemist, had visited East and West Berlin, and had done business at her factory.

Once qualified, he gave it up to run his own coach business. He trained to please his mum and dad, and they willingly accepted his change of occupation.

Elisabeth wished to bring up the whiskey question and asked Mary about the poteen. She said there were crates of the bloody stuff left in storage. The whiskey belonged to a family by the name of O'Kane. They weren't Irish; they were a kind of EEC family with lots of ethnic bloodlines from European nations. The chief of this dysfunctional family went by the nickname of Cockeye, Cockeye Kane.

Cockeye Kane was a poitin (poteen) seller and promised his sons he would make them prosperous. He would establish his own distillery and sell whiskey to the Irish in America. They set up their distillery during the 1920s, ever since prohibition had taken hold in America. A myriad of heroes of the War of Independence were residents, and like any patriotic Irishman, they liked a drop of the hard stuff.

'You know Elisabeth,' it is known as *uisce beatha*, which means *water of life*. It was credited with medicinal properties, and millions swear they feel healthier holding a bottle of Irish. Are you comfortable, Liz?' You don't mind if I call you Liz?' asks Ray.

'Elisabeth is such a mouthful, even if it is regal and an elegant name.'

'Liz will be fine, Ray.'

'What do you mean, Mary, it's got medicinal qualities? What does it do?'

'To tell you the truth, nothing. People here drink all day and live to a ripe old age. It depends on what your belief is. Is it the water, or is it the whiskey? Take your pick.'

'How much whiskey did this O'Kane make?' asks Elisabeth, 'and what did he do with it?'

Cockeye and the boys found themselves idle in 1923 or '24. They didn't fancy a stint in the new army, and neither did they wish to emigrate. Cockeye got a present of this mountain and its surroundings from the Free State in gratitude for his help during the civil war. 'What am I supposed to do with this monumental rock?' says Cockeye. 'Thank you kindly, Mr Free Stateman; I will knock it tomorrow. This bloody rock is too high anyhow, I might hollow the bloody thing out and create a fish farm, and I could sell the fish to the priests. They could give the altar boys a fish supper while busy bumming them.'

'You are getting into the spirit of the story,' Mariah says to me as I burst out laughing.

'It's one heck of a yarn from Elisabeth. Benedikta must have interviewed her with her consent. She recorded it and wrote it word for word. She probably did it for posterity,' I say.

'Storytime is finished, and I've had a restful kip,' says Becky.

I listened on. Cockeye set up his stills after complaining to the government that his family's compensation for their war effort was a pittance. He made it clear to the *Garda Siochana* that he would not put up with interference in the running of his business. He had the ear of one of the most influential men and had spoken to him personally in East Clare. He was informed that he and his sons could have a magnificent farm in West Meath.

'Have a bit of patience and make your whiskey as you've always done,' was the advice he was given.

He received everything he asked for to go into the whiskey business properly. The mountain was like Swiss cheese. It had been mined to death. Boats came in at ungodly hours and ferried whiskey to ships lying offshore. Nobody interfered with him. People said his whiskey was bland with an unfamiliar bitterness. It didn't taste right on the palate, but in the States, they blended it with stronger Canadian. It was reported that Jack Kennedy swigged a gill, spat it out, and made the sign of the Cross.

During the year, sales tailed off. It was noted by many who drank it that their skin remained unblemished and youthful for weeks later.

'You understand, Elisabeth? Certain regions of the world have people who are young at heart and in the body. Italy, Peru, Japan, and Russia have excellent districts for one's health. It's the water, they say, and there is much truth to that.'

'Natural spring water is excellent for one's health. You know what I mean, like spa waters.'

He persevered, knocking it out by the barrel load. He hardly made any profit. His sons had had a bellyful of it, and they planned to emigrate and make their own American whiskey.

By 1932 the writing was on the wall. Prohibition was dead, and Cockeye's brother came home from Germany with his wife, whom he had met and married after the Great War. He had never been discharged from the British army; he had upped stakes and went with this stripper back to Hamburg after the armistice.

The Von Schnapps family owned a string of knocking houses on the Reeperbahn. Brandy bragged to her father she could get him cheap whiskey. When the dad, Otto Von Schnapps, heard the price, he couldn't get them on a boat and out of Hamburg quickly enough to the Emerald Isle. He had visions of cases of Bushmills and Jameson's floating up the Elbe and leaping onto customers' tables for a few pfennigs. He could fill his customers with fine whiskey, and they would pay extra to ride his whores.

Take that fotze with you, bring back the whiskey, and leave him behind.

Chapter Seven

Brandy Visits Ireland

And so, it was Mrs O'Kane, the former Brandy Von Schnapps, who arrived in the County of Clare on the West coast of Ireland. She kept company with gunrunners and celebrated heroes of the Republic, not to mention the poteen makers. She placed an order for six dozen cases to be delivered to Dublin. The German Embassy would collect it, and payment would be given to Mr O'Kane or his representative. Mr and Mrs boarded a ferry at Dublin docks and sailed for Holyhead and London; their behaviour was severely frowned upon by the Catholic Church.

It happened when Brandy went to The Horse and Cart pub the following night after arriving and engaged in conversation with the neighbourhood tossers, who were glad to drink with her if she paid. Thirsty characters or barflies can be viewed in any bar in any town, anywhere in the world. They are perpetually there, continuously craving refilling at the expense of others, usually the state. With such pleasant company, Mrs Brandy O'Kane became engrossed in the male-dominated chatter. The conversation turned to her ravishing figure and what she did. The silly cow announced she was a stripper, and that was it; the questions came hard and fast, and the beer flowed freely. The barkeep, Haggis McCarthy, hurried the wife off to her bridge night, and the brandy flowed down Brandy. The Horse, Sullivan asked if she would do a dance for them, and Brandy agreed on the condition that she could get her burlesque kit. The alcohol had gone to her head.

Sullivan wasn't called The Horse for nothing; he drove Brandy back to the house of the O'Kane, where he gave her a stupendous shagging on the cold kitchen floor. She grabbed her knickers and ran up the stairs, telling him a bottle of brandy was behind the sink drawer.

'Where is that husband of yours?' asks Sullivan, concern registering in his brain. The O'Kane was a mighty strong family. They didn't take to having their wives ridden like horses by jumbo-tooled rakes like Sullivan. Down the stairs, she came in her burlesque costume, invitingly sexy in full makeup. The Horse couldn't control his cock, and for the second time that night, he shafted her on the kitchen floor.

'Stop in the name of God,' she yelled, 'I'm absolutely awash with spunk; for Christ's sake, I'm a married woman. I must stay faithful to my husband. Mein Liebling, you are such a vunderful lover.'

They headed out the door to the Horse and Cart pub stopping at the Slag and Peasant pub to let the clientele of six old fogies and a handful of dodgy tourists know she would be performing at the Cart a half-hour later. They went to the Cart, and she wore a racoon overcoat with a homburg hat and sat at a table. The place was choc-a-bloc, and not a woman in sight. Murphy, the fiddler, bellowed, 'Get up and get 'em off,' and she threw a bottle at his head, splitting him open. He slumped to the floor, where he was kicked into the corner where he might have died.

Brandy had busty busties, and the clientele wanted to ogle and grope them. Christ, it was exciting. Brandy jumped up on a solid oak table and started prancing about, and suddenly she threw her coat off. The punters became aroused and began shouting; what about no one cared? One thing was undeniable; they were horny and well aroused. Brandy swigged from a bottle and danced on the table with her long gloves and feather boa showing lots of legs in her black and pink cascade dress with ruffle trim. The men, sex-starved from their wives having overdosed on religion, could not help but take themselves in hand. Getting overexcited at the men's reaction, Brandy popped her tits out. She rubbed, squeezed, and tried to lick her nipples. The response was ridiculous. They took themselves in hand and spunked off all over the goddamned place. Randy Brandy threw caution to the wind, and off came her pink dress with the ruffle trim. She hit the deck, legs splayed wide open, inviting all and sundry to taste the pleasures of the flesh. The Horse Sullivan was first in and up her, and the rest followed. She was shagged stupid for over two hours. Eventually, they lifted and sat her on a chair, where she became semi-comatose with the spunk dripping from her truly shagged out fanny.

'My God,' says Sullivan, 'I'm off to Germany in the morning.' The door burst open, and the parish priest rushed in, effing and blinding. The clientele was shocked at the language coming from Father Dicks' mouth. It was disgusting. Brandy staggered to her feet, stared at the priest, and pointed at the men.

'What did you say?' screeches the priest glaring at her as she slurs her words. He's right beside her, frothing at the mouth, and snarls, 'What did you say?'

She draws herself up to her full height, legs wide apart. She shoves her tits out with the nipples hard, red, and erect and yells, 'They buggered me, they did the bastards, they buggered me, they did.'

He's beside himself with rage. 'How did they bugger you? These wretched men are too frightened of their wives. Have you seen their wives? I'm frightened of the bitches, and I spent twenty years in the darkest Africa. Get out; you strumpet, you harlot, you Jezebel, you daughter of Satan, take that yoke of a husband of yours and be gone from this blessed land, you spawn of Europe. Away with you,' Father Dicks says.

The Horse Sullivan was waiting as she stumbled out the door with a raincoat wrapped around her and her knickers and other bits stuffed in the coat pockets. The priest was still effing and blinding, and the clientele dispersed as they made their way home. There was terror on their faces. What would their wives say? What would they do to them? Hopefully, those harpies would increase their visits to the church; an extra few thousand Hail Marys wouldn't go astray.

'Where's your husband?' asks Sullivan. 'You need to get out of here.'

He follows her into the kitchen, bends her over the table, and gives her another decent shagging.

'*Ach Mein Gott!* Can you stop bumming me, you pervert? Leave me, you sex-starved alter-boy; I am going to bed,' and she shoos him out into the night like you would a cat and bolts the door. She gallops upstairs and jumps into bed, letting out a drawn-out watery fart, and within seconds she is fast asleep.

Brandy was woken by an urgent banging on the door at three or four in the morning. It was Father Dicks, and he was in a terrible state. Letting him in was her second mistake that night, for he ranted and raved about how beautiful she was. He had never seen tits or a pussy before, never mind shagging one.

He had been rammed into the priesthood at sixteen by his mother, who passionately believed Jesus Christ visited her at midnight and made love to her. She believed that little Tommy Dicks was the Son of God, and the priesthood was where he could hide from those evil Orangemen who might try to crucify him if word got out.

He was sweating like a pig and bollock-naked under his cassock. He showed Brandy his manhood, and she reckoned it was bigger than the Horse's. He was more endowed than the meterman, and that was saying something.

He was weeping, gnashing his teeth, and flogging his thighs with his cock. He needed help, he pleaded. He had fantasised about her all night; he had to have her to save her soul. She was Satan's daughter, and he would impregnate her with the divine juices of the Lord. He said his mother made love to Christ at midnight. According to his mom, Tommy Dicks was the second Son of God. She wanted to name him Rhesus after a Greek king she thought was a god.

'I want you, Brandy, to have my baby, it will be a gift from God, and the child will be Pope Patrick 1. Clare will be the holiest place on earth, and the Orangemen will have to kneel before the Pontiff and kiss his ring.'

Over the years, she had met a cracking selection of lunatics in strip joints. She was witnessing the mother of all lunatics jumping up and down in front of her. He was calling for God to bless his cock and give it the strength to shag the devil from her orifices and let his manhood wash away the sins of the sinners who had penetrated her womanhood.

'I need a cup of tea,' she said, 'and a Woodbine. I must wash my arse and make myself presentable for such a subtle invitation.'

Father Dicks was speaking in tongues, and he had found a whip he was using to lash his back and buttocks. His cock was enormous and swollen with enough blood to make a dozen puddings. She was puffing on a Woodbine compliment of W. D. and H. O. Wills, and she said she would be back in a jiffy.

Upstairs she dressed in a thigh-length skirt, leather boots, and blouse, and she was stunning. She was halfway out the window when her perverted mind desired Father Dicks's enormous cock. Down the stairs, she waltzed into the kitchen.

The poor man's arse was red raw. He was gibbering away as she took the whip and beat the living daylights out of him. He was crying and laughing. She grabbed his cock with two hands and wanked him with terrific speed and force. She could feel him getting bigger and harder. She knew he wanted her, he wanted to shoot his load, and she wanted to receive that load from this forty-year-old virgin.

She hitched her skirt high and forced her fanny onto his cock. It was grand as her love juice flowed; his weapon of mass production slid slowly but surely up her. He was deliriously happy and praying.

'Oh god, for what she is about to receive, may the Lord make her thoroughly thankful, for I give her the fruits of my loins.'

'I shall wash away the evil seed that men have fertilised her garden with and replace it with the finest harvest that any woman could or would seek.'

'Prepare yourself, my dear, for my stiff staff. Pleasure yourself, for the Lord Almighty has granted you the favour of receiving his holy water.'

He's holding her waist while shafting her on his cock. Cumming for him is immediate, and she called out, 'Oh my god,' to which he replied, 'I am here, Jezebel, my love. I will sodomise thee. You harlot of West Clare.'

Not likely, she thinks, as she cries out 'Mein Fuhrer, Mein Fuhrer,' and her whole-body orgasms, and the Holy Father keels over and is fast asleep, making noises like a sheep.

Cockeye's brother turns up at the house around ten and is surprised to see the front door open and Father Dicks lying in the cabbage patch with a turnip in each hand. He has a deco around the house, but there is no sign of Brandy. He goes to the hayshed where he meets the

Horse Sullivan with a pony and trap and who's sitting in it, but Brandy.

She shouts to him, 'We have to go; the priest is trying to shag me. Mr Sullivan was kind enough to lend us his rig to get us to the train station at Kilrush in time for the four o'clock to Limerick. We must hurry. The village women hate me too.'

'Well,' says Cockeye's brother, 'this is very strange, maybe you should dance for them, and they will appreciate your artistic talent.'

'The whiskey is on its way to Hamburg, and I think I'll follow it post-haste,' she says.

He jumps up beside Sullivan and asks if he had a busy night.

Sullivan replies that he has been in bed since six in the evening with a splitting headache. At seven the following morning, he got up to take confession as he likes to keep his soul spotless in case the big fella called. It being a beautiful morning, he had decided to take a detour by Skeritt's mill. He wished to pray at the statue of the Blessed Virgin for the souls of the drunks that had drowned there in the 1800s. Lo and behold, he noticed that the front door of the O'Kane residence was wide open; thinking that foul deeds might be afoot, he knocked.

'The good priest came out with a pair of turnips enquiring how much they were.'

'I didn't know what to say, a penny,' says Sullivan. 'A penny each, cash on the nail, and I'll be blowed, he paid me, and he staggered down the lane. Damned how he ended up in the cabbage patch, probably changed his mind and wanted carrots too, aah yeah, he wanted cabbage too, that's it that makes sense.'

'So, where did you find Brandy?' says Cockeye's brother, 'in her bed?'

'Good heavens, no, she prayed for you to come home under the kitchen table. The moment she saw me, she rushed upstairs, yelling for me to go and fetch my pony and trap and take her and place her in your loving arms.'

'You must have keen eyesight,' says Cockeye's brother, 'to see my door open from a mile away.'

'The Lord has blessed me with great hearing as well. I can hear that ould train chugging out of Lahinch.'

He gives the pony a crack of the whip, and they race along the old bog road, Brandy hanging on for dear life, her tits bouncing in the air. During the hour they are there, Sullivan tells Cockeye's brother to buy the tickets while he gets the bags to the train.

'Do you think he's on to us?' asks Sullivan.

'Maybe,' says Brandy, 'but my arse is sore. What is it with you and my arse? I'm glad the priest didn't bugger me too.'

'It was pleasurable fun,' as Cockeye's brother returned with the tickets, and the train could be heard in the distance.

'If you're ever visiting Hamburg, pop into The Crock of Shit and see me; you can dance with my sisters.'

'You have sisters.' And with that, the train is at the station, and they board.

Cockeye's brother smiles as two coppers holding bottles near the pony, and trap wait for Sullivan to return. He thinks that six wintertime months of breaking rocks will cool his ardour. They'll find more in his shed.

Their journey to London was uneventful, and they slept most of the way before booking into The Dorchester.

After a few shopping days, Brandy was well-healed and ready for a night on the town. They headed for the Windmill Club in Soho, where the models stood naked and motionless for ages. They were not allowed to move their bodies; otherwise, they would break the rules and be considered obscene. A girl with a slim body came on and did a fan dance, where she and another woman kept her body covered with fans while dancing naked.

Brandy was pissed and getting horny. She jumped on the stage and started doing one of her German stripteases. Off came the clothes one by one until she was naked, and she swung around the pole in the centre of the stage, throwing her legs open and thrashing the air.

She marched down the audience of two dozen customers, mostly British and a French diplomatic party, who caressed her tits and started to kiss her, muttering in French, Mon Dieu, Mon Dieu. Cockeye's brother was drinking champagne with two hookers. He never noticed Brandy as she dragged herself away from the frogs and started gyrating in front of the Brits.

'Vould you like to play vith mein pussy?' she said, giving them a taste of German English. 'Vot is your namen?'

'It's Archibald Penrose Caruthers,' he says, 'and my associate is Charles Fotheringham Ponsonby, and we work at the Foreign Office.'

'Golly gosh!' she says. 'Imagine little old me in the company of high-ranking civil servants. I say old chaps, would you like to take butchers at these bristols?' she says in a Cockney East End accent. 'Aah, I see, my dear Ponsonby, you are a pussy man,' as he gingerly puts his hand out to feel the merchandise. 'Go on man, for Christ's sake, it won't bite,' and he has a finger or two up her arse quicker than a magician pulling a rabbit from a hat.

'What is going on in these islands? Is everybody an arsehole bandit?'

She finds herself on her knees by Caruthers, and he has his cock down her throat. He's plunging away like a man desperate to clear a blockage in a sink. He's driving his cock in and out, a look of sheer anguish on his face while Ponsonby is stuck up the fan dancer. She was happily clutching a one-pound note.

The management had fired up the gramophone with its 78s, Swing was all the rage, and the club's half-dozen strippers were on-stage dancing and prancing around. One-pound notes were being waved at them. Opportunity knocks only once in a strip joint, and they took their shagged-out pussies to the one-pound notes making future Churchill signs which were readily understood, and wallets reopened; the music, the booze, and the crap lighting made it worthwhile.

It was an orgy. Another dozen hookers appeared with two dozen punters. The Charleston was blaring out, and everybody was dancing bollock naked. Tits were everywhere. Champagne corks were popping, and the stage was moaning and groaning under the weight of bodies. Cockeye's brother was banging the hell out of two arses. Brandy showed the women how to glide down a pole onto a cock with their legs splayed far and wide.

All night it went on, and at around five, the cops raided the joint. It was hushed up; you couldn't have Whitehall top brass doing the can-can with a shower of hookers. My God, the rest of the government would want to join in. Stiff upper lips should be maintained at all times. Sex and its pleasantries could not be let loose on the general population; no, women must know their place, and that's tied to the kitchen sink. Jesus H Christ, you can't have them expecting an orgasm from their husbands on a weeknight. Good God, no, that is not the British way. It was swept under the carpet, but people in the know still talked about The Night They Raided Windies.

Cockeye's brother and Brandy were driven to Croydon airport and flown to Germany. They agreed never to set foot on British soil again.

Chapter Eight

Baked Rat for Private Drew

'My God, Mariah, what an interesting story. I wonder if it is true. Whatever happened to Brandy? I've heard my granddad talk of Cockeye, a good ould poteen maker, powerful stuff. Never made anyone around my way look young, but they sure lived to a ripe old age. What should I have learned from this story of debauchery and illicit whiskey running?'

'We're here,' she says, twisting Becky's nipple. They park at the valet departure entrance, and in they go where Richard and Apsara meet them. Hands are shaken, and they head to the departure lounge, where I see Donald and what I assume is his family. The airport is crowded with all types of uniformed personnel and civilian families. Exodus comes to mind. The flight is on, and it's time to save one's bacon and, as usual, money talks.

There is no sign of Gordon or Austin. Dimitri and Yanni appear with another half dozen Spetsnaz warriors. With them is Private Murphy, alias Private Ivanovo, alias James Dempsey-foot soldier. There is no sign of Mutt and Jeff alias Fathead and Skeleton alias Rugosa and Sprangler. I wonder where Gordon is and his Texan sidekick Austin, the wood merchant. I think of poor Abilene with the delicate body lying twisted in the bed and the lovely Rachel, and hate fills my heart, and bile rises in my mouth.

I am here as part of the American Army. Just as well, I haven't got my other uniform, which would raise a few eyebrows.

Mariah's three-star general, General Hubert, marches over and speaks to Private Ivanovo, and they leave the building. Richard appears alone, and I'm dismayed that Apsara is not with him. I decide to go to the viewing levels and have a look. The place is alive with military helicopters, with a sizeable number of private aircraft, mostly Gulfstream 7s and C39As. I see their rotors motionless.

I can't hear engines either, everybody must be waiting for a bolt of lightning up the arse, and then they will stampede out, screeching and yelling to their aircraft.

I could fly one of those birds. Yep, I flew a Gulfstream 11 back in the late 1980s. What a story that was, and it made my reputation. I wonder how the march of the White Death is getting on and whether our furry little friends have been exterminated.

I head back to see Sheeree and see if she wants coffee. Why not invite Margo too? She's mighty young-looking? Let's see if she desires a bit of granddaddy cock in that new teen pussy.

Private Ivanovo, my beloved son, the giver of swollen eyes, comes to me and advises me to stay close to him and General Hubert when the time comes to leave. The government will open a slim air corridor for a temporary period. They fear anybody taking the White Death out, and they don't know how to stop it. It restarted movement six hours ago, and it's moving faster than a man can crawl. They have already seen hundreds of rodents mutating and growing; it's weird. To be honest, I'm scared myself. I don't want to die.

'Have you heard anything from your mum?' I ask James. 'How come you're so cosy with the general? You've not gone lavender, have you?'

'I haven't taken after you. I like a nice girl, none of your ladyboys.'

'What the hell are you talking about?'

'I've read your file; you have been under observation for years. Remember what I said, absent daddy, stay close to the general, and we will find mum.'

With that, he was gone.

He wants a family; he wants me.

I head over to Margo, who is talking to Sheree.

They are pleased to see me, thank God. Margo is beautiful and stunning. I can understand why women pay a fortune for what could be eternal youth. Why sag into a hag when you can be a jag with a tag?

'You are absolutely gorgeous,' I croon and hug them both. I look into their eyes — into an empty void, for there is nothing there. A shiver runs down my spine.

Sheeree feels it as she hugs me tight, and she smiles. 'Your soul is frightened, but do not be afraid; her soul will return. You will see it in her eyes.'

I look at Margo, who gives me an empty smile. What are they, and what have they done to them? Have they made a pact with the devil? I offer a nervous laugh asking, 'If Margo had sold her soul to the devil for worldly beauty and wealth.'

'Of course,' she said, 'of course I would sell my soul. I believe I have a soul, and it is mine to do with as I please. Yes, I made a pact with the devil; you can call him EARTHCO. You know him; you have seen some of his heads, and you are one of his hands carrying out his instructions. I don't want to be ugly and unloved. I want the joys of beauty and sex and to be admired; there is nothing wrong with that. Take models like Victoria Beckham, Naomi Campbell, and Heidi Klum. They still want the same attention as they did twenty years ago, and they are getting it thanks to EARTHCO.'

'Do you not want to make love to us, Patrick? Do you not want to undress Margo after a night out and make love to her? Faust wanted all the good things in life and sold his soul to the devil. In return, Mephistopheles gave him everything he craved for a term of years, but when the time was up, he took his soul to hell for eternity.'

'That's right, Margo, but your term is one year, and you are on a continuous renewable contract for millions of pollars, excluding inflation. What happens when you can't pay? It's the madhouse for you.'

'Aaah, that's where you're wrong,' says Sheeree. 'Gordon is in Ireland taking possession of his property through the courts. All those squatters are on their way to the mainland with their fishing nets, and they'd better stay there with their Provo friends. I don't intend to lose my beauty over a shower of useless, greedy inbreds. We are sending you over there to square it with your chums. Stonnage is mine, and I intend to keep it.'

Fire was in her eyes. Margo sauntered to the ice cream kiosk and got herself a cornetto.

I looked at Sheeree, and she said, 'You want to kill me? What if I kill you first, Major Dempsey? Yeah, major terrorist, this is how things will be in Stonnage, and there is nothing anybody can do about it. They have been paid over fifty million pollars, and that's in a deep recession; they can buy a mansion on the mainland and never work again. The matter is closed, and if they want to reopen it, I will close-shut their eyes, including their children's, forever. They are a heap of greedy pigs.'

'It's a lump of rock; they need to see it for what it is. We see it as a sanctuary, a place to hide while we receive treatment, a place maybe to go mad and die in privacy if we do not get our medicine. We will have what we need to remain forever young. We need the chemists from EARTHCO, and now this plague is sweeping the land of Wyatt Earp and Doc Holliday. EARTHCO is finished here, and so is Arizona; the military is waiting for the nod, and they are off.'

'The Pentagon is waiting to nuke this desert, and anyone left here will be a shish kebab. Thousands, maybe tens of thousands, will die in this state in the next seven days. Nobody is leaving on foot or by car. It will be turned into a giant graveyard all along the border. The army will napalm the whole border if the moat does not stop it. The government is broadcasting at ten o'clock. Don't miss it.'

'See if I'm right and understand how important twenty fishermen families are compared to what will happen to the good old USA.'

'The MIRA will hunt and kill that dried-up bollocks of a husband of yours. They have eyes in every country and will seek, find and destroy. If need be, they will blow that island all the way to New York, and your clap-ridden arse will be on Ellis Island a split second before your dried-up fanny touches down.'

'Why don't you use the word we, you shithead. We know you are MIRA, oh yes, we do, no need to feign surprise. Gordon remembers you and your daddy. You are going to Ireland to square it with, shall we say, Tom Dick and Harry, and in return, you will get you, your lovely Wendy. Tom and Dick will get a dozen anti-aircraft missile launchers compliments of Korea. Harry, all the rockets he could ever use. Your little army can blow up all kinds of things, which does not include Stonnage.'

'Is it a deal or not? Yes or no? Wendy and rockets from us. A blessing on the sale from your high command, and you and your whole tribe can continue to breathe God's clean air. Otherwise, it's curtains for ye.'

'But how did you find Wendy?'

'No more questions; when we get to Los Angeles, give me an answer, end of story. Get over there to Margo and have a feel of her tits. She has one hot bod, and it could be yours tonight. Remember, business is business; I don't mix it with pleasure.'

'Our day will come, and come we will,' and she squeezes my cock and goes over to Donald and the

Russian Spetsnaz. She could play Russian roulette with them in bed and discover which shoots first.

I fetch a coffee and wonder if she knows where Wendy is. I ask myself why I give a shit about this woman. She hid my son from me for years, and I wonder what crap she filled his head with. I must have a chat with him.

I wonder how Gordon knows who I am; I bet he is ex-SAS or Special Branch. He seems familiar. Maybe I ran across him in the past. I wonder what branch of the tree he belonged to. You mustn't forget the news at ten; it's gone seven.

Where is Margo? I see her from the corner of my eye, watching me.

I stand and look around, letting her have time to stop staring. I look at her and let out an excited smile and immediately start over to her. She rises to greet me. I hold her close, far too close, and tell her how I miss her from that night in the restaurant, how fantastic she is now. Not a day over eighteen/twenty, her skin is so white, milky white, delicate. Maybe she is a vamp and needs filling with blood.

'Sufficient compliments, do you want me?' she asks.

'Do you want to make love? Do you want me to enchant your cock and make him grow with my subtle touch? I am a married woman and would never dream of letting you stick that well-fed cock in my newly fashioned virginal pussy. Good heavens, no, what would Donald say when I stagger back to the marital bed, breathless and dripping with jiz? He would be very vexed and withdraw my mil-card.'

'On the other hand, do you want to see my breasts, thighs, buttocks, and magic garden? Do you want to caress them one at a time while I tell you the naughty deeds you must execute on my delicately sculptured private parts? Would you be Casanova enough to fulfil your mission?'

She moved in close to me, pushing her thigh right up into my crotch, leaving herself in no doubt that I had a weapon that was in sound working order.

'Yes, yes, I do.' I am engulfed in pheromones and in danger of going blind. Aengus, the great god of love, help me in bed if she is as horny as this and dressed.

'I must rest for a day and tank myself with vitamins. I want you. I hunger to get my hands on your body and my tongue in your crack to seek the hidden fruit in your magical garden.'

'You will find a sweet little cherry at the centre of my honey-scented bush. You can dip your tongue in the brook and feel that cherry floating there, waiting for a man like you to unhook it with his fishing tackle.'

'Margo, you have a way with words; when can we meet?'

'Later tonight, after dinner, we are going to get drunk, absolutely pissed. Donald and Richard are waiting at the airport for Apsara, probably having a strip search by customs; he came in on a military transport with lieutenant credentials.'

'Remember what I said: nobody is what they are considered to be. Donald is screwing that strumpet, Mariah. She is always hanging around. I caught him and Apsara drinking late at the bar, and Richard, the perv, already in his bed. I don't mind what he does as long as I am in the loop. I want you to keep an eye on him, for I intend to get my ration of dosh if he is going to toss me overboard.'

'I haven't slept with him in ages, pervert that he is; he tried to entice another woman and me to do it with dogs. It was nice with the woman; everyone should do it with the same sex, even once. Anyhow those dogs nearly clawed my friend's arse off.'

Blimey, she likes bestiality and same-sex shagging. I can't take any more of this. I need an immediate release.

'I need the toilet,' I groan with a knowing wink, 'you can jerk your gherkin yourself,' and she sits and orders a drink.

Arizona was doomed, but everybody was making money. An almighty explosion shook the airport, and sirens began to wail seconds later. The continuous boom of heavy guns could be heard amid the chatter of small arms fire.

'Let's go! Let's go!' screams Skeleton grabbing me by the arm as Margo races down the concourse towards Donald.

He, I presume, was searching for the missing Mariah. I could see Dimitri and the Russian soldiers outside with a lorry; the general and my son were there, as was Sheeree and a clutter of women and children scrambling to be the first onboard.

Donald was searching for Mariah when Apsara appeared and ran into Donald, who was running in all directions, his eyes everywhere.

'To hell with him,' says Margo. 'I knew I was right,' and she grabs me by the shirttails screaming, 'get me out of here, and you can do what you want to me; you will not be disappointed.'

'Double-crossing bastard, he wants to swap me for that bitch. I'll kill the cow. Shoot him before he divorces me; he wants to let me die screeching in my shit. I want the money, or I'm dead next year.'

She grabs an M16, empties the whole magazine towards Donald, and misses him by fifty feet. She's probably killed a dozen people and wounded scores. She's taken out soldiers as well. She is in peril of being shot, and I rush in front of her, shouting, 'Hold fire, hold fire, she has shot a terrorist.'

To be fair to Skeleton and Fathead, they take command immediately and disarm and lead her away to the lorry. Dimitri and Yanni grab Donald, who is crying his eyes out and lamenting the loss of his true love.

From the corner of that all-seeing eye, I see Mariah searching desperately for her bearings. She is a hundred feet away, and I rush to help her. I reach and grab her by the waist; I sweep her off her feet, telling her we must leave immediately. She is crying and clings to me tightly and kisses me full-on, thanking me non-stop.

'They are being eaten,' she sobs, wide-eyed with terror.

'You are safe; Donald is waiting for you. He is frantic with worry.'

'They are eating the passengers,' she screams at me, 'did you not hear me the first time? They are eating the passengers.'

'Where?' I yell.

'Out there, out there,' she points, and sure enough, I can hear the screams of people in terrible distress. Donald is with us by now, and he is dragging her back toward safety, yelling in her ear, 'Where is Becky?'

Hundreds of soldiers are on the concourse entering the building from where she was pointing.

What is going on? I want to see, but I know it might be the last sight my eyes might behold. I race back to the lorry. A sheet of flame greets me as I run out into the acrid smoke and dense heat. They have taken off in the lorry without me. The bastards must have taken off like greased lightning, and now I see the problem. The whole place is like the Montana Ranch, full of creatures great and small, but instead of eating cows, they are eating the US Army and a thousand passengers. The military is killing rodents by the bushel.

A mask and a pouch of grenades are thrown at me.

'Where is the bus that was here?' I shout at a soldier.

'It left minutes ago; it's going nowhere, just out to the desert. It's heading towards Yuma but will never cross the border.'

'It's heading for the planes,' I think.

Without warning, a massive horde of prairie dogs run across the tarmac, yapping and tearing at one another. A dirty sea of yellow is washing towards me in waves. These little mothers usually weigh a couple of pounds, but these yellowish bundles of fur are probably ten pounds. They change direction heading for me. I try to run inside, but the way is barred by hundreds of soldiers, and I nip smartly out of their way. Groundfire is being laid. I'm pushed behind. I join thirty or forty others who start lobbing grenades onto the runway. The whole place is engulfed with rodents, and I join everybody in dumping grenades onto the tarmac.

The noise is deafening as they explode, one-two-three at a time. I'm deaf, but I do not stop as a pair of earmuffs are wrapped around my head: One-two-three throw, and five seconds later, an explosion. The whole place resembles a butcher's yard.

Flamethrowers are melting the tarmac while the whine of rotor blades and the steady drone of engines can be heard as they taxi down the runway, all wanting to take off.

The inevitable happens. The runways become the graveyard for Gulf Streams, Cessna's, and Lear jets, as the pilots show inexperience under battlefield conditions.

The military C39s move with precision. There is no need to go tear-arseing down the runway unless little Yip-yap has a blow torch. He is not getting into the cockpit. The most significant danger is these executive jets crashing into one another.

The dozen that have taken off are not flying in the open-air corridor. They will be blitzed; they may as well land in Death Valley. Their chances of survival will be excellent compared to an Air-to-Air Missile up their tailpipe. Hopefully, the pilot will take note when he is buzzed by fighter aircraft.

I never saw Becky. I run inside to search for her. I ask another major where General Hubert is.

'He left with his staff to join Generals Rawlins, Kelly and Boyard on the border. The White Death has arrived about five miles from the border. It can't be held back, just slowed. The battle at the border will decide the future of the Americas.

Everything is left dead in its wake; it's been in a passive state for the last hour after gaining speeds of four miles an hour. The most prolonged concentration of firepower ever heard in Arizona will commence very soon as a massive army of mutant animals of all shapes and sizes descend upon the town of Nogales ahead of the White Death.'

Custer's Last Stand comes to mind.

'How come I wasn't briefed like you? Who briefed you?'

'Foxy Sky News Corporation. Why surely you didn't think our government knew what was happening for one moment?'

'I'm sorry for asking, but how are you getting out of here, Major Rundstedt?'

'That's the problem; we haven't been allocated any exit permits. It's a bit of Hitlerism: fight to the last man and the last bullet, then shove your head up your arse and roll down the nearest hillside, and with any luck, you will come to a full stop outside your front door.'

'In God we trust and the Yankee pollar. I would trust in a chopper at this moment; I have a family in Maine,' he says 'and parents in Kansas. I didn't sign up to be eaten by rodents. I'm going to hijack a troop carrier with the help of those appetising futuristic rodent dinners, pointing at a small group of Delta force.'

'I have a better idea,' I tell him, 'we could fly out of here through the air corridor, but first, I have to find my sister Becky. I don't want these boys cocking her a la carte while I'm saving their arses; no, Becky is mine and part of my family. Could you help me find her? We will sweep the concourse from north to south one level at a time. She is six-foot-tall with blonde hair, red lips and an Air Force uniform. Let's get cracking, please!'

'Isn't God kind to horny men? We found her machine-gunning away at a massive buffalo bouncing itself off plate glass windows. That girl sure has kissable thighs.'

'Rebecca darling,' I say, 'could you leave that poor beastie alone and accompany me out of this slaughterhouse?'

A crowd of passengers covered in squirrels and mink come running from a concourse exit and run into a flamethrower unit that tries to change direction and cause further casualties among themselves. There are bears, huge buggers eating a group of air hostesses in a McDonald's with a few staff members thrown in to make up a dozen.

I run like hell across the concourse, Becky's machine gun blowing in the windows of the fast-food joint, to be greeted by the stench of hot flesh and blood. It's a gruesome sight — a sight I had seen before, which changed my mind about the atrocities committed by fanatics in the name of God and freedom.

A beautiful face of an air hostess, rigid with fear and pain, stares at me. A cinnamon-coloured bear is devouring its way through the calf of her leg; she is trying to push its head away with her tiny hands. Major Rundstedt grabs an assault rifle, jumps on the bear, and empties the magazine into the bear's head. He produces a knife and slits the bear's throat. That helps enormously to remove the bear's gnawing hunger pangs as he opens his mouth wide and drops dead.

Sergeant Running Water cleanly amputates her half-eaten calf below the knee with one precision cut of a machete, one of those knives that would skin an elephant. He stretches and ties off the blood vessels and muscles; I reckon he is a surgeon. She never says a word.

Rundstedt is sitting there crying, cradling her head in his lap. He caresses her hair, talking gently about the farm he was brought up on and the animals she loved feeding and playing with. He later felt her grip on his hand tighten as her body shuddered, and she was gone on a very distant flight. It would be full tonight and every other night.

Before she was born, he had known her family; they were neighbours in Alta Vista, Kansas, where they owned small farms. Her father had enlisted with the Marines weeks after his eighteenth, and Rundstedt had followed the following year, enrolling in Wichita. Both had seen action in the North African Campaign and had won medals and promotions in the Antarctic Spring War of 2016.

He had no family of his own and treated Emily Rose as a daughter, and remained interested in her progress through life. Throughout Emily's twenty years, the families were best friends culminating in a celebratory party when she qualified as a hostess for International American Airlines.

Six months later, here he sat on a cold marble floor holding her lifeless body, to all intents and purposes of his daughter, who would soon be as cold as the marble he sat on.

She had been so excited about meeting him for an evening meal with her hostess friends.

How could he tell her parents what had happened? She was expected to die, screaming her head off as a plane plummeted to earth. The cause of death is terrorist outrage. Was that not why Homeland Security was so rigid in its dealings with the international community? It was obliged to safeguard its citizens and not put them in harm's way.

Instead, she was mutilated by a carnivorous bear in a McDonald's takeaway at an airport shopping mall. Why could she not have been in London, Paris, Rome, or any airport throughout the US?

Her father was on the Texan border, while her mother Dorothy would be alone when the knock came to the door.

I am a major in the US Army; I must be strong and continue to carry out my duties, he told himself, and every bear I see, I shall kill with extreme prejudice. Death was stalking Tucson and the airport.

A hippo came galloping down the concourse knocking everyone and everything flying. It was leisurely crashing in and out of the building, its body making mincemeat of toughened glass and steel. It was bellowing like a buffalo, with skin-like bone as the bullets bounced or stuck in its hide, sticking out like nipples with no sign of blood. I was facing a beast I had seen from a distance at night with its back glowing. This was a mutation, all right. It had a mouthful of evil gnashers as it sniffed at bodies on the floor. It moved on.

It was terrible news for the living. It likes living meat, and just to drive the point home, it picked up and tossed in the air a boy of around sixteen who had panicked and ran across his path. He grabbed him in its mouth, crushing the life out of him as blood spurted over the tiled floor. Putting its hoof on his head, he tore him to shreds leaving nothing but rags and bone.

It raced down the concourse, crashing out through another plate glass window.

I shook myself from my hypnosis and grabbed an M16.

I ran to the major standing there amid the carnage. The bears were gone, and the floor was covered with the dead. I could not hear a moan or groan, but the wounded shrieking outside could be heard in the terminal.

I knew we must leave before the airport would be overrun.

Hundreds of people would have barricaded themselves in the airport buildings. Sooner or later, they would have to make a dash for food or drink unless the animals wandered off elsewhere.

We head back to the terminal and meet the Delta boys and Becky. They are laying a crossfire to keep the furry creatures at bay. We head outside and run towards the planes. The National Guard has widened its occupation zone by hundreds of yards. At the same time, there are thousands of animals milling about, biting and snapping at each other. They seem put off by the one hundred thousand casualties they have suffered. I notice a dozen or so of those buffaloes among them.

'What are they waiting for?'

Sergeant Running Water has the answer.

'It's right behind you,' handing me a pair of binoculars.

Yep, that Death Snow is on the move, carpeting everywhere with destruction. We don't like it, and neither do they. They are not stupid these mutants regarding life and death decisions. One can always dine later.

A herd of deer could be seen racing ahead of the Death Snow. It's time to go. We troop across the tarmac, bundling into an empty flatbed lorry that has gnawed bones lying around. Go back and get those flamethrower boys; if the rodents attack, bullets are useless. We need to spray a carpet of fire.

I fire a burst into the air to the sound of an SOS, making one of the groups look up.

I wave to come over. This is dangerous play; we could be overloaded, and the army motto could change to leave one man behind. Three come running, reaching us within a minute.

'Where's the gas?' Runsteadt asks.

'It's around us, major, all-around us.'

They pile onto the flatbed, and one asks what's up.

I say we are leaving because everybody will get eaten. I point behind him to what's coming in. He is on his radio and demanding to know where the fuel is.

'Good question,' says I, 'good question.'

A fuel truck stops, and another two stick their heads out, wanting to know where we are going and how. I need a bigger plane looking at the two new recruits. They have spare flamethrowers. I have never seen one before. To the best of my knowledge, they were banned in the US in the 1970s. These ones are American-made for export. They will roast your arse at hundred yards and burn a hole in your eye at twenty yards.

A Gulfstream is a half-mile ahead, empty and sufficiently spacious to accommodate two dozen people. I shout to everybody to take up positions ready to repel boarders. Another jeep arrives armed with weaponry to wipe out the herd watching us. I feel it in my water.

They will take a gamble on these mutants as the buffaloes, bears and mountain cats advance slowly on us. They also see these animals, and without further ado, they jump from the jeep and start setting up bazookas. Everybody is out of the flatbed and rummaging in the jeep.

I grab a rocket launcher. Becky's got a machine gun which she deftly sets up on a tripod, and the flamethrower guys take up position ahead of us in a semi-circle. Major Rundstedt has got himself a machine gun. He has taken up position right flank to cover any unexpected visitors from the right. In contrast, Sergeant Running Water has done the same on the left. We should have a clear field of fire, and the flamethrowers should barbecue any that should reach our line. The herd of elk is far off, and I see through my field glasses that they are not alone. They are accompanied by foxes, cougars and other animals. The mutations seem to be random, but they are rabid and continuously snapping and biting. There are also wolves.

I hate wolves, and they don't look half-weird with their overblown bellies. I can see a mile behind them, and the White Death is on the move.

I must prepare the plane and inform Major Rundstedt that I intend to fire the engines.

'I will take the jeep, Rebecca, and two of the National Guard.'

'Like hell, you will,' he drawls John Wayne style.

'Rebecca stays here as insurance. Go now!' and he waves to two regular soldiers to accompany me.

'Be back here ten minutes after you fire those engines. I will be watching. I will blow you off the runway, so taxi over here slowly. Go, Major Dempsey, and carry out your mission. Make sure it's ready for boarding, and as a bonus, Machine Gun Rebecca will be first to board.'

There was nothing to be said as I jumped in the jeep with my escort. I sped across the tarmac and reached the plane in less than a minute. It's a C37, nice and big. Private Drew is up the staircase and into the plane. He is back in seconds, clutching a prairie dog with its throat cut.

'There are dead people in here. The captain has a skull for a head. Prairie dogs are having lunch, so excuse me while I teach these bloated little mutants table manners.'

He's gone, and there is a lot of cussing and yapping. We haven't time to fool around. I climb into the cockpit and drag the headless pilot out with the other private's help. His name was Krugeroff.

The plane is ready, and I fire up the engines and wait.

Looking through the binoculars, the herd has moved to within a few hundred yards of the flatbed. The engines run smoothly. The stairs are the problem. If I dump them, how is everybody going to board?

'Not a problem,' says Private Drew as he jumps back into the jeep and races back to his mates. The flatbed and jeep are full and on the way back with the herd.

Now that the proverbial has hit the fan, a semi-circle is formed in one majestic sweep as they jump from their transports and create a defence shield. A withering fire of bullets and flame cut the feet and hooves of thousands of animals. But they keep coming, and they keep getting shish kebabbed.

The major supervises the retreat onto the plane. Strangely the large animals are not attacking as the semi-circle contracts as people board the plane. Only hand weapons are taken aboard until it's just the major left fighting a rear-guard action with Private Drew at the top of the stairs.

'I knew it to be correct, but I could not believe it.' Rebecca said that as Rundstedt was about to be overrun by dogs, Drew shot him in the head. He signalled for the plane to taxi down the runway and slammed the exit door shut. Rundstedt could have made it inside with maybe a dozen or so dogs, and we could have dealt with them. Drew sat and lit a cigarette.

We were leaving Arizona, and I would seek out my son and his mother. The Gulfstream headed for the runway setting a course for Phoenix and north of the Colorado River. We would be buzzed into the quarantine area or shot down in flames.

Rebecca accompanies me to the cockpit, and I lock the door. I reached for the intercom. I informed them we would be over Phoenix, heading for the desert north of the Colorado River. We would land and be quarantined and debriefed. We could then piss off back to our own units.

Observe the seat belt signs and no smoking or shagging.

As we headed north past Phoenix, we were accompanied by six CU100s, a small cigar-shaped plane with computer-controlled flight and weaponry. Phoenix control tower informed us we were going on active service on the Mexican border. We would be dropped off at Tombstone by chopper and receive military hardware with instructions to take out any mutations like bison and bear and fight along the border at whatever point we chose.

'We have already done exhausting fighting at the airport; we need rest and recreation,' I inform the control tower.

'You can have it when this is over, but for now, follow our instructions, or you will be shot down. You can have as much R&R as you want while walking through the desert.'

How do you feel about that, Major? Who is your commanding officer?'

'I don't know. I was with General Hubert and Major Rundstedt, but he fought a rear-guard action and died a hero. He stayed behind to save our lives even though they were not under his command. General Hubert is on the Mexican border, and you should speak to him. I am here at the request of the US military at Fort Bragg.'

I left Rebecca in charge, saying I needed to stretch my legs, and went and sat with the others.

'Rosalina, the canteen whore, gave us a right dose of the clap in Tijuana last spring,' says Drew.

'I hope the flat-chested pygmy gets eaten by one of those buffaloes. On the other hand, she has a lovely arse on her. You remember Frankie when she wanted an extra forty pollars to let you shag her butt. She shat over Hugo when he stuck that monstrous tool up her. She thought it was you with your pencil. She didn't half squeal when he withdrew and covered him with shit. We should take a trip to that bordello.'

'Let's go somewhere quiet,' I yell.

'I don't want to shoot up another herd of crazed mutants. I'm tired and need fanny, beer, nosh, a bed, and a spliff to calm my nerves.'

'I'm thinking of deserting Frankie,' I say.

'I didn't come here to fight on this animal farm. To hell with Arizona and your bent cops. I've had nothing but misery since I came here. They can blow the place up if they want.'

Rebecca comes on the tannoy and informs everyone to prepare for landing. One half-hour later, we are on the runway and happy to be on the ground.

'See perfect landing.'

Rebecca doesn't agree for us to be separated. We will work as a team.

We were met by Colonel Potz, who informed us we would be airborne soon.

'Have a quick bite and be outside Gate 40 within the hour.'

'I can't get any reception,' says Drew waving his phone in the air.

'All communications have been cut with the outside world except for military chin-wagging,' the colonel yells at him.

'I have a satellite phone,' I whisper to Drew. 'I stole it off Major Rundstedt.'

'Did you really?'

'I requisitioned it without his knowledge, and well, he won't miss it, will he?'

'I have to phone my wife. Must find a private place; you can use it a bit later. Keep it under your hat, you tell anybody, and you don't get to use it. Agreed?'

Drew agreed with enthusiasm; he wanted to speak to his girl. I jog towards buildings being renovated and stick my head in through an empty door frame. There are building materials, and I find a roomful of electrical and phone boxes mounted in rows on further inspection.

There's a steel door; this will be one secure area. The walls are very thick and reinforced. I could howl at the wife, and no one would hear me. I find a bag on the floor with telecommunications written in block letters. I put a brick in and head back to the arrivals lounge, where Drew is loitering around the front, waiting for me to return.

We exchange a few words, and I return to the secure room, and he follows a few minutes later. I'm waiting, and he stops at the door; the sun is setting, sending its final rays of light and heat through the opening.

'There is no one out here. What are you doing in there?'

'Inquiring question,' I say. 'What am I doing here? Waiting to give you my phone. I'm going back to the flamethrower boys to get a bite to eat.'

I push past him and start walking back to the arrivals lounge. 'You need to be at Gate 40 in twenty minutes.'

'Hold on, hold on. Can I have the phone or not?'

'It's in there. Did you not notice I left it behind? It's no use to me now; I don't want to end up court-martialled.'

I slow without stopping, and I look him in the eye.

'Your girl doesn't deserve you.' I stop and light a fag, but he's already inside. I keep walking.

He calls to me, 'I can't find the phone.'

'For Pete's sake,' and I walk back to the door, 'over there next to that pool of blood.'

'What blood? I see no blood,' he says.

'Over there, murdering bastard.'

Going for his gun, he swirls around just in time to take a brick in the face. I shoot him in the kneecaps. I am going to kill him. It does not matter if he has half his khaki trousers embedded in the wound. It will make no difference; he will never see the inside of a hospital. I shoot him in the arms, hitting both elbows, and blood flows from his left arm.

'You are in deep shit.' I say. 'I bet you wish rats were eating you.'

'Major Rundstedt was the neighbour of the girl whom that bear ate. He was a nobleman on his way to telling her mother that her daughter was dead. Her husband is on the Texas border fighting for his country. She will receive that news on her own if I can't make it back in time. It's your fault.'

I kick him in the face breaking his nose. Blood pours, and he's screeching his head off.

'Stop screaming, or I will stop your screaming.'

I kick him hard in the balls. It only makes him worse; he is pissing, shitting and vomiting all over the place as he crawls across the floor with the strength of a desperate man.

'You want to live, do you? Well, so did Major Rundstedt. I will give you a chance.'

I drag two electrical boxes weighing fifty kilos each across, one to his left and one to his right. I wedged his arms under each box. No way he could shift those boxes, but he might. There is always hope.

'Let's get those legs tight together,' and I shove a bigger box on top.

He is screaming for the sake of screaming. I grab a pair of pliers and grip his tongue between the pincers. He looks surprised as I cut his tongue out.

'That will stop your yelling; nobody will hear you anyhow. With the amount of noise coming out of you, you would think you were being murdered. You are, for I have kept the best for last.'

I drag two squeaking rats out of a bag, their mouths muzzled.

'See what I have for you, Private Drew. I will cook them on that fat belly, and if you get up, you can have them for dinner. If not, they will have you for dinner.'

'Well well well, Mr Drew, your bowels are working overtime. You will have an excellent appetite for baked rodent a la pot flavoured with human blood and gut.'

I turn the rodents over belly down, holding their heads, and cover their bodies with the skillet. I remove their muzzles and push their heads into the pot. I bind the pot to his belly with duct tape. I think he's had a heart attack, for he is reticent. I pick up the electrician's blow torch and give the copper pot a good blast of heat. He regains consciousness, spewing blood over me.

The rats are busy as I throw away the torch. Bon, appétit you murdering bastard, and I head back to the terminal.

He won't do that again.

Back at the terminal, we are grounded for the night. We are bussed out to the Sheraton, where I hit the sack. I'm fast asleep in seconds.

I sleep the sleep of the dead, waking in a trance-like state.

The phone is ringing; time to get up.

It's time to kill God's rabid creatures.

Chapter Nine

Feast your Eyes

Saturday, 17th June.

I was dreaming last night. I could hear laughter from the clouds, the same laughter I had heard before. I listened to boys playing with soldiers. I recognised the voices, but who were they? I could not tell. A voice was lecturing me for not being a blessed person. I could not play with my friends, but I could redeem myself with charitable deeds. I must be punished and seek forgiveness from those I hurt.

My soul is a festering sickness covered in sores and boils. It is almost decayed; it can never enter the Kingdom of Heaven in this state. It must be cleansed and purged of the evil that has entered it. My sins must be washed away with penance. I must turn from my evil ways and preserve life. Hell, and eternal damnation await me and those who follow in my footsteps. Footsteps that will ultimately lead us to an eternity of mental anguish, knowing of heaven's joys but suffering the endless indignities heaped upon us in hell.

What if my soul is cursed with evil for eternity? It may return to earth periodically and continue to commit acts of corruption, plunging me deeper into the fiery pits. I will never rise to the first rung of that heavenly ladder and start my slow ascent to paradise. I will not earn the opportunity to walk the earth on the night of Halloween and meet the tormented souls searching for salvation. What chance do I have when the dead will be as numerous as the blades of grass on the green fields of Ireland?

I must do beneficial deeds to be remembered in people's prayers. Prayers help wash away sins but only in lesser amounts.

Scary dreamy lecture: I've not heard a sermon like that since childhood. The hellfire preachers would spout their homiletic rhetoric at Easter, scaring the wits out of the old folk with their fire and brimstone sermons.

Yeah, Drew's death was ruthless, but he deserved it. It was the best send-off I could provide for him with such short notice. That evil little bastard will get the same again if I meet him in the pits of hell. It's my conscience pricking me. He did say he did it to save us, but we could have coped with a few wild animals. He had dispatched four with his knife. No, he was a rotten bastard. He won't be the only one that will die by my hand.

I will take my chances with Satan; no one has ever returned to tell the tale. All we have is a guy called Jesus who promised us a cosy time in heaven if we live a miserable life and love our neighbours even if they crack us one across the face. If that wasn't enough, we should turn the other cheek and let them also have a crack at that.

But getting uniformed up and blessed by an overzealous priest is Ok. Our sins will be forgiven if we go to war and slaughter as many enemy troops as possible, even if they only have a bow and arrow. Genocide is Ok if the state sanctions it with God's blessing. It does not matter if they are innocent. It is God's will, and that is sufficient to go on a killing spree.

I remember the priest Father Dicks on Elisabeth von Feldt's DVD and how unholy he was. I bet he's in heaven chasing Gegania and the other Vestal Virgins around the Garden of Eden. He won't let their fires go out, that's for sure. He'll be there, pouring his holy oil into their hearth every chance he gets.

I wonder if that nymphomaniac Brandy made it there. I must get that DVD. What a story! Och, it's terrible to be fast asleep and have to listen to a voice lecturing you about the state of your soul. I shall say three Hail Marys and hope for the best. I will find a way back to my oversized wife and children.

Sheeree says she knows where Wendy is, so where is Wendy? I'm going to have breakfast. I light up a Camel and head for the dining room. The No Smoking sign reminds me of Private Drew...a great start to the day, memories of Dicks, Drew, and a sermon.

Everybody must have gotten up simultaneously because the restaurant is full. I'll have to wait. I push to the front, a sergeant gives me a dirty look, and I tell him to drop dead in front of everyone. I don't intend to hang around in this uniform.

I spy the flamethrower boys, all six of them sitting and eating a big breakfast. Becky taps me on the shoulder. She is in battle fatigues and is in the company of two privates. I remembered yesterday; it turns out it's

Frankie and Hugo, and they ask if I've seen Drew. I shrug my shoulders and say, 'No, I couldn't give a cuss about him; he has probably deserted.'

'No, he wouldn't do that,' Hugo says.

'Hugo, I don't give a toss about him. He shot Major Rundstedt, and he was a helpful soldier; that's why he was last to board the plane. He wanted us to be safe and out of harm's way, and that strip of rancid piss shot him. I hope the rats eat him.'

'I'm sorry, major; I didn't see the whole picture. Drew sure is a rotten bastard; the major did well by us. He didn't deserve what he got.'

'Too right too,' says Frankie, 'we are at your command.'

'Where is Colonel Potz, who wanted to send us to the border?' I ask.

'Follow me,' says Becky, 'I will take you to our leader.'

'Bloody hell,' says Frankie, 'he killed Drew. Drew would never desert us; he loves the action and a right Rambo our fat Drew is.'

'To hell with him,' says Hugo, 'never liked him. Let's go and keep an eye on the lovely Rebecca,'

He feels his nuts.

'How's yours, Frankie?'

'Never again will I let that sadist tie me up and suck my nuts; I'm half blind, and I feel cockeyed. I felt she would suck my eyes out through my arse.'

'I know,' says Hugo, 'after I shot my jiz, I was doubled up on the bed for ages. My balls are very tender; I hope a blasted rat doesn't make a play for them. It's weird that she wouldn't let us screw her. She has a lovely set of pussy lips, she wouldn't let me suck her pussy either, but I had a good slurp on those nipples.'

'I guessed you had been mauling them. She said they were sore and out of bounds. She said I could lick her arse, which I did, and I gave her fanny a few strokes of my tongue between those lips, and she punched me in the nuts for my trouble.

My nuts are tenderised; she boiled them in her mouth. Her mouth is like a microwave. My spunk was boiling; she potentially sterilised a billion babies.

She said she wanted to see us tonight. I am like a moth drawn to a flame. I want to suffer the pleasures of sex, yeah, me and my dick. I doubt if we will if we are on the Mexican border.'

Major Dempsey has got his written orders and is not a happy man.

'What's up, major?' bootlicker Frankie asks as I return with Becky.

'Go and get the flamethrower, boys,' I say. 'They have had their breakfast, and tell them to tool up and go to Chopper Red.'

'Chopper Red, what the hell is that?' asks Frankie.

'They have painted the helicopters in assorted colours. As you are going to be under my command, we have two copters. Ours is red and yellow. You, Hugo and Becky, are with me.'

'Call me Rebecca, damn you. How often do I have to tell you? Are you stupid or suffering from memory loss?'

'You can't speak to me like that; I am your CO.'

'Go and shove it up your arse,' she snarls.

'Hugo, go over to that sergeant and inform him that he is coming with us and take four of his best men, two with yellow and two with us. Tell him he oversees the yellow copter. Frankie, let's have breakfast, they can court-martial us later, but they won't do it now, not 'til after the border battle is won.'

The food is excellent, and we spend half an hour eating and drinking and take a bag of grub and drink with us. You can never be sure when we may get fed again. We head out to the chopper and collect an assortment of weapons from the trucks parked near bye.

A major general asks what the delay was.

I tell him I had a dose of the trots. Did he have anything to stop it?

He gives me a look of contempt and tells me to be a man and show some backbone.

Backbone, I've got more backbone in my little finger than he and his whole family have in their entire bodies put together. God blast him for thinking I was a coward. The lovely Rebecca is already in there with Frankie and Hugo. The other two rodent meals are Bill and Ben, two Oklahoma boys. Lucky old me and a smile runs across my face: who is in the cockpit but Fathead and Skeleton.

'How are you doing, boys? You be careful there, Sprangler, with your meaty fat head should those squirrels get to chewing on it. They will be mighty disappointed when they find that big nut is empty, and they, looking forward to gnawing on a fat brain.'

Skeleton is laughing like the idiot he is, but he is a kind-hearted idiot. That Sprangler is a dangerous mother, and he will kill me, given a chance. I will slice, dice, and package him home to his wife if he has one at the earliest opportunity. I wonder what Skeleton's wife looks like, given that she is Fathead's sister.

He is out of his seat and punches me in the throat. He is swift, and I'm left gasping for air; he is already back behind the controls. The bugger is a pilot as well as a fishkeeper. Surprises by the bucketful. I must get his curriculum vitae.

'I will fix you, Paddy, and fix you permanently; I will. Chew on that instead of a spud for a while, and remember, I'm the pilot. I'm taking you to meet gutter vermin like yourself.'

'Where are we going? Open your orders like a well-mannered Irishman and tell me where we are going. Chop, chop, get a move on; we haven't got all day. We are not on a Sunday picnic.'

Gasping for air, I tear open the envelope and stare him right in the eye with as much hate as I can muster. I'm sure I saw a shiver run down his spine. I will murder him in cold blood on the border. I feel happy with that notion.

'Right, you German sausage muncher, we are going to Rodeo, New Mexico.'

'Find it, set your bearings, and beeline there you beer-swilling kraut; wear your lederhosen next time. You will have no Oktoberfest unless you give the boys and me a number one blowjob.'

'That's it, *untermench*. I will kill you,' he snarls. But before he can get to me, I whack him with an iron bar, and he is out for the count.

'Help me get him out of here. I will fly this whirlybird,' I yell, and true to form, we are on our way, and Fathead is fast asleep. I wonder if they would object if I threw him out and let the buffalo suck his cock off. Skeleton has a smile on his face, and he leans over and tells me he will help me kill Fathead because he has a good reason to. He will tell me why someday.

Chopper Yellow has been airborne for ten minutes, and I need to get there on the double; the flamethrower boys are essential for our survival.

'Any idea where Dillon is?' I ask Skeleton.

'He was here at the airport with Gudjohnsen and Gordon,' says Fathead waking up. 'I should have gone with them, but the stick insect complained to his wife, my sister, who forbade it. I had to stay and chaperone him, big little snitch.'

'They have gone to Ireland, they are taking control of the island, and it's called Stonnage,' Skeleton says.

'I know what it's called. Who is with them?' Fathead snaps back.

'Gone to Ireland, have they? Well, at least I know where I'll murder them.'

'A group of ex-Delta force and SAS men will kill the islanders and the MIRA high command. You won't be able to play at soldiers up there in the Donegal Mountains.'

'They said you could have fixed it, but you were too interested in Wendy the slag.'

'Don't call her a slag, please; I love the woman.'

'No, you don't; you haven't seen her in donkey years.'

'I shagged her the other night; she is a useless old cow with a fanny like a sewer. She has gone with them to

Ireland; by the way, she'd copulate with anything that moved.'

'Look, agony aunt, continue with the info and let me solve my love life my way.'

'How would you like another punch in the throat when you land? Show me respect, you terrorist dog. I will ram Semtex up your arse with the help of your iron bar, and you can do your Riverdance and end it with a thunderous bang like they do in Belfast.'

We are hovering above Rodeo and spot Chopper Yellow on the ground. All the colours of the spectrum are there spread out for miles. The choppers are ordered to land within designated spaces and as close to their companion colours as possible. Company commanders are requested to be ready to be driven to the Controlmobile.

'I am in command here, and you, Private Rugosa, see that Private Sprangler does not injure himself while I am away. It might be an innovative idea if you march him around the desert. If he fails to carry out your commands, seek help and punish him as you see fit. I must emphasise to you, do not kill him. Stand to attention Sprangler when a senior officer addresses you.'

Sprangler pushes past me, whispering, 'Terrorist,' and I think, now is not the time.

'Check your weapons, link up with the flamethrower boys, and ensure you have plenty of sidearms and grenades. Find ones to set the timers on and see if you can find body armour, vests, bits like that, especially goolie protectors. I fear we are here for the duration.

Rugosa and Sprangler, can I trust you two to protect the supplies?'

'Sir, yes sir, bloody right you can, sir,' bellows Fathead.

I jump into the jeep that has come for me. At the Controlmobile, I am given the same briefing as the other commanders.

In a nutshell, a big nutshell at that, the White Death is one mile from the border and hasn't moved in two days. It's dormant, for it hasn't moved anywhere. There is no sign of that creeping fog or any movement from it. A herd of cows was forced to stampede through it, but nothing happened, and nothing could be gleaned from the samples taken. It feeds off vegetation and flesh to the best of the scientific community's knowledge.

It's just a fine mist of spidery webs or powdery mildew. Call it what you want; the military has named it Ari 50 in honour of the first state attack. What a dubious honour. They think it could be terrorist related. There is a wall chart over at Quantico, and the FBI has listed all the states, and Arizona is No 1. I can only assume they intend to tick off state by state as they die. William J. Petty asked for it himself, and it's right inside the foyer; you can't miss it if you work there. It's to remind everybody that this is a fight to the death.

The Marines have adopted a new motto of No State Gets Left Behind. The best guess is that it is a corrosive pesticide with the ability to regenerate itself. It's like a weedkiller programmed to destroy every living thing in front of it. Think of War of the Worlds with its red dust covering everything. That is what this chemical is, a destroyer of mankind. If we cannot stop it, it will overrun the whole continent of America in a month, a year, who knows. It will continue to devastate entire tracks of land and everything upon it. It's got no known chemical, biological, or physical makeup. There are traces of alcohol, sulphur, and sugar. However, in minute quantities, you would need a spectrograph to be able to read the information.

We don't know why it's inactive, but it has ceased movement. It appears dormant for hours, regenerates, and heads off in one direction. It no longer spreads like a pebble dropped in a pond; to sum things up, it could head this way this White Death. If it does, we are in a shit street because the ranchers in New Mexico and Colorado are driving herds of steer this way. They are clearing their land of cattle and whatever else they can put to flight or death. The herds are so vast that the government can't do anything; they will cross the state line today and tomorrow. Funeral pyres are already burning over the state of Texas.

Now's the time to get yourself a tasty T-bone.

Texas is siding with New Mexico and has promised anyone who wants a bloody nose will get one. It's nothing short of a rebellion. They are talking of secession from the Commonwealth if they are not allowed to protect their land and families in whichever manner they see fit.

They say Arizona is dying, and as many animals as possible should be herded into it and incinerated. Texas is the most vociferous in voicing its opinions and leading the shouts for secession from the Union. They say that the whole of Texas is now the Alamo, and they will make their last stand against this accursed plague and its mutant animals. They will kill everything that moves, and if the government interferes, they will be dealt with in the same way that Santa Ana was.

This, of course, has infuriated the Mexicans. They have asked and demanded a public apology from the governors of New Mexico and Texas. Senator Aloysius T McGinty has informed the President of Mexico that he will have to kiss his arse before he gets an apology. That will be over his dead body.

Philippe Honduras, the Magnificent, has challenged him to a duel but awaits McGinty's reply. Knowing McGinty, he will grow old waiting.

The fact that a million Arizonans are awaiting evacuation does not perturb them. There will be serious trouble if these people are not allowed to leave. The Hispanics and their descendants are smuggling themselves back into Mexico through the mountains. What a carry-on!

At present, people believe that all will end well as there is no movement in the Death Snow. However, if it goes on the march and heads north or in any direction with any speed, all hell will break loose, and you will see the panic and a border stampede.

I have been informed that Tucson is under attack from a plague of rats, moles, and prairie dogs. A rabid herd of steers has taken up position on Tucson's outskirts, probably six thousand strong; the mad animals seem to have an instinct for self-preservation. The town is being overrun, not by surface-living animals but by fossorial animals, which beggars the question, what is happening? The White Death is moving with millions of mammals, and the whole damn lot is heading towards Tucson with a vanguard five-mile wide.

A widescreen is set up, and we tune in to Starship Satellite which has cameras worldwide. Wave after wave of rodents sweep over the soldiers. Only a few have protective clothing, and soon a bloodbath is visible to the naked eye. They are being eaten alive, flailing their arms and kicking out in all directions. It's to no avail; they are dragged down and overpowered by the onslaught's weight and succumb to superior numbers.

Screams and curses can be heard, the cries of men in terrible torment racked with pain. A camera pans to a soldier who's screaming into another camera. 'My blood is on fire,' and he crashes to the ground.

What new afflictions await our heroes, our defenders of Tucson? Without warning, the cameras cut out, and all is quiet.

'Find out what happened,' shouts Colonel Potz as his adjutant legs it off to the communication room at double-quick speed and returns at a gallop yelling his head off.

'Did, did he say napalm?' yells the colonel jumping in the air, 'are they burning the town? I have just finished paying fourteen million pollars for my summer house. Who gave the order? It couldn't be the President, could it? I bloody know it was her, the napalm-loving bitch. I knew those Clintons were a shower of turds; she has burned my house, terrorist bitch. I will gladly give her to Osama, poor old invisible Osama. He is probably being held a prisoner in a dungeon by an American-paid terrorist cell.'

He strides off, effing and blinding, yelling that Monica Lewinsky should have shoved a monster dildo up Hillary's arse. She is talking through her arse, and now the bitch has burned my house. A satellite image shows a massive chunk of the city on fire. It's a tremendous firestorm, screeches a British journalist as she practically sucks the head off the microphone.

I can see people running, some on fire.

'Look!' she yells as the satellite passes over a vast herd of cattle in flames. Helicopters come into view, and they appear to be spraying fire and bullets at animals, all on the hoof and running for their lives. The satellite focuses on Tucson, but fire and smoke are all that can be seen now.

'Jesus Christ almighty, who ordered the burning of Tucson, it's a war crime.'

I've seen plenty. Time to go, time to save my bacon, time to find my boy, and I run for the chopper.

'Let's go, boys.'

Colonel Potz is beside me, telling me we are still in group G with black, red and yellow choppers; our destination is the White House.

'What?' I ask.

'Only joking,' he replies in an icy cold manner.

The White Death is on the move, forcing millions of animals of varied species toward the town.

I ask myself, where are all these animals coming from? Are they cloning themselves, or what? Sod this for a game of soldiers.

'We are to wipe them out and continue to strafe everything with four legs along the border,' Potz yells, 'and then we will go and visit that bitch in the White House.'

We will be supplied with munitions from depots flying the Confederate flag.

'Yee-ha,' he yells, dancing in the sand, 'where is Belle Starr?'

The country has gone mad, Confederate flags. Well, if it isn't Fathead and Skeleton wearing Southern secession cockades. Blow me gently. I can hear *When Johnny Comes Marching Home* from their chopper.

I recognise Galwayman Patrick Gilmore's song— three of the five helicopters are flying the Confederacy's battle flag and the other two the Confederate flag. Fathead is laughing, grabs and shakes my hand, and lets out a blood-curdling rebel yell reverberating around the choppers and is taken up by others. He drapes a Sons of Erin flag around me and tells me, 'Go, glory awaits you.'

Rotors are moving, and as they say, we are booted and suited and ready to die. I don't know about glory waiting for us, but my future is mothballed as I wrap the flag around my waist — what a weird gesture.

I will kill the bastard; he probably filled his trousers when I gave him the death stare. The world has gone mad.

Everybody is showing their colours. We will fight bravely, even if it is against a horde of crazed vermin. We check our weapons, and then one and all in good voice bellow out Dan Emmett's Dixie, another Irish/American, and we are on our way.

The colonel has jumped on board and is banging on about Hueys in Vietnam. He's old enough to have been there. He tells Bill and Ben that rat meat is delicious; the Cong used to eat it. He said they looked like rats and lived in tunnels far below the ground. Yeah, Charlie was a clever little rat. He kept nibbling away at us, and eventually, those yellow rats overran us. Clever little bastard, yep, he sure was. I never played Russian roulette with Charlie. Walkins did, I believe; he had a bit of The Deer Hunter in him.'

'Charlie didn't like deer. He liked rats. Permission to catch a rat-eater for interrogation?'

He was gone the next moment. We will probably be shot for rebellion, and I'll be shot as a spy. Whoever I am supposed to be spying for would never believe there is so much wildlife; they say you are never a metre from a rat. I can vouch for that.

Colonel Potz was running like the clappers across the desert. The chopper bursts into life as Fathead takes her up, and away we go to probably the most magnificent safari on earth. This will be no Daktari; these sick animals will receive an instant cure with the help of a flamethrower and other various remedies.

We are redirected to Benson to wipe out thousands of steers that have crossed over from Texas. They are drinking the San Pedro dry. None have shown any sign of rabies or even the mild form of rabies widespread throughout Europe and the USA. We arrive to find that the people of Benson have done the job and have set up an almighty barbecue. We are cordially invited to tuck in. Country & western bands are playing. Gallons of Hillbilly Piss, an excellent local amber brew with a knock-you-down effect, is available, compliments of the owner, Redneck Halloran.

He had managed to flog his brewing interests to a Chinese consortium that had failed miserably in their attempt to buy the Arizona Cardinals. News of this unexpected feast is circulating via the grapevine, and units from all over the desert gather by the truckful.

By eight o'clock, upward of 200-300 soldiers are setting up trestles and tables. Dozens of barbecues are pressed into service while a dance floor made of lumber from Gordon's mate Austin is set up. The locals are arriving with an assortment of extras.

There is a stunning selection of ladies without their husbands and a smattering of hookers so that all can feast on animal and human flesh.

I will make sure that Fathead gets a bit of marital extra. I hope he likes seafood because I'm going to find one with crabs. See how his wife likes that.

Frankie, Hugo, Bill, Ben, and the six flamethrower boys try to be Bronco Billys. They are doing their best to get their necks broken. They are riding steers, bulls, and one another. Frankie dashes towards a helicopter.

I practically fall over with the hard-on that jumps up in my trousers. A smile as wide as the Mississippi spreads across my face at the sight of the lovely and delectable Mariah and Rebecca. I come over all faint; it's too good to be true. Two attractive women at an alcohol-fuelled barbecue on a hot, sultry night with the sky full of stars and death awaiting us tomorrow.

Indeed, tonight will be the night.

It's that Frankie, and he's feeling Rebecca's arse. This cannot be, Frankie and Hugo shoving their cocks into my girls. No way, and I head over with determination on my face and a hard-on in my trousers. Hugo is on his way, as are Bill and Ben. If these boys have a foursome, these wenches will be useless for days to come.

'Hi, Mariah,' I call, striding up to her with a swagger.

'How are you? You're appetising in uniform. Are we going to have a drink?'

'Lads, the ammo needs sorting out in Yellow Chopper. Can you do it?'

'Hold your horses,' says Frankie, 'we know these ladies, and they are here to see us, isn't that right, Rebecca,'

He sneaks his head under her arm for a cuddle.

I could hear him telling her he misses her, and his coconuts were full of deliciously sweet milk, not stale and rancid like old men have. I should kill these little pricks. Frankie and Hugo are with Rebecca, whispering carnal pleasures in her ear. If any of their mates come over, I will do a spray job, and they can shag one another in hell.

'Did I not tell you two Romeos to go and check the munitions? What the hell is holding you up? Take your bodies away from those girls.'

Mariah whispers to Frankie, and he and Hugo, along with Bill and Ben, sneer and return to the chopper.

'What the hell are you flirting with those two yolks for? I want you, Mariah. What did you say to Frankie?' I ask.

'Ooh, he's jealous; he doesn't want those studs to be riding us. It will only make him look impotent, assuming he can get it to stand when it is his turn. Can you make him stand?' and they titter in that sexy way they have with the tips of their fingers on their lips.

'Do I see you tonight or not?' I ask in a determined voice, hoping they say yes, but instead, they ask, 'Is it one or both I would like? Should you not seek medical advice before such an undertaking? After all, you are on the wrong side of youth.'

An artillery captain turns up and gives Mariah an order. They immediately retire to a jeep and head for the Controlmobile. I wonder if Mariah would cross Donald and where he is. I can't be bothered to wait for their return.

I head back to the open-air barn dance, and a raven-haired-fortyish housewife offers me a beer with inviting boobs. We take to the floor, where we dance to hoedown music. Yee Haw! We spend the evening eating, drinking, dancing, and flirting and at about nine o'clock, she asks if I would drive her back to Benson as her husband will be due back in the morning.

A ten-ton tank of a woman is molesting Fathead, and as I approach him, he looks at me beseechingly to save him. I need to tell someone I will be AWOL, and I spot Alphonse dancing with another skeleton of a woman. I wonder what kind of shag they will have and whether they will play the guitar on one another's ribcages. As I reach Fathead, I lean over and tell ten-ton Tessie that he likes fat women. He will take two at a time. Make sure he performs, and give him alcohol. He's shy; loosen him up a bit and have a photo to show me tomorrow.

'Don't worry,' she says, 'he's not getting away.'

'You require me to carry out weapons check now,' he says desperately.

'No soldier, carry on as you are; you may remain in this woman's company and her friends all night if need be.'

'Paddy the terrorist,' he yells at me just before his head disappears into a pair of mighty heaving breasts. May God have mercy on his tool.

I head over to Skeleton, who is nervous and lets go of the woman, but she is like a limpet and hangs on. He practically drags her across the floor, but I am rubbing noses with him in seconds.

'Stand at ease, part-time soldier.'

Heads turn to see what the commotion is about.

'This soldier here is not enjoying himself. Fetch him alcohol and a chicken drumstick, Oklahoma fried,' which raises a titter.

'I insist you take this beautiful lad to her residence and invite yourself in for coffee, make sure Fathead knows where you are, and phone me on this number.'

We must be careful, or we could face a drumhead court-martial and end up buried in the desert.

A group of women are hijacking men and jeeps; before you know it, we have a convoy. I wonder whether these people are heading for outlying homesteads for a bit of how's your father?

The housewife's name is Grace, and she remains silent as we head toward Benson.

Chapter Ten

It's an Orgy

I have been thinking about my family in Seattle. Peter and Susan are teachers at Greyfield's College. I wonder how I will meet my son and where on the border he is. I feel lonely, and I look at Grace. She senses my eyes on her, and she glances shyly at me, and I wonder if I should.

She answers my glance by placing her hand on my knee and tells me, 'Her husband is in poor health but is convalescing up in Denver with his family. I returned to collect family heirlooms but have not been permitted to leave. The authorities are keeping the border closed, but everyone has been assured that everyone will be evacuated. Tens of thousands of people are allowed to leave each day after being quarantined.

'So, your husband won't be here in the morning?'

'You are a proper little fibber. Are you sure you are not luring me to your web, my lovely little spider?' and I give her thigh far up near her fanny a squeeze which makes her blush.

We drive to her house on the edge of town, where she makes coffee while drawing me a hot bath. Her bathroom is enormous, and she is definitely a woman of substance, as they say. The waft of scents and lovely bouquets greets my nostrils. The flickering light from dozens of colour-changing candles gives the place an atmosphere and a feeling of intimacy. The provocative bodies of pornstars on a widescreen 3D TV preparing to make love provokes my mind into a wild sexual fantasy of Grace giving herself to me.

Margo is beautiful and sexy, but she is old meat reborn to be used but not loved. Becky and Mariah appear to be a pair of sex machines for one's sport.

Wendy, what can I say about her, the biggest slapper that ever walked? She should be ridden and dumped.

Then, of course, there is the wife, but she is a raving lesbo. Sheeree is another manufactured doll for display purposes only, with sex thrown in. Only the lovely Rachel came close, and she was too energetic to keep on a leash, but Grace...Grace is beautiful with an attractive body **and** housewife material with cooking skills; the bedroom skills will come into play tonight.

I do not know why I should feel like this, for she had prepared the bathroom before going to the hoedown. She intended to drag someone back, and that is **OK** by me.

The mystical sounds of Enya fill this chamber of pleasures with the sweet sound of her voice and the enchanting strains of a harp. Grace enters with champagne and pills, and I recognise them as whackers as they make you overly sensitive to physical contact. The sensitivity of lovemaking is brought to a much higher plain. Without stoppers, the act of love would be over before it had begun.

I had not tried them. They could not be bought for love or money. It was impossible to duplicate the formula. Those who had tried had spent days in hospital suffering from priapism, resulting in an exhausted immune system, bringing delirium and death. I suspected cantharidin from Spanish fly was the main ingredient. That would have been the whacker; the stopper would have been the **sixty-four thousand** pollar question.

Obviously, Grace had contacts in the highest echelons of chemistry. She intended to be well and truly satisfied before the night was out. She didn't seem like a livewire, but you cannot judge a book by its cover. In this case, the book sleeve was of exceptional design. The reading promised to be very engaging unless looks were deceiving.

She asked if I minded showering after her, as she would like to dress and have drinks.

'Why not?' says I, 'it promises to be a delightful night,' the whackers are immediate, but the stoppers take an hour to kick in.

'So, how come you have such an alluring bathroom?' I ask.

She informs me it belongs to a madame who runs a brothel for the ranching community's wealthy clients.

'This here is the brothel, and I expect you will enjoy your stay. She started to cater to the South American and African ranchers who would study our Arizonan ranching techniques. We were enthralled by Anglo/Saxon/French period history, particularly the **sixteenth** and **seventeenth** centuries. With so much moolah floating about and whiskey and flesh being in abundance, it wasn't long before **m**adame discovered that megabucks could be made from our visiting guests.

She was especially interested in the Africans and the drug barons out of Juarez.'

'Pedro Alvarez was the worst for adolescents; he liked a nice bit of ebony in which to stick his ivory bone. He was a South African slave runner, dealing mostly with teenage girls he kidnapped worldwide.'

'He was madame's specialist supplier of fresh meat. He made sure that she had a well-stocked harem of girls, white, black, yellow, and Eskimo, he would supply at the cost of between **five hundred- thousand** and **one million** pollars per two-week hire, and if they were maimed/died, it was ten million.'

'She suspected a darker side to the business due to visits from a private undertaker.'

'Tonight's boys and girls are here for the pleasure of an African tribal chief who has had a bout of malaria but has recovered sufficiently for an orgy. There should have been other guests, but I have no idea whether they are late or have cold feet with all communication shut down.

They are coming from Juarez, and that kiddie-fiddler Pedro is with them. Tonight, I should be a million pollars in cash to the good, and you, my strong, adventurous friend, should protect me from unwanted attention if I should signal you such.'

'Madame and I had been at school together, and she had gone into the brothel business just like her mother. When she died, she continued to service the old lady's clients, there were forty-four clients, and she got in guest hookers for the cattle barons.'

'She offered me the opportunity to have paid sex with gentlemen of distinction, as she put it. I used to be a beautiful woman in my younger days, if you don't mind me being swell-headed. Still, I stayed with my childhood sweetheart. I lived a life of misery and poverty with no family and extraordinarily little sex.'

'I believe my husband was a homosexual, and the devil came for him many times, but the dying bastard would not let go of life. I'm not going back to him. I am going to Louisiana, where my friend has taken up residence in her early retirement. I yearn for a gentleman of distinction who will pay me to take up a beauty treatment at the EARTHCO clinics.'

'I will have the best part of ten million saved by tonight.'

'Oh, the 60/20 clinics,' I say. 'I can assure you they are outstanding, but they will probably go out of business because they started this epidemic.'

'Good lord,' she says, 'you really believe they will go out of business. What shall I do to enhance my body and keep it attractive?'

'You are lovely, and I am pleased to hear that you are not a hooker. I want to make love to you, not just have sex. I am surprised at what you have told me, but I will not hold it against you. I take it that I don't have to participate in this orgy. It's you I am here for.'

'It's you I want,' she says.

'Take me anytime, but relax and soak up the atmosphere.'

'There is an orgy here tonight for a chief Mogambo. You may join in if you wish.'

'What about the Jacuzzi?' I ask.

'If you want to use it, go ahead; I trust you are not full of morals. If you are, I am sorely mistaken.'

'I can't wait to get my hands on you.'

'What about a housecoat for me?'

'Don't worry,' she says as she exits the bathroom and opens the wardrobe doors.

'Help yourself; make sure you're suave and debonair. I want to feel used, abused, and taken for granted but in a gentlemanly way,' and she's gone.

I wonder why she chose me; it must be the uniform and the handsomeness, and I laugh as I pick a suit. A Ben Sherman strikes my eye. Having showered and shaved and now having a face as smooth as a baby's arse, I slip on a nice crisp white shirt and a pale patterned tie and admire myself in the full-length mirror.

Yep, I look sharp and polished in this attire; damned if I don't fancy a night in with myself.

I retire to a lounge. Tapestries depicting men and women in wild, depraved sex scenes with weird, erotic objects and animals bring my corrupt thoughts to the forefront of my imagination.

I stroll over to a massive tapestry depicting a **seventeenth** or **eighteenth**-century lady surrounded by a tribe of scantily clad **b**lack men in a jungle clearing. Four teenagers are holding her, naked except for a leopard skin skirt, and to be honest, it must have belonged to a week-old cub; it was so short.

I return to the drinks' cabinet and pour myself another Jameson's. By Jove, this madame sure knows her whiskey. It's an eighteen-year-old, it says on the bottle. It has a vibrant golden honey shade, giving you the feeling of holding a glass of valuable liquid.

As a boy, I could never forget its flavours, such as toffee, vanilla, and fudge. My father seemed to have bottles of it. My friend and me, best not to mention his name, often had a swig from the bottle, and we swore it was the most excellent apple juice we had ever tasted, even if it made us dizzy.

After pouring a glass, I returned to the tapestry to scrutinise this woman in bondage and study the other five scenes to see the outcome. The jungle drums' beat was getting louder, yet they were coming from another room. I wanted to investigate as I let my eye roam across the other scenes showing the lady in distress. She wriggled and fought to get away from the gargantuan cannibal chief, who intended to do more than eat her. All it needed was King Kong to come crashing around the corner with Johnny Weissmuller in hot pursuit, giving out his primal yell. That is where the drumming was coming from, from around the corner.

I followed the tapestry to its end; the doors opened automatically to reveal a scene from the tapestry. The drums' sound was now thunderous but hypnotic, and the air was filled with the scent of trees and spices. The lighting shone from the ceiling. It must have been fifty-foot-high with trees, flowers, flora, and fauna encompassing strange birds and animals that were possibly stuffed.

I have been through a time warp.

'Just getting myself a drink,' says Grace, 'I hope you like what you see.

Generals Higgins and Lorenzo like to act out their youth here using stand-in lovers. Of course, they are accompanied by their wives, who enjoy treating the ladies in a bestial manner. They are a right foursome of perverts.'

I see girls peering from bushes as day turns to night. A dozen Tiki torches are lit by another girl whom a warrior grabs. They dance provocatively to the sound of the jungle drums. I have noticed a constant chatter of monkeys in the background, accompanied by the odd lion and cheetah's roar with a female elephant's angry trumpet thrown in. It's all very jungly.

A babe waltz from behind a bush and leads me by the hand to a hammock filled with animal skins, and she offers me a drink that has the aftertaste of milk with a sweet-bitter taste. She sits on a tree branch and gently cools me with a wicker fan.

Grace calls and says that she will be back soon. I yell out to hurry as I risk taking advantage of a fantastically sexy goddess. She is gyrating in front of me.

The drums beat aggressively as six warriors in traditional Zulu clothing appear. They chase two nubile maidens who shriek out for help in their language; my lady companion translates for me.

She says to me, 'They said, '*UngangisizaNa*,' which means can you help me. You must remember it since everyone here may not speak English, and sex is free and never refused by man or woman.'

'You mean I could end up being buggered by those warriors?' I groan.

'I don't know what to say.'

'They are warriors who have won a magnificent battle, and these ladies must succumb and give themselves to them willingly or be taken by force.'

I ask her name, and she says, 'It is Zola, and I am overdressed for the occasion,' which I readily agree with.

I lose my coat and tie, and she unbuttons my shirt, and I remove it. Zola says, 'I am on safari and must save the white woman from the evil tribal chief's clutches, so I need safari clothing.'

She produces a short-sleeved buffalo safari shirt, a pair of Livingstone shorts, and a Barmah canvas drover's hat from a box.

'There you are, *Bwana*; put them on, and you'll look like Clarke Gable.'

I want to suck her nipples as she brushes her tits against my lips. She finished fitting the hat on my head, and the smell of her body increased my erection. Without hesitation, I let my tongue flick across her nipples. She draws away and tells me that the white lady is in danger and will need saving.

The girls are naked and dancing through the trees with exotic dancers impaled on their cocks. They release them to dance away to other dancers and go into a clinch, kissing passionately; the drums beat out a steady tattoo as the men thrust their penises provocatively.

I've changed, and short trousers are not the best at concealing a hard-on when warriors appear holding Grace, attired in **eighteenth**-century French costume.

'She is no *Bawanna*,' Zola tells me.

'Do you like MY dress? She opens her thighs and shows me her muff under her short grass skirt.

'You'll like mine better,' and she slides a finger between her fanny lips.

'I am *intombi emsulwa* for you, Irishman.' Chief says, 'You can have me instead of the white lady.'

'The chief will have her; the white lady is paid for and understands.'

'Would you like me?' She slides her body over mine to give off a smell of exquisite pleasantness; it's those damn pheromones.

I feel dizzy and want to hold Zola tight, but Grace calls out.

'Help me, help me,' she cries, and I can see the chief feeling her ample breasts as Zola tells me that he will strip her and take her for himself.

He is a pot-bellied chief, and 'Grace will be stripped to her underwear.'

'Do you not like her dress? It is a Marie Antoinette dress. The pinks give her an air of beauty and innocence. Do you not like those pretty patterns of pleats and trims? Do you not think her titties are ready to plop-plop out?'

'Chief Mogambo likes women with broad hips.'

'It gives him something pleasant to hold when he thrusts his cock inside.'

'A famous French actress last wore that dress. Do you not think the colour is striking?'

The warriors tie Grace by the wrists to a tree. The chief runs his hands over her breasts, squeezing them gently but firmly.

'He likes your woman, she is *chotygoty*, and he will teach her how to be his *stukkie*.'

The drums, which have been silent, break into a frantic beat. The dancers are flailing the air while the girls engage in *bukkake* and daisy chain sex. Grace draws a young buck's attention, lifting her skirts and peering at her underwear. Nope, one of them, two of the bucks, had disappeared under her skirts and were no doubt fingering her holes. The girls dance under a waterfall.

'Stop, stop,' she cries out, 'it's not a jam jar, you little kaffir,' as heads turned to give her the evil eye.

'I don't want those teen arses playing with Grace's fanny,' I tell Zola.

I grabbed her and headed to Grace, now doing a Highland dance. Zola barks an order sternly, and the little buggers pop out with her knickers. Then, when they see me, they waltz off?

Zola released her, and she ran to my side and felt my hard-on. She asked me to unzip her dress, which I did, and I kissed her passionately on the lips and neck. Zola fed me tablets as Grace stepped out of her dress, showing the loveliest legs in stockings and full breasts in a shallow-cut bra. She and Zola danced out to the floor and disappeared behind trees thirty feet away.

A teenager offered me a bottle of whiskey and started to undo my shirt. She unzipped and plunged her hand into my shorts and hoisted out my cock, which had grown to a size I had never seen before. Another lass and two boys joined her and quickly dropped to their knees. One rubbed her pert tits on my fingers, and I thought, damn it. I felt lips on my knob and another set on my balls. As if that wasn't adequate, one was trying to lick my ass, and I had never felt such pleasure. I greedily started to lick the nipples of this jailbait as I stroked her pussy, feeling inside her; she was wet and tight. I was hell-bent on ramming my cock up her quim.

Such an opportunity only knocks once on one's prison door. The whiskey and the drums had me in a hypnotic state, and as I peered down, two wondrous boys were busy sucking away at my magic rod.

I grabbed the petite boy, bent him over, and tried to plug his arse, causing him to cry. His cocksucking friend produced and rubbed what could be KY jelly on my cock and helped me insert it into the boy's arsehole, where I rode him gently but firmly. As I listened to his sobbing, I knew I had hurt him. However, I could not care less as I beckoned the girl and the other boy to assume the doggy position. I entered each, in turn, to be rewarded with the hot holes of teenagers born to be sex slaves. I bugger the boys with delicate strokes of my cock as I watch them get erections from their rape experience.

I fantasise about Apsara's arsehole. As I reach a point of no return, I push each boy away and turn the girl over on her back into the missionary position. She lays there, her eyes wide with excitement, her skin gleaming with sweat, her nipples inviting and erect. I suck them hard.

Gripping her ankles, I drag her to me, spreading her thighs, and she opens her outer lips. My hard-on is like a steel pole. I ride her with passion watching her face show signs of terror as I grip her throat tightly. As I orgasm, Grace strokes her nipples, and I flood her damaged pussy with sperm. What an experience.

'I want you next, Grace,' as I withdraw my cock.

I feel sexually liberated with the freedom to explore one's baser instincts.

I think of Rachel and those goons raping her and feel ashamed. But life is short, and that damsel's fanny will heal. She is already drinking cocktails.

I take Grace by the waist and dance to the middle of the orgy that is in full swing in the artificial jungle. I remove her bra and invite two other guests to feel her breasts, which they readily do. She squirms with pleasure as I finger her neatly trimmed fanny with little evidence of lips.

She is a delicate creature, and it would not be right to let her be abused. It doesn't matter that I have just raped a girl and two boys; after all, she is married to a disabled person and needs gentle servicing, or so I want to believe.

Zola slips to the floor, taking Grace with her, and they explore one another's vaginas with their fingers and tongues. The two men shrug and join some others smoking reefers in a booth.

I sit on a tree-shaped sofa and watch them do *soixante-neuf* on each other.

Another girl offers me a drink which she tells me is a mixture of milk, herbs, and rhino horn and will give me the physical and mental will to be a stud. She lowers herself onto my weary willie and rubs her fanny lips on my cock. He shows signs of life within minutes as she licks and polishes him with her tongue.

Boys and girls are licking Grace. The chief is standing over her, his penis enormous and swollen with blood, no doubt having left a trail of girls sore and disenchanted with the sex game. I can see that he wants to ride Grace, but Grace is beautiful, and I want her for myself, and the thought of that big, cocked Zulu sticking his weapon up her unused fanny makes my blood boil.

Zola notices this, and she slides across the floor like a snake coming to rest on my thigh.

'Are you jealous?' she asks.

'Is Grace a virgin? Do you think she has a tighter fanny than me?' She calls Grace, who is delirious with the pleasure she is receiving. She shouts and sprints over, pushing a boy away from Grace's fanny.

'Here, Bwana, feel Gracie's pussy,' and Grace lifts her hips with her hands.

I slip a finger inside her, and immediately the chief gives her oral.

A boy forces Zola's head onto his cock, and she starts to satisfy him. I am glad that Zola and I, French and Chinese, kissed earlier, for there is no way I will kiss her now.

Mogambo gets up, stands in the middle of the room, and waves his arms for silence; everybody sits. Zola beckons for Grace and me to sit. Drinks are served, and we drink merrily. Grace lays her head sideways on my chest. I stroke her nipples. One or two others are nipple-playing but are sitting, waiting for something to happen.

There is a roll of drums, and four men bring two white teenagers on a sedan chair/bed. The girls are blonde with delicate facial features; one is dressed as Little Red Riding Hood, and the other as Snow White. Chief Mogambo has put on his tribal wear, complete with anklets and armlets and is swishing imaginary flies off Grace's tits. The bitch likes it as she rolls to the floor as he flicks his swatch between her thighs and lets it wander up her stomach.

He looks at me, shakes his balls and wanders back to the sedan, where he lifts Snow White and places her on the floor. She stands there dazed and delish in her blue, red, and yellow dress, her legs in bright red heels and white stockings with red and yellow bows at mid-thigh height.

By Jove, you would love to plunge your cock between them. Her top is low cut to show perfect breasts, and her short yellow skirt trimmed with red lace complements her bow of red. She is truly a beautiful Snow White, and it wouldn't surprise me one bit if she is not gangbanged into eternity.

Mogambo beckons and she stretches out a red-gloved hand, and he escorts her to another room. We take off in hot pursuit, cocks and tits bouncing in the moist tropical air.

We are in a wood, lights shining through the trees and there to greet her are seven dwarfs. A cry is heard, and Little Red Riding Hood runs to Grace and tries to hide. The wolf's call can be heard above the drums as girls in chokers pass around reefers and spirits; we drink thirstily. I am stoned drunk, and I feel marvellous.

'Why did you bring me here?' I ask Grace, 'The chief wants you for himself.'

'I know,' she says, 'Mogambo has had his eye on me for a while. He comes here three times a year and feasts on happily married housewives who need money. Money can't buy love, but it can buy sex, and that's all the chief wants.'

'They know what they are getting into, and if they start crying rape, I believe madame would help them overcome their reservations with Rohypnol. It is better to go along with whatever happens here, or you may never go home.'

'He will take me tonight, and that is why no one else can have me. Those boys were checking my fanny, and no doubt he was pleased. I want the money, and you will get me out of here. I know who you are because your new friends come here, but tonight is a private show for the chief, and when it's over, I'm off in your company to colder climes with my sore fanny.'

'I should have a million pollars tonight; for that, he can abuse me all he wants. I will suffer the indignities, and I love it to tell you the truth. I wish I had joined **m**adame years ago instead of headhunting housewives. I see you are shocked, but you will get over it when I tell you where Wendy is.'

'We will speak later,' she says as Riding Hood gets to her feet in her little skimpy outfit of skirt and basque and adjusts her cloak. She picks up her basket and sashays to the trees and is startled by the howl of a wolf. She picks a posy of flowers showing her knickerless pussy to her audience. From among the trees, wolves appear.

She carries on picking her flowers as the lead wolf sniffs her fanny. He bloody well looks like a wolf to me as he mounts and thrusts himself into her. That brings her out of her stupor as her fanny is overflowing with that lousy wolf's cock. She screams as the wolf grips her tits in his claws and howls at the sky. Blood is trickling off her nipples. In a frenzy, the beast remounts and drives his rod into her. She wriggles like a worm on a hook but cannot get free. Watching him ride the Riding Hood, he has a stout bone. A gland at the base of his penis swells up and holds his penis firmly in the female. This time it is the fanny of this petite blonde that is full of wolf meat, and he won't let go of her until he has shot his jiz. Other wolves perform homosexual acts upon one another when more girls are ushered in by Mogambo.

He has a massive erection and makes a beeline for Grace. He beckons Grace to come to him, and he whispers in her ear, his fingers feeling her fanny. She smiles and kisses him, and she is gone. He waves his bollocks at me and tells me she is his, but he will send me one of his daughters.

'Treat her bad, and she will please you good. You have an upright horn there, white man; you like the wolf with the girl. Come with me, and we will have a beer while we wait for our women. I have waited seasons for this white woman, and tonight I will fill her with pain, suffering, and pleasure. She told me she had waited years for extramarital sex. Money has opened her legs in the end, and I intend to make her earn her pollars. She has stunning legs.'

Dwarfs are shafting Snow White. She is topless and knickerless. Others are in group sex, and the whole place smells of sexual activity.

We drink beer, and he beckons boys and girls over and indicates what he would like by opening his thighs. I do the same, and we stretch out on the sofa of skins and sip beer as the boys blow us.

A beautiful woman rides in on a horse, a delicate pink lace skirt high up on her thighs. 'My daughter Makosi,' he says as she dismounts and walks backwards to me, and lowers herself onto my cock. She lowers herself four or five times as she inches my cock into her pussy. She is covered in oils that smell of sandalwood and other precious Indian spice woods. She leans her head back, looks me in the eye, and smiles the smile of a man-eater. As Mogambo looks on with approval, I feel her nipples, tweaking them with my fingers. I hear Grace's voice from behind me, speaking to the boys.

Drums and flutes play the music of decadence as they lead Grace out in front of Mogambo.

She is dressed in provocative attire, only found on the latest Monasta music model. A little orange petite dress that clings to her stocking-clad thighs and a pair of nipple tassels is all she is attired in, all covered by thin veils. The chief is rubbing his knob. I feel jealous as he strips to his anklets and roughly plucks off Grace's tassels, making her wince.

Makosi is half-turned and kissing me, and I respond as she is hot and passionate. I look at Grace as she does a kind of perverted version of the Dance of the Seven Veils, pervertedly stroking her thighs and tits and all the other crap one sees the Monastas doing on stage.

The chief lifts and lays her on a table spreading her thighs high and wide. Mogambo penetrates her, and she yelps as his cock is forced in. He is running his hands up and down. Finally, he grips her by the throat and shags her with a vicious evil smirk on his face. Makosi speaks in Zulu, and he laughs.

I ask what she said, and she laughs and asks if I am excited at Grace getting shagged by Mogambo.

'Your cock is rock hard,' as she varies the squatting cowgirl position, the tightness of her fanny stretching my foreskin.

'I want to ride you on the floor,' I say.

She drops to the floor, and I enter her hungrily, wanting to avenge myself on his daughter. The chief has changed position, has Grace bent over the table, and is riding her doggy style. She appears to be in discomfort as she tries to lubricate. I notice her feet are off the floor.

'Makosi,' I say, 'assume the position,' and I withdraw and point to Grace. Makosi is quickly at the other end of the table, legs splayed, and she is guiding my cock up her arse within moments. She was ready for it. I drive him in hard, and she pushes back at me. I grab at a lass who has a plate of reefers in her hand. She cries out she is a waitress as I whip off her knickers, knocking her to the ground.

I remember Wendy and realise that I have had a bellyful of this sexfest, and I remove my cock and look at Grace. I strike two boys in the mouth.

Mogambo looks at me with hate-filled eyes, and I punch him in the throat and call him a jungle bunny.

'We are leaving,' I say, and Makosi whispers to take her with us; he is a horrible man. She grabs Grace's hand, and we run back to the main bedroom, where I'm dressed in a jiffy in my major's uniform.

Makosi and Grace are in the showers scrubbing their goddamn pussies. Only a pair of clapped-out bitches would do this at this crucial moment. We are likely to feel the wrath of Mogambo and could end up with sore arses.

I grab a pile of clothes from a wardrobe and drag them out of the showers.

'Get dressed, and let's get the hell out of here.'

Chapter Eleven

Baba Okeke

Sunday, 18th June.

It's six in the morning, and I should be back with the boys, ready to slaughter furry little creatures. Instead, two of the waitresses appear. Both are adolescents, wearing tiny skirts and no tops. They are smiling as the chief rushes in behind them. He grabs Grace by the waist, a gun in his hand.

'Watch this,' he screams, pushing her over the bed and kicking her legs open.

'Shove your arse in the air bitch,' and he pushes his raging hard-on into her.

I see the surprise on her face as she glimpses one of the girls sink her teeth into Mogambo's throat, the other her teeth into his gun arm. The gun drops to the floor, and the other one grabs it. He screams the scream of the demented and jumps back, striking the teen with a death blow with his right hand. The other teen has run from the room, leaving him holding his throat, blood pouring down his chest and between his legs, dripping to the floor.

'Help me,' he croaks as he offers me his outstretched hand, but there is no way that help will be offered, not after the orgy that has taken place. There has been rape, sodomy, and bestiality, to name a few.

He can die; he is no use to us as I turn over the unconscious girl, but she is dead, with no pulse. Her eyes are jet black with one red iris as she stares at the ceiling. Her skin has a marbled effect, white and red.

'Strange complexion,' I say to Makosi as I slip the gun into my belt. The women are dressed in jeans, T-shirts and trainers.

'Let's go,' says Grace as she comes out of the bedroom with a briefcase. Makosi disappears and re-enters, carrying another briefcase.

'He won't want this,' she says as we head for the door.

The jeep is waiting outside, and the sky promises a sweltering day.

'Leave the jeep,' says Grace as she heads across the road to a four-by-four.

'Let's hit the road and get the hell out of this place.'

A boy and a girl, the girl I recognised as the one I sodomised or was it the boy? Who knows, maybe both are running for the Land Rover?

'Frig off!' screams Grace, 'there is no room for you two wretched shags' as she slams the door in the boy's face, knocking him out. The girl stops, pissing herself with fear as Mogambo staggers out the door of the whorehouse.

'He will eat my heart,' she cries, desperation showing as she throws herself on the sandy ground, and she kisses my hands and pleads.

I draw the gun, a Smith and Wesson, and I empty the whole chamber into his blubbery gut. He's surprised the fat lump, as he sags to the ground and eats sand.

'That's got rid of your bogeyman,' and I lift her into the jeep. The unconscious boy, I pop onto the spare seat.

'We're ready to go.'

'We are going to Benson,' says Grace, 'and from there, everyone can go in their own direction, and you, Mr Dempsey, will come with me. Mr Dempsey's code words are Semtex and Wendy, so drive on, my good man and let us have breakfast.'

Another bastard who knows what's going on behind my back.

When we hit Benson,' she continues, 'you find your crew. You, Makosi and your two homies can slither back to Zululand or whatever slave colony you're from. I tell you, Makosi, you are a gorgeous woman, and if circumstances were different, I would have you as my friend and lover. As things are, we're pollar rich.'

She swings around and kisses Makosi full-on while her hand slips inside her top.

'I want you,' says Makosi lifting her T-shirt and exposing her tits, 'we can stay together and be happy. It's such an exciting business; we can re-invent ourselves, maybe in Europe.'

The girl is asleep semi-naked, and the boy is unconscious. I asked Makosi what we should do with them as we are almost in Benson, and if they decide to chatter, we will end up in the Browning unit.

'I'm not doing any pen time,' she says, pointing to a derelict smallholding. I turn off the road and reverse behind it.

'Get the boy out,' she says, and into the building we go, the door hanging by one hinge, and we lay him on the floor. He moves his head, and his eyes flicker and slowly open. He opens his mouth and lets out a blood-curdling yell. I reckon it could be heard miles away, and I run outside with Grace to see if anyone is within earshot, but all is clear.

The girl is awake and staring out the window with big, googly eyes. Terror etched on her face. We leg it across to the 4x4 as she opens the door and runs across the scrubland to Benson screaming. As luck would have it, she trips, and I grab her like a spider on a fly getting caught in its web.

She is a slippery little customer who wriggles free only to find Grace's hand around her throat. Recognition dawns on her face, and she cries, '*Bwana, Bwana*' as she stretches her arms towards me. Grace releases her grip. I see in Grace's other hand a small knife. The girl runs into my arms, and Grace breathes a sigh of relief, crisis averted, murder not committed. I cradle her in my arms and kiss her on the cheek. She loops her arms around my neck, nestling her body on my chest and stomach.

'Isn't love wonderful?' says Grace as we walk back to the house to meet Makosi. I immediately notice her nipples sticking out from her T-shirt, and her face is flushed.

'My God,' I say, 'you haven't been shagging him? He was unconscious a few minutes back, you sex fiend.'

'No, no,' she says, looking at me with an empty smile.

'He died in my arms, sobbing for his mother, and I said I was her. The boy told me he loved me, and then he gave up the ghost, so to speak.'

I've seen that look before; she's murdered him. But, on the other hand, maybe it's for the best. I'm in the company of two attractive women, and at any moment, they could slaughter the girl and me. I'm sure they will kill her the first opportunity they get; she is useless to them, just extra baggage with a mouth that could blab.

They saw her run towards Benson, but what would happen in Benson when soldiers and civilians surrounded her? It always surprises me how humanity has an instinct for danger, especially the type that spells death.

This girl knew instinctively that her life was on the line, and only I could save her, yet she knew I was contemplating murdering her.

She began to cry, the international sign of distress and the most recognised symptom of misery. Of course, it could signify happiness, but only a fool watching the present situation would think that. She wished to live and to show me her fear; she wet herself, her hot piddle wetting my trousers and my leg. I held her tighter, kissed her on the mouth, and told her I loved her. I would protect her with my life, and she burst into tears. This time, she flooded my chest, and I would swear on a stack of Bibles that I was drenched to the skin.

'Nobody hurts this girl, or I will kill them slowly and grotesquely,' I say, determination in my voice.

'We will dress her, and she will be OK. Is that OK with you, Makosi? If there is any problem, say so, and I will kill one or both of you.'

'It's cool,' they say as they jump back in the four-by-four. I place the girl beside Makosi in the back.

'Look after her. I will reward you with an exit permit from this godforsaken place.'

I need to tool up and, at the same time, make sure these two nymphos remain untooled. I decided to hide their stash, which should keep them under control. I shall tax their cash, and Mary can have a bumper pay packet. It will be on its way before nightfall.

We arrive in Benson and head for the Holiday Inn parking in the underground park; it's practically empty, and I send Grace ahead to check out the lie of the land. She takes her briefcase, and after twenty minutes, she returns with a bag in her hand.

'Where were you?' I ask, and she tells me, 'Get moving. The hotel is empty of guests, save for a few military personnel. Everybody was moved further north last night, and word has it that something big is afoot.'

She gives me the bag with a smile, and I lean over and kiss her, and she smiles and says, 'Later, I love you.'

I could taste the venom on her lips as I whispered words of love in her ear and hoped she swallowed them; it would be a relief to have only one poisonous snake to watch.

It's clothes for the girl in the bag, at least they are conservative, baggy trousers and a T-shirt, cap and trainers and I thank Grace.

'What is your name?' I ask, and she looks at me and says nothing. I ask again.

After a minute, she laughs and says, 'Baba, I forgot my name. It's Baba. Nobody has asked me my name in years. It's Baba, Baba Okeke. Baba Okeke, that's me, Baba Okeke,' and she is laughing and happy.

I remember where I had seen her before. She was the waitress with the reefers. I had fingered her pussy, and I said, 'Sorry.' She smiled as she dressed and placed her cap on her head.

She looked impish and could be mistaken for a boy.

The two women had gone ahead as Baba reminded me that my trousers were wet and dirty. We walked to the foyer, where I went to the receptionist's desk and picked up a key to a suite.

'I need a wash and breakfast.'

I tossed the two women an access key to the next suite. 'See youse here in an hour; if not, I will assume you have flown the nest, and I will make my own way home.'

I head for the lift, followed by Baba, who has refused to go with the women.

'Clothes,' I say to Grace, 'I need a change of rags,' and I head over to a boutique where I grab an armful, some bits and bobs and head up in the lift. The two bitches had their briefcases, but Baba was safe as long as she was with me. I phone Skeleton but can't get through.

Having found our suite to our satisfaction, we shower and towel one another dry. Baba asks, 'Would you like a blowjob?' as she has not had the experience of sex, but she has seen it done.

'No, Jesus, no, we must get away from this place, and you are not ready for depravity, and I am not ready today.'

'How old are you?' and she says seventeen.

'How come you are here at an orgy and you a virgin if I understand what you said?'

'My family sold my sister and me two years ago to a factory in Cape Town, and we had to work there for two years making jeans and T-shirts. My mother and father had AIDs and would die, they told us, and the village would kill us if we stayed. So, when a white man from South Africa came to our village in Niger, hiring girls to work in a garment factory for two years, wages paid in advance, and my parents sold us to him. Since nobody ever returned to the village, we did not want to go, but he showed us photographs of girls working and smiling in a factory. My school friend Kiki was in many photos, and she had sent money to her parents and even came home once.'

'About eighteen months ago, a woman came to the factory and asked for jeans to be made, and they would be sent to China; yeah, that's right, she was a China woman. We worked there for sixteen hours daily for six months and were always hungry. Girls would disappear, and they would tell us they had gone to another factory.'

'The China woman asked if we would like to work in her factories in the United States of America in New York City. We said yes, and she said she would pay the boss mucho dinero, and we could come to America. The boss told us that we would be going on a boat in the next few months, and we must work hard so that the order placed by the China woman would be fulfilled. She would pay us extra money for working hard when we reached her factory.'

'Six weeks later, we had to go to Durban, where we were to board a ship. There were dozens of boys and girls with babies. I knew something was wrong when I woke on the ship because I never remembered boarding. People were crying, and my sister was asleep. We were in a room on a slave ship with chains and a horrible smell. I was frightened, and I wanted my sister to wake up, but she wouldn't, and other people were asleep. I suspect we had been drugged.'

'The sea was rough, and people were seasick, and no one could get out of the trapdoor. When I woke later, the sea was calm, and we could see daylight through the cracks in the trapdoor. My sister was awake. Later, the trapdoors were thrown open, and the sun shone in, warming my face. A woman ordered us to line up a single file, come up the ladder, give her our names, and say nothing else. We trooped up the stairs and came out into the sun; it was roasting hot.'

'The girl behind me asked if she could have a hat to cover her head, and all she got for an answer was a beating from a horsewhip.'

'I can assure you no one else opened their mouths as they came up from the hold; the girl lay on the deck semi-naked, covered in cuts and bruises. Two crewmen grabbed her by the arms and legs and tossed her overboard, telling her the sharks would get her. The captain, a scar-faced Chinaman asked her if she would keep her mouth shut now. She nodded her head vigorously in the international language of dummies. I swear to God she never spoke another word while on that voyage.'

'One night, two crew members went into the hold and took two girls up on deck after tying their hands. The captain fetched the same girl every night up on deck, but this night, he returned early and found the trapdoor open and two sailors coming up through the hatch. He yelled for help, and the sailors were taken away by other crew members. Everybody was on deck when the captain came with the two imprisoned Jack Tars the following day.

He had them crucified in front of the girls and the crew, and while they were screaming in pain and terror, he cut off their balls and stuffed them down their throats with his own hands. He told the crew this could be you if you do not leave the girls alone; receiving a ten thousand pollar bonus should be enough. Then, he had four crew members throw the horny duo overboard.'

'He had stopped the ship earlier and had thrown blood and meat into the sea. He laughed as the sharks fought over the men. He went below to his quarters, and nobody touched us after that. We knew that we were important cargo and would not be killed.'

'The ship sailed for a fortnight, stopping at two ports, and eventually docked in Mauritania, and the boys were transferred to another ship. Doctors came on board and spent most of the day examining our bodies. He took blood tests and checked our pussies to ensure we were virgins. He dressed us in short skirts and blouses and later in maxi skirts and traditional African robes. The nurses photographed us naked and dressed, and a dentist examined our teeth. I knew that we were to be sold to men for their pleasure, or we were to be put in brothels in North Africa.'

'We spent months working in factories in the Spanish Sahara. Couples came to the factory and invited us to have tea with them. We wore nice outfits when we were having tea. We were told the night before that we were selected for a party and would have fun the following day. At times, there would be ten of us. There were other parties, but I was not invited.'

'Certain girls would leave, and we would be told they had a job working for these people. They would write to us, laud their benefactors, and visit, but they would not come or write anymore as time passed. I thought that something was wrong. We would say or do nothing because the factory's boss would tell us we would have to work elsewhere if we were not docile and hardworking.'

'One day, two girls had a fight, and to punish them, the boss sent them to a factory far away, and they did not return for two weeks. They were dirty and starving, and they smelt of piss. Their stay at the factory was a nightmare, they said. They only had rice and a bit of chicken to eat each day, and they had to work from six in the morning 'til nine at night. They never washed but slept chained to their machine. There were dozens of women working there, and the older women told them terrible stories.'

'The most terrible story was not of prostitution, slave labour, rape or beatings but of the baby hospital.'

'It was a grand house set in acres of land. When the girls reached puberty, they would be taken to this hospital, where they were expected to be surrogate mothers and meet prospective parents. They would be invited as dinner guests, and after a little chat, they would be asked to retire and wear the wardrobe provided. The clothes would be provocative, and the man's wife would be dressed to compliment the Mademoiselle's attire.'

'Most knew that sex was required, and being virgins, they would be upset. But one way or the other, the girls had sex willingly or faced the ordeal of being forced. This would continue for days and nights, excluding a period of waiting until she showed signs of pregnancy. The prospective parents would leave, wishing her all the best. As time passed and the pregnancy advanced, the girl would be transferred to the maternity ward where she would spend her time until the baby was born.'

'She would discover the evil she had been subjected to when her baby would be taken away and given to the new parents in full view of the mother. She would repeatedly be subjected to the same horrors if they were happy with the baby and wanted another. Later after she had produced a family for a rich barren bitch, she would be artificially inseminated to produce offspring for another woman or impotent man.'

'Later, she would be sent to brothels or spend tedious years in a sweatshop. Eventually, she would be deemed useless and murdered and dumped in a mass grave, come culling time for these factories of inhumane suffering. We must seek freedom, but not a word to anybody outside this prison, for we will surely be separated and murdered. May God help us in our quest for freedom and justice, said the old lady as she lay on her bunk and prayed for death?'

'We continued to work at the factory until one day about a month ago. My sister, six others, and I were told we were going to America. We were to be accompanied by a chief from Qua Zululand and a South African slave trader who turned out to be the same bastard that gave my parents money for us. We wanted to kill him, and the night before sailing, Mango, our overseer, told us that we suffered from a genetic fault, which was why nobody wanted to breed through us. She called it an unknown word, and it had to do with our kidneys or liver, but it wouldn't kill us.'

'We were to voyage to America to participate in an orgy and sleep with the chief and his friends. We would be set free with pollars in our pockets to take back to our village in Niger.'

'What if we get pregnant?' I asked.

'She told me to stick the baby up my arse and that Mr Botha will take us back to Africa.'

'Mr Botha was the slaver who gave my mother money. I served reefers at several orgies, and it was *streng verbote* to touch my sister or me.

'Anyone who doesn't want to go to America, say so, and you can continue to work in the factory. One girl said she wanted to stay, and Mango told her to return to her quarters. The rest were to bathe and prepare for our trip to a beauty salon where we would be prepped for our flights to the USA. We were surprised and delighted at the thought of getting on a plane. A dressmaker came and measured us for clothes. We ended up in the USA with Mogambo and his entourage of perverts and cannibals.'

'A week later, we were driven to Tucson, where we were transferred to Madame Fifi's house of unnatural delights. We were treated to chic attire, food, and recreation. She had us dressed and ready to be abused by fat Mogambo when she heard that he had taken to his bed with a bout of malaria. At the same time, a plague swept through Arizona, and people were leaving, including madame and her collection of boys and girls.'

'"What shall we do in Arizona?" I asked Madame Fifi. She informed me it's pronounced Arizona; there is no such place as Aritzona unless you are thinking of your shitty homeland. Mogambo will shaft you and your miserable friend's arse, and if you are kinky-winky, he will take you back to your dump in Arizona.'

'Be careful that he doesn't eat your heart, for he is a cannibal, and with that, she left me a bunch of keys and said to entertain him, for he is our way home.'

'Madame Grace came to the bordello two nights later. Mogambo fought with her in the office, but he was weak from malaria, and she hit him with a book stop and tied him up.'

'Later, they came out of the office as friends, and I saw him kiss and squeeze her tits. He spoke to her, and she lifted her skirt, he laughed, and she was gone. Three nights later, Mogambo told us he would have a party, and we were invited. We must pleasure Madame Grace's man-friend.'

'The rest, you know, when madame took you to the bathroom.'

'Where is your sister?'

'She's dead. Mogambo killed her the other night and cut out and ate her heart.'

'Are you sure? Seems a bit strong in this day and age?'

'He believed that by eating a maiden's heart after deflowering her, he would receive her unused sexual stamina and youth.'

'He was to do the same to me.'

'There are numerous strange things between heaven and earth,' I tell her.

'My friend said that boys and girls had their hearts ripped from their living bodies as their tormentors raped them. Because they struggled when the knife slashed into their breasts, a fountain of blood would gush over the rapist covering him from head to toe. He would then beseech the heavens to give him his victim's strength and sexual prowess.'

'Mogambo attacked both sexes because he wanted to be male and female and be as one.'

'He certainly is not a hermaphrodite.'

Baba looks at me, puzzled.

'He is like any other man to me,' I say.

'You like boys,' she says, 'you are a cruel man.'

'There is a little bit of savagery in all of us. God and the law keep it at bay,' I say, laughing.

'I do not especially like boys, but that was why they were there, and it would have been foolish of me not to take advantage of the situation. I understand what Mogambo did when he ate your sister's heart. In Ireland, long ago, there was a custom among my people that warriors would sacrifice and eat raw flesh and drink their victims' blood. They deny such things happened in prehistory.'

'Did you say you are Irish?' she queries.

'Yes, I did, so what?'

'Do you know Irish people?

'Maybe a priest in your village, a missionary; we are particularly skilled at sending missionaries to Africa. They want to fill your people with religion and your children's arses with rich monastic spunk.'

'Grace said that she was to meet an Irishman, and he would take her to Denver, where it would be arranged to send him to Europe as a soldier. There were several men and women here many nights with wads of money, and they had sex with one another and the women from here.'

'Madame Fifi had sex with two men at one time. I remember their names; one was named Gorgon, and the other Austin.'

'Gordon and Austin, those two bastards, what about the women?'

She remembers enough to convince me they are who I thought they were. I will take her to Denver; it's on my way home.

'Don't mention this to anyone, and stay close to me.'

She comes to me, and I kiss her on the forehead. She offers me her mouth, and I kiss her gently.

Damn.

'We must finish dressing,' which we do.

We head to the foyer where the two women are waiting, each carrying identical briefcases.

'Doubled your money. I'm happy for both of you, but I have my treasure here.'

I hold her by the hand.

'What is your name?'

'Baba, I told you twice, it's Baba,' and I wink at her.

'I know, but they know now, and it makes you human if you have a name,' I whisper. 'That's why prison camps have numbers, and the inmates have numbers; you are not classed as a human being but as objects.'

'Lot No 27, one pretty pubescent with mouth-watering titties and smooth thighs, will give new owner years of pleasure. Who will start the bidding at one?'

'Do you understand what I mean?'

We walk together towards the dining room.

'Yes,' she said, 'I will introduce myself to Grace and Makosi. I will make them like me. I will cook breakfast,' and she runs ahead.

The restaurant was empty, but she found the kitchen in a few minutes, and the rattle of pans and the clink of glasses could be heard clearly. She waltzes out singing with a tray of glasses and a decanter of freshly squeezed orange juice. She places drinks in front of Grace and Makosi and says to Grace, 'It's fresh from the fridge. I hope you like it, Grace, and you too, Makosi.'

'I will be preparing breakfast in the kitchen. If you require anything, please shout Baba. Thank you for helping me, and I hope to do the same for you someday, especially you, Patrick. I have to rush to get breakfast. I hope you like your eggs sunny side up.'

Grace asks what I intend to do with Baba.

'We can't have her as baggage; she is useless to me.'

'What do you propose, Makosi? Do you want to kill her?'

'I wish to be rid of her; she is excess baggage, like Grace says.'

Grace, the money-grabbing harlot, needs me to get her arse out of here.

'Why do I need you, you whore? Why don't I kill you and take your stash, your murdering bitch?'

With that, a rush of blood rushes to my head, and blind rage takes over. I have Makosi on the floor, my hands around her skinny neck. Her eyes begin to bulge.

'Kill her,' screeches Grace, 'kill her and keep her money.'

'Do her, don't stop, throttle the life out of her.'

I turn to Grace and see Baba hiding behind the kitchen door. I let go of the unconscious Makosi, grabbed Grace by her hair, and turned her head to face the kitchen.

'You want to kill Baba, do you?'

'You have brought me nothing but strife since I clapped my eyes on you; you promised me a naughty ride. I will have it now.'

I throw her onto a table, crockery and cutlery crashing to the floor. A murderous rage has filled my heart just as it did with Delano. Makosi and Grace are the recipients this time.

'Let's see what that old bastard liked. Was it your arse or that fanny of yours?'

I tear off her T-shirt. I undo my trousers, swing her head around, and shove my cock in her mouth.

'Suck bitch and do it well, or I will bust your gut.'

Her head hangs down from the table, and I clamp her head between my thighs. Unzipping her jeans, I tug them and her knickers off, her legs zigzagging like she was riding a bicycle.

'Now, for the main course,' and I swing her around the table.

I ride that fanny of hers hard and fast, giving her tits a right sadistic tweaking.

'Very nice, beautiful thighs, blimey, you are gorgeous. I wouldn't mind staying up there for an hour, but times ticking on, time for dessert.'

I turn her over, kicking her legs open.

'Let's see if this fine cock of mine fits that hole after Mogambo's been up there,' and I shove it in.

I curse myself for being an animal and stop immediately. I am no better than Winston Dillon and Swen Gudjohnson in the treatment I am meting out to Grace.

How could I be so barbarous and merciless after what they did to Rachel?

'I wanted you to make love to me, not rape me like you are doing.'

'I'm not a slag. I'm a housewife who has not had sex for a long time. Tonight I have been raped twice by men who knew my private parts were delicate. See the damage you have done me and atone for your actions by getting me to Denver and take your virgin with you!'

'You don't half spout a mouthful of bullshit wiping my cock on her knickers, an innocent housewife, my arse.'

She walks over to Makosi and cuts her throat.

'I loved that girl, and you know that. Any crap out of you, and I will also cut your throat. Let's go and get that chopper. I have a surprise in store for you.'

'But we have to go to the border,' I yell. 'They will never let us fly to Denver. Our best chance is to cross into

Mexico and head south. We could get a ship to the Caribbean islands.'

'I said I had a surprise for you,' she yells back at me.

'Orders will be waiting for you when we get to your Controlmobile. Remember I am your wife,' and she gives me a wedding ring.

'Where you go, I go?'

'What about Baba?'

'I will ask you one question; a yes or no answer will suffice. Do you want to leave Arizona, or do you want to die here? The choice is yours.'

'Fine, we will leave her here, but I will not murder her. I try to avoid murdering the innocent, but killing you would benefit society.'

'How could you do that to Makosi?'

'I fancied riding her again; that is a woman that knew how to do her Kigal exercises.

'Where's breakfast?' Grace yells as she strips Makosi and tries on her knickers.

'How come you haven't murdered your disabled husband?'

It dawns on me. 'You have not got a husband, you poisonous viper.'

'I have; he is crippled, and I love him.'

'Did you cripple him?'

'Yes, yes, I did, like in that movie Misery. That put an end to his nocturnal meanderings.'

Baba brings out the breakfast, too frightened to drop it, and having eaten, Grace tosses me a briefcase and yells at Baba, 'Let's go,' and we sprint out to the Land Rover.

We brake with a screech in front of our yellow chopper, and I spy most of the gang. I asked Skeleton when we would be on the move. He shrugs his shoulders, assuring me nothing is happening, according to an old potbellied general. The White Death is dead, there has been no activity anywhere, and scientists and chemists are swarming over the state, taking samples. Nevertheless, we are to remain on high alert and continue to wipe out all creatures, great and small.

'It better be dead, or those chemists will spread it over the country,' I tell Fathead.

Nobody can leave except through the shower curtain, the given name for the quarantine areas. Sporadic gunfire can be heard, but little seems to be alive. The new incinerators purchased from the UK after their foot and mouth epidemic in 2014 have made the open burning pits a thing of the past. Each oven can burn one hundred tons of meat an hour. With its reusable energy source, i.e., the animals, and it being a sealed unit, nothing is released into the atmosphere. Even the smoke and smell are burned. Energy is the key to the future, and the future is the incinerator.

Mariah and Becky turn up with the flamethrower guys and look at Baba.

'Who is she, cradle snatcher?' Becky asks.

She walks up to Grace and asks what she is doing here.

'Do we look like civilians?' she barks, 'well, do we?'

'I suggest you take your civilian arse back to Benson pronto.'

I step between them and see the glint of metal above Grace's sleeve, as does Mariah. Mariah is up behind her, two Glocks in Grace's ears.

'Drop it!' and the knife slides to the ground.

Becky retrieves it and looks at the dried blood.

'I see you have been busy doing a spot of population control, have we?'

I lower Mariah's hands away from Grace's head.

'It's all right, she is one of us, well kind off, and she's well in with Gordon and the rest of the bastards. She is going to get us out of here; let's play at being soldiers.'

'Could you find uniforms for our guests so we can have lunch? We can find out what's happening and make our plans accordingly.'

'Where's Colonel Potz? He must know what's going on.'

'I don't; I no longer know who is getting me out of here.'

'I don't know,' says Mariah. 'This morning, Captain D'Souza told me that while you were fornicating with the local yumyum, the Mexicans were causing trouble down New Mexico way. Something to do with a historical figure named Pancho Villa.'

'He was a bandit who raided Columbus and killed Americans back in 1916. The word on the street is that they will try and re-enact the march to Columbus, and we are to go there and order them to get back across the Rio Grande.'

'Troops will be integrated into depleted units, and roll call will be 15.00 hours. In the meantime, we are to spit and polish ourselves, and weapons are to be checked and ready for inspection.'

We troop to the field kitchen and eat burgers with lashings of onions and barbecue sauce.

'That should help us blow out our holes of stale wind,' I say, winking at Grace.

She gives me a dirty look and two fingers. I whinny like a horse.

General Hubert comes across with my son James, the giver of black eyes, and informs us that we will be under his command. He has been tasked to stop a march on Columbus by Mexican peasants seeking TV exposure.

We will meet the National Guard and help escort the wetbacks across the Rio Grande. We are to explain the danger they are putting themselves in with the New Mexicans, who are in no mood for any antics.

Hubert has an eye for Grace, and she's made it plain that she fancies him, and as with most men who spot a juicy fanny, he is prepared to eat a yard of her shit to have a peek at her arse.

Grace informs him that uniforms are needed and that it would be most kind of him to put his trailer at the girl's disposal, to which he readily agrees. She has given him a happy recipe because he has two guards on the trailer, undoubtedly keeping an eye on her bulging briefcases.

I must have a deco inside mine; best be careful opening the damn case. I have not opened Wendy's letter either. I am so busy with the fair sex.

As the day passes, I get to speak to James and ask about Wendy.

'He tells me she is in Ireland, safe and well, and on the island of Stonnage. He spoke to her briefly, and she informed him that she was in no danger. However, evictions have occurred, and the island is occupied by Ranger units. A final appeal is lodged in a Dublin court this week, which should settle the whole affair once and for all.'

'How do you know this?' I ask.

'Very easy; I have spoken to your father, who told me an interesting story. Don't forget that you have been on the US radar for years, and we know some dreadful things you have done. He said fifty heavily armed mercenaries landed on the Antrim coast and went to ground. It's reckoned that they are under the protection of the Red Leg of Ulster. On its return journey, the boat sent a distress signal ten miles from the Giant's Causeway that it was sinking. Flares were set off, and shortly afterwards, the boat blew up.'

'Unfortunately for them, a local fishing boat took a survivor ashore before the coastguard sailed into view. He was singing like a canary. He was blabbing about mercs here to kill the MIRA high command and end terrorism on the English mainland.'

'He said he saw military uniforms loaded onto the boat, and when the mission was over, they were to make their way to Stonnage and wait for evacuation. He babbled on for ages and died during the night.'

'He had fallen into the hands of a MIRA active service unit, and my best guess is that they made him sing and bumped him off. One way or another, there will be a gun battle between the MIRA and the mercenaries. I don't want my mother killed in the ensuing melee. Your new pals are there, and since you will be heading that way, I intend to tag along and get my mother out of harm's way.'

'Son, you'd better pick a side to fight with because I can assure you there will be no sitting on the fence. I'm going to phone my father to get additional details. I would appreciate it if you could get hold of a Trans Global Scrambler so we don't get our lovely heads blown off,' I said.

'Don't tell Mariah and Becky anything but bullshit and lies. Treat them like mushrooms and keep them in the dark because they are well in with those bastards.'

'It's sufficient to say they wanted me to go to Ireland to murder the high command, all for a rock in the Atlantic Ocean.'

'That rock must be special James, so important that dozens of people must die and millions to be paid out to occupy it. Check with Washington and see if there are any files on it; maybe it's an element they have discovered. After all, there are a lot of older women looking twenty and wanting to live there. Find out what you can about EARTHCO. They have a hand in it and remember what I said about Mariah.'

'Grace is getting us out of Arizona to Denver - as soon as we are out of here, I am heading home.'

'Look, absent dad, I am a soldier in the American Army, and I cannot desert, but I will find a way to join you.'

'James, I was listening to Mariah's CD about EARTHCO. I found it to be a wonderful story, especially about Brandy...damned if I can remember her surname. I wonder if she still has it. Still, she is one of them but not so evil, but don't take any chances, and don't forget her sister Becky. Call her Rebecca; otherwise, she gets nasty and aggressive. I have much to tell you, but now is not the time.'

General Hubert strides up with Corporal Grace and Private Baba in tow. I bet he fancies shagging both of them. I smile at Baba, and she comes to me and asks if I like her uniform.

'You look a real soldier in that uni,' I say.

'Doesn't she look fab, James?'

James turns on his heel and walks over to Hubert, who is circling Grace like a lion, ready to pounce on its prey.

'Has he tried it on with you, Baba?' I ask, but she laughs and says, 'No, I am yours; take me tonight, given that Grace likes Hubert.'

It's six o'clock, and the day's moving fast; I march up to Hubert, salute and ask if any orders are in for tomorrow.

'I will brief you in the morning; there will be big trouble in Texas tonight. The Mexican Army is camped out on the border, having siestas between fiestas and playing the Deguello, which roughly means no quarter given. They are taking the piss out of the Texans about the Alamo.'

'The jails are full of illegals that have been detained. Thousands are marching on Columbus dressed as Pancho Villas. This fiasco is turning into a nightmare for the National Guard.'

'The Mexicans are being heckled by hillbillies taunting them with, pour favor gringo, do not shag my Rosalita por favor, ai yai yai. Come out to play Rosalita.'

'Fights have broken out, and as yet, no guns have been used, but as the tequila and the bourbon kick in, the Wild West will be on display again.'

'That's over a thousand miles as the crow flies to the Alamo,' I tell Hubert.

'But we are going to Columbus,' says Hubert, 'with other detachments of soldiers from around Tucson. This mission is top secret, and Grace has arranged for us to be transferred to Denver, where further orders await us.'

'It goes without saying that the situation could deteriorate rapidly in Columbus if those tequila heads start getting uppity. I can assure you that orders have come from the President herself that no interference will be tolerated from a foreign power, namely Mexico. Their citizens will be removed with military force if necessary.'

'Keep that under your hat. I'm off for dinner with Grace, and if you would like to join us with your little Baba, we all can have an enjoyable night.'

'I am not sharing Baba with you, general, and it will do you no good pulling rank on me because I'll be pulling a gun.'

'Stay calm, Patrick; it's Grace I'm interested in.'

'Have you not noticed those legs?'

'Those tits are firm like her ass. I will enjoy her, for I've fallen in love.'

'General, make sure you know where you are going to stick that weapon of yours.'

He tells me to feck off as he strides over to his trailer.

As dusk draws in, a mobile field kitchen appears and parks beside the general's trailer. Trestles are assembled, and a half dozen Mexican women prepare the tables with crockery. A refrigerated lorry drops off crates and a block of ice and continues across the sand to the next trailer.

'Who's paying for this grub?' I ask, 'it certainly isn't Uncle Sam.'

'Not by a long chalk,' says Grace, 'but our good friend Makosi. After all, it wouldn't be fair if I kept all her wad. A little distribution in the name of proper digestion can be the most happy belly filler.'

A plethora of prostitutes join the half-dozen waitresses, but they are tasty hookers. Three are thin, three are fat, and poor Fathead is excited about having a choice.

Skeleton, with Bill and Ben, has already chosen their birds, but the flamethrower boys want to give them one to share.

'Screw youse thinking you can have three women; one will do you wankers; just fill her holes and be satisfied.'

A fight between Ben and the biggest flamethrower guy doesn't last long, and Ben puts him to sleep.

'I think one will divide nicely into five,' says Ben.

Frankie and Hugo are with Becky and Mariah, and I watch them giving Baba the eye. Grace is all over Hubert when the chuck-wagon dinner bell is rung, and like hungry urchins, we take our places at the table.

The beer and wines flow freely. Rare cuts of beef, fish, and pork appear whilst a sextet of musicians plays various country & western tunes from the fifties and sixties.

'Grand-dad music,' bellows Ben, and I give him the wanker's hand signal.

I think of Margo and wonder what happened to her. I would love to hold her in my arms and shaft her like the tart that she is.

Baba is poking me, and a charming waitress offers me a selection of meats.

I ask her name. 'Consuela Montoya at your service, and I am available for pleasure at your request.'

'Serve the meal, bitch,' snarls Baba, 'he will love me tonight. I am tight, I am a virgin, and I have not had love from any man. You, Consuela, can have any man here; you have sexy legs and breasts.'

Captain D' Sousa slips a hand underneath her serape dress and has a feel of her bush, to which he tells one and all that she has never had a pregnancy, in his opinion.

'She is finger-licking good.'

She slaps a plate of meats on the table and says, 'Eat, pigs.'

Grace slips her a hundred pollars and apologises for our ungentlemanly behaviour. She asks if she has any children.

She replies, 'No.'

Grace has her hand under her serape. Consuela withdraws to Bill and Ben. She treats them like lords, giving them titbits of everything, including asking them to nibble on her nipples. Conchita is another waitress who, according to D'Souza, had probably given birth to fifty kids. He could have worn a builder's glove, and she wouldn't have noticed that she was being fingered. The grub is coming hard and fast, and it's decided that everyone should strip the top half-naked because it is a hot night.

I am surprised how quickly Baba has her top off, and Ben is provocatively wriggling his tongue. He will have her given half a chance.

I am pissed as a lord, and I want Consuela. I need to speak to Mariah, but Baba is up in the air.

'I am going to screw your tight little hole tonight. Try and enjoy yourself in the meantime; try and avoid getting laid.'

I head over to Mariah. Ben is beside Baba, and Baba is looking at me. I shrug my shoulders, and she looks at Ben.

I reach Mariah and place a piece of Mesquite chicken in her mouth. Frankie is beside me with rage in his fists, and I knock him out with one punch.

'Are you married to him or what, Christ almighty, he is possessive?'

'Do you want to see me naked?' she asks, grabbing me delicately by the balls.

'You must be careful with my body,' she whispers.

'I doubt you are virginal, Mariah,' as I part her knees.

'I want to make love to you.'

Becky is leaning over me; her tits are brushing my lips.

'What the hell are you doing to my sister? Are you taking advantage of an intoxicated slapper?' she laughs at me.

I sit down and pass out.

Chapter Twelve

Otto's Irish Whiskey

Monday the 19th of June.

I awake the following morning with a sore head and an enormous hard-on, but it's caused by a bladder of piss. I stumble across a cactus tree and piss for an eternity, the chilly air freezing my naked torso. As I turn around, I see a mongrel dog foaming at the mouth; what the hell happened? I have no gun, and the mutt stands there growling. I stumble to the trailer and pick up an assault rifle, but the dog has gone.

Mariah and Becky are fast asleep beside a brazier, accompanied, not to my surprise, by Bill and Ben, the flowerpot men.

All are semi-naked. Mariah has a beautiful torso, indeed. I wonder where's Baba as I open the trailer door. D'Souza and Hubert are asleep with Grace and Consuela between them.

The growling of a dog can be heard from mesquite bushes, and the air is rent by a volley of semi-automatic fire. Out of the thicket, the flamethrower boys come having emptied magazines into the dog. It must be mincemeat as they are firing handguns, wearing gun belts, and nothing else. The cowboy film Young Guns comes to mind. They stand there reloading, their cocks hanging between their legs. The whores are sitting on the ground, chucking pebbles at the dog.

Hubert is bawling and yelling, wanting to know what is going on. I walk over to the thicket, leg muscles loosening. Fathead and Skeleton are in there with a fat bird. There are other soldiers with women, but I can't see Baba anywhere.

It dawns on me that Frankie and Hugo are not here either. They have shagged Baba; I will kill them when I catch them. Frankie has it in for me for fancying Mariah, and what the hell happened to me last night? I never pass out from drink; after all, I hadn't drunk much. They drugged me and rode the arse off Baba. I must find her, for she will be distraught, and I march to the trailer.

Grace, the bitch, should have kept an eye on her, but she was too busy getting her holes filled to be bothered. Grace is at the trailer's door, and I bawl at her, 'Where's Baba?'

'Do I look like a babysitter pisshead?' as she jumps from the trailer, her nipples hard and erect.

'She was drinking beer with Frankie during the night and must have gone off with him. What's your problem? Do you want me?' She takes me by the hand and walks me towards the trailer.

'Clear off!' I shout, 'You're no good; I want to find Baba.'

'Go then,' and she kisses Consuela.

'I bet your Baba has a sore arse. Take ice with you. She will need it, and by the way, Frankie will kill you given a chance. Let her go because we are on our way to

Columbus. Come in and see the news; it looks like there will be war with Mexico.'

I spend half the day searching, but there's no sign of her, Frankie or Hugo. I pray to God that they haven't hurt her or, even worse, murdered her. I climb into the trailer and fall asleep.

I wake up with a start; it's the same dream I had a few hours back. The sky is dark, and the weather is cold. I am naked and frightened, and I'm a five-year-old. A voice is telling me I am a killer. I must wander the galaxy of lost souls for eternity and a day. Then and only then shall I find my soul with the number 666 stamped on it with a branding iron. An iron so hot that such temperatures can only be found in the devil's fiery furnace located in the most bottomless pit in hell. A day is the length of my life on earth down to the last death rattle from my dying throat. I have to endure an eternity of wandering through these forsaken lands while hunger and thirst, accompanied by pain and cold are my constant companions. Occasionally, I see what could have been. As a boy, I see myself gliding through clouds of silk beneath a blue sky, playing games with my friends. Rachel is waving to me, and I hear the laughter of unseen friends at play, and darkness descends. A terrible feeling of loss fills my empty void where my soul should be, and I hasten my search in the most inhospitable places. I cry out for forgiveness, but I am showered with fire and brimstone, and I rush forward to find myself in a land of permafrost. I have awakened twice in the land of permafrost, and I clutch my heart, hoping to feel my soul.

I must leave this land of death and destruction; I can no longer suffer the evil that surrounds me, for everywhere, people wish to kill me and people I wish to murder.

Mariah comes to the trailer and tells me that we will leave at 18.00 on the dot.

'Did we...No, we didn't, and then again, maybe we did.'

Two choppers will be used with you, Grace, General Hubert, Colonel Potz, Becky, James, and the flamethrower guys in one. The other one will be little old me, Bill and Ben, and Captain D'Souza and Consuela to help us with Spanish.

I intend to knock lumps out of these two and make them tell me where Baba is.

'Thinking of leaving us behind, you scrawny-arsed slapper?' screeches Skeleton as he comes up behind Becky and cracks her across the arse with a baseball bat. Mariah produces a gun, but Fathead is beside her, a knife to her ear. A trickle of blood runs down her neck. They have taken us by surprise. They had crawled out from underneath the trailer.

'You did not read out our names; we are coming, and don't forget it,' says Fathead as he withdraws his knife and kicks Mariah square in the back as she tumbles forward, landing at my feet.

'We are all leaving Arizona and completing our mission for EARTHCO. Roll call is over, and there will be no more gab.'

'Have you got a problem? Because if you have, you terrorist bastard, let's get it sorted?'

I realise I made a terrible error of judgement on Fathead; he is a right killer, as is undoubtedly Skeleton. Dillon knew how to pick them, and if it's the last thing I do, I will find him.

'No, we hadn't forgotten you; you and Rugosa are with D'Souza.'

'Is that so child-killer? We will ride with you and Grace, the money-grabbing tart.'

'When you are ready to fly, we will give you your money,' he screams at Grace, and she is frothing at the mouth and threatening to castrate him with a rusty knife.

'Shut your face,' screeches Fathead, 'I will keep you close to me.'

He drags her by the hair to the trailer. A shot rings out, and he lets go and hits the ground, blood spurting from his foot. Hubert has shot him, and he yells at Skeleton to fetch that Apache surgeon, Chief Running Bear.

'Touch her again, fat bastard, and I will kill you next time. Make sure you remember what I said.'

He goes to Grace and helps her to her feet, and I can see the lucky bastards are in love. The day passes, as does 18.00 hours, and eventually, D'Souza tells us we are being stood down. We are tired and fed up, and there is no energy left in us. I sit and think of Baba.

Mariah comes over, and I ask if she is okay, but she shrugs and says it's all in a day's work.

'I can't believe that Frankie and Hugo have run off with that slapper.'

'She is not better in bed than my sister; maybe she has kidnapped them.'

'I assumed you were madly in love with Donald; where is he?'

'I don't know, probably with Margo in Ireland. Everything is up in the air. We still love one another. I have not been unfaithful to Donald. Over flirtatious, you could describe me.'

'Becky and I spent the night until about one o'clock with Bill playing cards. Ben had fallen asleep earlier, and you saw the rest; we were asleep near the campfire. I do enjoy being hedonistic, but not strictly in the all-sexual sense. Last night with Bill and Ben, we all went topless and removed our knickers but kept our skirts on. It was very exhilarating to be naked and yet not naked. We titillated the boys, and they wanked themselves off as we masturbated. It was a delectable gratification.'

'Maybe you and I could have a romantic entanglement in more tranquil times. It has been a hectic week, and tonight we will watch News International since there is paramilitary violence in Ireland.'

'Do you still have that CD you had me listening to?' I ask, 'I would like to hear more.'

'Mariah, you are so ravishingly beautiful and a temptress. I will carefully choose my time for maximum enjoyment. I could love a woman like you.'

'Yeah, sure, it's in my rucksack, come over to the trailer, and I will give it to you, the CD that is. Meanwhile, come and watch the news. Let's see how things are in Texas. Thank God that Death Snow is dead; things will return to normal. I need to get out of here; the stink is overpowering at times.'

'Grace has returned to Benson with the flamethrower boys in anticipation of finding your little friend. She said she was enslaved, and you had nearly shagged her, you dirty old man. She has lovely titties. I felt them last night. She is bisexual like your friend Grace. She, too, had fallen asleep before our finger-foursome.'

'I miss Donald. He sure knows how to make me feel special.'

He would go bananas if he knew what went on here, but he is not likely to meet any of the gang, but you and you will keep your mouth shut if I give you a passionate kiss.

'I don't care what you do, I want to find Wendy, and I wonder if I ever will. Grace says she is in Ireland in the company of fifty mercenaries. When I get her back, she will be a pin cushion full of holes from cocks or bullets.'

'What do you know about Stonnage, Mariah? What is so important about the damn place? Is it made from rejuvenating cream or what? EARTHCO seems to have a great deal of interest in it.'

'Listen to the CD, and all will be revealed. But first, I want to watch the news, then a field shower, and then I am off to bed beside that flaming brazier. There's no spread tonight, just iron rations, so I'm slimming.'

There is a commotion coming from the side of the Controlmobile as we join a dozen soldiers who are effing and blinding about Chicanos.

'What the hell are they yelling for? What is a Chicano?'

'I'm not sure,' she says, 'probably American-born Mexicans. I don't know or care because those Mexicans have been killing American citizens. Look at the death toll,' pointing at the television.

There is trouble on the Rio Grande border; trouble has been brewing with a death toll of 234 Mexicans and 97 Americans. It shows roads from California, New Mexico, Arizona, and Texas with heavy concentrations of vehicles, all illegals heading for the border.

The Mexican authorities will allow no one to cross but have asked the Americans to let their soldiers help police the camps. There will be a million by the weekend at the rate the refugees are advancing on the border. Mexican TV is sending streams of footage back home and to other Spanish-speaking countries. It is inciting its citizens into a frenzy of rage against atrocities in Texas and California.

On the other hand, the Americans are streaming the atrocities to their citizens.

The white supremacists are in full swing, with the Klan buying up the bed linen for miles around. It shows an interview with housewives moaning that their freshly laundered sheets have disappeared from their lines. There is no doubt holes are being cut in them at this moment.

Two boys in Wichita attacked their mother late last night, severing her jugular. According to eyewitnesses, the boys went out to the street and tried to bite a passer-bye. Seven other cases have been reported from around the US. These demented Night-Children are being kept in a secure mental facility. All are under the age of seventeen and behave calmly during daylight hours.

Further details can be found on our website at Nightchilds.foxynews.co.us.

In further news, Germany has warned Russia not to withhold gas supplies this winter.

In Ireland, the death toll from the gun battle on the Donegal border has risen to twenty, with other bodies expected to be found in isolated areas. The Irish Defence Force said the four soldiers among the twenty dead were not Irish army. However, one who spoke before he died gave his name as William Webb of Northampton, England.

The state of emergency will remain in force in Arizona. There are no further signs of the devastating Death Snow. Scientists are baffled by the lack of evidence for its cause and have assumed that it thrived on vegetation and living matter. They have not ruled out that it is dormant and could strike at any moment, but the signs are encouraging. The district under quarantine is expected to be reduced to a fifty-mile zone around Tucson.

An all-points bulletin (APB) is still out on the four CEOs of EARTHCO, better known as the Four Corners.

There are dozens of attacks by animals, but most are being killed. All animals are to be destroyed, and the penalty for harbouring an animal is two years of hard labour. The animal will be euthanised in full view of the family as an additional punishment. Citizens are asked to remain calm and not take the law into their own hands so as not to encourage extremist groups to take up arms.

Old newsreel of mass movements of people from the former Yugoslavia moving to their ancestral homelands can be viewed on the 10 pm special. Just like Yugoslavia, America has substantial ethnic populations residing in diverse areas. Hundreds of thousands of Croats, Bosnians, and Serbs were forced from their homes by ethnic cleansing, which will not be allowed in America. President Clinton has made it clear that ethnic cleansing in any shape or form will not be tolerated and met with severe punishments, including execution. Refugees are asked to return to their homes, where additional troops are being rushed to bolster the law-and-order forces.

'I must find out about Ireland,' I tell Mariah, 'I hope we get to Denver quickly.'

'Come with me,' she says, 'and I will give you your bedtime story, and we head over to the trailer. She rummages around in her kitbag and retrieves two CDs from a folder. Here's part one, and I want it back; I will have that kiss later.'

'Mariah, I saw you sleeping this morning with your sister, and I wanted to kiss your breasts and explore your body. You are stunning eye candy. Donald is so fortunate.'

Grace and Hubert jump from a jeep, followed by another vehicle with the flamethrower boys in full chorus. I look at Grace, and she comes to me and shakes her head in the negative. I say nothing but walk over to Bill and borrow his CD player. I rest near a campfire with his headphones on.

I fast forward and eventually stop near where I last heard Benedikta's voice talk of Brandy the slapper and how they were flown to Germany as undesirables after their behaviour at the Windmill Club in Soho, London.

Otto was delighted with their purchase. He informed his customers far and wide that fine Irish whiskeys would be served at his establishments of delight throughout the Reeperbahn in Frankfurt. Delivery was expected any day, and it would reach him through embassy officials.

There are certain things in life that one should keep to oneself alone. Liquor and women are two that spring to mind. In the blink of an eye on that warm autumn day in 1933, Otto's bargain whiskey collection was whisked away in the company of Ernest Rohm and his brown shirts. He would wait another week before having the nerve to ask a diplomat, a family friend, what happened to his whiskey. He wasn't left in the best frame of mind when told that Rohm had requisitioned the whole damn lot to celebrate the SA stormtroopers' rise to power during the Oktoberfest.

'Ach mein leben ist nur ein haufen kacke,' he screeches, throwing a bottle of slivovitch at a SA trooper who promptly tells him he is an arschloch. He will have him breaking rocks for the autobahn by Monday morning.

'Verpiss dich, you brown-nose,' and he shouts for his heavies to give the Brownshirt a good hiding.

Old brown nose isn't having any of this. He is roaring louder than Hitler ever could. As bad luck would have it, half a dozen blue-eyed blond Aryan supermen come out of the rooms. Within the half-hour, Otto was on a train to Berlin to spend no doubt a pleasant night in Wilhelmstrasse SA headquarters cells. He would be interrogated about what he knew about Rohm's sex life and what he was doing with fifty cases of Irish whiskey.

Did he know Irish people in Berlin?

He was frightened by the way events were unfurling, and he kept repeating that it was a mistake and not to mention the whiskey anymore. All he wanted to do was return to his clubs, and all would be forgotten.

He was told that his whiskey was in Berlin, and he was off to a labour camp.

'You can help build it,' and they threw him in a cell. Brandy said he died the first week he was there from a massive heart attack. Brandy left a Lithuanian belly dancer who had been a close friend of Otto in charge of the clubs for a fortnight. She told her; that her aunt Wilhelmina had died in Rome. She hoped the lady had left her, her string of knocking houses now that Otto was in Valhalla. She would need a madame to run them, and if she did a fair job here in Hamburg, there was no reason why she could not do the same in Rome. With war coming, there would be plenty of soldiers with wallets of money; shekels would also be welcome in her establishments.

She didn't trust that belly dancer. As far as she was concerned, the dancer had been robbing Otto since she met him. It was best to let this fotze think she was in for a big payday.

That night, she boarded a train to Berlin with Cockeye's brother and headed for the red-light district. She had been through a lot, and she wanted her whiskey back. To her, it was her whiskey, and to hell with the consequences. She told Cockeye's brother to clear off if he did not want to help. He fell into line quickly, hearing of the fanny around the Tiergarten. They spent a quiet night in a small hotel, hoping not to be recognised, and in the morning after breakfast, she was ready to reclaim her whiskey.

She found what she was looking for in the Hotel Adlon near the Brandenburg gate, having a late breakfast without his mistress, the beautiful but depraved Russian singer Molly Malonski.

'Guten Morgen, Oberst-Gruppenfuhrer Von Bulow. How are you?' giving him a perverted smile and a mental blowjob. 'You have not been to Hamburg lately.'

'Ah, Brandy, you look ravishing.'

'Have you met my husband? Yes, you have. May we join you? I would like you to tell me who is drinking my whiskey.'

'First things first, have your breakfast,' and he continues to work through his sausages and rye bread.

'I heard about Otto, he says. Terrible business, poor Otto.'

'How is Molly?' asks Brandy. 'Is she still dancing?'

'Yes, she is dancing, complaining that she should have been Lola-Lola in The Blue Angel film. Always complaining that Marlene Dietrich's voice was too deep and sultry, she could have sung Falling in Love Again much better.'

After breakfast, Von Bulow invited them to his suite of rooms for coffee. He would investigate the missing whiskey, make phone calls, and see what came back over the wire.

Molly comes out of the bedroom all silk and knickerless and sings to Cockeye's brother that she is falling in love. Brandy laughs and throws her skirts high in the air, giving Von Bulow her impression of the can-can. Molly is insulted by her behaviour.

In unladylike behaviour, Brandy punches her on the nose, drawing blood.

Molly marches back to the bedroom. Von Bulow tells them to go and come back later, and she, Brandy, better be in a friendly, loving mood, and she should make it up to Molly, and he gives Cockeye a big wink.

'What kind of a name is Molly Malonski?' says Cockeye to Brandy.

'She reminds me of an old tart that sold cockles and mussels on a godforsaken street in Dublin,' and he manoeuvres Brandy out the door. 'We'll be back.'

That evening, half-pissed, they returned to the Adlon to find that Molly was asleep and Von Bulow was drunk. Bulow groped Brandy and asked for a blowjob, to which she told him later.

'I need to have dinner first. I have been all over Berlin admiring the new buildings under construction on the Unter den Linden and the Alexanderplatz.'

Down in the foyer, she told Von Bulow, 'Our glorious Fuhrer will bring much-needed work to our downtrodden masses. Should mein Fuhrer and his cabinet of goons need blowjobs, I shall put my lips, top and bottom, at their disposal?'

She didn't notice the hotel receptionist giving her a look of contempt as she lifted the phone to her ear.

Having had an excellent dinner, including pork and sauerkraut, they retired across town to the Little Englander nightclub cum brothel, where it was mandatory for the ladies to go commando.

Brandy said the doorman slipped a finger in her pussy, and she had a sound mind to report the finger-licking bastard to management. However, he was cute, and she might let him screw her later.

Molly said it was best to lift your skirt and let them have an eyeful. Too many fingers poking too many pies, never know what you catch, and Brandy said she had learned a valuable lesson. Bouncers, you could never be sure what they had been feeling. She rushed off to the toilets to wash her fanny.

The club was packed to the rafters with men and women and some that were neither. As they moved across the floor, Brandy could feel hands groping her arse, and it was with relief that she reached a table reserved for them. She knew two men were interested in her and assumed they had done the groping.

Von Bulow wore his uniform, and the men avoided eye contact with him. He used his authority to eyeball their women. He took Molly to dance, and he changed partners six times in nine minutes, each time sliding his hand between their thighs while Molly obliged by dancing with the ladies' partners. None would feel Molly's fanny; such was their fear of Von Bulow. Molly would encourage certain Adonises to check her merchandise by placing a foot on a chair. Cockeye's brother sat at a table with a prossy on his knees in a dark corner.

Seeing him, Von Bulow strode across to a middle-aged couple, cut in on the man, and danced away with his wife. Molly filled the missing gap, but it was clear that this lady was refined. She fancied a bit of slap and tickle but definitely not the idea of being on her knees with her tits out sucking on a Nazi cock, especially an Obergruppenführer.

Across to the table, they danced to where Cockeye's brother was. Von Bulow unbuttons and tosses out his cock; to be fair to the man, it was a decent size.

She is beside herself with indignation.

Cockeye has his hand up her skirt. She can do nothing, as it is a club's rule. Finally, her husband turns up at the table. His wife is complaining she is being sexually abused by the jumped-up underclass, which brings a snigger from her husband.

'My dear,' he says, 'you have wanted to come here for months, and now that we are here, we should enjoy ourselves.'

He drops his trousers and invites Brandy, already on her knees with her tits out, to have a munch.

Molly unzips the protesting lady's dress and unfastens her bra while, all the while, Cockeye is fingering her clit. Molly takes her by the hand, and they kneel on the floor in front of Von Bulow. She gingerly takes his cock in her mouth. She begins to suck away, tonguing it deeper into her throat while Molly massages her tits. Molly takes over from her and takes Von Bulow.

The posh lady is free and can choose who she wishes. Molly knows that she will either go to her husband or seek fresh meat, which is precisely what she does. Later, she sees her in a booth bent over, legs wide open, and a group of naked men waiting to fill her. No doubt she will become a fully-fledged member of the swinging circuit and one that cannot read, for it said in enormous capitals in the booth, Ficken Verboten.

It's decided they will go back to the hotel for a nightcap. As they leave, Brandy and Cockeye are picked up by the security police and frogmarched to a waiting police wagon. Molly sees Cockeye getting hit over the head with a truncheon. Nothing is heard of them after discreet enquiries by Von Bulow; it is assumed that she has returned to Hamburg.

Best to let sleeping dogs lie, especially these nasty Nazi dogs.

The next time he would contact Cockeye's brother, it would be late November 1940, and Von Bulow was an Oberstgruppenfuhrer in the SS.

This morning, he was summoned to Heinrich Himmler's office on an important matter. Such requests struck terror into one's heart, especially if they carried out acts of depravity on the forced labour workers, which he regularly did. One could never be sure who might be a snitch. Feeling the urge to piss every few minutes, he headed for the office of the Reichsfuhrer-SS and wished he'd had a good shit as well. Secretaries and other paper pushers pitied him sitting there, waiting to be called.

Himmler did not like him because he had mishandled the fanny of a distant relative. The bitch should not have been in the club if she didn't want her tush felt.

Three men sat next to him.

One said, 'Wasn't it a beautiful day they were having,' which immediately conjured up pictures of damp, overcast days, graveyards, and coffins. He noticed that the man spoke German with an Irish accent, just like Cockeye's brother. He sat and wondered what had happened to Cockeye's brother. He didn't even notice the men going in to see the Reichsfuhrer. He was being called and getting a grip on himself; he marched in and shouted Heil Hitler enthusiastically. Himmler carefully studied a file as he eyed Von Bulow through his pince-nez glasses.

'Ah Bulow, I would like you to meet Darragh and Cormac McBride; they are from IRA central command. They are here, amongst other things we will speak of later, to locate a missing Irishman and his German-born wife.'

'His name is O'Kane, and from our files I note they were arrested in 1934. They spent a stint in a labour camp so that they could reflect on the gravity of insulting the Fuhrer and his cabinet.

I would like you to interview the camp commandant and find the necessary records to establish when they left and where they went. Unfortunately, she may be dead from overindulgence in sex and him from alcohol.'

'Brigadefuhrer Austerlitz, you are to find out what this labour camp is and why it is not on my list. You will report directly to me; here is all you will need,' and he passes him a sealed envelope.

'You will return my lettre de cachet to me immediately after completing your mission.'

With that, the meeting was closed.

Von Bulow exits with Austerlitz, who turns on his heel and informs him, 'That he will carry out his mission to the Reichfuhrer's satisfaction and he Von Bulow can clear off.'

He slams his office door in Bulow's face and calls immediately for his secretaries, one of whom he abuses. The other three look on with bored expressions and wait for him to grunt and finish.

He gives the gobbler the day off.

The camp turned out to be a forced labour camp outside of Leipzig with the appropriate name of Stalag 88. There are approximately one hundred Polish workers manufacturing shell casings for grenades.

Austerlitz sends two investigators to check the labour and financial records. He will follow them to the camp the following day, knowing they will probably not be given the information they seek. No doubt, Von Bulow will have stuck his bald head around the commandant's door prior to his visit. He will present his lettre de cachet when he comes, and everybody will jump to attention. He will find out what's so secretive about this bloody place.

He travelled by train the night before and was well-rested and breakfasted. He arrived with a military escort. The camp commandant is aware of his visitor and the reason for the visit.

'This is my camp, and I am in charge here,' he tells his guards. 'And no Reichfuhrer will screw up our little enterprise. I will send him back to his chicken farmer boss with the information he needs, and we will continue our business as usual.'

The camp commandant, Martin Riesling, is waiting for him.

He is escorted to his office, where he is offered a fine Burgundy and reminded that dinner will be at 14.00 hours. Nodding his head, he sits, opens his briefcase, and extracts a file.

He looks at Riesling, who is thinking to himself. 'I wonder if this bastard would like to participate in our forced labour programme and help our glorious Fuhrer achieve world domination.'

I shall sit and stare down at him as my chair is six inches higher.

'This Stalag 88 seems to be a bit secretive with its documentation. Our Reichfuhrer would like an up-to-date work schedule and financial records, and I would require them for the past five years.'

'You will have the accounts after dinner, but would you like a tour of the prison compound beforehand? It may whet your appetite to see our workforce labouring their arses off so we can have lebensraum.'

'Do you have any women here?' asks Austerlitz.

'No,' says Riesling, 'there are no women here, just a camp of eighty-eight men.'

'Is that why it's called Stalag 88?'

'What difference does it make? The Fuhrer gets his shell casings, and the Russians get them up the arse.'

'Come, let's have drinks, and I will introduce you to a sexy lady with a body to die for.'

'I thought you said there were no women at this camp.'

'I was expecting you today, so I thought, let me get the finest pussy in Berlin, in case our esteemed guest finds that his cock gets hungry.'

'I must advise you, Major Riesling, that I have a letter from the Reichfuhrer. It authorises me to do as I wish, even to execute you here on the spot for treasonable comments about our glorious Reich. Yes, I shall wine and dine with you and look forward to a meeting with this lady. I use the word lady loosely, but when all this is over, I will promptly expect answers and paperwork, or I shall have you shot.'

'You can't say fairer than that,' says Riesling, 'and would you mind putting this on a formal basis by showing me this letter?'

Of course, you may read it over pre-dinner drinks; let us retire to your private quarters and see this lady.

He asks to visit the production lines.

'You want to see the production lines,' says Riesling, 'very well, come with me.'

'What about your escort? Maybe they would like nourishment.'

'No, thank you, that will not be necessary, they can return to Leipzig, and I shall return by train later. You do have a staff car?'

'Of course, Brigadefuhrer, it will be at your disposal. When do you have to report to the Reichfuhrer?'

'The day after tomorrow at the earliest, but I don't expect to be here later than 18.00 hrs.'

'In that case, let us proceed post-haste; we have two production lines; one produces 50 mm shell casings and the other 40 mm casings.'

Entering the factory, he saw before him a workforce in full productivity. As he strolled down the assembly lines, he spoke Polish to several machinists. He crossed to the following line, where he picked up a shell casing and asked the worker in Polish a question.

Riesling saw the worker look at him, and he immediately crossed and asked him to speak German. He turned to Austerlitz and requested that further conversation is in the mother tongue. Austerlitz asked Riesling if he was a Polish-German.

'No, I am not; my family returned from the Urals years back. Why? Do you have a problem with my accent?'

'Let us return to my quarters. Dinner will be served shortly.'

They returned to be greeted at the door by a well-kept attractive forty-ish woman with striking features beneath a head of naturally blonde hair.

'Ah, my dear Brigadefuhrer, I have heard so much about you. It is a pleasure to meet you. Come, let us have dinner and acquaint one another with our choices of pleasure.'

Over a meal of suckling pig and crates of beer and wine, they got inebriated or pissed to the commoner. All three sat there smoking Cuban cigarillos while the well-kept forty-ish woman kept adjusting her bosom and skirt. Austerlitz did not let this pass him by, for the alcohol had made him very horny.

The lady was opening and closing her knees, and he could have sworn that her cleavage was all but out. Did she ask him if he wanted to screw her? She must have; he was sure he heard the word Ficken in a sexual context.

She was eating dessert; what was it? Bloody hell, bananas, and sweet cherries. She was definitely giving him the come-on. She was sucking the banana and flicking her tongue over the cherries, and she was a sucking and a licking.

The time to make his move was upon him.

Where the hell had Riesling gone? He wanted to squash him into a pulp and take his woman to bed; he wanted to feel her hot breath on his cock. Mein Gott, his cock was enormous and bulging from his trousers. She studied it with admiration, she wanted it, and she definitely would get it stuck up her. He felt he was in a stupor, but a damn pleasant stupor.

She was at his side refilling his glass, his hand touched her tit, and the damn thing was hot and soft and nearly made him come. He groaned with desire as she nibbled his ear. She whispered perversions and helped his hand up her skirt.

This was too much for him; she wore no knickers, just stockings. His finger slid through her bush. He felt wet flesh, and that was it: he shot his load. She kissed him hungrily and asked if he fancied her a wee bit, just a little bit. He needed to get away from the table as she placed her hand between his thighs.

'I do, I do, oh god, I do,' he groaned.

'I must find the bathroom, for I desperately need the toilet.'

She took him by the hand and led him to a bedroom, inviting him to use the ensuite.

'Oh brigadefuhrer, please forgive me, but I need to change my clothes as I allowed myself to be overexcited in your presence. I shall return in moments.'

As soon as she left the room, he was into the toilet faster than an African/American spotting the KKK on their way to his shebeen.

He dropped his breeches, and off came his pink frou-frou frilly knickers with their little red ruffles. Grabbing a sponge, he tossed his cock into the wash-hand basin and washed off the spunk.

He thought about the mind-blowing shagging he would give her.

Putting on his breeches, he lay on the bed and hallucinated about her wet pussy. He slid his hand into his breeches, played with himself, and dozed off.

Austerlitz was fast asleep, never to wake up, and his lettre de cachet was safely in Riesling's possession.

Austerlitz would be disposed of in the firepit by two inmates who would swiftly depart with bundles of Reichsmarks.

'Come Brandy, our work here is complete.'

Chapter Thirteen

Escape from Stalag 88

Riesling headed outside to the staff car with two bulky cases.

"Paddy O'Tooles's pub Gunther, and be quick about it! Biddy Mulligan is doing her cabaret act tonight, and I will speak with her. See if she can slip you in for the night if you get my meaning."

"Oh, thank you, Commandant Riesling, she has such lovely bon journos. I have dreamed of getting my hands on them for many nights."

"Tonight's the night, my lad; don't let her give you any blarney."

"What is blarney?" he asks.

"Oh, it's a long story. In a nutshell, if you kiss the Blarney Stone, which is a stone stuck in a castle wall in Ireland, they say you have the gift of the gab, or in other words, you could talk the leg off a table a bit like your Fuhrer."

"Where is this blarney stone? I would travel to kiss it."

"Don't worry about the stone. Concentrate on kissing Biddy Mulligan and make sure she hasn't been eating chicken soup, so to speak, you dummkopf."

I tousle his hair and give him a bundle of Reichsmarks.

"Just in case she needs money, and we pull up in front of the pub."

The pub was full of Liebstandarte with black uniforms and SS runes, drinking litres of Guinness served by buxom wenches showing lots of tits. I invited Gunther to stay with us to keep an eye on the innocent boy.

Helga bade me welcome, and I slipped her a wad and told her to find Wanda, the Polish knob-polisher, and get her to stay with Gunther as I had a bit of business to conduct. Effing and blinding were coming from the beer hall, and I knew it was the McBride's. We headed towards them to be met by a political inferno.

One German had a relative on a gun-running ship for the IRA twenty years before and claimed that the IRA was a shower of wankers who couldn't organise a piss-up in a brewery. They were not even capable of collecting a boatload of guns. The ship, the Aud, was scuttled, and his nephew was interned for the rest of the war, including twenty crew members and the captain, Captain Spindler.

Insults were being traded. I am sure the McBrides would have been murdered but for the timely intervention of Sepp Dietrich. He invited them for a pork, sauerkraut and Guinness dinner, and peace descended on the Third Reich.

Biddy Mulligan was on stage, ready to sing Lili Marleen to the joy of the Liebstandarte as they banged their steins on the rough-hewn tables. They were the sons of Germany, of the Fatherland, and they would sing the song that their fathers had sung in the First World War.

At the British government's request, Anglo/Irishman Tommy Connor would later write a version in English. It would be sung in many languages, most notably by Marlene Dietrich in English. How ironic, but tonight it would be sung in Germanrish accompanied by a tide of beer.

They are friends now, and Connor is conversing with Dietrich, and I can hear a reference to Himmler as I am within earshot. Actually, I am a foot away. Darragh is beside me, and I offer him my hand, which he shakes gladly. He is shocked when I take him aside and ask him, "How is poor old Ireland?"

He asks if I am Napper Tandy, to which I reply I am William O'Kane, better known as Cockeye's brother. He laughs and says, "I have instructions to inquire about your whereabouts, you pisswater maker. Your communications ceased six months ago, as did your annual contributions. So, it fell to us as German speakers to investigate."

"How's your brother?"

"I don't know, I've been running a forced labour camp with Brandy for the past four years, and we need to leave Germany."

"That is easy to arrange, we can have you in Spain within days, and we have comrades there from the Spanish Civil War. Didn't your nephew sign-up for the International Brigade in 37?"

"I was running brothels on the Reeperbahn in Hamburg. Ever been there? It's got ravishing German pussy, the finest in the land, and lovely hairy armpits."

"I see Brandy likes to get her kit off," says Darragh.

I look where he is pointing, and the bitch is in burlesque with Biddy. No doubt they will be entertaining the troops. No one is interested in us; even Sepp Dietrich is watching them closely.

Darragh gives Connor a nudge and points at me. "He is on the run," he says, laughing loudly.

"He wants to return to Ireland while half the country tries to escape the damned place. "Kaiser!" he yells at the barman, "Guinness and food."

Ingrid comes over and asks us to repeat what we want. Biddy is winking at Gunther, and it is only a matter of time before she takes him in hand. The Reichsmarks have reached her, and she is in loving form.

At about four in the morning, we catch the train which will eventually take us to Spain, but now, it's Mulhouse, a town on the border of Germany and France.

I have no intention of ending up in Ireland with those McBride's sniffing in my cases. It's New York or Boston.

Two days later, we are on the Spanish frontier and on our way to Pamplona to meet a mutual friend known as the half-crown. If events had been different, he could be king. I recognise him and wonder why he is sheltering us, probably hoping the IRA might help him to power.

The McBride's have gone, and they will meet us at the port of Bilbao at the Skin Headed Matador, a sailors knocking-shop-come-hotel. Brandy and I were soon out and about knocking back gallons of fine wines, mostly

Rioja, and causing no end of trouble with the hotel management over our antics late at night.

For several nights they boasted that Hemingway had gotten pissed with them. They had spent the night together as he described the bulls running through the streets in July. It's advertised as the San Fermin festival. Brandy yelled that she would stay until next year and outrun any bull. It was not to be, and we were on our way to Bilbao the following evening.

I knew it was risky meeting the McBrides as they would betray us to the Germans after relieving us of our valuables. They would no doubt collect a finder's fee as well. Iron ore was being shipped to America, and we intended to be on one of those ships.

The McBrides were pissed as coots at the Skin-Headed Matador and, with a great show of European camaraderie, gave us bear hugs and kisses. Connor took the opportunity to have a feel of Brandy as if by accident.

More blarney followed with, "Have a drink, and how was Pamplona?"

"Have you booked the Dancing Senorita Hotel? The paella is delicious, and your bed linen is changed daily."

"Yeah, right old Blarney talkers, you two," I say.

"You are a pair of traitors, and I know that chain of flea pits. I've known picture houses with fewer fleas, and you're staying at the Bilbao Senorita."

They turn to the Spaniards and start gabbing, laughing, and pointing at Brandy. She takes exception, and as in Ireland, she grabs a bottle hurling it at the bunch of laughing heads, striking two in one sitting.

Well, that's done it; Pedro, the hyaena, is up, blood pouring from a head wound, and he crosses the floor like greased lightning. A Bowie-type knife is in his hand with a Spanish notch near the hilt. I had one myself, and I recognised it immediately, as did Brandy.

"Siento," she says to him. "I'm very siento," and she offers him her hand.

Everybody is watching, and I have drawn a pair of German police lugers to ensure I can kill everyone if necessary. I have added a thirty-two-round drum for good measure. A Thompson machine gun would have been handy, but these girls are real bitches when fired.

She screams cono at him and sticks a stiletto in his bollocks. He lets out a piercing scream, sharper than the screech of a whore who has discovered a fake pound note and an arseful of Dublin spunk, and he legs it out the door.

"That's settled his love life for a year or so," she says.

All eyes are on William and his pair of lugers.

"Aah," she moans, "were you going to shoot me, darling?"

Connor and Darragh have skipped out the door and are on their way to anywhere but Ireland, a cowardly pair of Fenians.

"Buenos Noches amadans," says William as he pretends to spray the lot of them.

We head back to the Bilbao Senorita, and I sneak up the stairs; Brandy remains with the night porter, pretending to book a room. Suddenly, there are four shots in pairs, one second apart, and William is back at the reception desk.

"I'm not staying here," he says, "they are killing one another."

"They thought I was the porter. Best get going mate, go home and nowhere else," and we follow him onto the street where we head back to our hotel, collect our things and get a taxi to the docks.

The Pride of Genoa is ready to sail, and we are boarded. A bag changes hands, and the captain shows us our quarters.

"See you in America," he says.

Those McBrides will never embezzle funds again. They thought they could pull the wool over the Munster Brigades. They should know that we are like British Embassies; we have a branch in every country, probably more. A week later, we dock in New York and hightail it to Louisiana's French Quarter of New Orleans, better known as the Big Easy.

The embezzled funds, including a large donation for future years, are enclosed and given to a reputable politician.

The war years passed, the fifties came and went, and their little girl Katie grew up, beautiful and delicate of bone. It was 1953; she was ten, and Elvis Presley cut his first record.

Cockeye's brother (born 1898) dreamt of Ireland and his desire to return to the old sod. He was fifty-five years old, as was Brandy, and they felt their bordellos in New Orleans were in the hands of the competent Madame Fifi, la Putain.

They reckoned that the clear Arizona air would help with Brandy's increasingly bad asthma.

They bought a ranch of four hundred acres of pastureland and stocked it with Longhorn steers from Texas. The ranch turned out to be a goldmine with a workforce of forty men and a few women. Brandy's sexual appetite was insatiable, and many a cowboy found himself riding the remarkable and still beautiful Brandy O'Kane.

Benson became their home; Katie and her sister Gracie controlled large knocking houses in New Orleans and Mobile. Both had married brothers from the oil dynasty family of DE Vere-Rouen. The sisters lived with their families on their five hundred-acre estates outside Pensacola called The Rialto's.

They had built five exact copies of the Viennese Rialto Bridge, and each bridge linked each estate to the other.

The women were blessed with twins, Katie had two girls, and Gracie had two boys.

Life was good in 1970, and Brandy cursed the world she lived in. She was old and yet young at heart. She cursed her dried-up fanny and her wizened face and dry tits. She would give anything to be girlish.

She had millions upon millions of dollars and would spend it all for the secret of eternal youth. She would give up her whole life's work, all seventy years, for one week of teenage freedom. She wished to be a teenager and die in her lover's arms. William had gone blind in the late 1960s and spent his days singing rebel songs and becoming an excellent fiddle player. He dreamed of returning home as many Irish wished.

Maybe the Germans, French, Brazilians, and other nationalities, as they retired, would want to spend their remaining days in the land of their birth.

The devil greeted her in 1970; she met her on the main street of Benson. She was a fading beauty, and she too had a problem; she had reached the end of her youth stick. She had to renew it; she carried with her a secret.

Into Brandy's life walked this German immigrant who sought the elixir of youth. Her name was Angela Monke, a fifty-five-year-old housewife from Hamburg. She believed in eternal youth; she had witnessed it.

She had been a nurse in Berlin in 1945 when the woman gave birth. This woman remembered the rejoicing of the German army over the French. She had a baby in 1946 and the body of a 40-50-year-old...The story was true; too many people knew the woman, and she knew the woman. She spoke about whiskey, but it was the water. Find the water source, the old lady would say, and you have found the elixir of life; the other ingredients would be piss easy.

Brandy set up a factory in Phoenix to investigate Monke's theory using whiskey and water but drew nothing.

Then, early in 1972, they received a breakthrough when Brandy swore she felt twenty years younger after drinking an alcoholic tea made of Sumatran spices. The effects lasted up to twenty hours but showed no physical regeneration signs.

By 1973, she learned how to use its effects to her benefit. She got her body to behave like that of a forty-year-old. Her friend Monica, the German migrant, acted like a thirty-year-old. They laughed, cried, and swore that one day, they would be teenagers.

By the late 1980s, Brandy and Cockeye's brother were hitting ninety but were mentally alert and physically fit, as was Angela Monke.

Katie and Gracie were approaching their mid-forties.

Their boys and girls were ten when more Devil's disciples migrated from Germany.

Angela Monke accompanied Katie and Gracie to Benson to buy a property of an ageing madam. While having afternoon tea at the Dustbowl, a conversation was struck up between Angela and Elisabeth Von Feldt, a customer, about where they were from in the old country.

Please insert disk two, and I came back to reality and realised this was an incredible story. I would immediately search for Mariah and get the second CD.

I went over to Grace. She was cooking a pair of chickens she brought from Benson and asked if anyone was alive at the brothel.

She said, "No, but she had shot two rabid teenagers eating a man's entrails. They attacked when they saw us, but she shot them in the head. These children spoke and looked surprisingly normal but had a cannibalistic bloodlust."

I wondered if the old boy knew what he was picking up.

"I stand to lose millions of the property if things don't go back to normal, and it will be a miracle if they do. Stay and have chicken; we are leaving this place for Paris, France, tomorrow at the crack of dawn."

"I have been listening to a fascinating story lately, and I wonder, Grace, where is Madame Fifi, the whorehouse keeper?"

"You say that you stand to lose millions. Are you a Madame Fifi because I reckon you would make a distinguished madam?"

"Don't be daft; I was referring to my rodeo skills roping in sexy housewives for orgies."

"We fly on the morning wind. All those coming will be having dinner here," and she checks her watch, "half an hour."

She opens a metal box and chucks in the two chickens.

"Six should be enough." She opens other boxes to reveal salads and beer.

"What about my stalkers?" I ask.

"Skeleton and Fathead, they are coming," she says, "period."

"What about my son?"

"Lots and lots of questions from you, aren't there? He's coming too; happy now?"

"I thought we were going to Denver."

"Yes, we are, and on to Paris, France."

"I know where Paris is; I've been there."

"What a well-travelled man I have for a friend. Run along and see what's on the telly, and I will give you a shout when din-dins are on the table."

"Where are we eating?" I look around for a table.

"Grace, darling, you are pulling my strings. I'll have this spot here," and I sit on a munitions box.

"It's nice and comfy, and the print of your arse is on it."

"Are you saying I have a fat arse?" she yells, and I retire to the trailer.

"God, she's touchy about her arse."

The news is on, and there is trouble everywhere. Brazil has become rich over the past decade and is on the verge of walking herself into a war with Argentina and her northern neighbours.

Through the Monroe Declaration, North America guarantees South American countries independence. It has moved two aircraft carriers to Rio's Brazilian coast.

A pitched battle took place in Drumcondra, Dublin. Six soldiers were found slain, as were several MIRA battalion commandos. Northern Police stopped a lorry on the Newry Road and found four dead and six wounded men and women. Several were Red Leg of Ulster members, and two were English criminals. The government has denied that they are Irish soldiers and have openly accused the English government of sending mercenaries to murder the MIRA. Ireland has formally asked the European Union to investigate and station troops on the border if necessary.

The EU has warned Stormont that they will annex Ulster if England does not rein in its killers. Military personnel in Ulster have been increased to 150,000.

It's been announced by the American Embassy in Dublin that they will view any incursion into the Republic of Ireland by English forces as an act of war against the United States of America. Germany and

France have offered Ireland military assistance if the Dail requested.

There have been a further seventy-six attacks by teens on adults. The authorities are to close schools in Illinois, Kansas, Nebraska, and New York. Parents are asked to supervise their children closely. The affliction seems to take hold during the hours of darkness, and they are perfectly normal during daylight hours.

These children have the ferocity of the werewolf but none of the physical attributes. They are not zombies but have the carnivorous appetite of a zombie.

In Ogallala, Nebraska, two sisters aged twelve attended a party for a retiring teacher at their school on a Monday evening. The teacher had a mishap, a flat tyre and no spare on her way to the school, and the party was delayed for two hours. The sisters were clean and well dressed and neither smoked nor drank nor took drugs. Both had responsible parents. The girls attacked their teacher, a Miss Walpole, and tore open her thighs with their teeth without warning. It was impossible to save the teacher's life as she bled to death on the schoolroom floor. The sisters then attacked the medics. The police officers zapped both and had them incarcerated in the town jail.

The girls continued to howl and open and close their mouths in a biting motion. It was too dangerous to clean the blood off their faces, and it was best to allow them to work themselves out of this cannibalistic frenzy if that is what it was.

Even though the authorities monitored them closely, the girls started to weep and cry out for their parents.

They could not explain or recall their actions but felt they were on fire. They wanted to sleep, for the worms would stop wriggling in their heads while sleeping. It was four in the morning, seven hours had passed since the attack, and a pattern was emerging. A further statement will be issued soon, but tonight, we report the first case of a child dying from this unexplained affliction.

The first Night Child passed away peacefully in her sleep shortly after four this afternoon with her family at her bedside. She was from the town of Hard Rock in New York State, and the small farming community that made up the city had been offering up prayers daily for her recovery. They are shocked and cannot understand what evil had entered the child's body and inhabited her soul.

Meanwhile, in Arizona, no activity has been reported from the so-called Death Snow; the authorities are still seeking the CEOs of EARTHCO. They have employed forty thousand people to screen and search photos taken at airports, harbours, borders and any crossing point with CCTV. All countries are cooperating, and an incentive of one hundred million to the government and ten million to the finder has been sanctioned.

The threat of conventional devastation has helped enormously. The US government apologised for these draconian measures. However, survival is paramount and must take precedence over trivialities such as national pride.

I have much to ponder as I ramble over for my salad and cold chicken washed down with lukewarm beer. I sit beside Grace and tell her what I have heard.

"It's brilliant that we are going to Paris. I need to find Wendy and stop this bloodshed that is taking place in Ireland."

"Such small countries have often been the cause of global conflict," she says.

Consuela is here, and I know that our travel plans are in motion and our exit to Denver is imminent. Grace says she will leave soon to be with Hubert. The flamethrower boys are with Fathead and Skeleton. Mariah and Becky share their food and drink with D'Souza, Bill, and Ben.

James is the last to turn up with four privates who are not privates. I want out of here to start the hunt for that Gudjohnsen and Dillon, and I will carve that East End Gordon a new arsehole.

There is no sign of Baba.

I invite Consuela back into the bushes where I've hidden a large blanket; she collects beer and follows. We sit with the blanket wrapped around our shoulders and drink half a dozen bottles of Bud. We undo our clothes and quietly make love in the bushes without a word. Not a comment passes our lips. The deed done; we dress and fall asleep to be woken by Grace.

"Let's go fornicators, roll call," and everybody heads for two large trucks. Everyone is here, including Colonel Potz, but no sign of Baba, Frankie or Hugo.

It doesn't bode well; I fear the worst for all three.

It's late, but finally, we are on our way, and board our choppers, and fly towards the Mexican border. We land outside Tombstone and collect two suits, probably Homeland Security, and then we go again, arriving in Lordsburg, New Mexico, at 03:00 hours. We are to stay the night and chopper across to Holloman Air Force Base in Alamogordo in the morning.

Grace informs us that we will be attached to the 7th Fighter Squadron and flown overseas. I'll believe it when I see it. We hunker down here and there and snatch a few hours of kip before being woken by Reveille. Damn it; I'm tired, but we are directed straight to the choppers and climb aboard. I check my possessions, especially my briefcase, but all is well. I need to get this money to Mary if I am flying overseas.

It hits me between the eyes. Grace, Mariah, and Consuela are of high rank; otherwise, why would Colonel Potz and General Hubert be so accommodating? More to the point, why is there such a variety of soldiers mixing within the same company?

"Grace, what is your rank in this American Air Force, and how come you are a brothel-keeper?"

"I outrank you truck-driver, we are on our way out of here, and I will get my wishes, come hell or high water."

"We are flying out with the 7th Squadron to Paris very soon."

"Is that Paris, Texas?" I ask.

"It is," she says, "but don't worry, you will get to see Paris, France."

"Stop pulling my plonker and tell me when we are going to Paris."

"Which one?" she asks, and I squeeze her nipple.

"France," I say, "France, frog land, which is next to Germany, kraut land."

"You can kiss that tit better tonight because we are off soon to Paris, Texas, and our nice little arseholes will be in soft beds with luxurious bed sheets. I shall put Hubert to bed with a gentle winkwank; I shall wash my hand and return to your love-nest where you can administer first aid to my damaged tit. You'll be surprised where we are going."

"Grace, you are one hell of a sexy ride; I'm off to see James and see what news he has."

The permafrost had thawed a bit when I ran across him with Hubert discussing the worsening Texan landscape.

I gave him a manly hug, albeit not adequately reciprocated. We bade one another good evening, me in a merry and jolly way and him in a frosty and aloof manner. But things had improved. No black eye and a half-hearted "would you care for a coffee."

Things were on the up, and we headed to the campfire and poured a couple of mugs of steaming hot coffee. We sat cross-legged Indian style, and he asked me to tell him about his mother and what she was like as a teenager.

I rambled on for over an hour, telling him every detail I could remember about the disaster that befell me at the school prom. How I ended up married to the Incredible Hulk with an insatiable appetite for beaver. He laughed and got up and said we would speak more.

I went to get up but found my legs had gone asleep, and I thought I would drag the rest of my worn-out carcass to bed, and so I did. I slept the sleep of the tormented. I was in the land of permafrost covered in sores and boils. I was running scared, chased by dragons spitting flame and acid. It burned my skin, which fell to the ground, devoured by my children with cloven hoofs and impish faces covered in hatred.

They cried out I was evil and had made them the followers of Satan. I was the beast from the Old Testament and carried the number 666. I had murdered the innocent, six men, six women, and six children. They held up photos of my victims covered in blood, their eyes staring at bony fingers, with hanging fingernails pointing accusingly at me.

Their mouths lipless with grinning grimaces mouthing the words "murderer, murderer, a murderer of the unborn generations not yet conceived." They could have brought salvation to their helpless ancestors through prayer. They could have helped release them from the eternal damnation they suffered for their evil deeds. Deeds committed in the distant past when man was entombed in his primitive lifestyle. Now they must walk the earth on the night of Samhain (summer's end) with no food or drink left out to quench their yearly thirst or pangs of hunger. There is no one to intercede for their souls. Their graves lie unmarked in pauper's corners where the weeds long ago have obliterated any sign of their final resting place.

Only an odd rusty cross bears witness to a Christian site. Such was the snobbery in the olden days that a miser who spent his life ripping off his customers with substandard merchandize could afford to buy an extravagant final resting place. Yet, the hapless poor would be buried in useless inaccessible sites. The priests would not offer prayers for these paupers unless their palms were crossed with silver.

I see older women praying for the souls of those who have departed this life. Each soul will benefit from the invocations of the living, each receiving a microscopic piece of forgiveness that will enable them to move forward in the heavenly shuffle.

I saw my distant great ad infinitum grandparents hold their child's emaciated and lifeless body. I witnessed hunger and starvation and the Horsemen of the Apocalypse riding their hell-fed horses as they counted the souls of the dying that would be shipped to the underworld.

I saw banshees roaming the countryside, letting out their piercing screams to summon the souls of the Celtic-speaking families of Ireland.

Great-masted ships lay at anchor at Ireland's ports as the country's wealth was readied for shipment to the wealthy landlords overseas.

I saw families die with grass in their mouths lying at the side of unfinished roads. More perished on their tiny landholdings, their entrails hanging between their legs, resulting from starvation and eating the most obnoxious herbs.

Time passed rapidly as the clouds scudded across the sky. I saw hundreds of thousands of impoverished, near-naked souls pile onto coffin ships and sail to the Americas. I saw my distant grandfather's grandfather and his family disembark in New York City. They became part of the Mulberry Street gang at the Five Points, the most notorious violent slums that ever-graced God's fair earth.

This was riven with murder, rape, and robbery, where gangs vied violently for political ends. Protestants are still trying to dictate to Catholics, while both shat on the Black man.

His wife, disowned and sold by him to a brothel, lay on a soiled bed riddled with syphilitic sores, her teeth missing as she mumbled prayers for his soul to be saved. She died the same day as her husband, who had joined the 69th Regiment of New York. He hit the ground with a bullet between his eyes in Fredericksburg, Virginia. He had returned to his god in his hour of desperation as rifle fire cut his comrades to shreds in front of Marye's Heights.

Ironically, he was probably killed by a fellow Republican, better known as the Fenians from the 24th Georgia.

In the few seconds, his brain remained alive, he reached out his hand and was whisked away to heaven by his wife, who had died moments earlier. She clasped his hand in hers and soared onwards and upwards to the heavens, bringing her prayers to fruition.

They had lost their sons in the first week at Five Points (possibly through kidnapping or press-ganging). Two young men gazed upward at the cloudless sky from the wagon train that ground its way across the Wyoming plains. A sense of well-being swept over them as they felt protected from the heavens above, and they knew it would be a safe journey.

They ran ahead to the wagon and called out, "Pa, we will be fine, and so will Ma and our baby sister,"

Their father watched them with pride and urged the mules on. I could hear him say, "I am a lucky man."

I awoke with horror on my face, for it was the face of a beautiful woman with finely chiselled features, her hard life having eroded her beauty, but I could see it was my mother's face staring at me from that whorehouse bed.

I never thought about my American relatives, and a cold shiver tickled my spine. I knew that my mother was dead. I had to get out of this place, and tomorrow I would. Was I going insane as I was continually having these weird dreams? I was dreaming history, and was this story relevant to me? But then again, who do I know that is sane?

I sat up, kicking off the blanket to see Grace looking at me weirdly.

"It would be best if you never sleep because you fight a terrible battle when you do. I noticed you last night; you were tossing and turning and gritting your teeth."

"I want to see my mother, and I'm leaving here today."

"Fine, fine," she says, "let's have coffee, and we'll go."

Two hours later, we have two Lakota's at our disposal; we are airborne and land at Roswell.

"No Alamogordo," I pipe up.

"Sorry, love, maybe next time."

"Why don't you pop over to Area 51 and have a deco at that spaceman they keep in a jar?"

I said, "I want to see my mother; I am going to desert."

"Patrick, this is the only way to get out of this place. If you come up with a better idea, fine, but stick to the plan for now. Even if you had a plane fuelled and ready to fly you to Seattle, you would be shot out of the sky if you didn't land immediately, and that would be curtains for you."

"Please stick to the plan; it's bigger than your mother. Maybe your mother is well; it was a dream, a bloody nightmare. We will be on the move in a few hours."

Sure enough, by nightfall, we were in Abilene. A phone call confirmed my worst fears; my mother was at death's door and calling for me.

Chapter Fourteen

The Greek

Tuesday the 20th of June.

Early the following day, we took off, arriving in Oklahoma City. From there, we ended up in Denver. Grace arranged for us to be essential passengers on a flight to Seattle. She said it was not time to go to Paris, France, but to keep in contact. She gave me a satellite phone. We were to fly to New York when she said so.

"No tricks, or you and James are brown bread, no questions either," and she kissed me full on. Treacherous bitch.

"I love you, Patrick," and she's gone. The rest of the mob is tittering and laughing at me. Fathead gives me two fingers. I'll choose a fat slag for him in New York, one of those night-time fillies from Hell's Kitchen. After all, the place might have moved upmarket, but many women hadn't.

The flight to Seattle, Washington State, took less than three hours. James had already booked a car, and we were on our way to Skipton Lakes. We would call in on my parents first, and a sense of dread gripped my innards. What if she's lying dead in her finery and I had not visited in a year? How will I explain that to my father, and her relatives pointing at me saying what a useless bastard I was and how she had suffered for my sins?

I wished I were back in Arizona fighting those vermin, but it was too late now. She had never seen her FIRST grandchild either. We drove into the driveway.

On the lawn was our parish priest smoking a fag with a glass of whiskey and a face as sour as buttermilk. Fear gnawed away at my soul, and I panicked that I would smash his face if he put his hand out to tell me he was sorry for my troubles, but he didn't. I stood there rooted to the spot; my mind was racing.

Was my mother dead? Maybe she wasn't.

I needed the priest to put me out of my misery, and he said nothing.

I remembered the words of another IRA man turned writer Brendan Behan. There is no situation so tragic that a policeman turning up can't make it worse, to which I thought there is no situation so bleak that a priest can't make it worse.

"Is she dead?" I shouted at him. "Is she dead?"

"No, Patrick, she is healthy and cooking you breakfast, even if it is evening."

She asked me to bless her and the family after her short illness brought on by a bout of food poisoning. A mysterious caller informed her that Patrick Dempsey was on his way home for a full Irish and not to spare the pudding. She sent to Seattle for it; I believe she got it from the *Fado* pub. They have an extensive menu, but you would know that you pisshead.

I was happy as Larry as I rushed into the house, nearly knocking my poor father over, and grabbed my mum as she was about to put my breakfast on the table. She slapped me one across the chops and shouted, "patience, boy."

"I have been slaving over a hot stove all day preparing this fine meal; the least you could do would be to show some restraint. Sit and wait for your tea," and she grabs me and gives me the most loving hug I ever had.

James is standing beside me, and it's evident that our mystery caller never mentioned him; it had to be Grace doing a spot of homework.

I get another crack across the back of my head; it's my old man wanting to know where I've been and if I suffered from amnesia. Dad is studying James closely, and with paternal surprise, he announces, "I never knew I had another grandson."

He holds my mother by the hand.

"We need to sit down," she says breathlessly.

"He looks like you, poor lad. What is your name?"

"Who's your mother? Oh, dear Lord, it's Wendy, isn't it?"

"Where is she? Is she here?"

"She was such a beautiful girl, and you chose the incredible hulk. I heard from Mrs Borski that she belted Mr Patel in the eye and frightened the poor man so much he was terrified to serve her. His wife says that seeing her sends him to his bed trembling for up to twenty-four hours."

"Sit and eat your breakfast before it gets cold."

"Are you hungry?"

"What's your name? Well, what's your name?"

"Mine's Bridget, and over there is Patrick, and yours is . . ."

"James, that's my name, James Anthony Dempsey Ivanovo."

"What the hell," she says. "Are you Irish-Russian? Never mind, tell me later."

"Here, I have a second breakfast on the hotplate; tuck in; it will put hairs on your chest and yeah, lead in your pencil," says Pat, winking at him.

I eat breakfast ravenously and gaze at my mother. I am sitting here eating breakfast my mother cooked, and I thought she was dead. Wealth is indeed measured in love, and I have it in abundance. I am the wealthiest man in America, and I have the family to prove it.

I must hurry to the incredible hulk and see the rest of my offspring.

"There is a planeload of relatives flying in at midnight," says the priest as he pours himself a generous Bushmills.

"I suppose I should send Father Tom and Billy Joe to herd them to the Crown Plaza, and from there, the tribe can meet to discuss the merits of food poisoning."

I sat long into the night, talking to James and my parents. When the Bushmills were gone, the priest was gone. We went to bed at four in the morning and slept soundly when a loud knocking at the door reminded us that the world was still there.

Wednesday the 21st of June.

It was the Ulster mob with their morphology; it would be homely to hear the yees and youse and listen to them talking about the wee square fella. I told Mum I was off to see Mary, and hopefully, Peter and Susan would be there, and if all went well, I would drive the lot over this evening. It wouldn't matter if Mary got pissed; she would be in good company with the priest and Dad's brothers and sisters.

"Father Jack will stay out of the clutches of your sister, Dad, considering the sermon he received on the evils of drink."

I asked Dad to take a drive with me to Skipton Lakes. I have to ask him about Ireland, and I need to tell him about Wendy. I have no idea what he knows or doesn't know, but I know one thing: he is well within the loop.

All agreed, and we sat down to fresh fare and watched the news on the portable.

The government is facing a massive lawsuit for half-burning Tucson. Arizona and New Mexico threatened to expel Mexicans from every town if they offered further violence. The Mexicans say they have to defend themselves as upwards of five hundred were killed and thousands injured.

Texas is under martial law, and it's uncertain what attitude the governor will take if Washington orders troops from the northern states. The old sheet brigade is out in force in Louisiana and Mississippi, celebrating their 150th birthday and burning crosses here and everywhere. The Klux are insisting the Mexicans take a negro when they cross the border; the coloured are up in arms and have burned three Klansmen on their crosses.

The Gulf states are still smarting from the putdown they received from New York over their 150th celebration of the Civil War in 2015. In the past fortnight, the Civil War songs have seen an unprecedented resurgence, like The Rose of Alabamy, Yellow Rose of Texas and When Johnny Will Come a Marching Home.

Children have attacked their parents, and three teens attacked their babysitter, killing her by eating flesh from her body. One of the children was shot dead by the babysitter's father, and the police are seeking him for questioning. The other two went into hiding and have not yet shown themselves, even though it is past time to return to normal. People are asked to keep an eye out for the girls from Skipton Lakes. The Washington State governor is offering ten thousand pollars for their apprehension, alive and unharmed.

"Bloody hell," says Bridget, "there must be hundreds of these Night Children; they seem to go feral when darkness falls. They kept two in a darkened room, and nothing happened until dusk. They seemed to lose colour as the light faded. Their eyes went blood red. It didn't matter that they were in a room of dazzling light. They behave zombie-like, ravenous and murderous in their thoughts and deeds."

"Armstrong De la Ville of the Hamburger Factory, it's said, has a daughter stricken with this malady. He has her airborne 24/7, so she is in a daytime zone."

"Because he supplies eighty percent of burger bars internationally with meat, governments are reluctant to upset their fat-arsed electorate, so he lands where he wants. It's a minimal inconvenience as he prefers to keep his daytime landings to four countries."

Bernadette (dad's sister) says, "That she has it from the horse's mouth that the Yanks are planning a special hospital and town at the Poles. It is for the rich and self-important people who find that their offspring are considering snacking on mummy and daddy's arseholes."

Jack (dad's brother) says, "The burger meat was causing the problem. Mad cow disease is rampant among the lager louts of Dublin and Belfast. Have a look on a Saturday night. The coppers use cattle prods these days, and when they wake up, they slink off home with the piss and shit dripping down their legs.

The strange thing is they are back the following weekend for another charge, and at home, they go to their mammies covered in shite. I've heard these women say that their wee Jack drinks too much of the black stuff, and he should wear a nappy if they are going to shite themselves in the pub.

The women are just as bad but go commando in their leather miniskirts, and it's said the fountain in Trafalgar Square is a cesspool on a Sunday morning.

"Wadya mean? Wadya means?" says Dad winking at me.

"You don't mean they shite in the Serpentine, do you?"

"They would never squat and do it in public, would they? Well, would they?"

He asks Jack, "Would they shite in the fountain?"

"Listen," Jack says to Dad but is cut short.

Before he can finish his sentence, Eileen, his beloved wife, batters him with her handbag. She warns him to keep his filthy tongue under control. Otherwise, she will have to spend the following week in church praying for his miserable soul, which means there is no cooking or washing done like before.

"All right, all right for Christ's sake," he whines and gets another hand-bagging for taking the name of the Lord in vain.

"It's bad enough that I must listen to this godless drunken rabble, but I will not have you go to the dogs like Patrick and his kin. Speak the way the Lord would have you speak, and to answer your question Pat, you thick-sliced loaf, he was referring to the girls washing the shit off their arses and moneyboxes."

"Do you understand? You do, good, run along with younger Patrick."

"When you see your wife, the drunken wench, Patrick, tell her Eileen will be excited to meet her later."

"I've been looking forward all week. It did her well the last time I bumped into her."

Dad says, "Let's get ta hell out of this place. That woman is not a god-follower; she is a she-devil with pretensions of being a god-follower."

I think they're mad, and I grab my jacket and head out the door. We arrive at Skipton Lakes just as Mary returns from town with a bagful of food, probably mostly liquid in content.

"Where have you been?" she snarls, and more to the point, where are your wages? I've been living on welfare and credit cards for the past month, you tight-fisted git.

"I see you brought the other git with you."

"How are you spawn-maker?" she snaps to Dad.

He gives her two fingers and takes the key to her door.

"Can't open the door, you pisshead; you smell of piss. Have you pissed yourself?"

"Let me help you piss some more," and he takes a bottle of Jameson's from his pocket.

"An old soak like you deserves the best. Here shove that down your throat, make sure its bottleneck first," and he opens the door and enters.

"You are a stinking clipe of shite," she mumbles.

"I'd need a major bogroll to wipe you off my kitchen floor. Why don't you commit suicide?"

"Och, Mary, give it a break."

"What do you mean, have you not had money from me, not even severance pay? Dillon ripped me off; I'm owed a pile of money."

"Yeah, I bet you spent it on hookers and booze."

"I want a divorce."

"Oh no, Mary, I'm absolutely gutted. How will I live without you?"

"Please don't leave me."

"But, on second thought, why don't you have ten thousand pollars? It will take you to a homeless shelter for alkies."

"Let's make love," she says.

"I will wait for you upstairs, and she's up the stairs with a glass, bottle and the wad of cash; no explanation needed."

"Don't be long, passionate lover," and she's gone.

"It's a fierce-looking animal she is son. Were you a bit deranged when you married it? How did you get two slim kids from that obnoxious cow?"

"Don't say another bad word about Mary; she is the mother of my children and deserves my love."

"I could have been a better husband."

"Tell me about Ireland and what the hell is going on."

"I'll cut to the chase. Fifty mercenaries landed on Antrim's coast about two weeks ago. They headed for safe houses provided by the Red Leg of Ulster. They blew up the boat that was returning to the mainland."

"A survivor was picked up by a MIRA sympathiser and interrogated. They were there to murder the MIRA high command and as many of their soldiers as possible. The RA had let it be known that a meeting would occur in Donegal at a remote farmhouse, where several company commanders would be present. It was let slip to a money-grabbing double agent who fed the information to the security forces, who informed the killer squad."

"The encounter occurred at the farmhouse, where the RA had over one hundred men spread around the countryside. They killed at least ten in the ensuing battle, maybe as high as twenty, but the mercs laid a ground fire so accurate they blasted twenty-five of our men with exploding bullets. There were no wounded."

"The situation in Drumcondra was not much better. Last night, they killed another twenty men who had met to mourn their fallen comrades at a private party. These guys know their stuff; word has it they have received reinforcements. They wear FCA (Irish army uniforms)."

"They are trying to drag the Republic into a fight with Britain."

"America will not tolerate any bullying of its Irish parentage."

"Your friend Wendy is possibly on Stonnage, and the mercenary's benefactors are incredibly interested in retaining the island. What for, god only knows? It's a rock, just about capable of sustaining a dozen families, provided you want to live in the 1700s with no mod cons. Battery power has helped, but I like to drive a car."

"In the old days, a man and his gun found refuge there, but today its importance has waned since they discovered our little navy with its underwater arm."

"Many of the deccased have been returned to Great Britain and a few to America. Counteraccusations between the two governments lead nowhere. It appears it is an attack by NODA (Northern Orange Defence Association) to wipe out RASC (Republican Armies Southern Command, better known by the acronym MIRA). It's only a matter of time before another prisoner falls into our hands, and we will strike up the band and listen to him sing."

"Dublin courts have given full title to Stonnage to this British-American syndicate. Three days back, the houses and livestock were dumped in the sea. The animal rights movement was up in arms immediately. Two of the most vociferous members were admitted to the hospital with severe trauma from being buggered, to put it mildly. Animal Rights issued a statement the same night, stating that the information they had received was false and no further comment would be forthcoming."

"I know who these people are, Dad; I have wined and dined with them in Tucson weeks ago. They wanted me to go to Ireland to help eliminate the leaders. Who knows where their information has come from, but there is one guy, Gordon Thatcher, and I'm sure he is ex-security force or army. A lot of this is tied in with a health clinic called EARTHCO. They are responsible for the plague in Arizona. I've been face to face with a Night Child and seen what they can do. I tell you; the whole state of Arizona is a horror show of epic proportions, and I doubt if it's over by a long chalk."

"You must come with me to Tacoma tonight and tell this story to General O'Rourke. By the way, men have been snooping around, asking questions about your whereabouts."

"Was one a spade?"

"Indeed there was, a bald gentleman with a gold chain, no doubt to remind him that his forbears were once slaves."

Mary came down the stairs pissed and asked if we were plumbers.

"No, we are butchers from the local slaughterhouse," says Dad.

"We are searching for a fat pig. Have you seen one lately?"

"No," she says innocently but . . .realising that he was referring to her.

"Oh, we have a right comedian in my house tonight," she says, "how's your wife?"

"I hear her cooking almost killed her."

"Mary darling, he was only having a laugh."

"Having a laugh, was he?"

"I'll give him something to laugh about when he's done crying," and she aims a kick at his balls, and he retreats into the kitchen and starts making a brew.

"That bitch is dangerous. She should have a health and safety notice pinned to her."

Peter and Susan turn up, and after hugs and kisses, we settle in for tea and a good chinwag. Even Mary, who has become quiet and demure, joins the conversation. The chat turns to a vicious attack on the teacher at Susan's school. It turns out we know the family. The Trentinos relocated from New York suburbs some years back and have six children; the three infected are under thirteen. So far, it has struck the boys and one girl. All appear to be pre-pubescent; the strange fact is that they are in the age range of ten to fifteen and have shown no signs of any of the Tanner Stages on examination. The parents had consulted with medical experts, but they assumed they were late developers with no abnormal signs of underlying health issues. A register of pupils aged ten to sixteen was compiled to determine how these kids had not reached any Tanner Stages.

"Their sexual development is being stunted by something," I say.

"Have there been any cases overseas?" says Mary.

"It must be what they eat, and it's strange that they are cannibalistic and ravenously hungry. Why not eat a lump of meat? I bet they are mentally deranged," she says, getting up to fetch herself a drink, "they are lunatics, and they go by the moon."

"Do they rave and rant when there's a full moon?"

"No, they don't," Dad says, "that scenario has already been examined but thank you for your contribution. Is that Jameson's whetting your whistle?"

"I bet Bridget empties a few bottles of Red Biddy herself each week," she says to him, "and you, you old git, I'm sure you were a Bowery Boy. I bet you had fun with those fairy men in the bushes."

She staggers and mutters she needs a rest. She shouts back at Dad that, "He should have taken in the cabbage head in and left the ugly baby outside. You could have tried again, but you did not have it in you, did ya and . . .a hard man is good to find, isn't that right?"

"Wake me up when we go to see the Holy Mother and her collection of demonic angels," and she's up the stairs sticking two fingers in the air at me.

I apologise for Mary's behaviour, and they laugh.

"I don't know why you bother; we know how she is."

"She is kind when she's sober; it's the drink; it's got a bad grip on her."

We sat for another hour, and I filled them in on my exploits, keeping the X-rated parts to myself. If they knew what I had done, all three would have expired on the floor from massive coronaries.

I tell Susan my dad and I are off to Tacoma and should be back later tonight.

James, who has been talking to the next-door neighbour about the little cannibals, comes in and asks why we are going to Tacoma.

"I can't tell you," I say, "they would not allow it, but it has to do with us going to Ireland. I will fill you in when we get back. Find out what you can about these cannibals and see if anything new is happening in Tucson."

"I'm coming," he says in a final voice, and I shrug my shoulders.

""If you must, you must." We move towards a large people carrier.

"You have no idea what I have been through trying to trace Wendy's whereabouts. I need to locate evil bastards, and they need to be murdered in cold blood. Trust me when I tell you that death is the best visitor these rapists can meet, and trust me when I tell you they need killing. There is hardly a psychopath alive that is eviler than these two bastards. I can assure you that death will greet them when I meet them, so no interference from either of you."

"I would not be surprised if they are with Gordon and the rest of the mercs; probably, they are the ones knocking off the RA."

James wants to drive; Dad and I sit in the back and shut off James from us. The drive was uneventful, taking thirty minutes. During that time, I filled him in on the details of the Russian restaurant and Dimitri and Wendy.

I spoke about Rachel and how Dillon and Gudjohnsen murdered her before my eyes.

I told him about Gordon and Margo and their connection to the clinic and Sheeree, who was so sexy.

How I dreamt mum died, and how much I loved him and what a wonderful father he was. We hugged and promised to keep in contact twice every week.

We parked at a roadside tavern, boarded a boat, crossed the lake to the other side, and continued our journey to a log cabin. Sticking our heads in the door, I was delighted to see a friend from the old days, Tommy Clancy, alias Time Stopper.

Before firing the Barrett rifle, he would mutter, "Stop, your times up," and rest assured it was. Your brain would have a second to ponder where that headache had come from as it exploded into hundreds of sticky pieces.

In the cabin was a Chinaman who turned out to be a Vietnamese refugee. He called himself Paddy Murphy, better known by women as the Jackhammer.

He earned that name from sexual conquests because they said you felt like a jackhammer was drilling you. Murphy had this crazy way of drilling your fanny.

He had spattered the heads of many an army man as a mercenary for African and South-East Asian governments. He was five feet tall and a more affable chap you could not meet on a long day's walk.

His family came to England in the mid-1970s after the Americans were sent packing from Vietnam. They were the earliest refugees picked up by a British warship from a Chinese junk they had paid dearly for. The British were impressed with his shooting technique as they headed back to Gibraltar. He won the ship's shooting competitions, and MI6 decided that such a fine sharpshooter could not be wasted in the English community.

The English concluded that he could spy on the IRA and UDA, and off to Belfast they sent him in their infinite wisdom. Here he was, fresh from a small nation that had defeated a superpower, and here he was again with another small nation being oppressed by another superpower, albeit with their wings clipped.

He changed sides and became the first gook spook within the Provies ranks.

After a year, the spying business was not for him.

He asked to be an assassin for the government, to which they readily agreed. I doubt they cared whether he lived or died, but he knew they had another shooter waiting to remove his head if he cocked up. They gave him a passport with an impossible-to-pronounce name. Nobody ever bothered to check if he was the real McCoy.

"The Republicans provided me a lovely passport direct from their passport office, and here I am, Paddy Murphy."

He put out his hand to me, "*Cead Mile Failte*," and he bent over and invited me to "*pog mo thoin.*"

There are two men dressed in pullovers and jeans and two in suits and ties, none of whom I knew. There is also a refined-looking gent whom I assume is General O'Rourke.

"*Buona sera*, it is nice to meet you," says the suit.

Mr Italiano, I wonder who he is working for.

"What is it that you want to know?" I ask.

"Tell us about Gordon and Sheeree Thatcher; they sure got a real Provo-hating surname."

"He is probably behind most of the killing," I tell him.

"I recognise his face but cannot name it, and before you ask, I have racked my brain, but there is no recall. I reckon he was in the security services, probably retired but still active; I guess he is now active."

"He and three others bought the island of Stonnage, and I hear it is legally in their possession. Bought for cash I believe, lock, stock and barrel. He wanted me to negotiate with the Army Council to smooth the transition to new ownership; he knew it was a supply depot and hospital."

"There is something on that island that they want. A company called EARTHCO carries out enhancing treatments on rich women. They can turn a sixty-year-old into a beautiful twenty-year-old and leave you looking at her with the mightiest hard-on you ever had. I've seen such women. They want the island as a hospital clinic to continue their work as the parent company is in trouble in America."

"Yeah, but why do they want that island?"

"They could own a tropical island instead of a lump of windswept rock lashed by the Atlantic Ocean."

"Why didn't you try to find out? You knew it was important to find out, damn it man."

"Listen *fangula*, I don't need a shite like you to tell me how important it is."

I know your type, big man in a suit; you're a two-bit cornetto seller."

He spoke to the other suit and left the cabin.

"Where has he gone?" I ask his friend.

"Jonnie has taken personal insult and gone outside to cool off."

"If he has a problem with me, I will have it sorted now," and I crash out the door and stumble into Jonnie.

"Have you and I got a problem?" I bark.

"You hava insulted me," he snarls, "and I challenge you to a duel."

"Let me get you a glove, and you can strike me across the face, you nineteenth-century castrato."

"That is it," he says, "we will fight at dawn; bring a pistole."

"Yeah, sure, where do you want to be buried?"

I go back inside. Spaghetti-muncher throwing down the gauntlet, what a plonker. He won't try to murder me tonight; however, I best keep an eye open.

Murphy watches Jonnie from the window as he and my father converse deeply. I continued to tell the other Italian about the rest of the gang and what I learned about the mercenaries.

"There is something on that island that is precious."

"Furthermore, check out everything you can find out about Republicans from the 1920s. They lived in West Clare by the name of O'Kane; they emigrated to America. I have been listening to a fascinating story about the O'Kane's; they were poteen makers, two brothers and two sons, and a slapper named Brandy who lived in Germany."

"They have a connection to EARTHCO. Their ancestral home was in a market town called Kilrush, and they might have a relative alive that could cast light on Stonnage."

"One of the CEOs of EARTHCO, Elisabeth Von Feltz, a German, visited West Clare; she was looking for the holy grail, whatever that could be."

Murphy and the Italian pull guns on James and my dad without warning, and the two pullovers give me a painful hiding.

"Don't go round insulting our brothers-in-arms. We heard what you said," and he leans forward and squeezes my balls.

"I could make a castrato out of you. It's a mighty fine yarn you tell, and it's also the season for cock and bull stories. Learn your lesson, boyo, or you will be given a comprehensive re-education course. Apologise on the way out to Mr Brasco and make it remorseful. Bye now, and don't forget your manners in future; your father should have taught you better; just because you are a big man doesn't give you the right to be an arsehole. Remember, you blockhead, that it was not just the Irish who fought during the War of Independence, but Jews, Germans, English and Italians with a fair sprinkling of others. So, it was in the 1970s and 80s as well you know."

They were gone giving me a quick heel in the ribs. I admire them, for they are indeed a band of brothers.

"Watch your tongue in future," says Dad, "and you, James, learn from this fool's mistakes. Brave soldiers will forfeit their lives for one another, just like your Marines. Nobody gets dissed, and nobody gets left behind."

"We better head back to Mary's and get a takeaway."

"I'm going into Seattle for the night," I say. "I will see you in the morning."

Brasco has gone, and we jump into our boat. Thank God they didn't take it just to be real bastards! I change my mind and decide to stay at the Holiday Inn in Tacoma, and I wave goodbye as I catch a taxi.

I ask the driver to drop me off at the Midnight Clothing Store, where I get kitted out in fine apparel, and I hail a cab to take me to the hotel where I register. A quick shower and shave, and I am calling for another taxi.

I'm going to McChord Air Force base this time.

I yearned to meet up with Staff Sergeant Ontopoulus, a sexy woman if there ever was one. She was Greek and had flown the Lockheed F-16 Fighting Falcon for the Hellenic Air Force back in the late 1980s but had bad-mouthed the son of a diplomat, who thought she should drop her knickers for him.

Slapping him for not taking no for an answer, his dad moved heaven and earth to make her life difficult. Without getting any male support, she quit the Air Force and asked for and got American citizenship.

She packed her bags and headed for Washington state, but not before father and son were caught in bed with two underage girls. Career over poppa topped himself, and his son Spiros became a vagrant in Omonia or Syntagma Square, Athens.

He told everybody that his daddy would be the Prime Minister one day and could they spare a drachma for Ouzo.

He got spat on by the Turks, Albanians, and others who needed to clear their throats. She had since seen him thrice, and each time she gobbed and gave him a squirt of highly concentrated bleach.

"*Kalispera malaka,*" she would greet him and spray his face with the bleach, and he would recognise and threaten her. He would be effing and blinding, and the cops would drag him away, giving him a few whacks of a baton.

He would spend the night among the hookers and junkies in the alleyways leading to Omonia Square. The bent Muslim junkies would bugger him while the hookers would blow him for his drachmas. He no longer cared as the bumboys shot him up with smack and buggered him for fun.

Such was the story she told me years back as I headed for the security gate. The driver dropped me off with a "get another taxi if she's not there."

The gatekeeper or the sentry on duty, whichever you prefer, rang through, and in less than five minutes, a jeep pulled up and whisked me away. She was off duty and beautiful as ever. It was two years since she got engaged to a pilot, but I knew now it hadn't worked out.

"I am on my way out," she said, "it's party time at the Kalamari Restaurant, and you have come just in time to escort me there. Help me get pissed on Retsina. After that, you can take me home and abuse me."

"We kissed passionately, and I knew I would always love her. We will dance to Zorba the Greek, break plates, and shatter glasses, but we will make love above all."

She jumps into the air shouting Opa and dances out the door to the jeep, and the driver takes off as soon as we are aboard.

Chapter Fifteen

The Night-Child

The night wind is chilly as we snuggle up, feeling like teen lovers. The cold disappears. We laugh and talk about old times, remembering our drunken nights together. We celebrated St Patrick's in March and Greek Ochi Day in October. We would meet in various parts of Tacoma or Seattle and celebrate other nationalities' holidays. Pubs took up our holiday specials and became immensely rich from the experience. They would be crowded out with ex-pats to the extent they hired national bands from the respective countries and brought in the necessary chefs. Paddy's Corner, one of the largest pubs on the west coast, opened in 2012. A country's holiday was celebrated each week, culminating in a massive celebration on a Saturday night. By 2015 the joint would be packed to the rafters with politicians and Presidents coming to celebrate their roots. By 2014 there were franchised pubs in every state. The penniless immigrant Viktor Petrov, the founder of Paddy's Corner from Vladivostok, Russia, returned to his homeland to spend his millions on his wife, Barbara Putina-Petrova. A drunken Ukrainian mud-wrestler ran him over by the name of Marianenko, who was celebrating his Independence Day.

When told in the hospital, he said, "Uk's celebrating nothing. I should have come in September."

We arrive at the Kalamari to be greeted by the owner, an overweight Greek with a bald head, and he grabs Nicola and gives her what I would call hands-on kisses. I am beside myself with jealousy, and he knows it as he watches me from the corner of his eye. He is talking to her, and she is smiling, and I give him a big smile and take her by the hand.

"*Kali Nichta Luigi,*" I say, giving him an Italian name, and we head off to the table, which happens to be No 12, with spaces for eight guests.

Luigi steals her from me and escorts her to the table. He holds her hand, his arm around her waist, slightly above her arse, his fingers piano-playing. He dusts the seat, feels her arse as she sits, and she smiles at him. He calls me a *vlaca* and shakes his head, as much as to say, what the hell are you doing with that turd? Two people are already there, and we greet and take our seats. The table is spacious and round.

He comes back with a bottle of wine and pours Nicola a glass, the bottle he bangs on the table in front of me; "*a gapimou,*" he says to Nicola.

"I hope he's not coming back; he is taking the piss; I know Greek."

"Oh, I know you do; he likes you, he told me so," and before I can say another word, he is back with a pint of Guinness.

"Drink, my friend, and be happy. I have a beautiful sister, she will like you, she likes Guinness too, and she will come to you later. She is scrubbing the pots in the kitchens.

He offers me a toast. I don't know where he got another pint of Guinness from, but there he stood in front of me.

"*Yamas,*" he yells, "drink Irishman; it will help you make love tonight,"

He throws his head back and guffaws, and he's gone. I'm confused about whether to like him or loathe him.

"How long have you known him, Nicola?"

The man is nice to Nicola, and I better watch my step; I don't want those Greeks taking offence and reaching for their shotguns.

It's bad enough he is threatening me with his sister. I will need to have my eyes removed if she's anything like him. But, on the other hand, the ugliness might have been emptied into him, and his sister might be an absolute cracker.

I haven't noticed the other guests, three women, and one man, they sit, and all seven are laughing and blabbing away. Magic, I am the spare prick, and I gulp my Guinness and call for another one. A glass of ouzo is passed over to me by a dark-haired woman.

"My name is Andrea, and I am Nicola's best friend."

"No, she isn't," says the other woman, who has a beautiful head of raven hair, "she only thinks that she is her best friend."

"My name is Vasiliki, and I am Nicola's best friend."

They remind me of Spartacus. I look at the other woman who hasn't uttered her undying friendship phrase. I am her best friend.

"What's the occasion?" I ask, and she, that is Vasiliki, says, "it's your new friend's birthday; it's Adonis Papadakis celebrating his 40th birthday."

"Good god, you mean Luigi, I say," pouring double ouzo into my Guinness, "I haven't baked him a cake."

The foods were served plate after plate. Glasses are clinking, and the bouzouki band has turned up. More people arrive, and the place is overrun with children.

It turns out his name is Adonis. His father must have been having a laugh.

"When is his sister coming from the kitchen?" I ask Nicola.

"I want to meet her, I wonder if she looks . . ."and a kick tells me to shut up, and I go "aaagh," and pretend to pick a fishbone off my tongue...and cooks like Cat Cora."

"What do you think?" Nicola asks Vasiliki.

"Oh, you best ask her," and Vasiliki takes me by the hand.

"Let's go and see if she is in the kitchen," and she winks at Nicola.

She is greeted along the tables.

"You are the sister in the kitchen, aren't you?"

"You have caught me out."

She calls her brother over as he is laying out plates of food.

"He relishes the idea of walking me home tonight," she says.

"No, he can't the Romeo. He is with Nicola; I doubt if he could handle two women," and he throws his head back and laughs.

"Vasiliki, I never asked to walk you home. I prefer to be with Nicola."

Mrs Cosmos comes over to Adonis, crying.

"She bit me," she tells him, your girl bit me," and she returns to her husband, who gets up from the table and leaves the party with his wife, giving Adonis the Greek two-handed gesture, the *Moutza*.

"What the…," he says, pushing a waitress aside with plates of keftedes.

He runs out to grab Mrs Cosmos by the shoulder, only to hear a loud scream from inside.

Back in, he rushes to find two men restraining his daughter; she has blood on her lips, and her eyes are red. I run to be by his side. I recognise the eyes from the whorehouse in Benson, and they are Night-Child eyes.

A man comes stumbling in, clutching his crotch.

"I need a doctor," he yells and collapses to the floor, ending up on all fours like a dog.

She is deathly pale, and her eyes are a deep burgundy. She snarls at her restraints, breaks loose one arm, and sinks her teeth into the other man's throat.

He lets go and grasps his throat, blood spurting between his fingers.

Screams come from the restaurant's toilets, and I run back with a bottle.

Her brother's eating his way through a girl's leg. I hit him with the bottle, and he lies on the floor lifeless with a lump of flesh hanging from his mouth.

His sister is struggling with her father, who has a bite mark on his face. He is forcing her face down, and she is lashing her legs to and fro, trying to get free, and he holds her neck in a vice-like grip, horror etched deep into his eyes.

He was celebrating his birthday with his family one minute, and the next, he witnessed the destruction of his family. Andrea is beside him, wrenching his arm away from the girl's head, but her attempt is futile until he grabs his chest and falls backwards.

The girl sinks her teeth into Andrea's arm and runs from the building, leaving a bloody wound. The police arrive, and within minutes, the boy is restrained and on his way to a secure unit. Adonis, Andrea, and the other casualties are going to the hospital, accompanied by a police escort.

Adonis and others have become catatonic and no longer respond to stimuli.

Nicola and Vasiliki went to the hospital, and I arranged to see her tomorrow. I've agreed to search for the girl. Her name is Maria. She will be awake all night, probably searching for additional victims. I suspect she will use her sexual attraction to sate her cannibalistic desires.

No one, except a lunatic and a sex-starved lunatic, would allow themselves to be enticed into a sex act with a teenager covered in blood.

They do not become mindless, stupid zombies but remain calm and calculating when this affliction takes hold. She will attempt to clean herself so she will go home, and that is where I am going, but first, I need her address, and I return to the restaurant.

I phone James and tell him to get to Tacoma, the Night Children are on the loose, and I'm going after one. I wonder where the two Trentino girls are. I grab a taxi and head for the hospital. The lad will be okay, but there is a chance he could turn out a bit stupid after his bottling.

"Nicola, I need to find his sister; they will kill her."

"Who will kill her, the vigilantes?"

"Yes, they will be out looking for Maria and the Trentinos. Everybody at the party heard what happened. I reckon she has gone home; I need her address."

"Let's go," says Nicola, and we are back in the taxi.

The driver babbles on about the demon kids until we get to the girl's house. He asks if we would like him to wait, and he agrees to fifty pollars. We head up the steps, open the front door, and barge in; no point being frightened of a twelve-year-old biter. Her blood is in the shower, and the bedroom shows signs of hurried dressing. Her mother's makeup kit is on the bed.

"She will ensnare a man, and he will get bitten," she says.

"She will be at Spanker's Corner and probably take them to the park. We will go to the park Nicola; I don't think she will have trouble finding a John for the night; after all, it's pedestrianised there, so she won't have gone in a car."

The taxi driver is gone, and it's potluck that another one is coming down this deserted street, and we hail him, making sure he stops by standing in the street. We jump in, close the doors, and tell him where we are going. We will not give him the chance to drive off, and we say Spankers Corner.

"I can't drive there," he says.

"I know," I tell him, "drop us off at Skid Drive."

He pulls up ten minutes later, and I give him five hundred pollars.

"You can pick your taxi up at the corner, get out, or I will break your neck."

He is out quicker than a hungry cock spotting a vacancy sign outside a hungry pussy.

Five minutes later, I slip the keys under the seat and head to the park. We work towards the bandstand and the remains of tents leftover from last night's evictions from the tenement blocks. Everybody is gone. We look closely at a foursome near the bandstand, but no one else is there apart from the girls taking it doggy style. A few tents are occupied, but there is no sign of Adonis's daughter.

We go among the trees to be threatened by a pair of junkies with a rusty knife. I laugh, and Nicola asks if they have seen a girl here.

It dawns on Nicola that it's her tormentor; it's the politician's son, and from deep in her throat, she conjures up a ball of flem and lets him have it right between the eyes. It dribbles down his nose to the ground. It was a right old loogie, and she must have hocked it up with hate, for it almost knocked him off his feet.

Recognition dawns in his raddled brain, and he lets out a yelp, which makes his mate, a cross between Gollum and Shrek, jump in the air.

"Goddamn *poutana*, I am going to tear you open and piss in you. Look what you have done to my face, my lovely face, with your bleach. I'm going to bleach you and that *malaka* you are with. Imagine finding you here, and he opens a jar and swallows a mouthful of tablets."

"Get out of here," he screeches at me.

"I've heard so much about you, you twisted little wanker. Why don't YOU clear off?"

"What brought you to America, and how did you get here?" she asks.

"Why did I come here? I'll tell you why I came here; I came here to bum you up the arse; that's why I came here. My mother returned home, and I heard from her friend that you live in Seattle. I asked Mum for your address, but she laughed at me. Well, she isn't laughing now," I can tell you.

"What the hell did you do?" I ask, "you didn't kill her, you crackhead, and where has that monster-headed friend of yours gone."

He swirls around, bewildered. "Jason Jason," he calls out, "where are you?"

"We have you all to ourselves now," and I rush him and give him a hefty knuckle sandwich on the side of the head. He hits the ground, squealing like a schoolgirl.

"Have you seen a girl here?"

As I finish my sentence, I see her and two other girls with men through the trees. They head for the bandstand, and before they reach it, they stop. The boys give them a piggyback, and they run to the stand. I call out, and at that moment, I feel something cold and hard on my neck. It's Jason with a rusty Magnum.

"I want to kill him, I want to kill him, Spiros," he shrieks to Jason, but Spiros is right up beside Nicola.

"Clear off, turd," she says, "or I'll stick that knife up your clap-ridden arse."

"Be an obliging girl, and the *malaka* lives," and he cuts the buttons off her blouse.

"Do something Patrick, he is going to give me Aids. Kill him before he forces me. You and you're goddamn good samaritan act."

"Keep cool, Nicola. Listen, smackhead, how about if I give you a hundred pollars, you can shoot up all night and wake up dead in the morning?"

"I'll have your money, your woman, and your arse. How about that?"

I try to strike his hand, but he cracks me across the face with the gun and shoves it into my mouth, nearly breaking a tooth.

"Try that again, and I will doughnut you. Tell the bitch to strip; it's time for her to have her medication," and he pops more pills.

Jason is laughing and squeezing his bollocks in his tatty trousers. I am desperate to help her, but if I do, he will kill me, and her fanny is not worth that price, regardless of how much I care for her. He slaps her across the face and shouts, "to get her tits out."

He will take off the rest.

She is frightened, and she removes her torn blouse and stands there in her bra, her nipples stiffening from the cold and fear. Spiros cups one tit in his grubby hand and squeezes the nipple hard, which brings tears to her eyes, and she winces. His hand is beneath her skirt when a series of screams echo from the bandstand. Those girls have felt the urge to snack, and it's advantage Patrick.

Nothing is comparable to an eerie shriek to distract a smackhead rapist.

Like a flash, I have Jason's gun, and he is on the ground, his windpipe collapsing. There is nothing like the first-rate piledriver of a fist to the throat to help you deliberate on the merits of life and death. He is rolling on the ground, trying to breathe and to take his mind off his predicament. I give him one hell of a kick in the balls, just in time to see two men waving frantically at us.

I kneel beside Jason and think of Rachel. Holding his head, I snap his neck. Nicola had put her blouse back on, and there was no sign of Spiros the Spittoon.

He has gone to ground. I will have to kill him because he threatens Nicola's life.

I could not live with myself, knowing that two women I care about could be raped and murdered this month and my beloved Wendy kidnapped and held hostage. But for now, best get up there among those fine young cannibals.

We head across to the bandstand, and all three girls are there. The Trentinos take off immediately, but the other bloodthirsty neck-biter is still tearing at a biker's throat.

I recognise her as Maria. Grabbing his helmet, I bash her across the head. She rolls over and raises herself on all fours, her eyes red with blood and her face contorted with rage. She moves with speed, coming up behind Nicola, and springs on her back. Nicola has anticipated her movements and rolls across the grass, coming up on all fours.

The girl is semi-naked below the waist, which strikes me as weird as the bikers fully clothed. Nicola is waiting for the girl to pounce, and when she does, she is ready for her, pins her face down, and grips her hands behind her back.

"Get the helmet and put it on her; it will stop her from eating me alive."

"Damn good idea," I say, "if this continues, I will start manufacturing helmets. I could call them cannibal hats. I fit the helmet on, and it stays on, but she will rip it off when she is let loose."

"Find a cord to tie her hands with," but nothing is suitable anywhere.

"Here," she calls, "take one of these off, and that will do the trick."

She crouches over the girl in the doggie position. Her skirts riding high, portraying a fine pair of thighs in silk stockings, red-laced elasticated top bands, and blue French knickers. I never realised I would be relieving you of your stockings while the Trentinos and your junkie admirer hide in the bushes watching. The biker is sitting on the ground, dazed, bleeding, and crying.

"I hope the girls haven't eaten him," she says as I lift her skirt, revealing her hips. A hard-on grips me, and she can see in my eyes that I'm horny. I provocatively roll down one of her stockings and kiss the cheeks of her arse.

"Take me here," she pleads. I remove her stocking and tie the girl's hands behind her back. Maria has rolled over and is looking at me through the visor. I can sense her eyes on me, and she opens and closes her legs.

She crosses her thighs. Wow!

"There is no one here," says Nicola, "it's two in the morning."

"Take me like the junkie would have taken me," and there is excitement in her voice, raw sexual excitement, and she will have sex tonight with or without me, and I drop my trousers. Nicola has her hand between her thighs and is stroking her clit, moaning loudly.

I stand up and give my cock a pull and a squeeze making sure the girl gets an eyeful. I kneel and enter Nicola. She is as wet as a swamp, and I push in hard, making her gasp, and she's looking at the girl as I am.

The girl has closed her legs and is trying to bring her arms under her arse but can't. I'm riding her in an orgy of violent sex, and I feel the fullness of my cock against her pussy walls. I am looking at the girl, and Nicola asks if I want to ride her, and I say I do. Immature girls should not have such designer bodies, and I see Nicola beckoning to the girl, who is slithering her body towards her. She grabs the girl's legs, drags her sideways, and lifts her top to show me her titties. The girl is sitting up, and I feel Nicola needs to orgasm, which she does. I ride her hard, wanting to ejaculate, and I hope the thought of underage sex will wane if she is underage. Relief comes, the ebb and flow cease, and we lie on the grass.

"Take me, set me free, and I will love you," she says to Nicola.

I ignore her and go to the bandstand to find her clothes. I see her skirt and the partly eaten leg of a man, probably in his mid-twenties, and a boy aged twelve. They bled to death, and I could see two men lying on the grass dead, probably the two waving.

Everywhere I go these days, I am surrounded by carnage. It's too much for any human being to digest; it's no wonder I am perverted and a killing machine. I return her clothes.

"The little bitch has killed up there as well. It's hardly worth putting her skirt on. It measures seven inches in length, and here are her knickers and stockings. You dress her because if I do, I will shag her."

"Show me your teeth; how can you bite into flesh so hard."

I see nothing out of the ordinary; rubbing two fingers over her gums, they go numb. I wipe my hand on her t-shirt and empty a bottle of beer over my fingers, which eases the numbness.

"I think Nicola, her saliva can paralyse your body."

"Jesus, Pat, she is a teenage cannibal. Why would you want to do that to the pretty little thing, and you could have a nice blow job of her instead?"

"Very funny; dress her and let the cops have her."

She clips the handkerchief skirt around her waist and puts her knickers on, taking her time. The girl stares at me seductively.

"She is still Virgo intacta," she tells me, "Are you sure you don't want a new experience riding a virgin cannibal? We could keep her, and you could ride her without the helmet when she turns ravenous. You two could screw while she's trying to eat you; she could be the praying mantis."

"I'm going to tell the police what you have done," she says.

"Go ahead," and I tie her legs a half metre apart with the stockings.

"Your friends have gone."

We lead her across the park to Spankers Corner.

"They will find me," she says.

There is a smattering of people out tonight, all up at the Kalamari, no doubt. Not a sign of a cop when you want one, and I throw a steel dustbin through a whorehouse window.

"That will bring the doughnut-eaters running."

The alarm goes off, and we sit and wait.

"Say anything to the cops about sex, and I will kill you, got that virgin."

She doesn't say a word, and I check my watch; it's four in the morning, and I think of James. I wonder where he is. He is going to be mighty sore when we meet up.

"Throw away the gun," Nicola says.

"Stick to the truth," I tell her, "Obviously, we will skip the "how's your father bit," and I take the helmet off the girl, but she just stares at me.

"Not hungry, are we?" I ask. I squeeze her nipple, but there is no reaction.

"Pretty little thing, isn't she? She reminds me of the hookers in Benson."

At last, a car comes into view, its lights flashing. A T.J. Hooker clone from the 1990s police show alights, walks across to the knocking shop, and rattles the broken window.

"Looking for somewhere to sleep, are we? You'd better have a satisfactory explanation or face a four hundred pollar fine."

"I have Papadakis, the little cannibal, and she has eaten no end of people in the car park. She was with two girls, but they ran off. I found a gun in the grass; will you take care of it?"

"Get in the car!" he says, drawing his gun, "get in the car; these little cannibals are dining all over Washington State. There have been hundreds of cases in the past forty-eight hours. A news blackout was enforced to try to stop copycat behaviour."

"However, they are eating their way through mommies, daddies, and one another's siblings. I've called for backup and an ambulance. Where are the corpses?"

I walk with him to the bandstand.

"Yep, the same as over in Green Park, mutilated and dead."

"Why don't any of these victims fight back? We are waiting for toxicology reports."

"I haven't heard any sirens," I say, "and I think they paralyse their victims somehow."

"Well, you wouldn't. We are trying to keep it quiet, it hasn't worked, but there have been over twenty cases here in Tacoma alone tonight, with another thirty in Seattle. You and your friend must come to the precinct and complete a report. We have a whole pool of typists working throughout the night processing information."

"How did you come upon our little flesh-eater?"

Suddenly, I am in handcuffs, as is Nicola. I had forgotten about his partner.

"Sorry, sir, but we need to establish your identity, what you did when you apprehended the girl, and where you got the weapon. Is it yours, sir?"

"No, it belongs to a dead addict, and his friend has run off."

I tell him part of the story. No doubt his mate is grilling Nicola, but the stories will match; there is much to be said for staying close to the truth. I told him about the party, the girl and the smackheads, and how we went to look for her as Nicola was a close family friend. How the two chumps first tried to rob us and then attempted to rape Nicola ripping her blouse. I unintentionally put his lights out when I punched him on the nose, only for him to throw his head back, and he took it in the throat.

"Good riddance to bad rubbish, that's all I have to say about him, and may he rot in hell for all eternity?"

"Keep cool, sir, don't traumatise yourself. Your lady is safe."

"And there was screaming and all the dying people. It was horrible, so I put a bin through the window to attract attention."

If this doesn't satisfy him, we will be spending our old age on McNeil Island prison with the rest of the perverts, helping to renovate it.

"Yes, sir, wait until we get to the precinct, and we will get it all down on paper."

"I want to make a phone call, and I want our lawyers present. I'm not too fond of your attitude, and we have done nothing wrong except apprehend a violent runaway. We will say nothing until our lawyers are present."

"Very well, it is your right, sir."

Nicola starts laughing, and we look at her. "I guess you have lost your prisoner."

"Oh, damn it, Christy, why did you not cuff her to the wheel?"

"I did cuff her." He walks to the car to find the cuffs hanging off the grill. Taking his hand out of his pocket, he shrugs and tells his mate she has the key.

"How she managed that as if I didn't know."

"Did you molest her?" I yell at Christy. "I will have you done, you kiddie-fiddler."

I swing a punch at him, missing him by half a mile.

"I want to know what you did to her."

"Sod all," says Christy, "she played with my cock."

"She said you molested her; fancied a bit of her tight little arse, did we?"

"Were you out hunting for nonce food tonight with your very own noncegella?"

"I figure we should depart your company," says Nicola, "it's late, and what's done is done; no point in all of us getting arrested."

"Fine, shag off," says Christie, and they head up to the bandstand as Blues and Twos turn up. We are across the road and in a taxi and gone. We book into a hotel for the night or what remains of it and ask for a nine o'clock call.

Chapter Sixteen

Who am I?

Thursday the 22nd of June.

Nicola returns to the base the following morning, and I head home to my mother. I get grilled about what I did last night by the Belfast mafia and their American helpers. It's fair to say they cut me down to size, and I took my traumatised masculinity upstairs and went to sleep. Getting up the same day at four, I put a call to Mariah to come and help me escape, and she promised she would, but to remain strong in the face of the wolf pack.

Grace phoned to go to New York if I wished, but there was no chance to leave the US.

"Is Mariah with you?" I ask.

"Is she? Let me have a look." She says, "What do you want?"

"I want to know if she has that second CD."

She says she has.

"Come and get it and bring James. She wants to go drinking with him.'

"Mariah says she never wants to grow old."

I spoke to my parents and James and agreed to go to New York the following day.

Friday the 23rd of June.

Arriving at JFK airport, Mariah and Becky greet us.

"Hi, James," and they link arms with him and leave me to carry the cases.

I trot along obediently, swearing never to let my mother pack a bag for me again. God only knows what's in it. Arriving at the hotel, we sign in and head up in the lift. I am displeased not to have adjoining suites.

"Is Grace here?" I ask Becky.

"Yes, why don't you go and see her? See if Hubert makes you welcome.'

"We are going drinking, and guess what? You are not invited. So why don't you go up the Bronx and see if you can see any Irish?"

"What about the CD? Can I have it now?"

"No, you can't, and neither can you have the CD. Patience man and you will receive it once I open my bag."

"I'm not going up the Bronx; it's full of African Americans and Puerto Ricans. This zombieness won't affect them; they eat people anyhow; James gives me a dirty scowl."

"Aah, get a life, James." I head out the door and go to the bar.

A few arsehole tourists are checking in or out. The women are well past their bedding date, and I hail a taxi.

"Sorley's over on Seventh, I tell the Pakistani, and he grunts. Any students there these days?" But he doesn't know. We get there, and I give him his fare and deliberately wait for my pollar change.

He grumbles in Spanish, and I tell him, "Yeah, your one too; you know nothing."

In I go, hoping that it fills me with happiness, but after one drink, I leave. I got to find Grace and headed for Fifth Avenue to a steakhouse where I ate my fill and who walked past my window but Fathead and Skeleton. Doesn't Christmas come early for some like me?

As luck would have it, the waiter is at my table asking if all is well.

"Oh, it's top egg; take this; I will be back in minutes."

I give him one hundred pollars, "Be prepared for two extra guests. Your tip is getting bigger by the second as I speak. It's getting a hard-on."

A woman laughs at the adjacent table.

I rush down the street, catching up at the corner of 42nd and Fifth.

"Hey girls, guess who it is? It's Paddy the Irishman, and I have a surprise for you two. How are you, Sprangler, you German sausage muncher, and it's the lovely Rugosa, lover of pastrami and other delicacies of the Egyptian countryside? Cum cum Sprangler, let us all have dinner and go on a pussy hunt. Have you seen Grace?"

"Are you paying for the grub?" asks Sprangler, giving me a poisonous, but I am your friend, for now, smile.

"Of course, my friend, my German Wehrmacht friend, yes, dinner is on me," and I manoeuvre them back up the sidewalk and in the door. The waiter is still there gazing at the one hundred pollars. I tear it in two and give him half.

"Meet me in the jacks when I leave the table," and he goes to give me the half note back. I grab him by the shoulder.

"Good God, no; your arse has the wrong decorations in front of it. I want you to find me a woman for my friend, my fat friend, one that looks clean, is white with a shocking dose of the clap, preferably with Aids; I will give you the details later."

"I can't do that; I could be charged with murder."

"You could," says I, "but who will tell, not I? I could end up resting my lovely arse in Old Sparky, which would not help me reach pension age. My arse would be sizzling, no sir, my mouth will be shut tighter than a hooker's fanny at the sight of a poverty-stricken cock, do a sound job, and you get the other half. You can keep your arsehole for your girlfriend's rampant rabbit."

"When do you want to meet this dogass (dose of gonorrhea and severe syphilis), for I know where to find the very trollop? I finish in an hour, and I will take you to a club, not any old club but a club for ladies who operate by candlelight. That should keep your friend in the dark long enough for her to conduct her deed of mercy. He looks like a man who could give himself a good scratch."

They sat there scoffing through platefuls of steaks and all the trimmings washed down with a bucketful of Budweiser. When Fathead had gone to the jacks, I asked Skeleton where they were staying, and between mouthfuls of prime beef, he told me they were at the 'Hyatt, Room 902.'

"Watch your back with Fathead," and he smirks.

Fathead returns, his gut full of my food, and the waiter arrives at our table in civvies, and he has a few Buds at my expense. I wave for the bill and tell him to take them to the club, and he says, "It will cost two hundred plus."

From a wad, I give Skeleton a grand, "and I will want change and receipts. I'm going back to my hotel; I'm sick."

"Where are you staying?" asks Fathead.

"Mind your own business hotel, do you know it?"

I leave and jump in a taxi. A few blocks down, I change cabbies and return to Mariah. She gives me the CD, and I go to my room. I lie on the bed and doze off; the dreams come, and I wake up sweating. Jesus, Mary, Joseph and all the rest of his family, how can dreams be so real? Why do I dream of people I've never heard of, and why is my mother there suffering? Dreams can be as vivid as if you were there. Maybe we are. Who is to say? Our souls could be teleported; perhaps we see glimpses of our previous lives or that of our ancestors. Who knows?

I saw a sign. Medicine Bow and I knew it was Wyoming from the 1960s western show, The Virginian. I can still see Trampas acting the bollocks as clear as day and the Virginian saying to him, "When you call me that, smile."

A woman dressed in mourning with a white veil stood by an open grave, holding a boy's hand as two rough-hewn coffins lay side by side. Two workmen approached with shovels in their hands. She gave them what appeared to be silver dollars, and they started filling in the graves; she took from her skirts two guns, tossed them in, crossed to a rig, and returned with two gun belts, which she gave to the men. They placed them on the red earth.

Tom and Jack say, "Compliments on your work, gentlemen; you sure know how to keep a man down," she walks back to the rig.

Their job done, they strolled back towards the town of Medicine Bow, drinking from bottles of Redeye. She takes two photos from her pocket, and I crane my neck to see who they are. They are two Union soldiers in their twenties. They are with another thirty or so troopers, and everyone mounts up. We are out on the prairie surrounded by hostile Indians.

Skirmishing, we withdraw towards Medicine Bow, chased by the Indians into the town. They're Cheyenne, and they attack and burn the station, taking two white women and an Arapaho squaw. Captain Morgan takes off after them with most of the company, and he sends Tom and Jack back to the fort to fetch Bob Crochet, the Indian tracker, and a string of fresh mounts. When they pass through the town, they hear the missing women are Mrs Orlinbury, the local hardware store owner's wife, and Mathilda Jane, her sister.

Riding immediately to their sheep farm, they tell their dad, and he catches up with the main troop before dusk.

The hostiles are sheltering in the Medicine Bow mountains, and it will be difficult to flush them out without casualties. However, each man is up to the job. They find the squaw staked out in the foothills, her entrails stinking in the warm night air.

Old Bob confirms the Indians are skirting the edge of the mountains and suspects an ambush. A successful trap is a beautiful sight; twenty soldiers are wiped out in a minute by a flood of arrows. Hand-to-hand fighting ensued, and I stabbed left and right as I retreated on foot. It was over in minutes, and Tom lay before me, scalped. Jack ran out onto the plain, followed by two soldiers and hostiles on foot, while two women on horseback raced by. The soldiers die, and the squaws come from the hills to loot their bodies. I ran after the women's horses, and finding a stray mount, I rode back to the town. I staggered to the saloon, crashing through the batwing doors knocking a man to the ground.

I was out of breath, and he helped me up, and in between gulps of air, I apologised. He introduced himself as Owen Wister. I cried out, 'They are dead, dead, dead,' and I stood trance-like.

I was back at the grave watching this woman and knew who she was now. She was the sister of those brave men. She turned towards the grave, lifted her veil, and gazed through me, sending a shiver down my spine. I stared at my mother's face, agony etched into her cheekbones. I called out to her, and the boy seemed to cock his ear like a dog. I called out once more, and the boy seemed intent on locating the sound for a moment. He jumped aboard the buggy, and they were gone.

Who are these people?

I googled Medicine Bow and Owen Wister and came up with a date of 1890. Searching the records further, I discovered the woman's name to be Maguire. Checking the census for 1900, I learned there is no mention of a Mathilda Jane Maguire. Still, there is a Henry, Tom, and Jack Maguire buried in the cemetery and another grave named William Maguire, beloved husband of Mathilda shot in a dispute with cattle baron Augustus Hickey over water rights in 1891. It appears Henry is the father, but the mother is not mentioned.

So, it must be the same family that headed west in 1863.

I remember one of the boys shouting to his pa that Ma and his baby sister would be all right now. I strongly suspect she died on the journey; otherwise, there might have been another child or two. I promise myself a visit to Medicine Bow.

Mathilda would have been around thirty in 1890. I must have a chat with my grandpappy or with a psychiatrist.

It's two in the morning, and I fancy a drink at the bar. Who is there but Hubert, Grace and Mariah?

"Ah, Patrick," says Grace, "glad you are here."

"Tomorrow, we fly out on military transport to Paris. In the coming months, we will represent the US in the commemoration ceremonies for WWI. A quota of five hundred troops is allowed for each country. America, France and Great Britain will be the first to march in the Grande Armee of Freedom. Great Britain will show four armies due to its independent nationalities: the Scots, Welsh and Irish. These will be made up of their quota of five hundred in proportion to the population. You may choose to march with the Irish, but you do not hold any rank that any democratic government would recognise, and they laugh. If you can prove enough Fenians were in the British Army, they may let you and your balaclava friends march down the Champs Elysees. You could march with the German army in their commemoration service to their fallen. After all, I would like to hear from you, Fenian boy. Was it wrong to march in a foreign army for freedom?"

"Yeah, you could march in the Paddy Brigade," and I turn and receive a jaw-breaking punch from Fathead.

"Yeah, you could blow up the Arc de Triomphe and any flat tyres, you child-killer. How do you like that? Here, have another one; you look starved."

Before I can react, he lands one on my aching jaw and another in my guts, and that's me on my knees.

I spew up, and he sneers at me.

"Full up, are we? He kicks me in the knackers. That bitch was a clapped-out Polish whore. If I get the clap, you'll get a concrete head with a plate glass window so you can see yourself drown."

He speaks to the concierge and gives him a backhander, and I find myself tucked up in bed, semi-conscious.

Saturday the 24th of June.

I'm awoken the following morning by Mariah, who lifts the sheets and stares at my balls.

"Stop that, you hussy," and I attempt to smile.

"They're okay. I expected to see a pair of doorknobs," and she says, "Breakfast is on the way up."

"The doctor gave you the once over."

He says, "You'll be right as rain after a few days. Why don't you stay out of Fathead's way? He hates you."

I eat breakfast and am pretty surprised to be so agile. I thought he had broken my jaw, and I showered, dressed, sat and watched the news. The international news is terrible. The virus has shown signs of resurrection in Arizona but only in existing areas with no incursions into virgin territory. Plane loads of chemists, biologists and no-alls are descending in ever-increasing numbers on every town in Arizona. They believe that only they and they alone can solve this problem.

Rabid mutations have shown up in adjoining states but in small numbers. The authorities are keeping a vigil on herds of livestock and are ready to wipe them out at a moment's notice. The incidence of Night-Children or cannibal kids is increasing, with over two hundred attacks last night.

Germany is preparing its celebrations and has encouraged its allies to celebrate its soldier's bravery, the glory that was and still is Germania.

Most of the southern Mediterranean has now had temperatures above forty degrees since May, which has resulted in the loss of tens of thousands of older adults and asthmatics.

The freezing winter was responsible for another 2,700,000 excess deaths. Combined with the previous two inclement winters, this has reduced the population by eight million. The poor are being frozen out of society.

Dublin's massive carnage from the early morning bomb blast has caused the government to sanction the military's use throughout Ireland. Additional troops from the EU patrol every county town. The death toll from the Republican Army's battle with mercenary forces reached three hundred last night, with ten known Republicans and seven mercenaries killed. Again, there were no injured, and it is now recognised as an attempt to wipe out the MIRA hierarchy.

President Clinton has allowed travel overseas but is finding severe restrictions imposed on its civilians.

In further news, Israel...and I switch to the Simpson Bastards, a spin-off from the original series, where Bart has had a lobotomy and is openly living with Milhous in Springfield's sewers. Principal Skinner has impregnated Lisa. Homer's deceased, having been murdered by the Flanders kids, Rod and Todd, and Marge has gone on the game with her sisters and Edna Krabappel. Ralph Wiggum has taken over from his dad and filled the cells with imaginary thieves and cutthroats. His dad is presently on death row, awaiting the chair.

He buggered Uter and murdered Sherri and Terry, the purple twins when he caught them in a crack house with Comic Book Guy and Professor Fink. He arrests Lenny and blackmails Carl to swear that Lenny is the dealer; he forces them to kill Nelson and Jimbo, who have gone straight and were studying for the priesthood at the Roman Catholic seminary in downtown Springfield.

Tonight's episode is about Rod and Todd busting out of Springfield prison, helped by Snake and his girlfriend. The ungrateful pair murder Snake and gang rape his girlfriend. They sell her later to the sons of Cletus the hillbilly for cornbread. I head to the bar and run into Fathead.

"Good morning, Mr Child-Killer," he says, and he's gone.

Who is he? I know no Sprangler's or Rugosa's. I go to the bar, order a beer, spot Mariah with the flamethrower boys, and nip across to her.

"When are we off," she asks, "for I hear that we are on a C17 transport bringing over the hardware."

I think to myself, what a stroke of luck to have my munitions factory at my fingertips. I should be able to dump a load in England.

"We will go to England from Stewart Air National Guard base this evening. We will be accompanied by South American soldiers, who are too piss-poor to have their own intercontinental hospitality plane."

"Remember, we represent the USA, so no crapping on the neighbours; they presume they are in a special relationship with us. We are the ones who do the plugging, and they are the ones who enjoy the receiving. Don't forget they are a nation of puffs and kiddie-fiddlers, so try to be nice because their island is one of our fixed aircraft carriers. Stay out of politics. The Scots and Irish are spoiling for a fight with the English and their lackeys, the Welsh."

"Uniforms will be delivered at 14.00 hours; be ready to board at 15.00 hours. You, Mr Dempsey and a few more will be travelling as artillery pieces," and she laughs.

"End of briefing, Mr Dempsey."

Why am I bothering about Wendy, and what the hell am I doing up to my neck with this shower of murderers? Even the women are bitches, and I go and sit alone. I will murder the lot of them, especially that pair of Black and white rapists.

Grace and Hubert sit beside me.

"Fancy a drink, old boy," says Hubert, "we are now ready to undertake our mission to the Emerald Isle, that island of saints and scholars. It will be extremely hazardous; death will visit and maybe take us, but the reward will be eternal youth."

"The devil will have to wait for our souls, he says, for God will not be pleased that we have also become gods. Remember his first commandment: I am the Lord thy God, and thou shall not lay false gods before me. Thou shall not seek out false prophets or lay thy soul in the path of idolatry."

"So," says Grace, "at the end of the day, our souls belong to old Nick, and our arses to the earth. Therefore, we should remain on this planet and trust they discover a new world with exciting options for longevity sufferers. If we fail in our mission, we die by our own hand or the hand of our government."

"Patrick, what if Wendy were twenty? Would you desire her more, or has she stolen your heart over all these years?"

"Grace, I love women, as you know, but Wendy is special. She is my son's mother, and I must unite them in this life, even if it means my own demise. I fear for my son James, and I wish he were not here, but he is, and therefore his destiny marches in unison with mine."

"I will help you save her, as will Mariah and Becky, and you must help us win our battle against Gordon and his army of hired killers.

Gordon does not wish to share his discovery with anyone, yet he believes the Four Corners will share with him. They have the deaths of hundreds on their hands, as you will find out when you listen to disc two. The flame thrower boys are here for money, and Bill and Ben are but lapdogs for the girls. Hubert, my love is with me because I love him. The other soldiers are here because it is their duty. They have been chosen to represent America, a country I love with all my heart. I know your family also does, for the freedom it offers the oppressed masses. I believe you know that Gordon employs Fathead and Skeleton. I know that Dillon and Gudjohnsen are in his employ."

"You also believe that you alone know the whereabouts of the biggest stash of weapons in Ireland's history."

I'm flustered, but she says one other person was in the know when you flew the plane into that underwater cave, and you and the aircraft were never heard from again. You decided to leave your private army and go awol. You knew you could not retire; the only retirement you would have received would have been permanent.

"You decided to disappear off the face of the earth after hiding their weapons cache. It is true that North Korea sold them to you, and the Greek flew them halfway across the world?"

"She taught you to fly at the same time. She landed here last night."

"I know, of course, I know, she is my pilot, not yours, and don't forget it, Grace."

"You are on Interpol's most-wanted list. Your fingerprints were on those bombs, and you were ultimately responsible for the carnage. I don't have any sympathy for you. To be truthful, you turn my stomach. You are a murdering bastard, but we need you for that arms cache."

"I, too, am taking my army to Ireland to fight for that lump of rock. I intend to have it one way or the other, or at least have control of its resources."

"I knew there was something special on that island," I tell her.

"What is it, what is so important that hundreds must die...? Why is it so important to wipe out the MIRA? Is it because of Sinn Fein's rise to power, or do you fear the future under a so-called ex-terrorist organisation?"

"Aaah, don't worry about it," and she orders another drink, "tomorrow, we will not be here. Understand, Patrick; others have a say in what happens."

"They will not hesitate to kill you and your whole family, so cooperate fully, or you will be skinned alive and fed to those sex-perverted cannibals. Do not disappear, or your family will die; do not make phone calls except on the satellite phone, or your family will die. Do anything without my permission, and your family will die."

"You don't want to see your old mother taking it up the arse from a mad lunatic as he squeezes the life out of her."

"James is here too and is seeking his mummy; he knows the shit smells terrible, but he has no idea how bad the stink will get. He is a US marine, travelling to France legally and will probably never see that wild rainy country that spawned his murdering ancestors."

"We are going to be friends now, isn't that right, Patrick?" Becky comes over.

"He knows the rules; leave him alone," says Grace.

Becky bends over to kiss me, but I push her away.

"What did I say," says Grace, "what did I just say?"

"We are friends here now, so apologise and accept the kiss."

Seeing the writing on the wall, I said sorry. I tried to kiss her passionately, but she pulled away and said, "So you are hungry for me."

"Be patient; sex is a mental act carried out in a physical environment."

"I need to phone my parents and my family."

There is no point in Peter and Susan teaching this lot their timetables. I'm sure they know how many bullets they need to give you, one in the head and two in the heart, should you spot four people who require such treatment.

I wish Mary were here; she would bust their heads in her first attack, empty a few gallons of beer down her throat, and wash them away in a deluge of piss.

"I'm going back to my room to shower. Send my uniform up, pleasant peasant."

I leave them to murder me in their thoughts. I wonder if I will have any dependable friends or even one friend on this mission. We will land in England, not France, where they talk out of their noses and pretend to be impressive lovers.

The question is, why are we landing in England? There is no point in its favour.

"You wait for me, mademoiselles. I will show you what an Irishman can do with your petite fleur, especially when digging in your scented garden with his shovel."

At 14.00 hrs, I hear a knock on my door and a garment bag is handed to me. I unzip to find I am a private from the Republic of San Matador, a new republic hewn from Brazil's rump. I remember reading that Brazil insisted that it took independence and forced most of its Colocca Indians into it, with a fair proportion of its homeless.

I am a member of the poorest army in the world. I probably will have a bow and one arrow as our most up-to-date weaponry.

I lay the uniform on the bed and realise the colours are of puking drunks on a Friday night on O'Connell Street, Limerick. The browns and greens stand out, as do the yellows. I put my uniform on, and it fits me like a glove. I have a Heckler and Koch as a sidearm and feel terrific.

I head to the lobby, where Mariah is in a lovely cut Marine uniform, not necessarily cut for military action. She ranks as a sergeant and is extremely attractive to an enemy's cock. He would have no trouble discharging his weapon in her face and enjoying the close hand-to-hand combat.

Military vehicles are standard these days on city streets because of the Arizona crisis and the Mexican issue. A quarter million US soldiers and just as many from Mexico are on the border. The ethnic cleansing is in full swing, with sore-arsed Yanks dragging their damaged carcases across the border and Mexicans moving in the opposite direction. Body bags are in demand on both sides of the border.

At 15.00 hrs, the vehicles are outside the hotel. I march out with my head high. Fathead and Skeleton are snickering at me, and even Grace has a smile. I bet this isn't even a military uniform.

If the Chief of Staff designed this for San Matador, I could only say he is used to being shat on.

I spot Skeleton and Fathead.

"I am not travelling with 'em," I tell Grace, for if I do, I will kill them, and I mean it.

"Don't worry, they are not on the same transport, so you are safe, but you must cooperate in England. I shall have all of you fight to the death, and the last person standing will stay standing, and if you get seriously injured, you die. This is no picnic; we could die because of one person's vendetta. We are going out on the first C17 with one hundred troops and twenty piggybackers. The same applies to the next plane. You and a few chosen personnel, I like that word, personnel, are going as military equipment. We will lose a few troops on the way, and you and your comrades will take their places."

"They are counting the heads in; you can be sure the English will count them all out. Your head will be disguised as a Matadoran private. We don't want them to discover you are a crazy bomber, more dangerous than Osama-bin-bombing; they would lock you up and throw away the key."

"I didn't put that..." Yeah, yeah, I heard it all before; the bomb disposal defused it and put it outside the school to blast those proddy mummies.

"Grace, I know you. I need you to believe me, and I will hand myself in when this is over as soon as Wendy is free and safe."

Another truck is in the hotel car park. A dozen soldiers wearing my puke and vomit uniform jump out and start bladdering away in Portuguese. A sergeant comes and puts his hand out, in a give me your papers.

"I haven't got any papers," I bark back, and quick as a flash, he has a gun trained on me. He barks another order, and half a dozen soldiers train an array of M4 carbines on my noggin. My hands reach for the heavens, and I glance at Grace and Hubert, who look the other way, laughing.

"Lower your paws, frightened Irishman," he says, offering me his hand.

Finn Kennedy-Barros at your service, and I look at him with surprise.

"Wild geese, my boy, wild geese are what my forebears were."

I am relieved to be out of this jam; the only problem is that Finn is another of Grace's lackeys.

"Right," says Grace, here's the craic, as you would say. Get in that munitions box, and we will drill holes in it, hopefully not through your head. We will break the lock so it can't be opened, and you will be loaded without fuss. Hubert and I will be on the flight with you, as will the flamethrower boys and the Matadorans. Finn is coming to Ireland, and trust me, Patrick, heads will roll when we open up there.

"Don't forget what you are there for, Wendy and nothing else."

"We will whack East End Gordon and get your Wendy back, and you can play with her worn-out crack. Before that, you will do as you are told, is that understood for the final time."

"It is," I roar, "' it's sunk in completely. It's carved in capitals on my wooden head. I'm Grace's lackey."

"Good, now get in the truck and the box; you are not the only incognito on this trip."

I do as I am told. This mission will be worth tens or hundreds of millions if successful. Yet Grace can't believe in its ultimate success since she has taken that million; conversely, a million pollars should not be sniffed at but gobbled up instantly. Fathead is not here; he would block my breathing holes. Good old Grace must have thought of it. Finn takes roll call, fourteen Matadorans, six Flamers, Grace, Hubert, Becky, Captain Claus Monke and General Ignatius O'Kane, amongst others.

It's the O'Kane, Cockeye's lot; I've been reading about them. This is big, Brandy and William, also known as Cockeye's brother. I wish I had time to ask Dad about them.

"Grace, Grace," I yell out, and rifle butts start pounding on my new bijou home. I'm left with ringing ears but not enough ringing to block out the angry threats of suffocation and a dip in the Hudson if I whisper one more word. I best shut up.

I close my eyes and ponder Mathilda Maguire. Who could she be?

I doze off trying to picture Medicine Bow. It's windy, and the train is puffing into the station as Mathilda stands on the platform; flags and banners are fluttering in the cool summer air, proclaiming the third of July. Statehood is the reason for the banners, one day before the fourth of July. She and her son are the only passengers to board the train and a cloud of smoke billows as it puffs out of the station.

The smoke billows around, causing me to go into a coughing fit, and as the smoke clears, I realise that I can hear cannons and the cries of wounded men. I am lying in a muddy trench as bullets whine overhead, and I listen to the hurried breathing of men beside me. Where am I? I turn and stare at my uniform.

I'm in an army being shot at, which is certainly not an Irish or British uniform.

"Help me," a youth cries out, and I see a soldier holding his guts in with his hands.

"Mom, Mom, where are you? Help me, Mom, where are you," and I am grief-stricken at the sight of this boy; yeah, he is only a boy dying before my eyes. Other soldiers look on with apathy, and I turn and take his hand. He is fumbling with his bloodied hand in his jacket pocket, and I help him find what he seeks, a rosary bead set, and I place it in his hands.

He is praying, and I note that he is praying in Latin and beseeching his mother and father in a Bronx accent. I command the other soldiers to help, but they continue smoking and cleaning their weapons. They can't hear me; it's a dream, and the most terrible loneliness and helplessness grip me, and I know this boy had died decades ago.

I recognise the uniform and the insignia: the Fighting 69th, the incredibly famous Irish/ American Regiment that fought five wars and campaigns. A stretcher-bearer turns up, dragging a stretcher behind him, and he tumbles the boy onto it. I hear words being exchanged. He pulls a gun and shoots an insolent soldier; the other two grab the stretcher, and I follow the smoke, the cordite burning my eyes.

We are in open fields where lines of dead and wounded lie on the grass. Several have their eyes bandaged, and a priest blesses or gives the last rites to a soldier. I see it is the boy with the stomach wound. I hear the priest saying it will be tough on his mother and her bad health.

"I knew Mrs Maguire; she is a kind woman always available to help at the mission."

"I will recommend him for the Medal of Honour," and the smoke clears, and I see that it is two characters from my favourite Cagney film. Pat O'Brien and George Brent played Father Francis Duffy and Wild Bill Donovan. I wonder where James Cagney was on the battlefield.

"Did you hear that Joyce Kilmer died today," says the priest.

"I did. I wish I were with him," says Donovan, "this forest is causing death and destruction, but it will be over soon."

Donovan has Maguire's dog tags in his hand.

"Jimmy Maguire was a brave young man with his life ahead of him. He wanted to join the military like his dad. He fought the Plains Indians did his father, knew Armstrong Custer? Many of his men were Irish, and he liked them singing an Irish drinking song called Garryowen; he made it the song of the 7th Cavalry

Regiment. Comanche was reputed to be the only horse to survive the massacre. His owner, Irishman Captain Myles Keogh, was the lone soldier not mutilated by the Indians. The reason often cited was that the Indians assumed it would be bad medicine to mutilate a man's body wearing Papal medals. He fought with the defeated Vatican army but was selected for the Papal Guard. Seeking wild west adventure, he headed for the American Civil War, and as they say, the rest is history."

There is a great deal of noise and shouting, and I return to reality and realise I am being carried. I hope it's not to the Hudson.

"We are putting you aboard the C17, your old son of ma deuce," a gruff voice hollers through the air holes. It references John Browning's M2 machine gun, invented at the end of WW1 and still popular because of its accuracy and reliability.

"Keep your mouth shut until you are let out because we have Military Police searching for deserters."

"I need a shit soon," I tell him.

"You better hang on to it because we won't be loaded for another hour."

I feel the crate going up a conveyor belt, and I'm in. I lie there reflecting on Ireland, how I swore I would never return, and how events can change your life at a moment's notice.

A month back, I was a happy lorry driver with a lesbian wife, two grown-up children, and a bit of spare at different truck stops. I hadn't always lived with Mary. I had been away for extended periods, often months at a time. She was there when I returned, even if she had just feasted at a beaver-eating competition.

I was going on a hazardous mission, more dangerous than any I had ever undertaken, and I had made no financial arrangements for her future. Grace's pollars will be mine, and I will send them to her; yes, that will be my priority in England. Grace will have them with her because she won't return to America quickly.

I will relieve her of that worry, and I fall asleep.

I'm standing over a grave with a woman and two children; this is becoming a habit. There is also an older woman dressed from head to toe in black, reminding me of those Italian women trooping to the graveyard every week to lay flowers on their husband's graves. As I stand there gaping at rows of white headstones, I wonder whether they do it out of duty or love. Still, it is nice to be remembered.

This is a military cemetery, and I find myself gliding through the air and descending on the nearest headstone. The old one flicks a handkerchief, and I am lying on the ground. Satisfied with her work, she puts it back in her handbag. She takes out a pamphlet, opens it as they walk further, and stops beside a row of graves. In front of my eyes are three graves, William, Patrick and James, who died in 1945 and the surname Maguire-Dempsey.

Who the hell do you think you are, comes to mind. I am not just a Dempsey, a hero and a demon of the Irish Republic, but related to the heroes who fought for a free Europe. I'm a member of a family of international freedom fighters. This most incredible honour can be bestowed on any family.

The younger woman places a locket on the grave with the picture of two youngsters, probably the two with her, and the date is 1959.

The wind has picked up.

The souls of the dead whirl amongst the hundreds of relatives thronging the graveyard on this sunny day. It must be mid-summer. I wonder if people are as eager to visit during the frosty winter months when these soldiers may have died.

I seem to be in another cemetery or part of it, for I am at the boy's grave with the open stomach, poor lad. His name was Patrick, and he died in September 1918. I see him, fit and healthy, and with his three sons, gazing in admiration at the children and talking the talk of the dead. It is not for mortal ears; they are waving at the sky and beckoning someone to come.

Thunder rumbles overhead, and a flash of lightning in the distance beckons the clouds to darken the skies. I see Union soldiers, and I count three Confederates alighting beside the children, nodding and agreeing. They are happy with the fruits of their sons, grandsons and great-grandsons.

The wind is whipped up as the departed souls try to stop their relatives from leaving before the storm. All to no avail, they cannot hold a grip on them, and in their panic, they are knocking one another over. A gust of wind blows over the old lady. The woman helps her to her feet, her face open to the elements, her veil on the ground.

I am not surprised, it is my mother's face, and a fear gnaws away at me. Is she dead?

Inside the cemetery, other soldiers, hundreds to be exact, stand in different uniforms. Many young and older women in various dated outfits stand outside. The most senior soldier wearing a Boston minuteman uniform, tattered and probably from the wars of independence, either 1775 or 1812.

Only American heroes are allowed to enter this hallowed ground, and there is a noise like a door slamming, and light pours from the heavens, and I think the Lord has come for me. It is time to ascend to paradise, but I realise that my metal home has been opened, and hands lift me out.

"Where the hell is your brain, and you," says Grace, "you have a black darkness surrounding you. You look ashen. Have you been dreaming? You should have a word with your priest, you pagan; here, have a coffee; you give me the heebie-jeebies."

"I feel the creeping dead are climbing into my body and hiding in my soul," I say. "Grace, you know I have nightmares, now I have them in the middle of the day. I have been dreaming about a Maguire family; they have a Dempsey in the name now. I think they are my relatives. I've never heard of them. I've not heard of any relatives except my father's family branch; fascinating that I haven't been told of my mother's side."

"It's even more depressing that I never asked, never thought she had any. It's always my mother's face, and she is at a grave; she will be at my grave if this keeps going forward. This cannot be."

"I have news for you," says Grace, "we have been stuck here for the past ten hours, so you probably still dream at night."

Chapter Seventeen

To Kill an Orangeman

Sunday the 25th of June.

The city of New York is being eaten alive by little cannibals. There have been over four hundred reported cases in the last twelve hours. They are taking bites out of people; mummies and daddies are suffering the worst. The National Guard is out, including the Fighting 69th; they were the first to respond, just like 9/11. If we are unlucky, we will shoot black cannibals up in Queens and well-heeled white cannibals roaming Fifth Avenue. Hubert has gone to air traffic control to see if we can get airborne, and he has half of Grace's money.

Bloody hell, bribing the air traffic controller, I cross to the tower, but it's too late; he is on his way back. I mosey up to him and ask if the price was right, and he says, "Yes, but traffic is grounded for the next hour or twelve."

"So how much to get airborne?"

"Sod all, there is nothing he can do; we must wait."

"Get back in the plane, you Matadoran prick, before somebody asks you what the capital of Portugal is."

"You know what, General Hubert, I am going for a fat meaty shite, hot and steaming, and I shall let it slide out as if it was a torpedo."

I scamper off without hearing his retort, ".....ignorant prick; I hate the Irish."

Night falls, and the news is dreadful. America was entering the throes of agony, according to newsreader Elisabeth Horley. Riots continued on the border. The Texans were herding the Mexicans into cattle wagons, dumping them at the wall, and chasing them through gaps they had created. The Mexican Army was helpless, losing over a hundred troops in a skirmish with the Texan civilians.

President Clinton had warned Mexico to stand down or face them nose to nose.

The decision was taken out of her hands at 18.00 hours when the Death Snow re-activated along the border and inside Mexico. Texas and Arizona showed a continuous line on their boundaries. Large patches had shown up in Kansas, Utah, New York State, and Christ only knows where else, she whispered as an afterthought.

She was immediately suspended, and Gus Sissons took over. However, he laughed so much that it was a full minute before he could muster enough composure to continue.

At the same time, marauding packs of animals had turned up in these states, likely driven out into the open by the virus. Each site has teams of scientists searching for underground storage facilities belonging to EARTHCO.

An entire one-hour emergency programme will be shown at midday. Parents are advised to keep a close eye on their children during the hours of darkness. If necessary, they are to be cuffed and kept under constant supervision. Do not attempt to take them to the hospital, as they will be shot if they try to escape. All ex-military, police and security staff report to their nearest precinct.

All adventures have their ups and downs.

This adventure of mine was stuck in the middle. I had been going around in a circle since day one, and right now, I could see this shagging Colonel Potz on the way over to Hubert.

If I could read the shit lines properly, I would reach for a bog roll. Finally, a truck stops, boxes are thrown out, and I head across to Hubert.

"Us Matadorans want to be in the thick of things," I yell at him, and Hubert takes one look at my uniform and laughs.

"That surely will stop any little cannibal taking a bite out of your arse when he sees that attire. They will be at County Hall complaining to the Jewish lobby that they don't like the cut of your jib, which has frustrated their appetite for ready-wrapped meat."

"Permission to guffaw with you," I say in a retard voice.

"Ah, a bit of a Pedro Paddy, I see. Got that brogue accent too, have we," a voice spits out the words in a broad Belfast accent. Joining foreign armies are we, my old mocha. "You wouldn't be one of those new-style Ra-Ra's, those new Republican boys still wanting back the land for nothing, conveniently forgetting that they did not own it in the first place."

"Are you still trying to sell your miserable child-killing skills to those South American cocksucking pygmy Indians? I see. I will have to keep an eye on you, a watchful eye at that. Otherwise, you might get ideas above your station, you trench-digging navvy."

That was it; he was brown bread, and Hubert knew it. Hubert stood there, transfixed. I produced a machine gun of a knife from my boot and rammed it into him at least twenty times in twenty seconds.

"Piece of sectarian shite. Come with me, Hubert," and I go inside the plane.

"Where is everyone?" I ask poor Hubert, who is abhorred by the cold-blooded murder that has taken place.

"I don't know," he whispers, and I grab him by the shoulder and march him across the tarmac to a building with the words, award-winning cask and craft beers, wines and spirits.

I order two double brandies and pour one down Hubert's throat.

"You are my best friend now, Hubert darling, I tell him, and anybody picks on you, you tell me, and they are history."

Grace is staring out the window at the plane. I indicated to the barman to pour again and give another to Hubert. He swallows in one gulp and is as red as a beetroot, no doubt with an excellent feeling of warmth spreading through his belly.

I take my brandy and one for Grace, stroll across, and whisper, "Where is my Hubert," in her ear, and she turns startled.

"Where is he," she asks, concern on her face.

"You do love him," I say, and she nods, "because he is kind, not a nonce like you, and a murderer to boot."

"Oh well, that's grand, isn't it?"

"I just topped a marching drum. If the prickless bastard could make one, his son will be wearing the sash my father wore sooner than he thought."

"What the hell are you talking about," she snarls as Hubert comes over, staggering from the booze and fright. He tells her in earshot of Finn, "he stabbed him, Mon Dieu, he stabbed him. He's lying on the tarmac beside the plane, dead like a dodo."

"He needed killing. Kept calling him Paddy, amongst other things."

"Who was he," asks Grace.

"Don't know," I say, "thought he was one of your messengers from Gordon's camp."

"Gordon knows we are in New York; why did you kill him? We better get over there and see what we can do; maybe he's alive."

"Oh, he's expired, dead as a tyrannosaurus rex. He's like a sieve; he's lost all his marching blood."

"Who was he? Can't you go a day without killing?"

"We are supposed to be on our way to England in less than an hour, and we have a murder on our hands. The military will bang us up and keep us there until we spill the beans. Who else has seen this?"

"Nobody; he instantly disliked me as soon as I opened my mouth."

"He was a colonel," says Hubert.

"A colonel, oh well, that's ok then, he won't be missed, will he? After all, he is just a colonel, and they don't usually jump ship at the sight of a little tight-arsed cannibal wanting to suck their balls. Well, do they," and she was screaming.

Hubert fingered his holster and thought about shooting us; Grace was behaving very unladylike with her bawling. The colonel was crumpled up on the ground, and she rummaged in his pockets and found his wallet. She found a travel document and a letter addressed to a Lakenheath general. The whole troop was on the way over, and I didn't give a shit to tell you the truth.

Finn stood there and never said a word to his soldiers beside him. The flamethrower boys stood beside Hubert, battle lines were drawn, and the colonel lay in a pool of blood on the tarmac.

"He's the pilot." Grace dumps this bombshell on us. I look at the pilot and think that's torn it. We're up shit-creek without a paddle.

"Who will fly this crate," I ask, "what about the pilot that flew us here?"

"Patrick, can you fly this plane, snaps Grace."

"A short answer, Grace, is no; it's too large and new."

"That's bloody marvellous," she again snaps, so what pilots have you got, Dempsey, in your little black book of terrorism?

I know the very person who will fly this crate, no questions asked, but first, let's stash him in a munitions box and wash away the blood."

"It will rain very soon," says a Matadoran.

"Thanks, glad to see that we have a weatherman with us,' says I.

Fifteen minutes later, the sectarian bastard is cased up, and his blood is washed around the tarmac. Finn and his command head back to the bar after collecting a wad of cash from Grace. A jeep stops with a screeching of brakes, and a major jumps out and asks why we are booted and suited in our new uniforms.

"You are not going anywhere until tomorrow night. Give these orders to Colonel William Orr and tell him Ian was asking. I expect to see him soon. Where is he?"

"Over at the bar having a drink," Grace replies.

"Having a drink, he never frequents public houses."

"Maybe he's having a coffee."

Hubert orders a grunt to find him for the major, and he is off on the double.

"I'll wait a minute or so," says the major.

"Your detachment will be members of a famous regiment for tonight only; do not show yourselves up, just in case you will wear a blue shamrock."

I know we are joining the 69th of the 42nd Rainbow Division.

"I understood we were leaving tonight, Grace informs him. We will change immediately and be ready to deploy in half an hour. How many sentries should we leave on the plane? There is a large array of weapons aboard."

"Two inside and one outside, alternate every hour on the hour. Would you care to join us for dinner at the armoury later?"

"Indeed I would, provided we have not been eaten."

"Your man is taking his jolly good time," and away Ian goes, his driver putting the foot down.

"Right," says Hubert, "let's act as soldiers if we are stuck here," he orders the flamethrower boys to take the uniforms inside and get dressed.

I follow Grace, and we are re-dressed quickly, even the boots fitted, and there were plenty of uniforms for the Matadorans who were on their way back with the grunt who had a few beers himself. Finn gets them suited up and is ready for inspection in fifteen minutes. Finn will be crooked about rank, but Hubert immediately cuts the dissent.

"I am the commanding officer here regardless of your rank; this is not the time for throwing a tantrum. Let's get this night over and be on our way; the result is what counts."

Dissent could be misconstrued as failure to carry out orders in the field. One could be in the tank and not available for our mission.

I return from the airport security desk with a smile on my face.

"You would never believe who has landed at JFK," I tell Grace.

"Is this material to our military situation here or overseas," says Hubert, "for if it is, report to me and not Grace."

"Hubert is pulling rank on us all, and I agree with him," she says, "We must be a cohesive force; otherwise, we will be a rabble."

New orders are hand-delivered, and Hubert barks an order to prepare to move out.

"Where to," Grace asks, "a need-to-know basis," he rattles back.

I can't help but laugh out loud. "I need to know," I squeak.

"You will follow my order, says Hubert. Check your weapons and be prepared to march."

"I have a top gun on the way," I inform Grace. "She will cost you five million pollars and one hundred gold coins in Canadian Maple Leaf and American Eagles. She will take her payment of the top of the operation."

"But that's ridiculous," says Grace, "the coins alone are worth…"

"Over three million. She said you'd grumble but to remind you that she would want access to the clinic or another ten million. She said to tell you to bring a million with you as a part payment, and she would collect the rest in Ireland. She also said that if you have the correct information concerning her exploits in the past, she will be invaluable to the operation."

"I take it Nicola is on her way here; surely she does not believe that blarney you feed her when you are on the piss."

"Being spying on me up there in Seattle, have you," I say, my voice showing annoyance at her discovery.

"Yes, I have, and by the way, Tacoma is her hometown."

"Well done, Grace. You know she is top drawer and has plenty of mettle, so don't mess her about because she will kill you, and if not, I will."

"Have no worries about the money; those CEOs of EARTHCO have shipped billions over. Nicola can have the petty cash and tack along as a combatant and earn her stash."

"I agree with her financial terms. Patrick, I like her; she is an excellent pilot."

"You still don't know the grand prize, do you, me Greek shagging Romeo? Greet her for me if I am not here and ring me on this number."

"No need. She is on the way."

"Well, in that case, let us eat because I feel we aren't going anywhere tonight except for a kip on the plane floor."

"You can sleep with Hubert on the floor. Nicola and I have booked a five-star hotel, and you can't go anywhere without us, can you."

"Not only am I a pilot, but she is the dog's bollocks of pilots."

"You can't fly the plane, can you," she says, "you need a refresher course."

"Yes, I do, Grace."

As a matter of interest, where is the rest of your murdering mercenary gang? Are they residing in a bog-hole in the west of Ireland, waiting for the backbone of your army? You had not thought your pilot situation through correctly, Grace?"

"How could you hire a bigoted Lambeg drumbeater and knowingly bring a Fenian to the table? Did you expect me to digest his insults? he practically rammed them down my throat."

"Did you know, Grace, that the Lambeg drum is one of the noisiest drums in the world? However, you cannot be certain because an ancient African could be drumming away on such a drum made from his in-laws. He probably has a pair of Malacca sticks and is pounding the hell out of it, just like a missionary showed him years before."

"And do you know what, I tell her, pissed with the excitement of Nicola turning up. He probably has them wearing bowler hats and orange sashes. All marching up and down the jungle shouting, the Taigs are coming, and if we do not stop them, they will be coming in our women."

"You must have been fed buckets of bullshit as a child," she says, "for you can spout crap like a second language."

"Grace, I love you, and soon I will have you. Goodbye, baby, goodbye."

I head to the gate as a convoy of trucks arrives, and a sergeant bawls for the 69th soldiers.

"Yep, that's us," I say.

Hubert comes over and immediately takes charge. Soldiers grab their kits and get in line beside the two empty trucks. They start loading their gear, followed by themselves.

"Ready to rock and roll," bawls a Matadoran.

Everybody is aboard, and I am in the company of Hubert, Grace and a Matadoran major named Dunbar. He starts briefing Hubert on what's coming.

We are going to Poughkeepsie to examine a patch of the virus six miles outside the town and kill any animals we encounter. We are to keep our eyes skinned for teens that have gone carnivore.

"That word refers to animals," I say.

"They are behaving like animals, you kronk," says Dunbar.

"You can try vegetables on them and call them an omnivore."

"Jesus, I was only saying."

"Don't interrupt," Hubert bawls at Major Dunbar when your CO speaks. "Remember, you are a guest in my country. We have invited you and your ilk to our glorious celebrations in honour of our victories against the Hun and his sidekicks. Your president and his new dunghill of a country might be helpful to Mrs Clinton shortly."

Hubert dismisses me to the back of the truck, and I sit with Finn. He tells me straight up that he is going to kill Hubert.

"What kind of a name is Poughkeepsie?" says Finn.

"I don't know."

I take my mobile and connect to the Internet.

"Let's see; its name comes from an Indian word, which is supposed to mean a shack by the side of a stream called The Queen City of the Hudson." It's most likely got pink pavements and old queens, probably the village people sitting in rocking chairs, watching the arse go by. Well, blow me; nearly a hundred thousand cocks and pussies live there. I should have travelled further afield; what if my one true love resided in Poughkeepsie?

I look at Finn, but he is asleep, and I decide to have a kip myself.

I've watched Hubert buzz around Grace like a fly on a dunghill. I bet she has promised him masculinity and youth. I could do some of that myself, but Gordon and his cronies were old. After forty winks, I awoke to find the truck in Poughkeepsie, and police and ambulance sirens were going off all over the place.

"Out, you lazy grunts," shouted Dunbar, "There is work to be done this night, and I can tell you, it will be gut-wrenching work before the night is out. Get out, line up with the rest of the troops, check your weapons, collect a taser, and get steel fold-down helmets and cuffs. We are going on a safari, Matadorans, and he gives me a look of contempt."

"Try not to get yourself devoured by a child-beast," and he laughs and strides toward another major.

There must be upwards of three or four hundred troops here, mostly 69th from the Rainbow Division, Home Guard, and coppers, lots of coppers trying to be in command.

Grace has been given a sergeant's stripe, and I get a blue shamrock, which I stick on my arm. Ten of us are put under her command, and she heads up the town with us in tow. As we hit a large, sprawling, open-air pub, I break ranks and march beside her. The police are there in force, and teenagers are fighting.

Ambulances are whistling up the streets, accompanied by open-back jeeps with casualties screaming and crying. The town square is across the road from the pub, and a wall of screens is erected and welded into place. People arrive clutching various parts of their bodies, leaving blood trails here and there.

I see a pile of body bags – soldiers carry casualties from a lorry to a trestle table where an orderly is tagging and bagging.

Tag and Bag station in bold capitals is written on a giant board.

"Who is doing the killing," I ask Grace.

"Kids and animals, like in Benson, I suppose."

"What the hell are we doing here? We should be on that plane."

"Where's Nicola?"

I stare at my phone. "She should have rung me by now."

"Oh, she's fine, says Grace. She's over at the armoury rubbing shoulders with the top brass, and we poor schmucks are here waiting to have our nipples bitten off."

"How do you know that?" I yelp at her.

"It's my job not to let you lose yourself; otherwise, we are lost."

Profound thinking that. I wonder if Grace knows what she's on about because I haven't got a clue. Our thoughts are put aside as a crowd of teenagers come hurling around the corner, crazed and dripping blood.

I draw my sidearm, shoot the two leaders between the eyes, and re-holster my weapon. Both boys hit the ground, and the rest of the pack stopped dead in their tracks. They look confused, and I shout an order for helmets and cuffs and go get 'em, boys. I lead the way, taking down a fat-arsed teenager whose T-shirt is blood-caked. I give her a backhander across the cheek, busting her nose, and I leer and squeeze her fat gob into a hideous mask; her lower lip is protruding, and the blood is dribbling down her throat.

"Drink bitch, drink all you need, you cannibal."

I notice a soldier from San Matador has lost an argument with a petite blond, and she has taken a bite from his arm. He's squealing like a pig as his mate tries to haul her off, worsening the situation. I punch my bitch in the forehead knocking her out cold. I shove the helmet on, locking it firmly, and the cable ties tight on her meaty wrists. I roll her into the recovery position having a feel of her tits.

I go to the petite blond and grab her ungentlemanly by the fanny. She opens her mouth and lets out a yell with a distinctive meaning of let go of my fanny. His mate drags him away, blood gushing from his artery. I remove the necktie of a dead schoolboy and form a tourniquet using my knife sheath. We are down to eight men. The two bitches we chain together and leave them lashing out and blaspheming like the worst of troopers who have marched into the jaws of death.

Their eyes are red, accompanied by ashen faces. With the blood, gore, neon shop signs, and miserable street lighting, Dante's Inferno could be a scene updated to 2017.

Grace has dialled for a wagon to transport her prisoners. Two pick-up trucks trundle down the street, hankering for trouble. Men armed with guns could be seen in the back of the trucks, with more men flanking left and right, darting inside coffee shops and bars, searching for someone. A bad feeling comes over me, and she's yelling to get our prisoners off the street.

"These guys want their kids, and they don't give a damn that they have eaten their neighbours," says Grace.

"You shot two of the little beggars."

"Never mind, line your men up and make ready to blow them away. Take it as a bit of target practice for the near future."

A police van pulls up, and she hustles the chain gang through the doors. I take charge and line the Matadorans up behind our truck, and I step out and order the pick-ups to stop, which they do.

A bully boy New Yorker alights and strides over all Michael Gambon fashion. His coat flows out behind him, and he's cradling a shotgun.

"Who ya got there," he drawls cowboy fashion, and I sneer at him.

I want to kill the bollocks; where does he think he is. His friends jump from their pick-ups, and another two hang back, either being sneaky or yella-bellied. If it comes to killing, I will murder the lot of them. I take a machete from under the seat and pretend to clean my nails.

"Who are you looking for?"

"My daughter went missing this evening with her sister."

"Why don't you check at the Bag and Tag station? It's a few hundred yards from the next intersection," Grace yells at him.

"Why don't I have a deco at your prisoners?" he asks.

Grace whispers, "There are jeeps and pick-ups at our rear; we are cut off from the main body of troops."

I can only see a few soldiers and doctors at the station; they must be out in the field. There are over a dozen of us, three dozen of them, but we have big guns.

"Tell your chums to get back in their prams; this is a military area. We will use force if necessary."

"Look, soldier," he says to me, "why are you being so crooked? I want to see who you have, and if she is not there, we will vamoose."

"You're a liar; I will kill you if you don't leave."

I call for the Matadorans to show themselves, and Michael Gambon strides back to his pick-up.

"Take your limp and your face and be on your way."

"We saw girls in a truck," a soldier informs me.

Finn is near the red pick-up, and Gambon heads up the street to seek easier prey.

"What the hell do we do," I say to Grace, but she cuts me short and orders us back to Camp Tag and Bag, where more trucks are parked. I am delighted to see our flamethrower boys and not so happy to see Fathead and Skeleton. General Hubert is with Colonel Potz and Nicola and two women in their late twenties with piercing blue eyes. A staff car pulls up, and out steps Mariah and Becky with a couple of Navy Seals and an old geezer who must be hitting a hundred and his wife. A police captain demands assistance to set up a roadblock, and volunteers take out three snipers.

There have been sightings of rabid animals on the outskirts of the town.

I see Grace busy talking to Colonel Potz. Our plane is on the apron, fuelled and ready to go. I don't want to stay here. There will be wigs on the green if they find that dead bollocks. I bet he is not even airforce; probably a commercial pilot tanked up on King Billy's piss, ready to fly us into the sea. I'm going to drag him out and kill him again.

Trying to wipe out the competition, are you, Gordon Thatcher? I am coming to get you. I will ride that wife of yours like a Dublin jackeen would on Smack and Guinness.

"Stop that grumbling," says the colonel. "Take six men and go and scout the outskirts. Report back if there are any wild or house-trained animals abusing the local population.'

"What if there is an army of our furry friends sneaking up on my lovely arse using the cover of darkness," I enquire. "I will need grenades and flamethrowers."

'Sure, sure, get them, and there are boys yonder attached to a flamethrower unit, says Potz. Go and choose a couple for picket duty."

"What about those two there," pointing at Fathead and Skeleton. "They could hold a whole zoo back."

"Yes, yes," he says, "just do it," and heads across to Finn.

Later, Finn tells me he will man the barricade at the intersection and shoot to kill anyone breaking the curfew.

Mariah and Becky are across the road in McDonald's, munching burgers with the two old codgers accompanied by the steely blue-eyed women. Soldiers from the 69th have turned up at the Bag and Tag station and have taken Hubert and Grace away in a military bus.

"I'm coming with you," the colonel says, jumping into the driving seat.

"Good," says I, "you can lead us to the killing fields, but first, I must have a quick deco at the casualty list."

"Crack on then, boy, and I will meet you there. We will mosey around the east side and see what's moving; that White Death hasn't shown up on that side yet."

"Have you ever seen a rabid animal," I say, "no sir, should I be worried?"

"You certainly should be worried; they can devour your head and arse in one sitting. Terrible thing to see an animal dining on a soldier, and he so traumatised he can't shoot, but I will," he screeches.

"I will blow his paws right off."

"Well said," Colonel, "let's get 'em like Floyd used to say in advertisements back in the last century, might have been in the eighties."

"Yes, let's," he says. "I hate dogs, cats, rabbits, bears, squirrels, horses, sheep, and all kinds of four-legged things, and most of the two-legged variety, not to mention three-legged bastards that prowl the alleyways seeking vanilla-flavoured horseshit."

"Are you sure you haven't been on a duck shoot lately?"

"Your face looks familiar."

"No sir, been on no duck shoots; you must be mistaken, must have been somebody else. I've got a familiar face. My father had a bike and got around the villages a lot. He could be a bastard relative."

"Come with me," he says, "let us ride on the lorry at the back. We can see them sneaking through the grass and hanging around alleyways, waiting to pounce on an innocent grunt doing his duty for our glorious, war-mongering president."

"Mrs Clinton is not a warmonger; she believes in détente."

"I'm not talking about that Chinese belly dancer," he says, spitting into the air.

"I'm talking about Lyndon B., the mad bomber of Texas, sure made Charlie into an excellent tunnel digger. So keep your eyes peeled; they will be on top of you before you can yell, nuke a gook."

We headed to the intersection with four trucks and left Finn and his men behind. I was glad to be in the back with the flamethrower boys, even if it meant standing beside the lunatic colonel. Fathead was in the other truck with Skeleton and some unknowns.

I hatched a plan to kill them and blame it on a dumbo-man or animal. What possible use could they be over in Ireland unless they were there to whack me when I had done the necessaries? That would be a double death sentence, for Wendy would be murdered. No, I must kill those murderers.

The colonel was going ultimately off his rocker. First, he was standing like Napoleon with one hand in his shirt. Then, five minutes later, he was giving the Hitler salute. Then, he started talking in Italian and taking up the

Mussolini pose. I'm getting tired of being surrounded by killers and lunatics.

We drove for a couple of miles until we reached the town limits, and we split up at the forked road and agreed to meet up at the Knocking Knockers lap dancing club five miles further on. The darkness's greyness gave the surrounding countryside an eerie half-light effect. The car lights from the distant freeway flashed across the treetops and hillocks.

The colonel was pacing backwards and forward, muttering to himself in French. He grabbed me by the shoulder and informed me that Dien Bien Phu would be relieved when De Gaulle gave Napoleon his marching orders. A piercing screech rents the night air as I and everybody else jump twenty feet. The colonel didn't flinch but told me the Cong were probably disguised as rabbits and foxes. Blood-curling screeches could be heard in the distance; the flamethrower boys and the Matadorans looked at me for guidance.

My eardrums nearly burst with the colonel's yell, and the trucks halted.

"Mutants," he shouted at a Matadoran, "go get 'em," and he shoved him out of the truck.

"Colonel, they are miles away," I tell him.

"Yes, yes, but we must put out pickets, call for reinforcements, and arc lights. We will advance when the reinforcements are deployed, leaving a staggered picket line. You will go to Poughkeepsie and return with orders from my captain regarding battalion strength and current deployment. Bring the local fuzz so that I know the civilian strength here. Heavy equipment is to be deployed post haste. Staff sergeants are to come here immediately. Inform the National Guard that the battle will commence in a few hours. Inform the Governor of New York that the enemy has been sited, and the White Death lurks in the bowels of the earth."

"Hurry back; you shall be my Aide de Camp. Are you sure you have not been on a duck shoot? Inform the armoury to send a Huey," and he gives me written orders, and he's gone to the second lorry. He runs back, don't forget the field kitchen, don't forget what our Emperor Napoleon said, an army marches on its stomach. He quickly goosesteps back to the lorry, yelling in Italian, and I wonder if the flamethrower boys will shish kebab him while I am away.

He seems to be a complete lunatic with his head screwed on. He certainly has no bolts loose as regards tactics.

I'm met by another lorry, and I reverse back on the dirt track and wait and see who has turned up. It's Rebecca, Mariah, Hubert, and soldiers from the 69th.

"Where's Grace and Nicola," I ask Hubert.

He turns on me and shouts to address him correctly and to tidy myself up as he practically rips my jacket off. Otherwise, he will have me for insubordination. Bloody Irish always supposing they are an army in themselves. Where do you think you are off to? I see the colonel heading across, and I'm sure there will be fireworks.

"Why are you still here," he says, "advance, or you will be court marshalled."

He turns to Hubert and tells him to clear off.

"Mein Gott," he yells at him, "you have lost my army to a Russian peasant," and he cracks him one across the face.

"The enemy is sneaking up on us. Why don't you reconnoitre further out and report back to me, you useless *fils de pute*?"

You can imagine Hubert's reaction; he blows a gasket and goes utterly red in the face like he's having a heart attack. A stream of profanities spews from his mouth in a cascade of spit and foam; he gulps in the air while frothing and dancing around the colonel.

"What's your name, you melted bastard," Hubert yells at him, "why is your name not on display, you bastard? You will hang for this, you bastard, too right you will you bastard, I will see to it you will you bastard, how dare you speak to me like that you bastard. I'll teach you manners *sac à merde*," and I notice they are fingering their sidearm holsters, but no one has opened theirs yet.

"Colonel Saunders of the Kentucky Rifles," the colonel says, "on secondment to the 69th Infantry Regiment."

"Are you now," Hubert replies and turns on Mariah, who's laughing with Becky. He then tells the colonel, "Saunders and Kentucky; I'll give you Kentucky fried chicken. *Va te faire foutre! Imbécile!*"

"Bye, Hubert," the colonel says, "must dash; the enemy is at the gates knocking to get in."

"Place that man under arrest," Hubert bawls at the two Matadorans.

"Ah, go and toss yourself, you French *connard*," and the colonel pokes me in the ribs to get a move on. An almighty cacophony of screeches, yelps and roars can be heard on the horizon, and lights can be seen heading towards us, lots of vehicle lights. Whatever is on the march is driving the human population ahead of it.

I don't relish welcoming this menagerie when it sweeps into Poughkeepsie. I ram the truck into gear and return to town at breakneck speed. The colonels whipped himself into a frenzy, shouting that the sandstorms would come, and Fallujah must be taken before breakfast. I will not kill him if he doesn't go all Stalin on me and send me to a Gulag. I am sure there is more to this man than meets the eye.

I promised myself I would take a hiatus from killing, but it is exceedingly difficult with killers trying to get you to meet your maker. I hit the town in record time with the colonel doing a chicken dance in the back. Hundreds of people are milling around the town square.

The colonel is out of that truck like a sprightly twenty-year-old and demands to know what the furore is about. I descend and stand beside him as an aide-de-camp should do. A police captain tells him New York City is in chaos, with dozens of teenagers running amok, biting, and eating people. The butcher's shops have been broken into, and the meat stolen. Whole blocks are sealed off on Fifth Avenue, as is the case over the five boroughs of Manhattan, Queens, Bronx, Brooklyn, and Staten Island. They are to be used as safe havens for the inhabitants, as there is no point in quarantining the little cannibals.

They are attacking one another. Thousands of children are fine and have been evacuated to Ohio and Pennsylvania, where they can roam in open-air camps.

These vicious little cannibals must be caged quickly to contain fatalities between innocent and infected. We have a few of our own afflicted, but the influx of parents with teenagers exacerbates the situation. The local hotheads have been beating up the parents amid reports of sexual attacks on boys and girls, even kidnapping.

I recognised the Michael Gambon imitator. Grabbing an Uzi, I headed across to the truck with the colonel and hit him with the rifle butt, leaving him dazed. Two shots rang out; the colonel had shot two of his compadres for attempting to shoot me in the back. Another three jumped from the truck. One caught his leg in the rope that held the tarp and fell, hitting his head on the ground. The other two made a run for it firing their handguns as they ran, but they ended up on their arses, blown away by a volley of bullets from the boys from the 69th. Their other truck was further up the road, and I shouted to the 69ners to go and requisition it. I untangled the foot of my unconscious prisoner.

More soldiers came running and asked where their comrades were going.

"They will apprehend the truck's occupants," the colonel informs them.

"You help load these prisoners into the back of this truck and assume a position with a view to a kill."

I outline what is coming to the town: an army of rabid animals.

"Let's see how our home-grown cannibals deal with that meat feast."

Two soldiers come back and tell the colonel, "he should have a peek in the back of the truck. There must be a dozen boys and girls semi-naked trussed up like hogs," they shout in unison.

My sister Theresa is there with my girlfriend. My father rang the police after she bit Mum. My girlfriend agreed to take Mum to the hospital, as I had been summoned to the armoury.

The colonel legs it to the back of the truck and climbs up. There are the faint sounds of forced breathing, and he reappears, hauling two girls by the legs. They are bound with duct tape with their noses exposed and tied back-to-back, leg to leg, arm to arm. I have seen this type of bondage before. One girl in her Night-Child mode has the affliction signs, while the other is quiet and fearful. We gently lift the two of them to the ground and place them in a war blanket. He calls for more blankets, and when they arrive, the rest of the girls and boys are wrapped cosily.

The two kidnappers have regained consciousness, and he orders them bound, gagged, and tossed in the back of the empty truck. Four blokes and a woman are taken from the other truck with three captives, two of which could be called milfs. The captain has radioed in, and ambulances and extra police arrive and fit iron masks on four of them. The captain, police officers and a truckful of grunts join us.

We park up and drag out our five prisoners; they are conscious and aggressive, spoiling for a fight.

"Let's give them a sound thrashing," says the colonel, "and see if they find it sexually fulfilling."

Everybody starts knocking ten bells out of them.

"Enough," shouts the colonel; they are bloodied but not subdued. They continue effing and blinding, and a Matadoran grabs the weakling. Another one hauls down his trousers and castrates him, shoves the knife up his arse, and chucks him in a dyke. The rest are terrified, and we force them back into the truck and drive back to base.

A collection of vehicles have turned up full of occupants.

Hubert is busy making up a convoy, and as soon as we arrive, he gives the go-ahead to move towards Poughkeepsie.

About fifty men stay behind. Hubert orders us to advance to the Knocking Knockers Klub. To my surprise, the colonel salutes him and shouts to his men.

"You heard the general? Move out at the double and await your general."

He goosesteps over to the lead truck and jumps in, beating Hubert to it. Hanging out the door, he's waving his hat in the air, yelling, hurrah, Stalino, hurrah, Stalino! He charges over to me and puts a gun to my head.

"Are you my aide de camp or not, are you? Well, are you," he yells, goosestepping back to the truck and shouting *ella ella*? I follow him at the double, keeping an eye on Hubert, who plans to murder the colonel.

"My horse's name is Bucephalus," he tells me, "and you will accompany me in the saddle while my troops hide in its belly."

He imagines he's Alexander the Great; I hope he doesn't take a shine to my arse.

Hubert has already commandeered another lorry and takes off as if the devil is nipping at his heels. The rest of the troops follow him, cutting me up and sideswiping me into the ditch. I have spun the lorry out of the damn hole when several trucks tear past full of troops and searchlights. The colonel is around the back of the truck shouting to give the non-combatants a severe chastising.

I must admit I put a few good punches in myself. The Matadorans grab one and castrate him in front of the other three, who are shitting themselves.

These Matadorans are vicious bastardos.

"The colonel has the three survivors lashed to the lorry's outside. The castrated nonce is left with the knife up his arse and thrown in the ditch like his other mate. When discovered, there will be hell to pay."

I have no sympathy for these would-be rapists and am glad they suffer hideously.

We reach the Knocking Knockers, and the place is busy. Isn't shagging a fantastic pastime? Men will do anything for it. Here we are in the arsehole of nowhere with a plague on the way, rabid animals and brain-damaged children and music blaring. The strippers are having a field day with dozens of vehicles randomly parked. It's dusk, and tourist families are drinking pop, munching burgers, and arsing around.

"How far away are the animals," I ask Hubert; he says, "he doesn't know."

Nothing has been heard in the last half hour, but everybody knows they are out there.

"I know one thing," says Hubert, "I 'm knackered and dying for a shit," and he heads towards the jacks.

I meet Mariah and Rebecca, and they tell me Grace and Nicola are on the way.

"We must leave no later than mid-morning, or we risk being shot down, otherwise, there is no chance of exiting. We will never be allowed to land in England or anywhere with an anti-aircraft gun. Orders from Grace are that you do not endanger yourself and stay away from the so-called front line."

"I hear you have nonces in the back of the truck," a Matadoran demands of me. "Let's go and have a peek-a-boo,"

I walk away. I think these Matadorans are handy with a knife. I see two Matadorans coming from the woods, and instinctively, I know what they have done as they march up to me.

"Your friend is dangling from a tree with an extra-large arsehole on him. Before he died, he begged me to tell you he had hidden another lorry load of underdeveloped beaver. It's parked down the road at the back of that house with the cider for sale sign. Did you notice it because I did? I love cider."

"Let's see this truck, soldier."

I ask Hubert's permission to check the truck, only to discover the colonel is doing an Apache war dance while chanting war cries. I believe he is making whoopee.

"Hubert warns me to watch myself and my scalp with that lunatic and kill him if the mood takes me."

I look at him, and he is serious. Whom does he want me to whack, the soldier or the colonel? A station wagon stops, and a guy shouts wild animals are coming across Dillon's plateau.

"Where is that?" I yell, and a copper informs me it's a ten-mile-wide strip of land that leads up the valley, bottlenecking between these two hills here, widening and sweeping towards the town.

"We are standing in the bottleneck, and it is the better place to stop a stampede. Anything that gets past will continue to Poughkeepsie and on to wherever it fancies."

"I see you are alone," says the colonel.

"Yes, they are all dead. The racoons got them, and Tom Hertz got his head bitten off by a bear. Would you believe it?"

"General Hubert, would you permit me to send pickets to pinpoint the enemy," shouts the colonel. "We should ambush the little furry darlings."

"Yes," says Hubert, stunned at the colonel's about-face, "take the flamethrower boys with you and the Matadorans."

"Find Finn the pisshead," he orders a Matadoran, "and ask him to lead you to victory." Hubert says, "Go and check that truck and wait there; I understand Grace is on the way with our pilot, a friend of yours. Meet and greet them."

I pick an open-top truck with high sides and an even higher tailgate, and I station soldiers inside with machine guns (LMGs) and one flamethrower boy.

He isn't over the moon about being separated from his buddies, but I tell him that no one will notice you filling your breeches when the attack comes. We drive up the road; I ruminate on returning to the airfield once I have Nicola in tow. Grace will accompany us as I need her stash of cash. How did I miss this place with such a big Cider for Sale sign? I kick in the front door and pick up a Granny Smith's Cider bottle. The house is as empty as a

Scouser's arse after a dose of the trots from overeating craggy munch.

I head out the backdoor like a steamroller, taking the door and frame with me, and ahead lies a barn. When I prise open the door, I know I will be greeted by a lorry, an addition to my transport fleet.

Shots plough into the ground a yard ahead of me. In the twinkling of an eye, mind you, just a twinkling, the flamethrower boy sends a sheet of flame up on the roof. Moments later, a screaming, blazing, I'm unable to fly assassin comes tumbling down and rolls around on the ground. We ignore him and storm in the barn door, and there is the lorry. A soldier named Pingo jumps in the cab and reverses, taking the wooden wall with him and drives over the sentry's smouldering remains.

"Some sentry," he laughs.

Breaking the locks with a sledgehammer, he whacks open the doors and leaps inside. A half-track rolls into the yard, and Grace and Nicola climb out with a hillbilly in civvies.

"Greetings and felicitations," he drawls. "I thought I might mosey along with a couple of my old-time friends who are seriously aggrieved by your aggressiveness."

"What can I say? What friends are you talking about? I am working here and don't know you from Adam."

"Come and meet them."

"They can wait."

"I see what they mean about your aggressiveness," and he goes and talks to Nicola, who has not had a chance to open her mouth.

Grace is beside me and says, "We have to leave as soon as possible. New York City and half the cities in America are in turmoil because of this infection spreading through the teen population. The White Death is active in Arizona and has crossed the border to Mexico. A dozen or so Mexican children have the Night-Child virus. The Centre for Disease Control in Atlanta has confirmed that it is linked to fast food. The meat in question is from specially bred wild animals. There is a high protein count, which is alien to the domestic food chain."

"The country is going to the dogs and will be torn apart, and I intend to leave with my family." Grace goes to speak, but I say, "I know, I know it is impossible, but I will take them out when I get the opportunity. I do own a boat, you know."

"Oh, we know, that is why you are here," she says, and I wonder what she means. I return to the truck, but the Matadoran has rescued and unbound seven girls and two boys. He is the flavour of the month, the way they crowd around him, and I can't believe what I see in front of my eyes.

It's Baba, and she immediately runs to me crying, "*Bwana, bwana,* you came to save me."

Grace purrs, "If it isn't the virgin pussy so-called," and Baba gives her a look of fear and stands closer to me while smiling at the Matadoran. She is keeping her options open, clever girl.

"Where's Frankie and Hugo," I demand of her, "did they take you to this rotten apple."

"No," she says, staring at Grace, "they are dead. They buried them back in Aritzona and put me in a car."

"Who did, who did this," asks Grace.

"Mogambo's men did it; they are here."

"Talk later," says Grace, "let's move on."

One of the boys is rabid, blindfolded and gagged, and Grace walks over and shoots him in the head. Shrieks and cries accompany the shot, and the rest runs off into the darkness.

"Right, let's get back, I say," and we load up, taking the other truck with hard skin sides.

Grace shoves Baba into the transport and guns it down the road.

"Grace says we are going to the airport as soon as possible."

"I can't wait to get the hell away," I say, and we pull in front of the Knocking Knockers and barge in.

"Let's booze and round up our passengers," she says, beckoning Hubert and Mariah over. Becky follows the flamethrower boys. Finn takes up the scent, as do his boys. Fathead and Skeleton are there drinking with Consuela. I had forgotten Connie and her friends, Bill and Ben. Everybody is here except Nicola.

"Where's Nicola?" And I head for the door and bump into her and the hillbilly.

"I wondered where you were," and she laughs and kisses me.

"I'm fine, I'm fine; this here is Jeremiah Halloran; he had a brewery down Arizona way."

"I say aye, I remember you, flogged it to the chinkies. I thought you were older."

We shook hands, and we went back inside. Some local tarts had gotten up on stage, stripteasing while burlesque dancers drank neat gin at the bar. Gunfire can be heard in the distance, and Grace tells Finn to send a scouting party and see what's happening. The civilians are scared, and Hubert orders them to get ready to leave. Some ignore him, but others take his words as an order and beat a strategic withdrawal back to town.

I tell a sexy bit of flesh to head towards the Midwest; the cities will be overrun. She walks on, head held high, and I ask if she would let me bum her. She declined to comment.

The colonel bursts through the door, shouting that the hour is nigh and America expects every man to do his duty, especially Poughkeepsie. He has a patch over his left eye (it should have been his right). He now imagines himself as Admiral Lord Nelson, the hero of Trafalgar.

"Move it," he yells at Hubert, "the enemy is closing in and snapping at the heels of the stragglers. All flame throwers and their handlers to the front line immediately. Crop dusters will spray the bottleneck to a depth of two hundred yards with a chemical BLT69. They have assured me we can have as much New York frazzled rabbit as we want for our early morning brekkies. Instant BBQ," he says, "scratch a match."

We will draw our line of defence five hundred yards behind that. All the vehicles are to be staffed by drivers ready to pedal at a moment's notice. Soft-skinned transports to the rear.

"Hubert, take command and remember the Alamo. We are going to be different from that lot. As soon as the shit hits the fan and our lines are stretched, we are off. Do you understand, Môn General?"

Hubert sticks two fingers up at him; he is too tongue-tied, and the colonel is at the bar ordering a drink.

"We'll get Bugs Bunny and his crew," he shouts to me, "they must be nearly here even if they are hopping along. Jessica Rabbit will be in the rear, slowed by those impressive melons she carries. Take her prisoner, for I want to nibble her butt."

He throws his head back and lets rip a rebel yell, which Fathead and company take up.

The air smells of marzipan, and I wonder what concoction they have sprayed the area with. There is a smell of boom-boom, and I want to keep my arse rigidly attached to my backbone.

"Where are the pickets," I ask the colonel, and he retorts, "I left them to get roasted, you idiot. What the hell do you think I did? I brought them back in, so I'm having another drink. No one is to go past that red flag. Yeah, it means danger, stay out, do not enter, eintritt verboten, non-passe. The whole place is sprayed with a volatile oil; it's made from Belfast putty, you know that, don't you, you big old Leprechaun," and he takes a chunk from his pocket lights and tosses it at me.

"If I had a spud, I would stick it in it and sing you Happy Birthday."

It's my birthday. There is scuttling in the darkness, accompanied by animal noises.

I'd swear I heard an elephant trumpet.

"Hubert, someday I will ram a grenade up your arse with a thirty-second timer and leave you with a breadknife."

"Oh, Patrick darling," says Grace, "would you come in from the chilly night air and help poor Nicola make up the beds for the night? It's only war blankets, and we need to get a kipping if our furry friends haven't got the bottle to cross over that lovely carpet of death laid out for them at great expense."

"Yes, I would," I have not spoken to her all night, and I practically run into the motel-type lodge that is an annexe of the dirty dancing club. I go in the door to be greeted by a wall of cheers and a well done for reaching the acceptable age of twenty-plus. Have a beer, a whiskey, a burger, a tit, a shag, a blow, an arsehole filler. Everything was on offer. Everyone was amicable, but there was no sign of Grace and Nicola.

"Where...and I'm told to drink and be merry, for afterwards, you will make love in the boudoir of delights. My imagination knows no bounds."

A Dita von Teese burlesque dancer comes with two of her friends and does a dance called the Martini Glass, made famous by Dita twenty years before. Her friends do another named the Chair and the Table, which is trendy in the Far East.

After all that, a bell rings, and the flamethrower boys carry me to a door titled Paddy's Lament. Two naked women open the door, and I am enveloped in a reddish fog, erotically charged with oriental spices.

Two of the most beautiful women I have ever known appear from the mist. It is the amazing Grace and the attractive *koukla* Nicola. I'm led to an oversized bed overawed, and I lie down and smile. I stretch my hands out, and night overtakes the day. I try to stay awake, but I cannot. I claw my way to the light as the darkness overtakes me, and I surrender and fall asleep.

"He shall have something to lament in the morning," laughs Nicola.

"Morning does not come without the night horrors for him," says Grace, and they close the door on me.

Chapter Eighteen

Rendezvous at O'Neill's

The horrors came for me with a vengeance that night. I awoke several times, the first time when the older Italian woman had died. It said Arlington Cemetery; there were crowds of top brass, even one of the Kennedys. It might have been the President, but I can't be sure, for I was far away; the fog was like a peasouper. I drifted towards the coffin draped in the American flag, and beneath, I could see the Tricolour.

My mother's face floated from the coffin, and she waved to me to leave; startled, I glided backwards, passing through the dark-veiled woman with the two teenagers. She made the sign of the cross, shivered and held her kids close to her. A general was saying how brave she had been; she should have died with Edith Cavell, whom the Germans executed in 1915. Edith was a nurse who worked in Belgium and helped over a hundred prisoners escape to freedom, including the old dead woman. Having been caught, Edith was found guilty and executed.

He told the newspaperman to ensure her heroic exploits were printed on the front page. It's all doom and gloom; with the Cuban missile crisis and the Berlin wall less than a year old, we'll all be going to hell in a wheelbarrow.

The newspaper said she was spying in the South Atlantic during the forties. As three shots rang out, I could not hear him as a bugler played the last post.

"Who are you, and where are you from? Who's your mother?" I keep hearing myself say to the two teens.

"Please don't return to where you came from," a soldier tells me. I knew your great-grandpappy here on the other side; I sure did. I bought my ticket at the Battle of Bunker Hill. They had made me an indentured servant. I lay there for days until all the blood had drained from me. I died a free man.

Hands are shaken, and the veiled lady leaves with the boy and girl. She looks through me to the row of headstones behind, and I turn and see the names of Maguire, lots of them and a couple of Dempsey's.

"Oh, there is more," says a soldier to me, and I recognise him. He is the soldier from WW1; you may yet live your eternity here. We are one family.

The wind is picking up as the souls are like will o' the wisps and are popping up all over the graveyard; they are known as corpse candles and are like little burning lights or small fires dancing. A major in an ancient American uniform speaks to me in an Anglo/Irish language; the majority of the words are Irish, which I speak fluently. He says they are the condemned souls; they burn in hell and must be redeemed by prayer. So when you next see these lights, they will be coming for you; they will wait for you and drag you to hell, where you can repent at your leisure for your evil deeds. You are a wicked man; try to redeem your soul, for it is lonely here. There is company in the lands high in the zenith of the heavens that is of my bloodline. Bloodline is everything *mo buachaill beag*, and do not forget it, *oiche mhaith.*

Flames burst around my feet and enveloped me, and I cry out and wake to beat the air with my hands. I glance around the room, and I hear music and laughter. Grace is sitting at the end of the bed with my grandmother, who's been buried for donkey's years. Water, I plead, but I faint with the pain. Bombs are raining from the sky, and everywhere is on fire—painted black by Mick Jagger and the Rolling Stones blasts from a burning Huey. Soldiers are shouting at one another to move backwards; our air force is carpet-bombing us.

A sergeant laughs at me and says, "Are you not a bit old to be here, Granddad? Have you time-travelled from Iwo Jima?"

"The little yellow monkeys are way up there eating rice; we have a nest of rats called Charlie. You don't want to be caught by these rats, Granddad."

He is gone, and he seems familiar but too young. I am in Vietnam, and I run back into the jungle and jump into a foxhole beside a marine who punches me in the mouth. "Mind where you are plonking your feet."

"Sorry, sorry," I say, but he ignores me, and I stare at him in astonishment. It is me, well, kind of. He seems a bit like me and punches me in the mouth again.

"Eyes forward for the enemy," a sergeant yells, "you two stop fighting and keep it for the Cong; they will be coming to gander at that chopper."

"Where is your weapon, and where is your uniform? Where have you come from?" the sergeant yells at me.

"You are mighty weird," says the puncher. He jumps from the foxhole into a barrage of bullets and falls back riddled.

"You are not here," he tells me, "you are not real; you are from the future."

"Tell my Julie I love her, tell her that Ben will be healthy."

I held his hand, but he kept saying, "Don't go, stay, tarry awhile, pray with me for your soul," and he died.

The sergeant had put a Camel between his lips and commented on how many he had helped to take up smoking. A soul-destroying loneliness crept over me, and I cried out, "Who is Ben," as explosions rocked the ground, and the gunfire reverberated in my ears.

I'm falling and going to die, and I awoke dizzy and scared.

Monday, the 26th of June 2017.

The rat pack is on the move, and so is the Death Snow—it's time to abandon this pass. Three hundred Spartans we are not, and this bottleneck is not Thermopylae.

It's Finn, "time to live or die," he says, "time to go."

I follow him outside, and the day is like Dante's Inferno; a boundless wall of fire is burning. At the same time, pocket-sized explosions rock the ground, which is being consumed by the flames. Rats, squirrels, boar, deer, and all animal species come through the fire and run in all directions; they do not attempt to have lunch at our expense.

"Let's get the hell back to town," says Grace.

"What the hell happened last night?" she asks me.

A sloth of bears comes tear-arsing through the flames. They flee through the car park and in the open doors of the Knocking Knockers. Nicola has turned up from nowhere, toting half a dozen pistols tied around her waist and a machine gun.

"Oh, wouldn't you like to know?" says I, "because I definitely would. Those bears are a bit late for the strippers, but I'll tell you what happened; you two bitches drugged me and had it off together while I lay there having nightmares."

A couple of teenagers come tear-arsing out the door while screams and yells erupt from inside.

"I'm going in, but guess what, Grace, I will soon have caught up with myself; I can't have far to go now; it was the mid-sixties in my dream last night. I'm sure I will be at my funeral tonight when I sleep. I am not staying here any longer. I will swim back to The Cliffs of Moher and climb the bloody things. I might even cadge a lift on the Queen Camilla ocean liner."

"Who knows, who cares?" she says. "You can never tell who you might meet snorkelling on the high seas."

"If I meet another shower of sociopaths like you lot, I will drown myself," I snipe with hatred in my voice. I have reached the door, and Grace has drawn a pair of grenades and is ready to flick the pins—three seconds and boom. I can see Dita in a vast glass suspended from the ceiling, and she looks none too happy.

"Mick Jagger was singing in my nightmarish dreams last night," I say, glancing around nervously, but there is no sign of the bears.

Grace and Nicola exit the rear entrance after the bears. Dita yells at us that the bears have taken the girls and two boys.

"I was born in 1962, bloody hell, which makes me fifty-five; last night was my birthday, and there I was in the Mekong Delta in South Vietnam, watching myself or a relative of mine die. Who is Ben? Is he me, and was that soldier my dad? What the heck is happening to me?"

"Get her off that ceiling and stop your prattle, Grace demands. We will meet at the trucks.'

"A soldier died. I must discover who he was; he had my facial features."

"Just as well he's dead then, isn't it," Grace says.

I give her an authentic mean look.

"Patrick, it's not the time and place; we will speak later once we are airborne, today, we are leaving on a one-way ticket."

"They will never permit us to fly now," I say.

"I know, all pilots are in so-called protective custody, and the planes are grounded, but not the military ones," she says.

"We can't get a military pilot," says I.

"But we have me, the best that Greece can offer, so we will fly," gloats Nicola.

"They'll blow us out of the sky," I grumble.

"No, they won't, you're a yella streak of piss with coward written through it. I am American Air Force. They won't shoot at us once we are in international air space."

"We are technically dead, as everybody else will shoot us. What's the point of flying if we get blown out of the sky?"

"That's where you come in," Grace says, "you will take us the rest of the way."

"But," I say.

"Never mind your but, you are a murdering terrorist; we know about your boat or should I say, the IRA's navy."

I'm astonished as she lashes me across the face with her hand. It stings, and she holds her hand in pain. I grab her, only to get a poke in the ribs from the colonel. Finn punches me in the face saying, "Sure, tis grand to hit a bollocks like you."

Fathead and Skeleton pick me up and throw me at the feet of the flamethrower boys, who stand back and ignite their flamers.

"Do you fancy a roasting?" Says Hubert, flanked by Bill, Ben, Pingo and the hillbilly. "We are not bringing you along because we like you; you are here primarily because of the RA's Kriegsmarine. You know where it is anchored and how to captain it. You are not the only one that can be a captain; you will arouse the crew from their slumbers when I tell you."

"Sometimes, a man needs encouragement to cooperate; would you not agree?"

"Oh, by the way, Mummy, Daddy and your fat wife, what's her name? Yep, Hairy Mary and your spawn are in our custody; you understand that word, don't you, you killer of children."

Fathead rushes at me and kicks me up the arse.

"They will be boiled alive one by one, starting with the oldest; that's your grandpapa if any crap is forthcoming from you. That other bollocks you spawned are searching for you, so we will pick Jamesy up at the airfield, where he will be waiting to greet his papa."

"The deal still stands; money a plenty for you and scrubber Wendy, and new bodies if required. I would recommend a facelift for your mother, the haggard bitch. We can bump your wife off or leave her with your spawn.'

I am boiling with rage and can no longer contain my hate. I grab Grace by the throat in the fastest throat-grabbing manoeuvre that has ever been performed in the last hundred years, and I start to squeeze the life out of her. Horror is etched on her face, and she knows she is brown bread, but Hubert knocks me cold with a rifle butt, and when I wake up, I am lashed to the front of the truck like a trophy from a hunt.

We are coming into Poughkeepsie, and the streets are full of vehicles heading north toward the Canadian border. Parking, Fathead jumps from the truck and cuts my ropes.

"Be a compliant little Fenian now," he says, "and we will let you have the best seat in the cinema later."

Dazed and cowed, I nod and collect my weapons as more trucks arrive. Hubert is talking to a police captain who is giving him a right load of guff. When he's finished, he calls us over to an empty café and provides us with the lowdown, which would leave anybody feeling low when he said all he had to say.

"So, in a nutshell, we will leave this land of uncertainty and go to a land which will bestow fabulous wealth and youth upon us," says Hubert.

"In an hour, a tide of rabid animals will pass through here, he continues, followed by an ever-increasing swathe of the White Death, and this is the news for New York State. New York City does not have the Death Snow due to the amount of concrete. However, feral teens are eating their way through the adult population. There were reports of wild animals in the suburbs. So, to put it in another nutshell, you can have your cock eaten by a dog or a teenager. Either way, it will not be pleasant, and if you survive, you will be a eunuch, praise the Lord."

He threatens me with death, and he knows I'm cowed. "You will be an obedient boy now, and I will get you a nice Leprechaun to play with."

I am going to drown all of them, I tell myself. Grace turns up and stands beside him, a brace on her cock gobbling neck. I should ram it down her throat and let her choke on it. I never really hated that bitch, which reminds me of Baba.

Grace gives me a stare of pure unadulterated hatred and a thumbs-down. Then, she says, "Going to the pictures later, are we," and a sense of foreboding fills my body and soul.

"The screening," she says, "will be a horror movie."

The Matadorans are at the 'cash and carry' looting whiskey and Hersey bars. The police officer patrolling the street tries to arrest them while calling for help, only to get shot. That brings a rush of officers, and the four Matadorans are seized and cuffed.

"Kill them," shouts Mariah, "we haven't time for this shit."

The colonel is across there trying to explain that they should be under guard with the military, but to no avail. There are four shots in rapid succession, and they are dead, not to put too fine a point on it. Finn and the hillbilly stride across the road with Barrett rifles slung over their shoulders.

"Who killed my prisoners?" the police captain's bawling.

"Why put them on trial for an old lesbian judge to give them a lollipop each and send them back to their shantytown," screeches Mariah.

"Yah, sod 'em," mumbles Bill and Ben.

"Strip them and leave them on the sidewalk. They will feed the host bearing down on this city," says the colonel, and a police officer on a motorcycle stops and tells the captain there are animals further downtown.

"I can't even remember how I ended up in this town," I tell Finn. "We are murdering our so-called friends that are here to help us. This cannot be right, but who cares about a shithole in Brazil."

"I presume you are here for the Yankee pollar," he says, a boiling rage showing on his temple veins.

"Did you know," he yells, "that all the scum of Ireland were secretly deported to Brazil, where they took up the profession of bumboys for the forest Indians?"

He knew how I would react, and he meant to put the frighteners on Fathead and his bag of bones companion.

He intended to kill me.

I went ape shit, as they say, and as he tried to land a killer punch on my chin, I kicked him in the balls, missed and kicked his hip.

He grabbed me by the throat and reined blows on my head. He flung me out onto the street where a crowd of civilians had gathered. The coppers will wait for the fight to finish, so they can wade in and hammer the rest of the shit out of me. He flung barrels at me, missed and hit a few civilians. That went badly with a couple of them, and they rolled up their sleeves and headed towards Finn, who quickly put them to sleep with broken necks.

"Anybody else wants a bloody nose," he shouted, knocking two teens unconscious who were busy videoing the fight. I am back up on my feet, sufficiently regretful of getting in a fight with a fellow Irishman. He has now started to show all the traits of a psychopathic homicidal maniac.

I am his main course for the evening. God damn me for rising to the bait that this bastard fed me, and I decided to stab or shoot him.

"No guns or kitchen cutlery," barks Hubert. "I will shoot you myself," he says, "and that goes for you too, Finn. Fists and boots, Marquis of Queensbury rules and other tittle-tattle. Fight on, boys and make it last."

He places a wad of cash with Colonel Potz, our crazy colonel.

"Just in case you don't know, Paddy, Baba's tight little quim is the prize for the colonel here if you lose, and then everyone can have a bit, starting with Finn. He is going to shaft that daughter of yours too, a busy bee he is going to be."

Finn wades in and pummels me with a series of jabs to my rib cage; he grabs my throat and starts to throttle me. A shot rings out, and Finn stumbles and loosens his grip on my windpipe. He pulls his weapon, but before he can discharge it, he is reshot in the neck by Grace.

A gun battle ensues between the Matadorans and everyone else. Everybody is fair game in their eyes, and the whole place is rapidly turned into a slaughterhouse.

Civilians and coppers are mown down as machine guns and assorted weapons are fired with a devil-may-care attitude by people with no reason to live. A dozen Fighting 69th died without a fight. Two flamethrower boys are wounded, while the other four barbeque most of the Matadorans. The police captain is a flatliner, as are most of his officers.

Grace and Nicola are behind a flower trough with the hillbilly, who's busy spraying all the windows along the street. He has a whale of a time with his hooting and hollering. This will undoubtedly be a great yarn to tell his inbred family when he returns to Arizona or whatever mountain domain he slithered down.

Strange though, I like the man, and I wave to him and give him the thumbs up. Then, he starts to blast the other side of the street, sending rocket-propelled grenades through Wal-Mart's shop windows. Glass shatters, adding horror to this gorefest. The loud barking of dogs can be heard, accompanied by the roaring of bears. This is not good.

"Get to the half-tracks," Potz is yelling.

"Waiting for us," a voice says behind me, and I realise it's Fathead with his shadow by his side, both adorned with enough hardware to impress a small government.

Jeremiah joins me as a menagerie of frightened animals comes sweeping up the street. A couple of bears must have had a high school education. Seeing the army uniforms, they change direction and head through the plate glass windows of Stonkin Donuts, sending Raskin-Bobbins's customers out the side door.

Their slogan hangs from the window frame, **have you dunked and creamed today?**

Ten of the Matadorans are still alive, four of them injured.

"Whose relatives are these," Redneck asks, but they shrug their shoulders, and he dispatches them with a shot to the head as if they were vermin. Considering where they live, they probably might be.

"Strip them and leave them on the street for the necrophiliacs."

The civilians are going bananas at the sight of the bullet-riddled corpses and the murder and mayhem taking place. They can say what they want, for we are not coming back. A couple of cops attempt to arrest him, but they are shot dead. The place is going crazy. If the authorities discover what is happening here, they will send an extermination squad. It will be for us, for we are worse than the rabid animals. To add to the excitement, teenagers turn up with dark red eyes, bloodied faces and hands and are tottering along exhausted.

"It's a tough life being a zombie," I tell one as I rip off her top, revealing a pair of bloodied titties. She sways unsteadily, and I think of my daughter and feel terribly guilty. I vomit and begin to cry. I take a dying woman's coat and cover her with it as she makes gurgling noises while opening and closing her mouth.

"Restraints," I holler to a police sergeant who chucks a pair.

The Matadorans have a couple of civvy girls in dog-graspers, and they push them towards a shop called The Choco Box. The girls are protesting loudly, and I decide to kill them if they rape them.

Wild horses and steers foaming at the mouth come galloping into the square, followed by a pack of wolves that have taken up company with every stray dog for miles around. The place is awash with squirrels, cats, gophers, rats, and mice; you name it, it's visiting Poughkeepsie. Only a few dozen are rabid, and they are quickly dispatched.

"We have to get out of here, Nicola. I still love you. Do not let greed become your lover, for you will never satisfy him, even if you have collected the last sou in the world."

"I am with you, Patrick; do not doubt my loyalty; go and help those girls,"

I can hear their muffled screams. Drawing a pair of Glocks that I had strapped to my waist in a Billy the Kid-style gun belt, I kicked in the door.

What a surprise! All four Matadorans were in there with two others from The National Guard, and they had stripped the girls. One girl was being raped in a sandwich. I despatched her tormentors with shots to the head, splattering the girls with Brazilian brains. The two

National Guards ran for the door, the yellow-bellied swamp rats. I emptied the Glocks into their arses, their screams drowning the animal's noises who mistakenly thought the Poughkeepsie square was a safe place to venture.

I had to admit these two perverts had the imagination to shove Mars bars up the girls' arses, and judging from the wrappers on the floor, there was a few up there. I could hear them cursing for not keeping their weapons close to hand.

"Aah, now boys, Bill and Ben would never have been caught naked like you two twix prix. No, they would have carried their sidearms holstered and unbuttoned in case of snakes like me slithering up on little pervs like you. Now your fun is over, and it's time to ask these girls if they had fun too."

They can turn fast, for in the blink of an eye, they went white-skinned as if wholly drained of blood. Their eyes were a deep burgundy. I was witnessing the transformation of a schoolgirl into a flesh-eating fiend. I noticed that their areoles were dark, whereas before, they were tan, probably a hormone reaction to the body change.

One with choccy bars up her arse made for her tormentor, and I made for the door as the Brazilian stood there transfixed. He had never seen anything like it before and would never see anything like it again. She tore a substantial chunk off his shoulder, dislocating her jawbone.

I descend the steps to find myself stepping on all kinds of rodents.

"What are you waiting for," I yell. "Clear the square, use those flamethrowers and let's get out of here?"

"Where is Grace, the melted bitch? I must thank her for saving my life."

"Here I am, let's go," she calls to me from a truck.

"It's about time," sez I.

"Right, you, Dempsey, Nicola, Bill, Ben and Police Captain Thompson, and your hillbilly friend Jeremiah, go in the half-track and prepare the plane. He likes to be called Redneck. Nicola knows the orders, execute them and do not put yourself in harm's way like a good lad. Enjoy the movie, and remember next time, do as you are told."

We climb in only to find Pingo has shoved his arse in with us, and it's now crowded. He and I have our puke and vomit uniforms, and I say to him, "It is time we switched armies." He readily agrees.

"The rest of us will follow soon," says Grace, "so quick march on the double."

"Well, well, well, it's the Flowerpot men," I sneer.

"Who's shit themselves," I start yelling, "It smells like a sewer in here. Stop, stop the bus. I'm going up top; I'd prefer to freeze my bollocks off rather than sniff this air."

"Good idea," says the hillbilly, "I'm going up top too."

"Fine, fine, stop the wagon," says Hubert, "let them go up there; it's probably an Irish stink."

Climbing up top, I lit a Camel and offered one to Jeremiah, who said, "I don't smoke, but heck, I don't think I'll make it back from this adventure."

"Been on many adventures, have we," I say sarcastically, and he laughs.

"I remember you; yes, I have, and I am braver than you. I have killed a centuria of men, civilian and military, and there is no pride in my voice when I say so. I have been a soldier and a mercenary. Like Rutger Hauer in Bladerunner, I have seen battleships burning in the Gulf of Tonkin. I have seen light beams shining on the burning tanks in the Sinai desert, and I have seen the skulls of nations lying in the jungles of Rhodesia and Cambodia."

"I have loved and raped my way through the virgins of exotic continents and stolen treasures of civilisations long lost and buried. Those moments of glory are now, but memories are lost forever when I have explained my life to my maker. The dirt farmer who has spent his life tilling his land and loving his family will be waved through to the Garden of Eden to await his final temptation."

"I will be ejected to a garden of desolation, where I will learn to reap what I sow. Believe you me, I will learn fast when I reach that godforsaken garden and a bountiful harvest will be the fruits of my labours my very first year."

"You certainly have a positive outlook on the afterlife, Jerry, but I can't remember you from anywhere."

"Don't worry yourself at this stage; let's have another of those toxic sticks."

"Sure Jerry, how come you ended up on this expedition?"

"Money," he says, 'money.'

"I got a pile from the Brewery sale, but I wanted enough to buy a hotel, and I shall have the luxury of the penthouse suite and be waited on hand and foot. I shall have whiskey and heroin on the drip and sexy blonde hookers to roll the finest cigars for me on their thighs. I will be happy. I will not die alone, forgotten and eaten by the rats. No sir, they will find me quickly and apply immediately for their severance pay."

"Not a bad idea. I, too shall buy a hotel across the road from you."

"Excellent," and he produces a litre bottle of Jamesons and swigs a few gills.

"Fancy a slug," and I take the bottle, and he listens to the glugs, and I hand it back. "Well-matured medicine," I say, and he knocks back a few more.

"You know, Patrick, when I was sixteen, I went to America and enlisted in the army. I got sent to Vietnam, where I ended up with the Aussies combing the Cu Chi tunnels. I had never seen a gook while I was there, but they sent us to the Gulf of Tonkin, where I was seconded to the Marines, who used me as cannon fodder in and around Hanoi. I got shot in the leg and was shipped back to Boston to my uncles."

"When my two-year stint was up, I collected my American passport, left for California, and loafed around surfing and shagging. I fell in with some Jewish lads, Israelis, and we went to Israel for a stint on the Kibbutz. It was September 1973, and the country was at war. My friends were conscripted, and I enlisted as a soldier in the Israeli army with a bit of a sleight of hand. It was a short war, for the killing was fast and furious, and it was there that I witnessed the destruction of the Egyptian army, complete with tanks."

"The Israelis rumbled and deported me with a medal and a bundle of shekels. Contacting the old IRA, they connected me with a young man who has climbed up the ladder quite a bit. He gave me names and treated me like a dog," he said, "sanitise and don't come back if you don't."

"I worked the mercenary game in Angola, hoping to kill a murderer who had slithered over there after participating in the Bloody Sunday massacre. Instead, the Angolans executed the lunatic for murdering his men. There were a few Irish there who gave an excellent account of themselves. After that, I migrated to Rhodesia to take up the offer of free land in exchange for killing those independence-seeking Rhodesians. Having killed plenty, I never got my land; just as well, the place has turned into a hungry dump."

"Spent a few years in Central America training various army types, married, and stayed until that dark day in '85 when those rebels murdered my family. The war was over, but the place was awash with unemployed soldiers, and they chose my family to rob."

"Over the next two years, I hunted and executed over four hundred soldiers employed by the Donna Valla drug cartel. The last ones to die were the self-styled Generalissimo Vasquez, his bitching wife, and seven grown-up children. When I showed him pictures of my family murdered by his henchmen, not one said they were sorry, and for that one word, I would have let them live."

"His daughter Maria laughed and called them *escoria*. I allowed Maria to live after I abused her for two days. I placed her with a convent of nuns who were happy to teach her the error of her ways for the rest of her life in exchange for a huge stash of drug money. I understood that they would have her legs amputated and her eyes and tongue removed to help her see the vision of God more clearly. I wonder what happened to her and if she kept my baby. I must go back someday, maybe when all this is over. I am too old for adventure; this is probably my last hurrah."

He starts banging on the roof with the empty bottle, shattering it as the half-track comes to a halt. I had listened to his story and wondered what had brought him on this expedition. He is truly an evil man, eviler than I have been, and I remember how I made a rat meal out of Drew. He is across to the 7/11 at the double. Two potheads are smoking ganja and start mouthing, "What you eyeballing, man."

"You're bleeding balls," Jerry yells and shoots them in the crotch and into the shop he goes. I draw my gun and aim it at the door, and in a few minutes, he exits with a carryout, closely followed by the Pakistani protesting he had not been paid for his merchandise.

I knew Mr Patel, or whatever his name might be, would regret his bravery and live to regret it. He did. Jerry grabbed him by the scruff of the neck and banged his head off the lamppost. He retrieved a bottle from the bag and broke the neck on the post. He shoved it down Patel's throat, probably breaking his teeth and slicing open his tongue.

The two potheads were up on their feet with knives, giving it all to Jerry in Jamaican patois. Drawing a bead on the first, I shot him twice in the arse and turned my attention to the second one, who was now undecided about his survival chances. I shot him in both legs. As they lay crumpled on the sidewalk, Jerry relieved himself. Squeezing his cockhead he fired jets of piss onto their faces.

"Hurry up, let's go," I shout. He kicks Patel on the sidewalk and picks up the bag. He rifles through their pockets, finds what he wants, and is back up top, and hands me another bottle. He calmly rolls a fine spliff and sits there smoking, drawing the weed deep into his lungs and letting it out with the mellowed aaah you would hear from a satisfied wanker.

"Good gear," I ask.

"I can see the Blue Mountains and Bob Marley eating jerked chicken," he says.

"I say to him, damn fine visionary you are, but I can see the Wicklow Mountains and Nadine Coyle. She's eating bacon and cabbage. Thanks to the Jamesons, I can see her twin. I'm getting rid of one and putting Kylie Minogue in her place. I'll feed her Marley's jerked chicken and watch the grease trickle down her belly, and she can have my banana for afters."

He starts laughing and won't shut up. He has the giggles and will laugh himself to death. At the speed we are travelling, it will take us all night. We pass a retail park, and I bang on the roof, and again we halt. This time, everybody piles out and makes a beeline to Satellite Burgers with the corny slogan, They **are out of this world**.

"They better be," says Bill and Ben in unison while Nicola and Captain Thompson head to O'Neill's Roadside Tavern.

"Very astute of the owner to come up with a slogan like that," Jerry says.

"You don't mind if I make a play for that little arse on legs, do you, Pat."

"No, Jerry, knock yourself out, rape my Nicola, and I will castrate you real slow, so be a gentleman. I love her very much. I'm going to get myself a sheepskin coat from this boutique, and then we'll drink."

"I'll get you one in."

I head in the door, start rifling through the coats, and remove a leather trench coat from a rack. I see its Italian design and manufacture, and it has the feel of soft lamb Nappa. I collect a pair of leather trousers, a shirt, high-heeled cowboy boots, and all the bits to make me dress like a gay man. Plan B for Bum is in my mind, but we must wait and see. There is not a soul in the boutique, which saves me the trouble of robbing the place. I open the register and see a handful of visa card foils. Whatever happened to dosh, good old dosh? I go to the Roadside Tavern, which is packed with civilians eating and drinking.

"Jerry, what is going on? Do they not realise it could be their last supper if the animal stampede comes this way ahead of the Death Snow?'

"Pat, call me Redneck. Everybody in Tucson does. and I like it. It gives me a feeling of freedom and wild mountain living."

"Yeah, sure, Redneck, you old mountain goat, would you like me to remove a few of those teeth to give you that Cletus Simpson-Spuckler look."

Captain Thompson is trying to get inside Nicola's knicks, and she has three Tyrconnell single malt whiskeys on the table before her. I bet it is twenty or fifteen years old. I know what she drinks, and Tyrconnell will only take her knickers off by her own invitation. Redneck has gone over, takes a glass of her drink, and asks if he may find it a home. Whether he knows what it is, I do not know, but she says okay, and down the hatch, he puts it.

"I do love a pot still whiskey," she says, "but this barkeep has only single malted, which is drinkable.' She picks one up in each hand, shouts Slainte at Redneck, and swallows each in one gulp. Bill and Ben are with Becky and Mariah, and I feel a hard-on growing for her.

"I missed you, Mariah," I say, all pansy-like, and she says, "I haven't missed you at all. Take yourself to the boggeries and relieve yourself over a mental picture of me spread-eagled naked over a bed of chicken feathers."

"Oh, Mariah, my hard-on for you would cripple a pussy for life. Take it now while it is hot and raging."

"God damn," says Grace to Nicola, "have you ever heard such a mouthful of wanking material like that in all your life."

"I'll get a round in," I say, heading to the bar embarrassed and asking for a pint of Red Sox and whiskies for the ladies.

Damn it all to hell; I could have had both for my birthday.

"I've got a gun, and I'm not afraid to use it, and I felt a cold muzzle under my shirt. Turn around slowly and kiss me passionately."

"*Shalom,*" I say. "Is that you, my little gun-toting gangsta."

"Aaaah, mein Irish schmuck, how are you, Patrick, and as I turn, she flops her arms over my shoulders and kisses me. I saw you helping yourself to my merchandise, you secret teapot."

"Ach, I would recognise your sexually repressed squeal anywhere," I tell her.

"I live here in Poughkeepsie with Ruth's son, Moshe. Imagine meeting you here."

"Bloody hell Pat aren't you the popular little bollocks in this tavern," says Redneck, as he and Nicola toss back whiskeys.

"This here is Elisabeth, a toe rag was blocking her happiness, and we flushed it away one fine day, and from what she has said, the blockage is well and truly gone."

"In other words, you murdered him," says Jerry. "I presume it was a he so you could clear the way to sample her beaver."

"No, it was not," I take her hand and pull her to the bar.

I'm still horny, and I want Elisabeth. Jerry was right; I want her beaver. I will have her, but it must be soon; otherwise, we will be gone.

"It's marvellous to see you, Elisabeth. However, it would be best to leave because all kinds of animals are maurading this way, and I have seen them in action. This place will resemble a slaughterhouse when they have finished."

"How is Rachel? Are you together, or has she run off?"

"She's dead, murdered, and raped by EARTHCO's hardmen. I am on a mission to kill and mutilate them for my revenge. I shall make them suffer for all the rapes that have taken place in the history of womankind. Starting with the rape of Eve after the Serpent got her pissed on apple juice and slipped her a length that all women crave."

"By YHWH, there is infinite evil in your heart; you must fight this evil and forgive them their evil deeds of greed and murder and their thirst for power."

"I will; I will, I will cut the evil out of them bit by bit, and when I'm finished, Allah won't want anything to do with them. They never gave Rachel the chance to live after her ordeal. She was never given a chance to forgive. She would have forgiven them on the second, maybe third pleading. I would nail them to the floor and make them plead one million times, and each time I said no way, I would snip a piece of flesh from their bodies."

"You're a killer, all right, that I saw when you iced Delano. I see you still talk, and you can walk the walk. Let's drink, sod it, beer and whiskey chasers," and we toast one another with *slaintes and l'chayims*. Nicola appears jealous, and I think to myself, isn't life grand to have pussy on tap for one's hungry cock.

"What do you want the clothes for," she asks.

"I might give myself a change of character when I go to certain B&Q nightclubs in the promiscuous un-united counties of Ireland. The Rumper Rooms and Queens of the South are the places to be."

"What, are you going gardening, or are you doing a spot of DIY?"

"Oh, it stands for bent and queer, and that's where I will lie low, but never mind, drink up. I want to make love to you."

She looks at me, surprised and angry, and starts to laugh. "Irresistible chat-up line, why certainly, sir," and we laughed, drank, and got pissed, and we could hear screams and yells above the din.

"Top floor now, secure the roof," I shout to Mariah, but they are already on the way.

Everybody is milling around lost, except us. I climb onto the flat roof.

"Mariah, we need to get to the hard skins and make haste to Stewarts. It is the rendezvous point, isn't it, and the plods will be left behind if they are not on time."

"Replacements will be waiting for us in Ireland," she says, "they will be Irish, so no questions should be asked."

"To tell you the truth, Patrick," says Grace, "I am sick of it. I never realised there would be so much killing when those women made me that offer in Tucson that sunny June morning. I had heard of the brilliant drugs that could keep you youthful, so why not, I thought? I'm getting long in the tooth. I roped in Austin and his wife, and they found the rest of the gang."

She then gave me her version of what was happening in Ireland.

"The Irish and English governments were having kittens at the thought of the New Sinn Feiners getting power ever since their vote had increased in size since 2010."

"With the centenary celebrations of the Easter Rising, and the mass redundancies forced on the public and private workforces, people began to envy the migrants and began to grumble, he has my job, and I have to immigrate, sod that, I want my job back, and he can emigrate back to his bread and dripping economy."

The New Sinn Feiners advocated mass repatriation with the help of a size twelve boot. In by-elections, their vote increased dramatically, winning seats. In the Dail, they began to eat into the old-timer's seats, who seemed to be dying with increasing regularity. They had been cleverly murdered, and the old political parties knew this. Over the past year, the mercenaries have been taking a toll on the New IRA soldiers, now known as MIRA, with little interference from Dublin or Westminster. They wanted them downsized, preferably six feet.

Since the MIRA assassinations had intensified in early 2017, the bombing had stopped. Gordon had agreed to liquidate the sleepers on the island of Stonnage and purchase it for EARTHCO's laboratories. Both governments gave it their blessing with reservations. Good ole Gordon found he could kill three birds with one stone and get paid treble."

"Grace, my heart bleeds for you, you poor, impoverished murderer. You and your gang of Anglo-Saxon muttonheads can go and play with yourselves. You will release my family long before you free Wendy, or I will scuttle *das boot*. Hear that and hear it well, or you will hear the sounds of your own drowning."

'I'm not interested in your clinics and your politicking. You will all die in the end, for you certainly don't believe the short murderous campaign you are carrying out will end MIRA. Bloody hell, woman, they have fought since 1798 and have suffered defeats and victories. They have reinvented themselves from their ashes every time throughout the centuries. The spirit of freedom can never be extinguished in a nation. It can only be dampened like a fire. The slightest breeze, created by a voice crying for liberty, equality, and fraternity, will fan that spark, still smouldering in the embers of past freedoms. Suppose hundreds, thousands, hundreds of thousands, millions, all calls simultaneously, the hurricane unleashed will fan that spark into a raging inferno that will burn away dictatorship. In its wake, democracy will flourish.

"Damn it, Patrick, I'm impressed with your cocksucking speech. When you get there, teach them about democracy and Saint Patrick and his shamrock," Grace says mockingly.

"Look at the Arab uprisings; the entire father and son dictatorships have been deposed, and the families brought to book."

"Yeah, that's true," she says, "but it will lead to Israel nuking the place. Let's do pest control. I could kill these furry little creatures day and night. Poor animal rights movement must be having kittens watching the slaughter. I will send them a video with me as a chief pest controller eating a juicy lamb kebab."

Gunfire reverberates around the street, and looking over the parapet, I see the locals taking potshots at skunks and racoons on their way towards Poughkeepsie. A stampede of steers accompanied by white-tailed deer passes the building, pushing cars and people aside. It takes a few minutes, and they leave bodies and wrecked vehicles in their wake. Panicked people are coming up on the roof, and Elisabeth is shouting in my ear that she wants to go home. Jeeps pass by the Knocking Knockers, and Pingo is effing and blinding.

"What's the matter with you," I ask, and he says he needs a shit.

"Have one," and he asks where.

"Stick your arse over the parapet and hold on to the coping in case you fall over when you release that big steaming turd."

"Excellent idea," and he climbs up, drops his kecks, fires off a pile of scutter, and goes aaah. I peer over the parapet to see he has shit on the National Guard boys who are about to fill his arse with lead. I drag him off the parapet as a volley of bullets ricochets off the stone, throwing up little clouds of dust.

"Thanks, man. I owe you my life and my arse. I am indebted to you."

"By the way, they intend to kill you as soon as they have done with you in Ireland, before if it is possible. I heard them talking about killing your grandfather tonight or tomorrow, so you will do as they say."

"Who said that?" I bawl at him. He points at Bill and Ben, and I call them over.

"Look who I see below," and the two National Guard boys are cleaning their tunics.

"Wankers," I yell and pull my head back in.

"Who is it," they ask.

"It's two naked girls blow-jobbing a…," and their heads are over the parapet.

"What can I say?" As I turn to Pingo, a couple of shots ring out, and the two boys are dead as doornails, a stupid grin on their faces.

"What the hell is going on here," screams Mariah, looking at Ben's head in horror. "Who killed him?" I point over the parapet but advise against sticking one's head over.

"Murderers," she screams, running for the stairs with Becky close behind.

"Clear the way, shitheads," she yells at the men and women.

One grabs Becky by the arm, and Mariah turns on him and shoots him in the face.

"I said, get out of my frigging way," and I can see a geezer aiming. I let loose a 9mm shot from a luger with an excellent suppressor, and he slumps to the ground. No one heard him die. The girls are gone, and we follow. The game is up when we get outside, for Becky and Mariah are against the wall, weapons lying on the ground.

"Keep walking and do not look back," says Pingo, and I take his advice and head towards the hard skin. Shots are fired overhead, and we stop in our tracks.

"What is it, soldier? What is all this bullet-talk?" Pingo snarls.

I approach them, noticing another five National Guard and other grunts at the burger bar.

"Where are you two going?" says the one with the smoking gun.

"Come here, join these murdering bitches."

Sniper shots blast the boys in the back of the head, and they hit the ground lifeless. Mariah and Becky quickly grab and train their guns on the other soldiers after lining them up against the burger bar windows.

"Keep staring at the menu and work up an appetite," she says.

I can see our blessed saviour up on the roof.

It's Elisabeth, that chip off the gangster's block, and she waves to me.

I run to the roof where Elisabeth is standing over the body of Grace.

Chapter Nineteen

To the Airport

"Is the bitch dead?" I ask Liz, but to my disappointment, Grace answers.

"Sorry to disappoint you, Patrick, but your whole family will be murdered if I die, as it is your grandfather's demise has been filmed. Here's the movie," and she tosses me a mobile, which I fail to grab. It hits the ground, battery and cover flying across the deck. I pick up the pieces and ask, "Did you have him murdered on your order."

"Yes, I did, and next time, be a humble servant and do as you are told on the double, and no whinging or the rest of your nesting tribe will get it. You have become pally with Pingo; don't forget he is disposable; he is along for the money, as was your friend Finn. Reinforcements will be at the airfield, so don't fret that you will be in danger."

The sounds of trucks can be heard below, and looking over, a convoy is heading towards Poughkeepsie. I wonder where Nicola and Redneck are. I need my friends now. But, on the other hand, no friends, no double-cross. I descend the stairs, accompanied by Elisabeth, and head for the half-track. I call over to Pingo, but he stays with Mariah, and we jump in and speed off.

She has had my grandfather murdered.

I'm flying out from Stewarts, and I'll see who's waiting, probably more homicidal maniacs. Let's see who that bastard is; he must be important. Maybe he can save my parents. Perhaps he is there under duress with his chequebook; he's certainly not a fighting man.

Elisabeth shouts to take her to Moshe.

I yell, "Yes, yes I will. I will stay with you for a while. I need a rest."

Reaching Poughkeepsie outskirts, she instructs me to turn right into a dead-end road. She owns the house on the hillock, a prominent property with double-fronted windows.

"Must have cost you a few shekels," and she smiles as I swing into the driveway. In the driveway are teenagers, and I recognise them for what they are: little cannibals.

The lights are on, and I see a woman at the window. She disappears, and the front door opens. The teens dash forward only to find the door slammed in their faces.

"There is only one thing for it," she says, removing a pair of handguns from the glove compartment.

"I never liked those wopeens," she leaps out, shooting four between the eyes. A boy comes running towards her, and she blows his little goolies off and finishes him with a headshot. Elisabeth sure knows how to hand out doughnuts.

"Let's make love later, Ra-man."

"Certainly, my little shekel collector."

I drag a machine gun out and set it up on a tripod by the front door, thus giving me a considerable swathe of ground to cover. I could wipe out a whole army with this.

I hang a pair of grenades with rigged pins. I set up a few tripwires with Vesuvius grenades.

"No time for sleep," she says, giving me some tabs.

"Take us with you, I have money, and my pussy is delicious."

We go inside, "I want to return to Israel, and you are going to Europe. I will watch your back, for you have many enemies."

"Okay, but it is not up to me."

I am almost deafened by an explosion, followed by an adult cursing.

"Billy Bob is dead," a voice yells as a barrage of bullets rips through the door.

"The gun's jammed," a hysterical voice yells, but I know it is not; it is one of my safety devices, wouldn't want some amateur cocksucker blowing me away when I'm on a mission of life and death.

"I'll kill the bitch; she's murdered my boys," and I hear the windows blowing in.

The baby screams his head off as Elisabeth follows the woman across to a side door, beckoning me to follow. As the front door crashes in, we descend the steps and hear voices threatening to rape her and her sister. I notice the resemblance, and she nods towards a trap door and tells me it leads out to the front of the house. The baby's screaming can be heard up top, and they shoot through the floor, missing us by inches. We run to the trapdoor and watch the bullets ploughing into the tiled floor. The door opens at the top, and she puts her finger to her lips. "Wait, wait," and two stupid dickheads start descending the stairs while a wiser head peeps around the door jamb.

"Take out the head," she yells as she blasts the two on the stairway. The door slams shut, and another volley of bullets rips through the floor. She gives the bodies an extra dozen shots. "Best be sure, bulletproof vests and military jockstraps."

"They are probably dead now," I mutter; "Their heads are minced."

"It's only a matter of time before they kill us," she says, "they can't have any grenades. Otherwise, we would sit on a cloud waiting for St Peter to give us the thumbs down."

"Too true," I say, "wait here; I will surprise them if they are all inside."

I gently open the trapdoor and peep out, but no one is in sight. I climb through the bushes and dense weeds to the front door. The machine gun sits there lonely and helpless, and I start firing through the door, blowing it to bits. I sweep an arc of bullets around the entrance hall, killing several intruders. I beat a hasty retreat to the bottom of the steps, crouching behind a massive lion's head, guns ready, waiting for the departure. A handful of Rambo's exits slowly, crouching and sneaking about. A fat lot of good that will do them hiding. I fire at point-blank range, killing a lot of them.

Gunfire comes from inside, and then silence except for someone moaning at the bottom of the steps. A shot to the head, and all's quiet. Seconds pass, long and drawn out like time stood still; the trapdoor is flung open, and a voice shouts, "How ya doing Fenian," and I call back, "All right, you gangster's daughter."

She exits the trapdoor with the baby in her arms, followed by her Uzi-toting sister. She must have been going somewhere posh because she has an adorable dress that shows off her curves and sexy legs. My cock is springy. The violence and the inviting flesh have given him a generous budgie bulge, and Elisabeth notices it and smiles.

"Would you like to make love to my sister? Why don't you offer? I see you admiring her thighs, you dirty, perverted man."

Her sister is watching me, and I feel a right plonker.

"She is yum-yum, and I can talk for myself. Come on, let's get out of here. I have a bad feeling about this place."

I heave the machine gun back into the lorry.

"What's turning children into cannibals," Elisabeth's sister asks, and I ask her name.

"Ruth and I want to return to Israel; I hate this place with its two-faced Jews and Ities. I am re-joining the Shin Bet. Take us with you, and I will kill your enemies. You come to Israel with me and enjoy the radioactive atmosphere."

"I will not. I am on my way to Ireland to save a sexy slapper who was once the love of my life and to kill a collection of has-been British soldiers."

"Would you two like to join me, and you can have a million pollars apiece for your trouble?"

"Don't mind if we do, kind sir. Will we be travelling steerage, or have you a fine Leer jet waiting to fly us to the Emerald Isle?"

"You know the place," and she says, "yes. I have heard of the land of leprechauns and banshees."

"Piss-taker," I snort.

"Years back, when I was an ordinary soldier, I met UN soldiers from Ireland; they told tales of the old country and its struggle for independence. They do not like the Israeli state. They say that we stole the land from the Palestinians and turned their homeland into a ghetto."

"Ah well," says I, "I fought in the Yom Kippur War, didn't know that, did you."

A Range Rover slewed across the lawn and halted, and us with no weaponry. The door opened, and a fashionably dressed woman in her early fifties pointed an Uzi at me. Elisabeth ran to protect me from a stream of bullets.

"He is my friend and Ruth's lover," the woman lowered the gun. Ignoring me, she spoke to Elisabeth and exchanged the gun for the baby. She smiled and said something to Ruth.

"Do you know Captain Louis Meyer, a bald Bolshevik from Rostov on Don?" I ask the lady. "Louis sent many martyrs to shag their seventy-two dark-eyed virgins when they blew themselves up. They couldn't wait to die, never realising they would be prickless when they arrived at Heaven's gate."

"By Allah and his band of marching shahids,' Ruth shouts with excitement welling up in her voice; it is you, the Irishman."

"I remember him, Elisabeth. He was the man Dad took to stay with us when we were living in Ashdod."

Elisabeth smiled, ran, threw her arms around my neck, and kissed me.

"I promised to kiss you as a flirtatious adult, but you never came. I waited for years, and as I grew older, I knew you would never return. I suppose I secreted you away in the dark recesses of my mind, never to recall you or your memories again."

"By the Lord Harry, it is a small world. Where is your dad now? I would love to see him. I owe him my life. If only you had mentioned your father at Delano's."

"He is in Tel Aviv growing tomatoes amongst stinking weeds, but we know better because he's in cloud cuckoo land at dinner time. He says he needs to detach his brain from his stomach to tolerate mum's new cooking. She has been at it for years; he calls it latrine cuisine, and the local takeaway is grateful for her culinary skills."

"I doubt you can come with me, but who knows, strange things happen at sea when you are dancing with exotic women or words to that effect; halleluiah should make that sentence palatable."

"So, we can come with you; fine, let's saddle up and go to the airport."

We jump into our miserable war wagon and the lady in her SUV. We head towards Newburgh, approximately fourteen miles away, and chaos reigns as we enter the town. An SUV is parked skew-ways, and a couple of soldiers are having their balls chewed by a pair of teens. They don't like their blowjobs because they are screaming blue murder. I don't blame them, for experience has taught me that those girls are not sucking but munching their nuts, which has never been recognised as part of the fellatio process.

I shoot all four in the head and peace reigns. We hit the main thoroughfare to be met by another crowd of teenagers trying to eat their mamas and papas. To add spice to the dish, a bear is lumbering across the road into the SUV path.

With inches to spare, I swerve past the brute. I head toward the airport, the roads eerily empty of traffic. I sped down those couple miles at a healthy sixty mph to Runway 40. I saw our transport sitting on the apron guarded by the spirit of our dead drummer boy.

I stop at the plane, its loading bay doors open and not a sentry in sight. Hard-skinned vehicles are parked randomly on the tarmac two hundred yards away. I assume that bitch Grace is here with Nicola. I wonder, for the umpteenth time, how I was swept away in this tide of greed, sex, and murder and ended up in this situation.

I was driving my truck incognito, minding my own business, and no one knew who or where I was. I could have ended my life happily in the company of my pig of a wife and my two grown-up children. I could have grown old, never thinking of my spent military career. No, that would have been too easy. I now end up going back to Ireland for an Irish version of Custer's Last Stand, and the result would most likely be the same. I would be Custer, and I would be dead.

"Roll call and who are these bints," chuckles Mariah, "and where do you think you are going," she says to Ruth, "to the ball, I think not."

"For Christ's sake, Pat, you have brought a baby; we don't have a crèche, bit old for a mother," eyeballing the Uzi-toting-baby-carrying granny.

"Bit of a late starter was we, or was it a long birth?" and she laughs with Becky. "Go back to where you came from; Grace won't stand for it."

"She will; let's wait and see who else is here."

"Nobody, says Rebecca, "except our four guests and the pilot, who is not alive."

Redneck arrives with a truckful of fifty young and fit grunts, all from New York regiments.

"My sons, Tom, Austin, and Richard, are amongst these soldiers," says Redneck, "and they are all dependable boys; our backs will be well protected."

"Who's your son?" I ask, and he puts a finger to his nose, and I know that he will not tell me.

"Security," he says, "so watch your step."

After speaking to Mariah, he barks out an order to load the weapons and munitions. She starts writing names in her ledger from a sheet he has given her and says, "Twenty-one places left, and you lot are not coming."

A jeep stops, and I see Grace, Hubert, and Captain Thompson.

"Aah, Thompson," I say, "thought you were dead."

"Captain Schultz is on his way," says Thompson to Mariah.

"Eighteen places left," and she smiles at me.

The wind is cold, and I ask Mariah if the three women can wait on the plane, and she agrees and orders me to start the engines and see that all is tickedy-boo.

"That is a bit of a tall order starting the plane; let's wait till Nicola's present."

She says, "I knew you knew nothing," and walks off.

I climb into the cockpit and start checking the controls. I want to fire the engines and taxi down the runway. I turn, startled, and see Nicola sneaking in on the quiet. She winks at me knowingly and fires up the engines.

A jeep is heading towards us from the control tower, and Becky meets them; a man and woman join our aircrew, and Mariah hands over a briefcase. They walk across to the plane with Grace close behind. I noticed the geezer visited his mate earlier—a nice bit of bedroom material his wife is.

I step down the airstairs to be met by the leering Mariah, "Twelve vacancies left."

"Who's here," I ask.

"There's your lover, Nicola, your friend Pingo, and the last of the Matadorans, all four of them, but don't worry, there are more essential passengers on the way." I mutter a variety of swear words as the Matadorans drive four Defence Force jeeps into the hold.

"You looking for Colonel Orr," I shout, remembering his name was Ian, another bigot, no doubt. He is as stiff as a cock that has spied a virgin's fanny.

"What are you on about," says the middle-aged man in Air Force uniform, 'answer me immediately.'

"Why, who the fuck are you, you self-important afterbirth."

"My name is Major Ian Donaldson. What do you mean, he is stiff as a cock?"

"I killed the drum beater."

He attacks me, and we are rolling on the ground, fighting like two drunken Scotsmen.

I land a flurry of blows to his head and torso, and he reciprocates with a couple of kung-fu kicks and a punch to my head that leaves me dazed. The end comes for him quickly as I cut his throat and drag him under the plane, blood flowing everywhere.

"Oh, this is great," howls Grace, shooting the woman in the face, "you have only murdered the co-pilot. What is it with you and pilots?"

"I better put Nicola in protective custody, but there is no need for that because you are shagging that well-rounded arse of hers, aren't you?"

"I'm sick to death of killers trying to murder me," I whine.

"You are a dead man talking," she says.

"Walking, not talking, ignorant bitch," she laughs in my face and says it's best to hear it her way.

"Oh, by the way, you have a film to entertain you later, titled Death of a Leprechaun."

I am boiling with rage, and she knows it, and she says, "Cool your engine, or you will blow a gasket." I head to the hangar, intent on getting a whiskey bottle and checking the authorisation Redneck has to command fifty men.

He must be Gordon's man; care is the byword with him and his stories. He knows me, he said, but I can't remember him. On the other hand, he could be a patriotic soldier soldiering, and be a helpful friend to me at the same time.

A police van reverses beside the plane. Captain Schultz alights with his wife and daughter, and two officers drag large trunks and store them in the hold. They board the plane without a word to the scribbling Mariah.

"Seven left," she says.

"Eight," sez I.

"I am counting, and I say seven."

"I'm not going if they are not coming, and that's that."

"Listen to who's talking; you are killing people every hour. This mission encompasses wealth and power, not you and your scrubber, Wendy."

A sleek limousine purrs to a stop right in front of me. I never heard it glide up; what a car, what an engine. A chauffeur opens the door, and out jumps Colonel Potz, Baba, and, to set the mood, Gordon and Sheeree Thatcher. I thought they were in Ireland. The hardbacks drive over, and Donald and Margo hurry up the air steps with their sons and wives. Apsara is in the company of Mariah's brothers, attired in sober suits. Two trucks are driven up the ramp. Austin is not present but could be on board with other personnel. On the other hand, his wife is deceased, so he could be in mourning with little interest in military proceedings.

"We have the army on our heels; close the exit doors. Let's go," shouts Gordon.

Chapter Twenty

Gunfight at Knockdown Castle

Mariah rushes up to him and says something, probably about my passengers, and he yells at her NOW, and she runs up the ramp. We are heading towards our nemesis and off to meet our Waterloo. I discover a cosy corner to kip between crates with boxes of parachutes. Baba gives me a watery smile, and I give her one back. Elisabeth and Ruth are further up the plane.

Nicola has a co-pilot at her side (a bit of a yarn about how Redneck kidnapped him with the aid of a policeman's uniform.) The plane taxis down the runway, turns and moves to its take-off position. I doubt if Nicola informed the control tower of our imminent flight. She opens the throttle, and I feel the speed build as she races along the runway, and we are airborne and climbing. I see the sky blue and clear as the sun sets, and once more, I am laughing as I swim amongst the clouds and try to glimpse my friends who are laughing with me.

My grandfather appears, his head protruding from a cloud, and he says to turn back, or he will have no option but to prepare my final resting place. The clouds part, and I see a sea of blue and stars and realise someone has fisted me in the head.

My eyes open, tired and bloodshot, and one of those Matadorans is standing in front of me rubbing his knuckles, and Gordon is beside him with Grace.

"So, you like killing my men," he says, "especially my pilots. Ian was Margo's brother."

"Well, to hell with him and you and the rest of these mercenaries. I will deliver you to your destination, and then I will kill the fucking lot of you, understand this and understand it well. My relatives will be free before I dock the boat. I heard you threatened to kill my grandfather, and if that is true, I now threaten you and your whole family with death."

"You don't seem eager to view the home movie I gave you. Here's a copy," and he takes a phone from a pocket, scrolls, and gives it to me. I watch it. I go pure white, white as a sheet, Redneck later tells me. The shock was too much, and I fainted.

When I recovered from seeing my grandfather murdered, I informed him that my grandfather, his age, would have ripped apart a dozen Gordons. He would have tortured the whole damn lot together for such a crime, probably in some cave. He would have a few beers and a smoke, record their screams, and play them back while they screamed some more, increasing the volume until he could no longer stand their stench and pleadings. He would have emptied a gallon of gasoline over them and chucked a match. A small explosive charge would have sealed the entrance, and a few bushes planted here and there, like blackthorn and privet, once growing, would have concealed the entry for eternity.

"Does Nicola know about this?" I ask Redneck, and he says, "No, only Grace and Hubert and, of course, Gordon and his wife, probably others."

Margo didn't know; she is distraught at the murder of her brother Ian and has sworn vengeance on you. Murder does not lie well with everyone; that is the knowledge of a murder committed. To kill in cold blood takes a particular person; committing mass murder requires a unique person.

"I have never killed for pleasure," says Redneck, "There has always been a reason, even if it was greed or revenge. I never killed for the sadistic pleasure of killing, if you know what I mean."

"How come you didn't know? You were pally with Grace. They must have said something, and I reckon you are well in with them."

"You stay calm, Ra-man, or I will have to decommission you if you offer violence to my superiors. We are on a mission, and my job is to be the commander of our military forces. I have no superiors except the Four Corners, whose word is law; even Gordon has to take orders. There may be several clandestine armies operating within one army," he says, "but at the moment, it is all for one and one for all."

"This mission is enormous as regards the result. It could mean riches and possibly eternal youth, definitely a postponement of old age."

"Yeah, yeah, I'm aware of this, but the murder of my grandfather is beyond the pale and was unnecessary."

"Patrick, my popish son, stop killing our men and women and knuckle down to the job in hand, and hopefully, we will survive. There will be blood spilt, gallons of it, and I don't want it to be mine. I will kill you if you become a threat to the operation, yet I will be your friend if you want me to be. I tell you, I had no idea they had started killing your family, and if you doubt my word, so be it."

"I believe you, Jeremiah."

"So, you should," says Gordon, "you have brought misfortune on your head yourself. You had to be awkward and sectarian. You could have had lots of money to take back to that flappy-lipped tart, but instead, you chose to muck me around."

"I know who you are. I've known for some time, you murdering bastard. Don't know me, do ya? It will come to you. Any more whinging crap and your mummy and daddy will get a double roasting. I can assure you the movie will be thirty minutes this time."

"Do you reckon that your old mother could scream for half an hour, or would you bet on Daddy having the better lungs? If you want to find out, try doing your own thing."

"I am Captain Gordon Thatcher of the Special Boat Service, and I first clapped eyes on you that St. Patrick's night at the Pregnant Beggar Pub in Dunrannon town. Do you remember such a night when you murdered five SBS men?"

"Well, well, well, what a turn-up, Gordon Thatcher, I am flabbergasted. I do recall that glorious execution. I cream my pants, fantasising how you balaclava-hooded terrorists roamed my country and how I sent two dozen of your pals to hell, not counting those scumbags that night."

"Five male hitchhikers and one girl, wearing expensive hiking gear off the shelves at Harrods, rambling along country lanes. All decked out in their finery and the yarn they had to tell. Oh, we have trekked from the Ring of Kerry through the midlands all the way here to Dunrannon town. Of course, an imbecile could see they were not what they said they were, so they could only be one thing, Brit soldiers seeking directions to the next world."

"How did you figure they were SBS?"

"The girl told me in between gulps as she sucked on my virile Fenian pecker that they had left her at the...what's the name of the most bombed hotel in the world? The Europa, yeah, that's it. They had left her for the night because she had a dose of the trots from eating undercooked shellfish."

"I was ordered to find out who they were and to make sure they were not half a dozen Hurray Henrys from Cambridge, having a weekend in sunny old Ireland. She opened the door, and to make a long story short, I opened my flies and invited her to have a little munchie, which she seemed reluctant to do. Still, as soon as I said I would stick it up her arse minus the Vaseline, she quickly hit the deck and started munching and crunching, all to my heart's delight. She seemed confused when I took my cock away from her mouth, and I realised she was a right-happy slapper, and she threatened me with her brothers and his mates."

"Special this and special that," she said.

"They are on the way to take her to the pub, so best be away while I can, or they will castrate me. She liked me," she said, "but her voice got meaner and crueller, and I thought, damn you. I flung her across the settee- arm kicking her legs apart. She turned with surprise in her eyes, and you know the rest."

"I do, and I will kill you with pleasure for what you did to her and my brother. She was my sister. You have no idea how long I have searched the world for you, and imagine my surprise when I saw your face in that hotel that night."

"It was during the morning dickhead."

"Whatever, says Thatcher, you said your name was Patrick Dempsey, and I thought he still has the same name. I got Sheeree to prod you for information, and you gave her sufficient to locate your whole tribe here and back in Belfast. Twenty years have passed, and the agencies are still searching for you. As Humphrey Bogart muttered, *of all the hotels in all the Americas, you had to drag your arse into mine,* or words to that effect. Now you're preparing to sail to your doom, just like those cheery Hitler Matrosen on their U-boats."

"You have significantly changed your appearance, Gordon Thatcher. I have known no Thatcher except Maggie, and she had no love for us rebellious Fenians. I now can fit those eyes into a head, but not that head you carry on those shoulders. Have you redesigned your noggin? Where are the scars?"

"I'm going to kill you, Thatcher, for being a nuisance. I don't blame you for trying to kill me; after all, I sent your relatives on a hellish journey. If only you had a little courage that night, you could have saved your comrades."

"Yes, you are right, Dempsey, but I felt scared when I saw her lying on the settee. Tom was not, and he raced in to attack his sister's tormentor only to find himself staring down the barrel of a Kalashnikov. I ran back to the campsite for help, never thinking that I should run to the police barracks, and when I got back with reinforcements to the hotel, Tom and Maisie were on the floor, bound and gagged. I knew that you had sodomised them. Tom kept saying he was ashamed and would kill himself if anyone discovered what had happened. Maisie was eager to hunt you, and she said you knew who we were and where our campsite was."

"We never went back; we phoned our handler and informed him our cover was blown. Not knowing that his cover was also blown, he directed us to Knockdown Castle, where we would be picked up by helicopter and flown back to England. It took us hours to reach the desolate ruins of that medieval wreck, only to be informed the chopper had engine problems and would not arrive before midday."

"Of course, you knew this, and you spent hours waiting. You had your prey trapped but were unsure how to kill it and get away with it. More choppers would be airborne once gunfire could be heard, particularly by the rescue chopper's downing. It was the most exposed castle in Ireland, with grassland low and level for miles; a fly could not have sneaked up on us, yet you and your murdering thugs did. I suppose it should have been obvious a castle has escape ways, but it was unheard of except in stories like The Three Musketeers and other bedtime tales."

"A few lads from 3rd Para came to see us with a couple of foot-sloggers, a bucket of Donegal fried chicken, and a crate of Sligo beer. Maisie was alright about it, but Tom was in a morbidly dark place, and to be honest, his arse was sore as hell. I'm going to cut that prick of you and feed you your balls, Dempsey, one at a time; you should have the opportunity of sucking your nuts before you die."

"Thanks for the invitation, but to be frank, can I be frank with you, Gordon, you paedophile, you will be guzzling my balls, and a superb job you will make of it, and you will plead with me to shag that arse of yours. I will ride Sheeree and give her a mind-blowing orgasm when I finish with you."

"Now-now, keep calm and eat your porridge Fenian. Let me tell you the story, even though you already know it, for it was my finest hour also. It gave me the greatest pleasure to watch those Biddies walking behind the coffins of their sons and husbands as they were buried in... what's the name of the republican plot in Dunrannon?"

"I don't know, and I don't care. I'm sick of the murderous killings."

"Hear the story, Ra-man. If memory serves me right, the chopper came from Lisburn to pick us up."

"A bit of dementia kicking in, Thatcher, you East End cockney."

"No, Dempsey, I have been many places, but you have not been a mile from a cow's shit. The chopper swept in low, making the grass dance in its downdraught, and suddenly it was downed in a shower of flames, a SAM 7 up its arse. Earlier, my mates chased me away from where I was crapping in a foxhole. Too close, they yelled, your stink will gas us and leave us too frightened to shit. I had my crap far away and swapped foxholes for a clean one to ponder how to kill you and your noncy RA friends. I must have dozed off, and the next thing I heard and saw was the chopper in flames. Everybody stayed put as reinforcements were called in, and two Saracens brake a half-mile distance with a dozen squaddies. Of course, we are outside the castle walls standing in the tall grass, our arses exposed to the whole Republican army. Five minutes pass and nothing."

"There is no sound, not even a bird or grasshopper chirping. Then we see the rotor blades of another chopper coming in and an armoured personnel carrier keeping pace with it. Two specialist observers were supposed to scan the grasslands for IRA activity. They reported the area clear to land as no thermal heat had been detected. It should have been the bloody castle they should have been eyeballing because the ruins of that place were alive with republican terrorists and murderers."

"Still, to be fair," says Thatcher, spit forming in the corners of his mouth, that day the IRA fought and died like soldiers, a famous victory for them but a victory that Whitehall strenuously denied. Two SAM missiles hit the chopper and the personnel carrier. Everyone hit the ground, burrowing themselves into the grass, but it wasted time. I saw a dozen men open fire from within the castle walls."

"Bodies jumped in the air as the bullets ripped into them. The Saracen survivors were shredded by the flurry of grenades thrown as they raced to the foxholes. SAMs slammed into the burning vehicles, and I knew the RA had fight and spirit as they emerged from the cover of the castle and gave battle on open ground. In their first charge towards the foxholes, seven, maybe ten men were killed. They died yelling their war cry, **Faugh a Ballagh,** destiny was calling, and they ran to meet it, the words of the Foggy Dew singing in their ears. ***It was better to die beneath an Irish sky....***"

"I saw Tom rise from his foxhole and slaughter three of their number before buying his ticket. There was no sign of Maisie, and I hoped she had found a hole big enough to hide, but she was dead; a spray of bullets had removed her head. At the rear of the fighting, I picked myself up and ran towards the castle, coming in from where the old drawbridge had been. Seeing two men with rocket launchers, I opened fire, killing both. I searched the castle bailey-ruins but found no one else, but I did find a hole in the ground. Later, I learned that this trapdoor led to an underground tunnel to a river. The whole place was built, including its tunnels on the valley floor and covered with thousands of tonnes of earth. The castle stood high on its artificial mound overlooking the countryside. Still, the advent of the cannon had made it pregnable, and it had fallen to Cromwell during the 1641 Confederacy."

"The locals knew there were tunnels, but the dampness, slime and rodent infestation had made them undesirable to explore. However, that day, the 18th of March, had made it necessary for those boys to make the journey that would surprise the enemy. Help was on its way, albeit by ground forces only. I assumed they had run out of helicopters. However, they had sent a few truckloads of grunts. The IRA were retreating towards the castle. I heard over six hundred people gathered with umbrellas at the Weasels Hole to give cover minutes before they were expected."

" Five men ran up that hill, says Gordon, and five terrorists died with surprise on their faces; they would not be going home. I sent them to the inner pits of hell. Forty-five men lay dead and wounded on the grass, seventeen of them terrorists. It had been a battle fought between men, which explained why you were not there, Dempsey, you snivelling rat. I refused to return to England until I had hunted you down, but I accepted Elisabeth's VC pinned on my chest that Mayday."

"Aren't you the brave Brit?" says I. I knew who you were. I believed that killing you, Thatcher, would be a disrespect for a war hero, even if you had sneaked upon them from the rear, but all's fair in love and war. I agree with your actions; they needed killing. After all, they had shot the arses of your bedmates. We did not want to make you into a bigger hero. Oh no, we did not, but when you went undercover posing as the Tullamore Jew, which allowed me to give you a protracted kicking."

"You remember that pauper's graveyard, do you, and the kicking you took and that cock up your arse. Well, the kicking was mine, and the cock belonged to Raymond the Cocklicker, the other tramp local to that area. He was bloody well annoyed by your behaviour collecting pennies on his patch. He said, Gordon, you were already an arsehole bandit. You had robbed him of the opportunity of sticking it to you with excruciating pain and little pleasure when you had involuntarily come round to his way of loving."

"I shot those men face to face, so I did."

"Yes, you did, Gordon; you were courageous, your shots were fast and accurate, and they all died on that patch of grass. The only reason I allowed you to live and never told anyone else who you were was the respect you had shown to the fallen. When you returned from the first aid station and discovered the paras had piled the bodies into a heap, with their faces in a semi-circle, you shot the officer in the kneecap. Even though they gave you a VC, you were cashiered from the army by collective agreement with your pension rights intact."

"Yeah, you are near enough to the truth, Dempsey; I donated my pension to the hundreds of soldiers left legless after the battle of Lambruso. Having surrendered, the Lambo army amputated their legs in a massive field hospital, leaving the survivors for the European Army to collect. Eight hundred Englishmen suffered that fate?"

"Yes, as did many Irishmen. I volunteered to help repatriate the wounded. It was a terrible brutality to inflict on any soldier, especially teenagers. The French soldiers they castrated by the hundreds, fifteen hundred, I believe, for spreading the anal boils. They didn't even test to see if they were carriers; they took the words of harlot Lambo women."

"Those Lambo whores had taken to having sex with the crossbred pony dogs who had carrier spores in their sperm ducts. It ended European land-grabbing, but not before the EU army levelled Lamboland with no hut left standing. A UN statement made it clear that any external forces that tried to occupy the devastated wasteland would be annihilated. Of course, there is always one, and the Kiwananese invaded and found their shithole country also devasted."

"It had been intended to warn the European nations the more troops they sent, the heavier the drain on their economies from disabled veterans. It was a lesson from history. The Byzantine emperor Basil II crushed the Bulgarian army at the Battle of Kleidion in 1014, capturing about 14,000 soldiers. Basil II had blinded all, except one in every hundred or two hundred, depending on who said what. Still, the cold fact of life was the Bulgarian economy was bankrupt for years afterwards, having to feed and tend to these blind soldiers. It was said that Emperor Samuil dropped dead from the shock of seeing his blinded army pleading for his help."

"So, tell me, Fenian," says Gordon, "did they build a shrine to your heroes at Knockdown Castle? Is it one of those haunted places where Provo's fear to tread, for the ghosts of those English warriors, will appear and scare those cabbageheads to death?"

"No, you East End pufter. Cocklicker told me about you. He said you had a bummer's arsehole, and you got a boner when he shoved it up you. Did you never go back to Knockdown Castle to reminisce on your sexual fulfilment that day?"

"No, I didn't. That whole episode gives me the creeps, and I am not yellow."

"That's correct, Thatcher; you stood your ground with that stiff upper lip stuff, don't shoot until you can see the whites of their eyes and all that Boy's Own crap."

"I will tell you what happened, Gordon Thatcher. A Texan, it would have to be a Texan, bought the site for a million dollars at the time. In true Irish/American fashion, he turned the place into another tourist resort, complete with shops, pubs, and woollen mills. It cost him a fortune to rebuild the castle, and the Orange boys blew the place up since he was of Catholic ancestry. Mr Clint Carter-Bush was not a happy bunny when Downing Street rang and informed him that his goldmine was rubble."

"He had teams of builders set to work, and the place was up and running four months later, and it a hundred times grander than before. While work was in progress, fishermen on Lough Leagh netted Loyalists by the score. The last one was retrieved on opening day, bringing the total to forty-seven, excluding their families. Since then, the castle and its surroundings have enjoyed a bomb-free environment."

"Of course," says I, "Cocklicker was castrated a few months later as if he was a bull. It is called Elastration, tying the scrotum or balls to you to stop the blood flow."

"Thank you, Patrick, for that lesson in castration. I know how to castrate a man."

"I suppose you do, Gordon, for it was you that castrated Cocklicker after buggering him; I heard it from Ernie Smalls, your part-time bum boy."

"Would you like me to castrate you; you wouldn't be able to ride that old bag, Wendy."

"Where's my son," I ask.

He laughs at me, "Got you by the goolies I have, haven't I? He's in a safe place; he has a suite to himself to lock from the inside. A pair of hungry lions are outside to stop intruders from getting at him. Guarding those lions are a pair of vicious pufters, and protecting them is my right-hand man, Luther White. He will slice and dice you in the twinkling of an eye."

"I knew a bastard named Winston who had a mate from Eskimoland named Sven. Is that the mothers you are talking about, or is he one of your mother's any daddy kids, you being the one she found under the bush, where she emptied her shit bucket every day?"

He jumps at me like a leopard would when trying to drag down its prey, but I knock him senseless with a punch to the temple. I yelp from the sheet of pain that ripples up my arm, and I stamp hard on the side of his head, but it doesn't bust. I'm grabbed and thrown against the side of the plane. I venture further into the hold and discover Elisabeth, Ruth, and the baby eating tinned apples. Beside them sat Hubert, no doubt gleaning information to use on me. Why he should be nosey at this stage, I do not know. Troopers surround him, many asleep, and I notice Redneck watching me with interest.

"What, what are you staring at me like that for? I don't fancy you, Jeremiah Halloran." Grace, the vicious granddad killer, swaggers down the aisle, and I grab Hubert by the neck, giving it a quick twist.

"Was that how you had my grandfather murdered, knowing full well it was not."

"No, it was not," she says, "We did him in a personnel jihadi way, or they did. They removed his fat, empty head with a sharpened spade. Cut it clean off his shoulders as he knelt there praying to God to take his miserable soul to heaven. His heart was knackered, for he only gave a little spurt, probably a bit like his lovemaking."

"May the curse of God be upon you, you hell-bitch; I'll break your scrawny neck."

I throw Hubert to her, his lifeless eyes open, and it reminded me of Rachel, and rage consumed me. I rose to get up, only for the bitch to zap me thrice with a Taser. Lying on the floor doing the Riverdance on my back, I heard her say in a loud, shrill voice. "Taser is not a word in English; it stands for Tomas A Swift's electric rifle."

With each word, she kicked me in the balls, and a group of misshapen monkeys appeared and carried me away to the land of cuckoos.

I could hear music in the darkness surrounding me, and I started moving my arms to the left and right, hands clenched into tightly knitted fists, and I thought I knew the film. I realised I was marching with the Chinese army, but I was a militia girl, and I thought everyone would laugh at me. I laughed and thought, hmmm, I don't half look sexy in this uniform of pink with its miniskirt and jacket and my white gloves and beret. I had a type 56 AK47 rifle clutched to my chest, and I peered at my white boots and shouted, "Not one fat arse can I see."

A Zulu warrior rushes from the crowd of Chinese dignitaries and jabs me with his *iklwa*. Then, he yells, "Be quiet, dog of war, why are you marching with my wives," and a mist descends over the square.

I'm standing in Red Square beside the Kremlin, and the Mayday parade is in full swing. Vladimir Putin is giving me the two-fingered salute. An Englishman comes to me in full plumage and regalia and tells me to stop pissing on the lions.

"They are a present from the Trafalgar Square Pigeon Fanciers Association of Little Britain and Rural Ireland (excluding the Hebrides). Be a hero and get the Sagallo Colony back for the Russians."

"What are you talking about? I know you, Rexy; they sent you packing as the Governor of the Falklands."

"The Gulf of Tadjoura," Rexy yells at me, "that is where Sangallo is, on the coast of Djibouti, that is in Africa, spud eater. Go get it back, and the Ruskies will help us eliminate the Chinese from Africa."

"But there are no Chins in Africa," I explain. "Bloody Irish, they are always telling me what to do. I was frogmarched to my boat like a common criminal by an Argentinian Irishman. He was Patricio Dowling, the Chief of Police. So I lost my job in the Malvinas, no no, the Falklands."

An Indian arrives, sits beside us, and tells Governor Rexy, "I am your *char-wallah*. Would you like tea? I have head of cabbage for you Irish *mensaab*," and they laugh at me.

"Raghead coolie," I say, "have you got a Bacardi Breezer with cool organic ice in a long-salted glass with a blue-tinted rim."

"Of course," and he opens his pot and hands me one.

"That is five hundred Euros," and I say, "I have no Euros for you, you smelly *aavaara*."

So, he punches me in the face and yells, "Go get them." I crash land in the Kit Kat Klub, Berlin, and watch Sally Bowles performing her cabaret act.

"Hi Sally," says I, "fancy meeting you here; what's the *craic* like?"

She laughs and says, "Be here when I get back."

"But you are not real," I say, "you are a character in Christopher Isherwood's novella."

"All characters are real, whether fictitious or not," she says.

"How do you know whether I'm real, have a feel of my tit and tell me, could you never imagine yourself sucking on that nipple? Of course, you could; it is a beautiful tit; my name is real, but am I?"

"If I'm not real, you are stone-raving-mad talking to yourself like that," she says. "Are you insane?" She punches me in the head. "Did you feel that, oh you did, you are crying? Did that answer your question? I'll be back soon. Observe my act from over there," and she tosses me into the audience, and I land beside a couple who take no notice of me.

Her act is decadent and pansexual, and I feel horny watching it. The show continues to intermission when much of the audience troops to the foyer for beer and schnitzels. I see Sally in the company of the couple sitting beside me.

"The show will not continue until Sally has eaten," they sing soprano.

She invites me to sit and have Bratwurst and Knockwurst, accompanied by generous helpings of potato dumplings and spaetzle with sauerkraut and red cabbage. I could have a choice of sour or sweet for my palate.

While eating, the woman speaks to the man, ending the sentence in *mein liebling*, and he answers back in a thick Irish brogue, ending in *mavourneen*. They both mean "my darling" in their respective languages. I have the strangest feeling I know who they are: Cockeye's brother and his German dancer. They look me in the eye and say, "You will meet us when we are old."

I realise they are the older people on the plane.

"Is it you, Brandy?" I ask in a quiet voice, "But you are so youthful."

"Yes, but so was Oisin, and time, my friend, can pass in the twinkling of an eye, yet a minute, even a second, can be years. Who can say as one waits for the inevitable."

I'm choking, and Lili Marlene is beside me as I lie on the floor, trying to breathe.

"Help me," I croak, and her fingers are plucking at my tongue, and I begin to breathe. I see Gordon, Grace, Elisabeth, Ruth and Jeremiah anxious, and I close my eyes and drift asleep to continue my nightmarish dream.

I lie paralysed as a hellfire preacher stands with his congregation of frightened peasants. He points a bony finger at me and shrieks in a high-pitched eerie voice, "The Lord giveth and the Lord taketh away, and in your case, he giveth you FUCK ALL, and what you have, he will now taketh."

I am lying on the floor, cold and weak from hunger, bollock naked.

"Begone unpleasant peasant, killer of children," weeping and wailing, the congregation exposed themselves to me. I drag myself to the rear of his flock and leave; the door is opened for me by a naked female bi-sexual dwarf who crouches over me and pisses on my face.

I awaken thanks to Grace, the bitch empties a bucket of water over me.

"We need to land this plane, or we will be ditching in the briny in less than an hour," she yells in a sharp, clear, concise voice, her vowels cutting into my brain. Two fighter aircraft are buzzing us and will undoubtedly down us once we enter Scottish mainland air space. Even this far out from territorial waters, we are being warned.

"The coordinates, the coordinates, the coordinates," I hear the words repeated nonstop.

"The leprechauns are dancing Ceili at the crossroads," I yell.

"He is delirious," snaps Gordon, "did you have to taser him? Did you have to kick him in the balls a million times? If he dies, I will boil you alive in a cast iron pot I bought in Uzbekistan; go and get Nicola; they are close friends, and get Austin on the line and Wendy quickly. We are in shtuk; bring that girl up here to be with him, NOW, you pox-riddled bitch."

"Right, right," she says, "I'm on it, and I have not got the pox."

"You will have every disease known to humanity if you don't get this sorted and get Margo up here. Leave them to it, and we will stay away, especially you, useless strumpet—hundreds of millions of pollars at stake, more likely billions and the fountain of youth thrown in. I would never tire of being a teenager, and you are screwing it up. Every government is after the secrets that these people carry. It gives immunity from the plagues sweeping the US of A, and we are fleeing. If they find us, they will make us sing like canaries, and we don't know the innermost secrets of EARTHCO. I bet you a billion pollars they will build us our own Guantanamo Prison. America does not like to sanction murder unless the bastard needs murdering."

Margo is restraining Baba, fearful that Gordon will murder her in cold blood. Margo could be many things, but killing was not in her repertoire. Baba cradles my head and tells me we must land the plane or die.

"Good," I yell. "I want to swim with Poseidon and encourage him to shake the sea so mountainous waves devour Stonnage."

Nicola comes from the cockpit, and I sneer at her, "Who's flying the plane, you venomous bitch? Bugger off at the double, you Hellenic Medusa."

"Next, please, let's see what they have to offer," but no one comes. NO... I collapse; some say I died and came back to life frothing at the mouth with my eyes on stalks.

I had a wicked visit to the nether regions where the skin was flayed from my children and grandchildren.

They roasted the skin until a hideous beldam appeared with a carline's face and the body of a diseased demon. She cut and sewed the burned skin with her bony, nimble fingers until she had fashioned a facemask. Slicing my face off with her razor-sharp nails, she sewed my new look on and dragged me deeper into the pits of Hell.

I awoke to find Gordon dragging me to the cockpit. He put a pair of headphones on my head, slapped me violently across the face, and yelled, "Listen, and answer with numbers only. Can you hear me?" he cried, and I nodded.

This is the end; I hear the desperation in his voice; we will either crash or be downed.

Grace is beside herself, consumed with greed, knowing that her dreams are fading. Nicola is on her knees, imploring me to give the coordinates. Rebecca and Mariah are weeping and lamenting the turn of events. Grace is ranting, raving, and mourning her wasted time, jockeying for position. Prostitution, racketeering, murder, dirty groping old men, girls murdered after having too many babies, all experiments now useless, this indeed was the end.

She knew the end was nigh; she could feel the fires of hell beneath her feet. She silently prayed for God to forgive and reunite her with her parents, whom she had forsaken in their hour of need. They were kind, poor, dirt farmers from Minnesota who had received the human race's ultimate curse, Alzheimer's. They had spent their final years confused, hungry and lost in their past thoughts, never knowing what day it was or what year. Confusion and violence had reigned on their farmstead, and the neighbours had left them to their own devices, as had the government agencies. Social Welfare had contacted Grace to see if she could help, and she agreed that she would return home to be their caregiver. She never had any notion of doing such a deed. She continued her search as a lackey of the corporation for the elixir of life.

Having been ignored, her father phoned the Sheriff and then shot his wife and himself in a moment of clarity. They forgave their daughter for her parental neglect and begged her forgiveness for asking for her time to reduce their burden.

She did not travel to the simple funeral; their neighbours, ashamed to show their faces, buried their heads in the sand and pretended to be the Chinese monkeys. She never came to the farm, too busy to attend to the animal's welfare on what was now her land. The neighbours, never a lot to miss anything *buckshee,* took the animals and even the building's wood. At the end of the year, six months after their death, a visitor would never have guessed that a house and outbuildings existed.

Eventually, the government took the farm for back taxes and added it to their land bank.

In a rage of pure unadulterated hatred, Grace cursed me, yelling, 'That death will arrive for me and my ilk, yeah, you can be sure of that, every one of you. There will not be a trace in the annals of history after 2017 that any of you mangy, cocksucking slags abortions ever existed. The shit that breathes god's clean air will be exterminated with such pain that Christ on the cross would have reckoned he had a slight headache with a stabbing pain to his side.

"Period," growls Gordon, pointing a finger of death at her. "Enough said," and turning to me, he looked me in the eye, and closing his mouth and breathing through his nose, he wagged his index finger at me and never said a word. It's now or never, I thought. The loudest word I ever recall, never spoken, has been conveyed to me in silent language. Yet, its meaning was as clear as the skies that once covered the North Pole. I understood perfectly well what the future held for my family and me.

"Put her on," Gordon says, and she is on speakerphone. Then, with terror in her vocal cords, Wendy's soft voice whispers in a loud and frightening squeal, "Tell them what the coordinates are."

I say nothing. I sneer at Gordon and Grace.

Ruth pushes past Grace, followed by Elisabeth. Elisabeth offers up the baby, and Ruth places her in my arms. "Save this baby for the love you carry for Rachel and her murdered unborn child."

"57 degrees north, 7 degrees west, no minutes, no seconds," I say.

"The Hebridian Archipelago and the island we seek is *Innis Cnoc.*"

Elisabeth runs to the cockpit shouting the coordinates, and quickly disappears through the open door. Gordon stares at Grace, and she slowly shakes her head.

"You, Dempsey, are one dark horse," she says.

"Help me to my feet, Baba, and seat me with Ruth and Elisabeth, and you stay out of my way, Gordon Thatcher.

You have redesigned your ugly mug, you lecherous murderer and rapist of children. Developed a taste for the macabre after viewing Tom and Masies ravaged arseholes, have we."

Nicola makes her way down the aisle, followed by Elisabeth, who sits beside her sister.

"How long before we are in Scottish airspace?" I ask Nicola.

"Almost there, you are taking me back to the Hebrides; why would you want to do that? There are hundreds of the fucking things. What is the island's name, for Christ's sake? And don't tell me it has an Irish name."

"It has; its name is *Innis Cnoc*, and who is flying this bloody crate, eh, Tom Clancy?"

"That could be his name," she says, grinning, "ask Jeremiah; he press-ganged him."

"Use this map," I give her a pen, and she smiles.

"Patrick, my dear, you still believe in the power of the pen."

She twists the biro, unfolds a map and studies it momentarily, looking more perplexed. But these islands are big rocky rocks with nowhere to land using these coordinates except number 42; you have put an x on it."

After giving Elisabeth the coordinates, I hadn't decided whether to provide you with this info or sit and watch us being shot down. Well, you better get it to our reluctant pilot ASAP."

She passes the map to Gordon and says, "She will be along in a minute; tell him it is number 42."

"It's flat," I say, "Not all are rocky; this one is special; it has a runway from one end to the other. It was built in '42 for damaged planes to land, and the labour was free. No one has been on the damn place for years, and it has a deep-water inlet that goes right under the island, a massive cavern. I doubt if anyone knows it's there except the chosen people, and I am not referring to the Jews," and I smile at Elisabeth.

"How did you find out about it?" she asks.

"Italian prisoners of war built it. They stayed behind in jolly auld Scotland, eating their haggis and learning to speak Glaswegian. Many became fine soldiers of the Republic and carried out missions in the fifties, mostly culinary, but you must understand that an army marches on its stomach. Isn't that right, Gordon? So you and your boys took it literally and slithered along on your bellies, keeping a squeaky bum profile. You let the ordinary Tommy do the work for you?"

"You are a bog-soldier," he snarls, "left foot straw foot; you don't know your arse from your elbow."

"I know where my elbow will be later, and I bet you'll enjoy it immensely."

"Enough," snarls the old man.

I knew he was Cockeye's brother immediately; what was his Christian name? I pondered and muttered, "How are you, William."

He ignored me, turned to Gordon, and spoke. "Bit of a bastard, are we Special Boatman? There will be no more orders from you because your son, oh, you look surprised; we knew about that little fucker years ago. You didn't think that lovely first wife of yours would divorce you and forget that you knocked her sister up in a drunken stupor after plying her with gin, did you? We kept an eye on you, waiting for the day we needed to turn over a Brit just like you and guess what? Your day has arrived."

"That's excellent fighting talk, you grizzled bogman, but you can fuck off. I am in the direct employ of EARTHCO's CEOs."

"That I know; tell me something I do not know. Have you met my wife, Brandy? Come and speak to her; she is not as agile as she used to be."

"Move, Gordon, I whisper in his ear, for your life hangs by a thread, and I am considering your life expectancy value. I know this man, and I suspect his word carries the strength of a dozen fine men or women." Taking a cue from my warning, Gordon heads down the aircraft, sits beside Brandy, and offers his hand in friendship. Lifting her head, he sees steely blue eyes and the face of a woman who carried much beauty in her youth.

"I have chosen to die with my husband. We have a combined age of nearly two hundred and fifty years, almost the length of time that Oisin was in *Tir Na Nog*. You will see to it that we reach Stonnage. You will receive your payment as agreed with the CEOs. Understand Stonnage is the rock that EARTHCO was built on, and those four CEOs are the pillars that hold up the edifice to the all-grasping world."

"The world has changed a great deal in the past hundred years, and it is now changing for a final time before the day of Judgement. Global warming was the third warning. The first was the Industrial Revolution, nuclear weapons were the second, and the final warning, number four, was the death of a continent caused by mankind's greed for beauty and longevity. This time, it was coupled with women's vanity, which unleashed an unstoppable plague upon America. It may consume the whole planet, for we sought eternal youth and beauty. But, in our search, we broke God's Commandments, and now we race like frightened rats to abandon the sinking ship before we are dragged down into the vortex."

Gordon never said a word but listened intensely to every comment from her faltering voice, and tiredness swept over him. In his eyes, she saw a man who wished for a quiet life, like having a beer in his local after an evening tending his garden. To go home to his wife, watch the late news, and repeat the same thing daily until the devil gave him a shout, and he would pack his soul in brimstone and offer it to Old Nick whilst his earthly body would be consumed by fire.

"You have lived a long time," he said, "Has it been a fruitful life, or has it been a life fashioned by the seven deadly sins?"

"I have fallen by the wayside long ago, having cloaked myself in the pleasures that the capital sins gave me. I shook hands with the devil, and I think he knew I was his daughter. I always had an impulse to break the lord's commandments, and I have broken them to smithereens."

"You are the Queen of Darkness, and the fires of hell burn in your irises," he says.

"You will die, Gordon Thatcher, you will surely die, and it will not be of natural causes, for Judgement Day is upon us. The American Dream is fast becoming a nightmare...

A massive explosion shook the plane.

The End

About the Author

John Woodmount was born in Ireland, the eldest of four children to Irish parents. Emigrating to England, he took an interest in the property market. Divorced with an adult son and daughter. ARIZONA DYING was written in 2008, the first book of a trilogy. Several other books took shape, yet with the pressure of business, editing and publishing had to wait. The writing was on the wall for a period, but now, it is firmly back on the pages.

www.ingramcontent.com/pod-product-compliance
Lightning Source LLC
Chambersburg PA
CBHW070337170726
48291CB00001B/89